WAKING THE SLEEPERS

Tony Irvin

Equator Press

Equator Press, an imprint of Write Now! Publications.
Copyright © 2018 Tony Irvin

Design and typesetting: george@wickerswork.co.uk

Kindle ISBN: 978-1-912955-06-0
Paperback ISBN: 978-1-912955-07-7

By the Same Author

Operation Fruit-Bat (humour)
Highway of Darkness (literary fiction)
It's Hell in the Tropics (short stories from hot places)

For Younger Readers (middle-grade fiction)

African Safari Adventures

Volume 1 – The Ant-Lion
Volume 2 – The Elephant-Shrew
Volume 3 – The Buffalo-Weaver
Volume 4 – The Leopard Tortoise
Volume 5 – The Rhinoceros-Beetle (in preparation)

Teenage fiction

Cobra Strike (thriller)

"Terror fear over killer virus spread by bats:

Roosting in one of Africa's national parks are some of the world's deadliest animals: fruit bats carrying a lethal virus which could pose a global threat if weaponised. Death from shock or organ failure usually follows quickly after infection with the Marburg haemorrhagic fever virus. During the Cold War it was rumoured that the Soviet Union had developed a strain of the virus as an air-borne powder: a single particle of which could kill."

The Times (London); 22nd December 2018

Prologue

Extracts from the journal of the Reverend Huw Williams, 1975-80.

My first impressions of Lokinang are that the heat is unremitting, the rainfall negligible and the scenery spectacular. Most of the vegetation appears inedible, except to goats, and uninteresting, except to witchdoctors. The few people who live in this remote village in northern Kenya are sustained by the meagre produce of scrawny livestock and the hope they might find food the next day or the day after. I thank the Lord that he has entrusted me to bestow his bounteous bread of life on these destitute people.

The villagers have few visitors, other than marauding bandits who steal the goats, rape the women and kill the men. This is a godless place.

My wife, with her nursing background, brings much comfort to these people. The noxious potions she dispenses are combinations of modern pharmacy and Welsh nostrums, and are much in demand – the fouler their taste, the greater their undoubted potency.

Today was one of great joy. Despite its perilous journey from Nairobi in the back of a pick-up, the harmonium arrived safely and is now installed in our little chapel.

Praise the Lord, the chapel was packed this Sunday to hear my wife play the harmonium and accompany me singing Cwm Rhondda with all the passion I could muster.

I find increasing solitude and peace as I roam the hills with a guide, camel, notebook and camera, recording all I see for the memoirs I will write when we return to our Welsh homeland.

Today, my guide and I detected considerable activity around Lokinang Mountain, but he refused to take me there. It is a bad place, *bwana*.

Some men brought a sick boy to the mission today. He was strapped to the back of a donkey and suffering from a terrible rash, fever and bleeding in his eyes; a disease which the men said he had contracted in bat-infested caves on the mountain. My wife had never seen the like before and was unable to save the poor lad. That night we committed his soul to the Lord.

We experienced an earth tremor in the night and the cross fell off the altar and broke.

It is with great sadness, I note my flock has dwindled almost to nothing. The only ones who stay are those to whom I pay a small wage to work in the house or tend the mission's sheep and goats. It may be time for a change.

Should these random jottings come to your attention, dear reader, I trust you will not think unkindly of this poor sinner. God moves in a mysterious way his wonders to perform.

Chapter 1

Northern Kenya – 1980

It was the softest of sounds: the whisper of wind on sand, clouds brushing against each other, the rustle of butterfly wings. But it was always there. During the daytime other sounds intruded and Dima could only hear the rasping of tiny jaws if he put his ear to the wood. If he tapped, the termites would pause. 'Go away,' they would say, rattling their heads against the walls of their tunnels and sending a shiver through the colony. He would smile. The termites would then resume their ceaseless gnawing and the sound would return. One day, their persistence would be rewarded and the hut would collapse.

***

Dima lay beside his mother on the bed in the servants' hut, listening for the whispering rustle which would lull him to sleep. Tonight, though, there was an uneasy stillness: the sound of silence, the sound of stress, the sound of…

Shots!

Close by. At the mission house. Their echo hung in the air: brittle, harsh, terrifying.

Dima clung to his mother.

The termites listened.

The echo drifted into darkness. Silence tiptoed back. The howling of a distant dog edged into the silence. Still the termites listened.

'Mama, what is it?'

'I don't know. Something very bad.'

Another dog. The sheep and goats restless. A rat scratching in the roof. His mother's terrified panting. The pounding of her heart – and his. Whisperings. Men among the animals. Frightened bleats. The clonk of a bell. A muffled curse.

'Mama, they are stealing the animals.'

'Sh!'

'We must stop them.'

'These men will kill us.'

'But Mama—'

A crash against the door of the hut.

The lock held firm.

'Hide.' She pushed Dima away.

A volley of shots. The lock shattered.

His mother gasped. Dima scrambled into the rafters.

The door flew open. Moonlight flooded into the hut. A man stood in the doorway.

Dima's mother cowered against the wall.

The man dropped his gun. Came towards the bed. Stood looking at her; then—

She screamed.

Dima dropped from the rafters and sank his teeth.

The man leaped from the bed. Yelled. Tried to beat him off. But Dima was a leopard and clung on with teeth, arms and legs. He tasted the warm saltiness of blood. Ignored the pain.

The man staggered outside. Other men. Sheep and goats milling round. Dogs barking. His mother screaming.

Flashes in his head. Agony. Blackness. Silence.

The termites resumed their labour and the whispering rustle returned.

***

When Dima came round the silence was soft and soothing. The pain was harsh and merciless. Something warm and strange against his face. He picked it up.

An ear – a human ear!

He hurled it away. Pain, so much pain. He remembered and stumbled back to his mother.

'Mama.'

No answer.

'Mama, Mama.' He shook her.

She groaned and struggled to sit up. A spasm shook her body as she hugged him.

He pulled himself free. Forgot his own pain. 'Mama, what is it?'

'I am paining so much.' Another spasm. 'They were bad men – very bad.'

'They are now gone.'

'And you saved me. Oh, Dima, you saved me.'

'But Mama you are hurt.'

'A shot went into my body and is paining me… paining me so much.'

'And that man?'

'He has gone with the other men and… and taken the animals.'

4

'My sheep and goats.' He dashed tears from his eyes.

She remained silent, her breathing ragged.

'I will kill those men.'

'No. You must go... go and bring your... father here to—'

'You must come with me.'

'I cannot move. You must... must go alone. You must not fear the... dark.'

He looked sharply at her. 'I do not fear the dark.'

'It is you who must care for me now, my son.' She paused to regain her breath. 'You are now a man.'

He thought for a moment. 'I will go and tell Baba to come.' He crossed to the door and peered into the night. The brilliant moon showed a dark shape lying in the shadow of the missionary's house.

'Dima,' whispered his mother. 'Come here.'

He knelt beside her.

She took his hand. Pressed it to her face. 'Go safely, my Ridima.'

He withdrew his hand. Slipped through the door and closed it as best he could with its shattered lock. He waited in the shadow of the hut, studying the shape on the ground and its surrounding stain – black in the moonlight.

I am now a man. He fought off the fear which made him want to rush back to the embrace of his mother.

He crossed to the shape. The *bwana's* wife. She had been good to him. Taught him Swahili. Given him some lambs and kids to care for. Given his mother a good job in the house.

He had seen death before. But never a white person.

There was no sign of the *bwana.*

A strange yet familiar sound. His mother singing. Words formed themselves into those of her favourite hymn – the one from which she derived his name: "*Guide me, oh thou Great Redeemer.*"

He slipped off into the night protected by his mother's blessing.

***

Dima's father was a *Ndorobo.* A man with no cattle, a honey hunter, a wild man, a man who lived in caves and knew about poisons and other dark secrets. A man who wore animal skins on his body, a dagger on his belt, a bow and quiver over one shoulder, and a bag of hyrax skin – containing who-knew-what evil – over the other. A man of the forest and of the night. A man feared by the villagers and loved by his son.

Dima reached the cave in the great mountain called Lokinang, the cave his father used as his base when hunting. He listened for elephants which also visited the cave, travelling from far away to scrape salt off the walls, gouging deep grooves with their tusks.

All quiet.

He crept into the cave and gave the call of the scops owl.

Echoes wandered through the tunnels which honeycombed the mountain and died away.

I am now a man. I am now a man.

He repeated the call.

A faint light deep inside. A reddish light which flared to yellow. His father appeared and embraced him. 'What is it, my son?'

'You must come. It is Mama.' Dima forgot he was now a man and his story tumbled out in a torrent of tears.

'And the *bwana*, the man of God who lives in the big house?'

'We heard many shots, Baba. I think he is dead. And I saw the *bwana's* wife. She is dead.'

'Who did this thing?'

'Very bad people. They stole the sheep and goats.'

'Come.' He led Dima to a ledge deep in the cave and put dried sticks onto the fire. It flared up, sending strange shadows dancing round the walls. He took his bow and arrows, and those he had made for Dima, and set them near the fire. He reached into a crevice and withdrew the precious tin containing black sticky paste prepared from the roots of the *egales* tree, the recipe for which he had taught Dima and made him promise never to reveal.

Many times Dima had watched the procedure in the cave with its dancing shadows and lingering smell of bats and elephants: the smearing of the paste on the arrowheads, the binding of the heads with strips of dik-dik skin, the careful placing into the bark quiver. But this was the first time he prepared his own arrows. The first time he applied the poison. The first time he would use a man's tools to do a man's work.

***

Dima led his father back to their hut and took his mother's hand. 'Baba is here.'

She gave a faint smile.

His father examined her wounds and his expression hardened. He sent Dima to collect some aloe leaves, broke their stems and smeared the sap on the wounds. 'We go to find those men,' said his father.

'We will kill them, Mama,' added Dima. 'Then I will come back

6

and care for you.'

'My Ridima,' she murmured.

***

They caught up with the men that night, drawn by the smell of roast meat drifting in the air.

Four men. Three, with guns beside them, sat by the fire chatting and roasting meat – one of Dima's precious goats. The fourth lay with a cloth tied round his head. Beyond them, a makeshift enclosure of thorn branches penned the animals.

Dima fingered the arrows in their quiver.

His father touched his arm. 'Not yet. They are too far.'

They watched and waited.

The great scorpion rose in the night sky and the men lay down beside the fire. The man with the cloth round his head had not moved. He had not eaten.

Dima's father pointed to a lone rock between them and the men. The signal to attack would be the call of the scops owl. They would rendezvous back at the sand river they had crossed earlier.

A cloud drifted over the moon and his father was gone.

Dima shut his mind. Raced across the open space. Dropped behind the rock. Waited for the shouts and the gun fire.

Nothing.

He extracted two arrows from their quiver. Unwrapped the skin covering the poison: poison which could kill an elephant. What chance did a man have?

He laid one arrow on the ground and notched the other into his bow. His breathing had settled. His heart no longer pounded. He was now a man.

The cloud moved on. Moonlight flooded the scene. The scops owl called.

Dima rose and sent his first arrow into the body of the man nearest the fire. He notched the second and…

The man with the head cloth was gone.

A burst of gunfire. Bullets tore into bushes, ricocheted off rocks. Screams and shots shredded the darkness.

Dima fled.

He threw himself down behind a tree. He had failed. His father trusted him to do a man's work and he had failed.

The shooting stopped. The screaming continued.

A crashing in the bushes. The sheep and goats had broken out of

7

their enclosure. They raced past him and tore off into the night.

Dima followed.

***

Dima opened his eyes. Warm sun filtered into his hiding place above the sand river. His head ached. His body ached. His muscles had stiffened in the night.

'Baba,' he whispered.

No reply.

He sat up, startling a ground-squirrel scrabbling nearby.

'Baba.'

He was a bruised and frightened boy alone in the bush. But a bush filled with joyous birdsong and the whispering spirits of trees and rocks: 'You are now a man. You are now a man.'

Dima peered out from the screening bushes, slipped down the bank and dug into the sand river with his hands. Water seeped into the hole. He quenched his thirst and washed his face.

The alarm call of a francolin.

He started. Turned his head. Listening, smelling, searching.

Scent drifting on the air. Not an animal. A man. Not his father. A man who smelled of stale sweat and wood smoke. A man following his tracks.

Dima would not fail this time. He turned and ran, making no effort to conceal his tracks. He ran until he was clear of the surrounding bushes and in the open among rocky outcrops. He chose one with vegetation which offered shade and concealment, and settled down to watch and wait.

And wait.

He was thankful of the shade from a gnarled acacia which gave some protection from the remorseless sun.

His head began to droop.

A movement.

The man was there. At the edge of the bushes. No cloth round his head. But on one side, the ragged and bloody wound where once there had been an ear. The man would be reluctant to follow Dima's tracks, reluctant to approach too close. A hidden boy with poisoned arrows was more deadly than a man in the open – even if that man did have a special gun called Kalashnikov.

The man hid in an adjacent outcrop.

Dima watched and waited. He watched harvester ants carrying grass seeds to their nest, an agama lizard posturing with its blue throat to its drabber mate, a sunbird probing the flowers of an aloe. He watched the place where his foe lay, his rifle glinting in the sun. And he watched the blazing sun beating down as it moved across the sky. By the time it was overhead, even the industrious ants ceased their activity and retired underground.

Dima struggled to keep awake as he watched a dust devil weave its haphazard way across the surrounding plain. Then, as though with some demonic purpose befitting its name, it rushed at Dima's hiding place. He clapped his hands over his face and threw himself to the ground, bracing his body against the roaring monster which tore into the outcrop, hurling sand, sticks, leaves and birds into the air.

When he cleared the sand from his eyes and peered out, the dust devil had resumed its aimless wandering but the glinting rifle had gone.

He had failed again.

***

When he reached the sand river it was almost dark. Some warthogs had been during the day to drink from the waterhole, but no sign that his father had been there.

He was past caring. 'Baba,' he called. 'BABA.'

His cries were swallowed by the bush. He slumped beside the waterhole and buried his face in the wet sand, heedless of the coarse grains he sucked into his mouth as his body took over the task of restoring itself.

He raised his head and listened.

There it was again.

He answered the call. A pause. The call was repeated.

His impulse was to rush towards the sound. But perhaps it was a real owl. He called again. Again it was answered. His father was out there calling to him.

Other things were also out there: leopards, hyenas, lions even. They were dangerous – particularly if hunting – but they were predictable. The man with one ear was different.

Dima picked up his bow and arrows, rose to his feet and crept off into the advancing night.

He reached a sand gully bordered by sparse bushes. He was about to squeeze through a gap, when…

A dark shape. Moving in the gully towards him. The shape came nearer and… And passed beneath him – so close he could have touched it. There was a bark of alarm as the leopard picked up his scent and fled into the night.

Dima breathed out.

This time his owl call was answered from nearby.

He strained his eyes. Nothing resembling the outline of a person. Had he been deceived by a real bird?

Very faintly, he heard the whispered word: 'Dima.'

His father lay hidden in the thickest part of the bush. They hugged each other, tears coursing down their cheeks.

'Baba, that man escaped. I have failed you.'

'No, you have not... failed. I am... proud of you.'

'Baba, you're sick.'

'It is... nothing.'

'But...'

'Be still, my son.'

Dima slipped into a dreamless sleep.

***

Dima woke to the sound of chopping. He opened his eyes to see his father cutting a throwing-stick.

'Come.' His father smiled.

Once again, father and son were hunting at first light with the mist rising from the mountain called Lokinang. As the mist dispersed in the morning air, the fear lifted from Dima's mind.

His father hurled the stick.

Dima rushed forward and picked up the luckless hare – just as when he was small and his father was teaching him the ways of the bush. Except, it wasn't.

His father slumped to the ground gasping and clutching his stomach.

Dima flung the hare aside. 'Baba, what is it?'

'One of the... shots from that man hit... me.' Blood oozed through his clutching fingers. 'When... when I threw that...' He paused, panting. '... threw that stick, something broke... inside me.'

'I will help you, Baba. I will get medicine.' Dima rushed off.

He scrabbled leaves and berries together to make the medicine his father had taught him. When he returned, his father's eyes were closed. Blood was darkening the sand around.

'Don't die, Baba. Don't die.'

His father opened his eyes. 'It was the... man with one... one ear. He was—'

'I will kill him.'

His father gave a faint smile. His eyes remained open. They were still open an hour later but a film had formed over them.

Vultures circled overhead.

Dima closed his father's eyelids. He kissed his brow, picked up the hyrax-skin bag and walked away leaving the vultures to carry his father's spirit into the sky.

He walked all day, indifferent to thirst and hunger. As he approached the village, a flock of sheep and goats wandering unattended through the bush, rushed to him with joyful bleats. He barely noticed.

His mother lay as they had left her. The hut was filled with buzzing flies. Dima pulled a cover over her body, picked up the paraffin lamp and matches beside the bed.

The flames engulfed the hut, cremated his mother and incinerated the termites. He turned away and, followed by his faithful flock, walked off to an uncertain future. Now, he *was* a man.

Today was his eleventh birthday.

Chapter 2

London – 2001

Colette struggled with the front door. It closed at the third attempt and a piece of masonry fell down narrowly missing her head. She leapt back and glared up at the crumbling façade and the creeper which seemed to be holding the house together; then turned her attention to the tiny garden – pretty sad, really. The blue tits, which had been nesting in the back of the piano, had recently flown. It was her excuse for not having the thing taken away – or the mouldering sofa through which a buddleia was growing. But the excuse was wearing thin, even though the tits did come back each year, and the buddleia was wonderful for butterflies.

Paul said if you tidied your front garden it encouraged people to think you had something worth stealing. What, his weights, his rowing machine, his... his tackle? Where was Paul, anyway? He'd said something about a new contract but she hadn't seen him for over two weeks and was beginning to have doubts.

She checked her car and was mildly surprised to find it still in one piece: the steering lock in place, the windows intact, a wheel on each corner.

A leaflet was tucked under the windscreen wiper. She pulled it out:

Shah's clearance services.
All forms of household goods removed by sympathetic and friendly professionals.
House, garage and garden clearances a speciality.
No job too small.

Why not? The tits had flown.

She rummaged for her mobile and called the number. Then had to run to catch her train.

Her brain was in neutral as she rode the escalator at her arrival station but it snapped into gear when she noticed a smug-looking Paul in skimpy underpants. She scrabbled in her briefcase, put on sunglasses and hoped that none of the fifty thousand other travellers would notice her blushes.

There he was again, and again, and again. Every third poster, exhorting London's population *to feel confident when it matters*, portrayed

Poser Paul. God! – it was probably the same at every station on the Underground. And who was that beside him? – the bimbo with the inflated superstructure, the belly of a greyhound and the straying hand.

The next thing she knew, she was lying in a heap at the top of the escalator with feet stepping over and round her. People tutting and muttering. She snatched her sunglasses out of the path of a large foot and some of the words filtered through her humiliation.

'Give me your hand.'

She looked up. A tanned face, blue eyes, a concerned expression.

'I guess you missed your footing.'

'Yes, I was…' She held out her hand. 'Thanks.'

'Are you hurt?'

'Only my pride.'

He gave a lop-sided grin. 'Sure you're okay?'

'Yes – and thanks.'

'No sweat.' He disappeared into the crowd.

Hey! Aren't you supposed to invite me for a drink or something?

Another bloody poster! Graffiti scrawled across it read: *May contain nuts.*

She fought her way to the exit.

She reached the Zoo twenty minutes later, headed for the Unit of Comparative Medicine and let herself into an office with the nameplate *Dr Colette Fraser, Virology,* on the door. She dumped her briefcase on the desk and slumped into her chair.

The light on her answer-phone was flashing. She pressed the replay button: *"Colette, one of the new colobus is off its food, can you come down?"* It was Eric, her assistant. The light continued flashing and she waited for the second message. *"I'm really sorry. I don't know how to say this, but Binty and I have this thing going. I think it's best I move out. Sorry."*

'Binty!' She swept Paul's photograph off the desk. The glass smashed.

She snatched up the phone and punched numbers.

"Hi, this is Paul, I'm busy right now."

Doing what, I wonder?

"Leave your number or call back later."

What – when you've finished?

She drummed her fingers on the desk. 'Hi, this is Colette. I'm *not* going to call back later. Just make sure you and your tackle never

13

come into my life again.' She slammed the phone down and felt better. 'Tosser!'

She switched on the computer and allowed her mind to wander while it booted up. Realistically, the relationship couldn't have worked. Perhaps she felt relieved – too early to say.

There were two new e-mails: the first reminded her to attend a meeting about the Condor Programme – whatever that was. She deleted it. The second was from her boss. She thought he was in the States, but this was from Kenya. "*Call me urgently on this number. Don't forget we're two hours ahead of you.*"

She got through at the third attempt.

'Carter,' said a man's voice.

'Jeff, it's Colette. You asked me to call.'

'Thanks, Colette. You busy right now?'

'Well, there is the—'

'Good. I want you to get out here on the plane tonight.'

'Tonight?'

'Yes. The Petes have gotten a problem.'

'What sort of problem?'

'I'll fill you in when you get here. E-mail me your flight details and I'll meet you at the airport. You're booked into the Fairview.'

'Jeff, my dad's quite ill and may have to go into—'

'Get a three-month excursion. Charge it to my travel budget.'

'I'm really tied up at the—'

'See you tomorrow. And bring your sampling gear. Any problems, call me on this number. Leave a message if I'm out.'

'Yes, but—'

'Thanks Colette, really appreciate it.' He cut the call.

Damn. He'd caught her off guard. Why hadn't she resisted? She wasn't ready to go back. The memories were too painful. And what was that about the Petes? If they had a problem they could contact her direct. Why was Jeff involved?

There was a knock on the door and a young man with a wispy beard entered. 'Morning, Colette.'

'Hi, Eric, I got your message.'

'You okay?'

'I'm fine, why?'

'It's just you look a bit sort of like flustered.' He noticed the broken picture frame. 'That's a shame.'

'I, er, knocked it off with my briefcase – careless.'

14

'I'll get a dustpan and brush.'

'Leave it, Eric.'

'It's no trouble.'

'I said leave it.'

He held up his hands. 'Okay, okay.'

'Sorry.' She gave a rueful grin. 'All right, I am a bit uptight – not my day I'm afraid.'

'I have days like that sometimes.'

With posers in pants and bronzed Samaritans? I doubt it.

***

They went through their respective units, and changed into hospital greens before entering the quarantine area reserved for all new arrivals. The black and white colobus monkey – one of the new batch from the Berlin Zoo – crouched in the corner of the cage, hunched and listless. The others seemed fine and raced through to a connecting cage.

She and Eric put on surgical gloves and facemasks. Then, with a mixture of persuasion and coaxing, managed to get the monkey into a crush-cage so she could carry out a proper examination.

The monkey had a high temperature, signs of respiratory distress and – most disturbingly – conjunctivitis. At least, there was no evidence of a rash – yet. She gave it broad-spectrum antibiotic – not that it would do much good, but it was a gesture. They carried the monkey in its cage to an isolation room. Normally, she alone would attend to it but in view of her imminent departure to Kenya, Eric would have to take responsibility.

'Are you okay with that?' she asked, when they were back in her office.

'Yes, I think so.'

She opened a drawer in her desk and took out a business card. 'If it dies, call this number.' She scribbled down the details. 'Ask for Dr Alan Davies.'

'Who's he?'

'Someone else who specialises in primate viruses. He'll know what to do.'

Eric frowned.

'It's okay. I'm just being ultra-cautious.' She gave an unconvincing smile. 'I'm sure the monkey will be fine.'

'But this Davies person…?'

'As I said, nothing to worry about. I just want to be sure you've got back-up if you need it – which you won't.' She repeated the smile.

'What if...?'

'It's okay, Eric. We've got it covered. Now, are you clear what to do while I'm away?'

'I suppose so.'

'Right, then. Thanks, Eric.'

She gazed at the closed door. Was she being alarmist? That conjunctivitis, though? And the temperature? Could it just be stress? Should she alert Alan?

She turned to her computer and typed in the address on his card. A screen flashed up: *Porton Down is home to the Defence Science and Technology Laboratory, an Executive Agency of the Ministry of Defence. The site is one of the United Kingdom's most sensitive and secretive government facilities for military defence against chemical, biological, radiological, and nuclear warfare.*

She shuddered.

***

She managed to get through her routine work but her mind kept going back to the monkey. She paid two further visits to the isolation unit. The monkey hadn't moved and its food remained untouched. Perhaps she wasn't being alarmist.

At lunchtime, she grabbed a journal from her bookshelf and went to the main cafeteria: a place of cheerful chips and children's chatter. She collected some food, found a spare table, propped the journal against a pot of plastic flowers and shut out her surroundings.

'Do you mind if I sit here?'

She glanced up. 'No, go ahead.' She went back to the journal.

'It's rather crowded.'

'Hmm.' She started munching a sandwich and continued reading. The respiratory infection, the conjunctivitis, the high temperature... Please, God, no. Perhaps she'd missed the rash. She'd have to check more thoroughly.

'I can see you're busy but haven't I seen you somewhere before?'

'I don't think so.' Nice try, Sunshine, but— 'Good grief. What are you doing here?'

'I could ask you the same question.'

'I work here.'

He raised his eyebrows. They were unusually fair against his tanned face.

'You all right, now?'

She managed to switch off monkeys and smiled. 'I felt such a fool.

Thanks for coming to my rescue this morning.'

'I guess your mind was elsewhere.'

She was at a loss for words.

'What are you reading?'

She showed him the article: *Differential diagnosis of Marburg and related haemorrhagic diseases of non-human primates, by A. Davies.*

'Not exactly light reading.'

'It's my job.'

'You a vet?'

'Sort of.'

'What's a sort-of vet?'

Stop blushing, you stupid cow.

'I am a vet but I now specialise in this sort of thing.'

'Isn't that a bit scary?'

She examined her finger nails. It was scary sometimes – bloody scary.

'I'm sorry I interrupted your work. Just ignore me.' He pulled a newspaper from his brief case.

Ignore you? Fat chance.

'Do *you* work here?' she asked. 'I don't often come to the cafeteria so it's hard to keep track of people.'

'Hell no, I'm a visitor. I was invited to give a talk.'

'Not the… what was it?'

'Condor Programme.'

'Have I missed it?'

He nodded. 'It was this morning.'

'Come on,' she said, closing the journal. 'Let me get you coffee in the Fellows' lounge. It's much quieter.'

'I don't want to impose.'

'No, I need a break. Besides it's the least I can do to repay you for saving my life.'

A few minutes later they were settled in a more peaceful and refined environment.

'I'm sorry I missed your talk,' she said, 'but we have so many meetings, I'd never get any work done if I went to all of them.'

'Sure.'

'So you're involved in condor conservation, then?'

'No ways. Condor is a corny acronym. One of the donors dreamed up the name.'

'What are you conserving?'

17

'Wildlife regions of Kenya.'

'Is that new?'

'No, but the funding is. At last, we're getting good backing from the donors and a chap called Jeff Carter, who's—'

'Jeff! You work with Jeff?'

'A very persuasive guy,' he said, with a chuckle.

'Don't I know it. But how's Jeff involved?'

'He's been brought in as—'

Her pager buzzed. She checked the message. 'Damn. Can you excuse me a moment? I'll be right back.'

'Go ahead.'

She hurried off to meet Eric in the primate isolation wing. It took longer than expected and when she got back he'd gone. The woman, who was tidying away the coffee, told her that the man – "*such a nice man*" – had to leave to catch a plane. He'd said he was really sorry he couldn't wait.

Such a nice man – and she hadn't even learned his name. The only consolation was the sick monkey was now eating. Perhaps the antibiotic was working or perhaps it was travel stress. She felt foolish over her alarmism.

She went back to her office and stared at her computer: chance encounters with someone who had sun-bleached eyebrows and worked in Kenya with Jeff on some conservation programme or other, and who…

Just book the bloody flight.

But what if her ex was still there? He'd stopped sending her Christmas cards but had he moved on? Perhaps she should tell Jeff the flights were full. He'd never believe her, though.

She swept up the broken picture frame, consigned an unsatisfactory relationship to the waste bin and booked the flight.

***

She reached home and was pleased to see the front garden had been cleared. She put her key in the lock and opened the door.

Bastards! They must have discovered the spare key hidden under the brick.

She found the crumpled leaflet in her briefcase and called the number.

'Can I speak to Mr Shah?'

'Which Mr Shah you wanting?'

'I don't know.'

'You wanting to leave message?'

She gazed round the sad empty room. What's the point? 'Just tell, whoever, that he's left a broken chair.' At least, Paul's stuff had also been taken. That was some consolation.

They hadn't bothered with her clothes. She'd had her passport and laptop at work, and had arranged to collect her ticket at the airport.

She changed into jeans and a simple top then climbed into the loft and dragged out a suitcase, stuffed some clothes into it and went to the bathroom – also untouched. She studied the twenty-nine-year-old with the brown eyes and sleek black hair gathered in a pony-tail who peered back at her from the mirror.

'Your nose is too big. God, wrinkles!'

She scrabbled things into her wash bag, shoved it in the case and hurried downstairs. She checked the essentials were in the small rucksack to carry onto the plane, had a last look round and locked the front door – that was a joke.

She set off for the airport, wondering what it would feel like to be thirty in a couple of weeks' time.

Chapter 3

Nairobi – 2001

Ian tried to ignore the phone. It was no use; they knew he was in. He snatched up the receiver. 'Sinclair.'

'Ian, I know it's Monday but...'

'Sorry, Helen, what is it?'

'The High Commissioner would like you to come and identify some birds.'

'He what!'

'He'd like you to come and identify some birds outside his window.'

'Good grief. Is that more important than national security?'

'Sorry?'

'Nothing.' He scowled at his reflection in the window. 'Okay, on my way.' He adjusted his tie, took the stairs to the top floor and smiled contritely.

Helen looked up from her desk. 'Perhaps you need a break.'

Office work getting him down? Was it that obvious? He shrugged.

The turquoise top suited her, complementing her blonde hair which was tied back revealing discreet jade ear-pendants. Her slim bronzed legs protruded from under the desk. She'd kicked off her sandals and was wiggling pink-painted toes. He wondered why she wasn't wearing her wedding ring.

'How's it going?' he asked.

It was her turn to shrug. 'Go on in.' She inclined her head towards the inner door.

He knocked and entered.

Sir Aubrey Gilmore was a tall angular man with bushy eyebrows, a prominent nose and Prince-Charles ears which probably went with the post. He stood peering out of the window as though surveying a missionary field.

'Morning, sir,' said Ian.

The High Commissioner turned. 'Ah, Ian. Good man. Thanks for coming. Tell me, what are those chaps?' He pointed to some iridescent purple birds which were jostling the other birds aside in the pink blossoms of a cape chestnut tree outside the window.

Ian followed the High Commissioner's gaze. 'They're violet-backed starlings. The purple and white ones are the males, and the brown ones are—'

'Thanks, I must remember that – most attractive. Take a seat.' Sir Aubrey returned to his own seat and began shuffling files on the desk. 'Busy day? Keeping well, are we?'

'Can't complain.'

'Splendid, splendid. Any good safaris recently?'

'Well, I—'

'Ah. Knew it was here somewhere.' Sir Aubrey passed over a bulky report. 'Do you remember this consultancy?'

Ian read the title: *Conservation in Developing Regions of Kenya – Report of a Multi-Donor Consortium.* 'Yes, some of the team came and spoke to me about security issues.' He passed the file back. 'They seemed to have some pretty radical ideas.'

'Well they certainly haven't pulled their punches. They say there won't be any African wildlife to speak of within fifty years unless there's an international effort to address the problems.'

'They could be right.'

'Well you know more about these things than I do, but the consultants seem to have convinced our lords and masters who've accepted most of the recommendations.'

The report on Ian's desk began to seem less important.

'I plan to go back to London with my own endorsement,' continued the High Commissioner, 'but with one proviso. That's where you come in.'

'I see.' He didn't.

'Our Department for International Development is proposing to pledge a not inconsiderable sum – twenty-five-million pounds to be precise – over the next five years for wildlife conservation in Kenya, provided the other key donors – US, Japan, Germany and so on – make similar pledges. Coffee?'

'Er, no thanks.'

The High Commissioner took off his glasses, held them up to the light, polished them on his tie and peered out of the window again. 'Violet-winged starlings, you say?'

'Violet-backed.'

'Ah, yes. You'll see that one of the main proposals is to set up a number of task forces to tackle different wildlife aspects.' Sir Aubrey looked up. 'Cynthia will be most interested.'

The High Commissioner's wife interested in the operational aspects of a conservation programme? Ian didn't think so.

'She's keeping a record of all the birds she sees at the residence – bet the violet-winged starling isn't on the list.'

'Backed.'

'Backed. Must remember that: violet-backed.' He smoothed his eyebrows. 'Anyway, the consultants recommend that each of these task forces should be jointly led by a specialist nominated by the donors and a Kenyan counterpart. On this basis I am proposing that you help lead the force concerned with security and anti-poaching. Let's say for a year – should be enough time to get the show on the road.'

'Right.'

'Let me explain,' went on the High Commissioner. 'I've already had a number of informal discussions with other heads of mission while the report was in draft. With such large sums of money being proposed, we are unanimous that there must be strict and transparent accountability…'

Ian's mind began to wander.

'…joined-up thinking… coordination of inputs… poverty focus… multi-pronged attack… maximize resources… Are you with me?'

'Yes. You want me to be an accountant.'

'No.' The High Commissioner wagged an admonishing finger. 'Well, no, not exactly.'

'What do you have in mind, then?'

'Well, it's, um, we need to make sure that a tight watch is kept on the funds. We don't want any misappropriation; politicians lining their pockets, fingers in the till, shopping trips to Paris – that sort of thing.'

'But appointing a military attaché to manage budgets?'

'Ian, the whole point is that you are appointed to the security task force on the basis of your military background – and, I might add, your considerable knowledge of wildlife. You are not being appointed as an accountant.'

'But that will be my role.'

'As far as the British Government is concerned, yes. But the Kenyan authorities won't see it that way. Besides, there may be more to this security aspect than meets the eye.'

'Meaning what?'

'Eyes and ears, Ian. Pre-emptive focus.' Sir Aubrey leaned forward and lowered his voice. 'Let's say the Americans are getting jittery.'

'But they've been like that ever since the Embassy bombing.'

'Yes, yes, I know. It's just that the, um, the Ambassador button-holed me at a recent function and mentioned some satellite images their fellows sent her which appear to show some unexplained activity in a remote region of northern Kenya.'

'What sort of activity?'

'She didn't know but... Who's your opposite number in the Embassy?'

'Felix Rossi. Italian father, Jamaican mother.'

'Is that relevant?'

'I'm sorry?'

'His ethnic background. I wouldn't have thought that was relevant these days.'

'It isn't.'

'Precisely. The Kenyans can be quite sensitive about such matters.'

That's why I mentioned it. Ian was glad he hadn't mentioned the mother's profession.

The High Commissioner sniffed. 'Anyway, get on to him. See what he can tell you.' He leaned back in his chair. 'I expect to hear from the Minister for Environment and Conservation, within the next day or so, who your counterpart will be.'

'How's he involved?'

'Daniel ole-Tomeno is the Programme's patron.' The High Commissioner removed his glasses. 'We were at Cambridge together.'

Ian pasted a polite smile.

'He's a Maasai.'

'Is that relevant?' – *sotto voce*.

'Good runners the Maasai. Daniel won the varsity cross-country three years on the trot, if you'll pardon the pun. No one could touch him.'

Ian's gaze wandered back to the birds outside.

'Well, yes, enough of that. Anyway I took the liberty of mentioning your name and he was strongly in favour of your involvement.' The High Commissioner wrinkled his nose. 'Incidentally, I've offered to host a party at the residence just before the formal launch of the programme. Quentin can organise it. He's good at that sort of thing. Start off on the front foot as it were.' He passed the consultancy report back to Ian. 'Get up to speed on that and we'll start things moving. Nothing urgent on your desk just now?'

23

'The report on airport security. You wanted to see the first draft before the—'

'Your deputy? Remind me.'

'Tim Hollis – he arrived last month. He's heading the Kenya Air Force training unit.'

'Ah yes, Squadron Leader Hollis. Pass it to him – probably more in his line, anyway. Tell him to come and have a word. He can be acting attaché while you're on this assignment.'

Ian rose to leave.

'One last thing, Ian. I'm pleased to say that my own, er, modest contribution to the programme has been accepted.' The High Commissioner gave a slight cough. 'I, um, suggested the acronym "Condor" for the Conservation in Developing Regions programme. As you know, this large bird symbolises many conservation successes in the Americas, and would I believe convey the connotations of what the programme will be seeking to achieve here in Kenya.'

'Most appropriate.'

'I presume you're familiar with the condor.'

'Yes. It's related to the vultures.'

'Oh. Well, let's leave it there now.'

'Yes, sir.' Ian wished he hadn't mentioned vultures. Before he could leave, there was a brief knock on the door and a man with a flushed complexion, black unruly hair and a rumpled suit, swept in. 'Melhuish reporting back for duty, sir.' He gave a mock salute.

'Quentin,' cried Sir Aubrey. 'Splendid. When did you get back?'

'Straight off the plane. Duty calls.'

'That's very conscientious of you. Good trip?'

'Well, these things can be rather tiresome but one has to... Ian, my dear fellow, didn't see you skulking there behind the door. How are you?'

'Fine.' Ian found it hard to warm to the First Secretary.

'Must say you're looking disgustingly fit. What is it: yak's milk, clean living, press-ups before breakfast?'

Ian gave a pained smile. 'Where have you been this time?'

'Just waving the flag, old boy. Someone has to do it.'

'Yes, I suppose they do.'

'Everything under control here? All that cloak-and-dagger hush-hush stuff we don't talk about.'

'Yes. All under control.'

'Jolly good. Reassuring to know we can sleep safe at night, thanks to you chaps. That right?'

Ian shrugged. He didn't do bogus bonhomie, particularly when blended with pretentious after-shave.

'You coming to our next production?'

'What next production?'

'Phoenix Players. We're doing *The Mousetrap*. I play the lead. How many tickets would you like?'

'I'll, um, let you know.'

Quentin swept back his hair. 'They'll sell like hot cakes. Don't leave it too long.'

Ian checked his watch.

'Put me down for a couple,' said the High Commissioner. 'Front row, if possible. Cynthia loves Agatha Christie.'

'Marvellous,' cried Quentin.

Ian cleared his throat. 'If you'll excuse me, sir, I should be...'

'Yes, yes, of course,' said Sir Aubrey.

'Off to exercise the bloodhounds?' asked Quentin.

'Something like that.' Ian closed the door behind him and raised his eyes to the heavens.

'It's his style,' said Helen, noticing his expression.

'What's he do on all these trips? He never seems to be here.'

'He waves the flag.'

'You're very loyal.'

Her smile betrayed nothing.

He grinned. 'That *Phalaenopsis* is nice.'

'That what?'

'The pot-plant on your desk; it's a *Phalaenopsis*.'

'I thought it was an orchid.'

'It is. Sorry, just showing off. Take care.'

She turned back to her computer. 'And you,' she murmured.

***

Ian returned to his office. Why had he let himself be talked into it? Eyes and ears. Pre-emptive focus. What was all that crap?

His gaze strayed round the room and he wondered vaguely why he wasn't entitled to a hat stand. Quentin had one. Were military attachés junior to...? For God's sake, hadn't he anything better to think about? A photograph caught his attention. It showed a rather more youthful Ian and a pretty dark-haired girl with a ponytail, bottle-feeding an orphan cheetah. That had been his introduction to African wildlife. He didn't know why he still kept the photo. He thought for the umpteenth time of the what-might-have-been.

The phone rang.

'Good morning, sir,' said the switchboard operator. 'Can you take a call from the American Embassy? A Major Rossi.'

'Sure. Put him through.'

'Ian?'

'Felix, you old reprobate.'

Chuckles down the line. 'Say, Ian, you know anything about orchids?'

'Orchids?'

'May be nothing, but could be interesting.'

'Well, I know some of the names.'

'That'll probably do.'

'Look, Felix, what is all this?'

'Get your ass down here and I'll fill you in.'

'I hope you're not wasting my time.'

'Trust me, Ian.'

'Give me a couple of hours.'

'Okay, I'll tell the guys to fast-track you through security and expect you around twelve. I'll get Grace along as well.'

'Grace? Does she know anything about orchids?'

'I doubt it but I guess she might want to learn. See you later.'

Orchids? Was Felix losing it? And why Grace? – better known for her Olympic achievement and now something in Special Branch.

For the next two hours, he immersed himself without enthusiasm in airport security; then scribbled a note to his colleague: *Tim, the Old Man has asked if you can handle this. Grateful if you could check the draft, then bung it up to him. Thanks. Ian.*

He tossed the document into his out-tray and left for the Embassy.

Chapter 4

Colette wheeled her trolley into the heaving arrivals hall of Jomo Kenyatta International Airport and made her way to the smiling figure dressed in a bush shirt and faded jeans. With his sleek black hair and natural tan, Jeff reminded her of a Bollywood film star.

'All set?'

She kissed him lightly on the cheek. 'All set.' She liked working for this no-nonsense, up-front and talented professor, for whom life was too short for platitudes and pleasantries – and the encumbrance of a partner.

'I thought you were supposed to be in the States,' she said.

'That was last week.'

'Last week, the States; this week, Kenya. What is it next week?'

He laughed. 'Let's go.' He led the way out to the car park and stopped beside a new Land Rover with the words *Condor Programme* painted on the side.

'So it's true?' she said.

'Meaning?'

'You've got a new job.'

'Who told you?'

'Someone came to the Zoo to talk about the programme. Said he knew you.'

'Good talk?'

'I'm afraid I missed it. I was very busy at the time, one of the monkeys was sick and—'

'Right.'

She could have kicked herself. He hated pathetic excuses.

'Hop in.' He unlocked the door then loaded her luggage into the back.

'How's Paul?'

Jeff making small talk? Perhaps he realised he'd been too brusque.

'Cocky as ever.' The pun was intended. 'But he's history.'

'Sorry.'

'Don't be. He was a prat.'

'I agree.'

She glared through the windscreen. A *matatu*, one of the local mini-buses crammed to bursting, had stopped in the middle of the

27

carriageway to defy the laws of space-time and pack in more passengers. Jeff hooted and steered round it.

'He really was a prat,' she said with a rueful smile, 'and an unfaithful one.'

He grinned. The tension evaporated.

'So what's your role on the Condor Programme?'

'I'm the coordinator. I haven't told the authorities at the Zoo yet but I guess they won't mind. I'm due some sabbatical.'

'So who's going to do your job while you're away?'

'You want it?'

'No.'

He smiled. 'I thought you'd say that.'

She tried what she hoped was a casual question. 'The, um, person who gave the talk at the Zoo; who would that have been?'

Jeff glanced at her, the smile still on his lips. 'His name's Sean Paterson. He manages a wildlife ranch up near Samburu National Park and is advising the programme on integrated approaches to wildlife conservation and sustainable rural livelihoods.'

'What bollocks. I'm glad I missed the talk.'

'Hey! Not my fault I have to go along with all this donor-speak crap.' Jeff hooted at a cow which was weighing up its chances of getting across the dual carriageway unscathed. 'What it means is he's advising on how to manage wildlife in ways which don't conflict with the needs of local people.'

'Wildlife and locals living in harmony?'

'If you like.'

'I can get my head round that.'

'Approve?'

'Very much.'

She looked out of her window to see if she could spot any animals in the Nairobi Park, but most of the view was now obscured by warehouses and other buildings which had been crammed in between the road and the park fence. She wished the city planners were stricter. Apart from the new buildings, not much seemed to have changed since she'd left around four – or was it five? – years ago.

'What's that great edifice, Jeff? That's new.' She indicated a large white building set back from the road. 'Looks like a fortified doll's house.'

'Pretty much what it is. That's the new US Embassy. I guess they felt security would be better if they moved out of town.'

'After the bombing?'

He nodded.

She stared unseeing through the windscreen. August the seventh, 1998, the day of her birthday. She'd been home on leave and was celebrating with friends when they'd seen news on the TV about al-Qaeda bombing the US Embassy. No one felt like partying after that.

'One of my friends told me he was caught up in the bombing,' she said.

Jeff slowed to allow a small child to chivvy some goats across the road. 'Someone I know?'

'Possibly. He was in admin when I worked at the Primate Research Centre.'

'What name?'

'Omar, Richard Omar. We've lost touch but I think he got a scholarship to do a masters somewhere.'

Jeff glanced across. 'I guess you're going to meet up again.'

'How come?'

'He now works in ole-Tomeno's office.'

'Whose?'

'Ole-Tomeno's. He was Dean of Science but he's now Minister for Environment and Conservation. More importantly, he's also the patron of the Condor Programme.'

'And Richard?'

'He's the link person in the Ministry working on the Condor Programme – ole-Tomeno's assistant.'

'Good for him. He was always ambitious.'

They came to the outskirts of the city. The hibiscus, frangipani and oleanders were in flower, and the bougainvillea-lined carriageways were splashed with colours from an artist's palette. The air was filled with exhaust fumes.

Jeff drove into the Chiromo campus of Nairobi's university and parked in a space reserved for the Zoology Department. He led the way along dingy corridors and into an office piled with scientific papers, journals and unwashed coffee mugs.

'Your office doesn't get any tidier,' said Colette.

Jeff chuckled. 'The department lets me have this, thanks to ole-Tomeno. I still have a few projects going.'

He led her through into a small laboratory where microscopes, centrifuges, water-baths and incubators jostled for space. A man in a white coat was peering down a microscope.

'How's it going, Henry?' called Jeff.

'Not bad, prof. Come and see.'

'Henry, Colette. Colette, Henry,' said Jeff, completing formalities.

'Hi.' She waved a tentative hand.

Jeff peered down the microscope. 'Colette, take a look.'

She adjusted the eyepieces and studied the image. 'Malaria?'

'I've found parasites in all the slides, prof,' said Henry.

'Looks like we've gotten to the bottom of it, then.'

'I didn't know you were getting into malaria,' said Colette.

'I'm not. The Petes sent these blood slides down. Some of the monkeys there are sick.'

'These are from monkeys?'

Jeff nodded. 'Colobus. The Petes darted some of the sick ones in the forest where they're working – near Tandala Ranch, Sean Paterson's place.'

She turned back to the microscope and examined different fields; then repeated the process with other slides. She looked up. 'This level of infection wouldn't make the monkeys sick.'

He studied her, seemingly lost in thought.

'Benign infections are common in forest monkeys,' she added.

'Right.'

'The parasites are called *Hepatocystis*, if my memory—'

'I'm taking you up there on Thursday,' he said. 'All arranged. Tomorrow is ole-Tomeno's meeting – briefing about the Condor Programme. We leave for Tandala the next day. Sean's driving us.'

'Sean Paterson's taking us to the ranch?'

'Sure. He's on one of the task forces and will be at the meeting.'

'I see.'

'I've sent the Petes a message.'

She gazed briefly at a noisy colony of weaverbirds nesting in the tree outside the window then rounded on him. 'Jeff, just what is going on? You drag me out here on some lame excuse, telling me to bring my sampling stuff. I've loads of work I should be doing back home – not faffing around attending meetings I've no interest in, or gallivanting off to the bush when the Petes could perfectly well send samples to the Zoo – as they've done before.' She snatched a breath. 'And my dad's not well.'

Henry shuffled his feet and fiddled with the microscope.

Jeff avoided her gaze. 'Just bear with me.'

Chapter 5

The tall marine rose from behind his desk and engulfed Ian's hand in one the size of a dinner plate.

'Ain't you hot in that thing?' said Felix, who looked cool and relaxed in sandy-coloured trousers and matching shirt with open-necked collar and the words: U.S.Army, and Rossi, embroidered on the respective breast pockets.

'No.' Ian stuck out his chin and adjusted his tie. 'I'm used to it.'

'Sure.' Felix gestured to a chair beside the desk. The computer screen showed an action photo of the Dallas Cowboys.

'That you?' asked Ian. Even among big men, Felix stood out.

'Year we won the Super Bowl.'

'Impressive.'

'Yeah, well.' Felix indicated the slim girl with the braided hair who was watching the two men with an amused smile. 'You know Grace?'

'Of course. How is it, Grace – *namna gani?*'

'*Nzuri sana.*'

'Hey, cut that out,' muttered Felix.

Ian winked at his Kenyan colleague. 'So what's all this about orchids, Felix?'

'Dunno but take a look at this. Mentions orchids.' He passed Ian a photocopy on which the title of an article had been highlighted. 'It's from the Frederick News-Post.'

'The what?'

'Local press. Frederick, Maryland, the home of Fort Detrick.'

'I see.'

Grace glanced between the two of them. 'Can you tell me what you're talking about?'

'Sure,' said Felix. 'Fort Detrick: the US Army Medical Research Institute of Infectious Diseases. It also keeps a watch out for bugs which might be used in warfare. May be nothing. Still, as you two are here I thought I'd run it past you.'

Ian looked up. 'Does the word "Mlala" mean anything to you, Grace?'

She shrugged. '*Lala* means "sleep" in Swahili. *Mlala* is a person sleeping.'

Ian gazed out of the window overlooking the adjacent Nairobi

National Park. 'That's what I thought.' He skimmed the rest of the article then passed it to her. 'What do you think?'

'*Soviet Defector Dies of Mystery Disease.* So?' She shrugged and tossed the article back on the table.

'Let me fill you in,' said Felix.

'Please do.'

He regarded her coolly and pursed his lips. 'This defector guy, name of Alexei Borishenkov, used to be director of a lab in Russia – place called Stepnogorsk – thought to be carrying out bio-weapons research: dirty bombs and suchlike. Leastways, seems he started getting a conscience about what his pals were doing, and when he went over to the States on some high-powered delegation – something connected with all that *glasnost* stuff few years ago – he sought political asylum and started spilling the beans.'

Grace sniffed and checked her watch.

'You make anything of this orchid thing, Grace?' he asked.

'No.'

Felix muttered something about pushing water up hill and jabbed at the article. 'Someone apparently sent orchids to the paper with a note saying: *In memory of Alexei Borishenkov who died of Marburg disease. He also liked orchids.* It was signed Mlala. So what's that tell us?'

'I thought it was customary to send flowers on such occasions,' she said.

'You trying to wind me up?'

Ian stepped in. 'Do we know when he died?'

'Week, ten days ago, seemingly.' Felix scowled at Grace who had adopted a choir-girl expression.

'So presumably none of this would have come out if the paper hadn't been sent the flowers and started digging?' said Ian.

'Damn right, it wouldn't.' Felix got up and made his way to the window, feinting left and right to avoid imaginary tacklers. 'No way Fort D folks want to draw attention to what they get up to.' He peered at some animals which had come into view in the Park. 'What are those guys?'

Ian joined him. 'Kongoni – a kind of antelope.'

'That so? Funny-looking horns.'

'Don't let me interrupt your game-viewing,' said Grace, her cherubic smile clinging by its fingertips, 'but much as I'd like to learn more about someone I've no interest in, working in a place I've never heard of, I do have more pressing things to do. Can we get on?'

'Hang in there, Grace.' Felix returned to his seat. 'All the Fort Detrick folks have said, is that Boris worked there as an adviser and they've sent their condolences to his family – the usual horse-shit.'

She smiled sweetly.

'CIA, though, have been keeping him on their radar since he arrived.' Felix returned to his keyboard. 'When I quizzed them, they sent me this: *Soviet defector, Alexei Borishenkov, was formerly head of Russia's Biopreparat programme at the Progress, Scientific and Production Association in Stepnogorsk, in what is now Kazakhstan. He claimed that development of Marburg virus as a biological weapon had reached an advanced stage. Independent confirmation for this claim is lacking but at least one laboratory accident, which resulted in the death of researcher, Olga Levkova, may have been due to a bio-engineered variant of the virus. Following Borishenkov's defection, it is thought the programme closed down, but the whereabouts of its lead scientist, a US-trained Pakistani Dr Qasim Chaudhry, is not known.* Then there's a bit of background on this Marburg thing: *Marburg virus takes its name from the town of Marburg in Germany where it was isolated from workers at a pharmaceutical plant who contracted a fatal haemorrhagic disease from monkeys imported for research from East Africa.* That's probably why my guys sent the cutting – possible Kenyan link.' Felix turned away from his keyboard. 'Any thoughts folks?'

'Perhaps it's a wake-up call,' said Grace.

'Meaning what?'

It was her turn to wander over to the window.

As he and Felix waited, Ian recalled the image of the tall Kenyan athlete – who could only be called Grace – powering over the line in the final of the Olympic five thousand metres.

She continued gazing out of the window and seemed to be talking almost to herself. 'Not all those involved in the Embassy bombing were captured or accounted for. Some are still out there – sleeping.'

'We know that,' muttered Felix.

She ignored the comment and indicated the photocopy on his desk. 'A story like this is going to be picked up by the international press, and it won't be long before some sharp-eyed reporter in Nairobi spots it and blows it up into something for the papers here.'

'Kenyan link to mysterious death of Russian defector; that sort of thing?' said Ian.

'The papers will love it: a deadly virus from Kenyan monkeys and someone with a pseudonym of possible Swahili origin. I think this Mlala person could be using the press to give the sleepers their wake-up call.'

'I like it,' said Felix. ''Cept I don't.'

'What do you think, Ian?' asked Grace, returning to her seat.

'That there are a lot of unanswered questions.' He counted off on his fingers. 'Who's Mlala? Who are the sleepers? Is this a call to wake them? If so, why, and why now? Who's pulling the strings – orchid-boy Mlala, or someone else? Was Borishenkov's death an accident, or did orchid-boy organise it? Again, why?'

Felix sighed. 'You sure as hell don't make things easy.'

'They're not.' Ian's smile lacked humour. 'Felix, get your people to lean on Fort Detrick. Find out more about Borishenkov, who his contacts were, exactly how he died, how the news got out.'

Felix scowled and folded his arms.

'I imagine someone like this would have been watched like a hawk from day-one. FBI, I presume. Also see if—'

'Okay, okay, I know my job,' growled Felix. 'Grace, those Ninja jerks; what they up to these days?'

'Njia Mpya?'

'Yeah, them.'

Ian glanced between the two of them. 'Who are we talking about?'

'Njia Mpya,' said Grace.

'My guys reckon they could have had some involvement in the Embassy bombing,' said Felix.

'First I've heard,' said Ian.

'Or maybe not.'

'Why haven't I been told?'

'Like I said; perhaps they weren't involved.'

'At least tell me your thinking.'

'Aw, hell.' Felix rubbed his hands over his face. 'You folks want some coffee?'

'Please.' Ian nodded tersely.

'Tea for me,' said Grace.

'Right, I'll go grab them.'

Ian sat glaring at the table. 'Okay, Grace: Njia Mpya.'

'What about them?'

'Who are they? What are they up to? Why have they suddenly popped up?'

'They haven't.'

Ian ran his hands through his hair. 'Christ, I thought we were on the same side.'

34

'We are.' She studied him for a moment then smiled. 'Njia Mpya means the New Way or Path. Until recently the group was nothing more than a bunch of Somali kids involved in petty crime who adopted a fancy name to make themselves sound important.'

'Are they?'

'Are they what?'

'Important.'

'A few days ago, I would have said no. Now I'm not so sure. They seem to be better organised and—'

'Who runs their show?'

'Don't know.'

'Come on, Grace, you can do better than that.'

'Listen, Ian, I don't know – repeat, don't know. *I* don't know. *We* don't know.'

'But they've come to your attention and to Felix's people?'

'Yes.'

'Why?'

Felix returned with three over-full mugs from which the contents were slopping. 'Jeez, that's hot.' His eyes swung back and forth trying to follow the words swirling round the room.

Grace sighed. 'It's possible that some of those who evaded capture after the Embassy bombing have joined the group.'

'And why it's now better organised?'

'Perhaps. But from now on we should factor them into our equations – isn't that what your people would say, Ian?'

Ian picked up his mug and shoved his less charitable thoughts back into his pockets. 'From now on, you also factor me in. Okay?'

'Sure, sure.' Felix chuckled. 'We'll keep factoring.' He shut down his computer. 'Which brings us to—'

He was interrupted by a knock on the door. A marine in uniform, rimless glasses and a crew-cut entered. He consulted a piece of paper and whispered in Felix's ear.

Felix frowned as he jotted down some notes.

The man seemed to notice Ian and Grace for the first time. 'Hi, folks, how you doing?'

'Fine,' said Ian.

Grace said nothing.

A cat wandered in through the open door.

'Jeez,' muttered Felix.

The man shooed the cat out and followed it.

'So much for friggin' security,' muttered Felix.

Ian caught Grace's eye and smiled. 'What's the cat's name, Felix?'

'Piss Off. Leastways, that's what I call it. Ambassador – it's her cat – probably calls it Tiddles or Pussykins or some such. Seems to go just where it likes.' He glared at the closed door. 'Let's move on.' He looked down at his notes. 'Seems like our investment might have paid off.'

'What investment?' said Ian.

Felix leaned back and studied the ceiling. 'Following the ninety-eight bombing, the Embassy assisted Kenya to install improved surveillance systems at the major entry points into the country. These systems are linked to computers here and also in Special Branch which…' He flapped his hands and sat up. 'Hell, you know all this.'

'So what's new?' said Ian.

Felix tapped his notes. 'Seems some smart guy at Immigration felt that one of the jokers from a Pakistani Airways flight didn't look right and flagged him.'

'What name?'

'According to his passport: Faisal Malik. But guys in there—' Felix jerked a thumb. '—tell me Malik used to call himself Qasim Chaudhry when he worked as lead scientist at Stepnogorsk.'

'Jesus,' muttered Ian. 'And now he's pitched up here?'

'And I don't reckon it's for bird-watching.' Felix looked up as the door opened. 'Yes?'

The man with the crew-cut was back. 'Best we can do for now, major.' He passed Felix a grainy photograph, 'but we've gotten Langley working on it.'

'Thanks,' said Felix, as the man left. He laid the photo on the table. 'Taken from the airport CCTV. What you make of it?'

'Not a lot,' said Ian. 'Tall man with a beard. Narrows it down to a few million.'

'Yeah, yeah, I know. Let's see what Langley comes up with.'

'Langley?' said Grace.

'CIA headquarters.'

'Oh.'

'But now we get to the juicy bit.' Felix pursed his lips. 'Seems friend Malik was met by an African male, name of Richard Omar.' He paused. 'And Omar just happens to work for the Minister of Environment and Conservation, guy called ole-Tomeno.'

36

Chapter 6

Northern Kenya – 2001

In the dry season, sun congeals on black rocks and blisters tortured sand. Vistas shimmer. Plants survive if they are steeped in poison or covered in thorns – or both. Others – if they haven't been eaten – die. Dust devils roam. Frogs retreat underground and become entombed. Hunger prowls.

Now was different. The rains had been kind, gullies filled, water courses flowed, frogs emerged from their tombs and chorused nightly, rivers revived. The scent of acacia blossom, damp sand and new beginnings hung in the air. Lifeless trees sprang into leaf, grass grew and set seed. Birds ate the seed and raised young. Butterflies jostled round flowers. Sheep and goats gave birth, crickets sang, dust devils slept.

The landscape glowed in the beautiful-people colours of evening, lighting up the distant mountain of Lokinang. People said many vehicles were now coming and going, but Dima wasn't interested. He'd no reason to go there. He sat relaxing in the remains of the day proudly watching his family. His two young sons were shutting the sheep and goats into their pen for the night. His wife was milking one of the goats, and his daughter who was beginning to toddle, played nearby. He smiled as he watched her, his *swara mdogo* – his little gazelle – tottering around with her new mobility, taking an interest in all about her.

His last hunting trip had gone well. Perhaps he should have asked more for the leopard skin he'd sold to the Somali trader, but the money had enabled his wife to buy food for the family and hunger no longer threatened.

This was a good life. Always, though, he was haunted by the memory of the man who, all those years ago, had killed his parents. Sooner or later, he would find that man – the man with one ear. He would not fail again.

A hornbill began calling in the tree above his head. He smiled at the comical bird posturing to its mate. His daughter pointed to them and laughed.

He waved and returned to the scenery, breathing in the peace of cool evening air.

Screams!

Screams shredding his peace.

His daughter had stumbled near the fire. Upset a pan of boiling maize gruel.

He rushed to her. Frantically scraped the scalding food from her arms, face and chest. Ignored his own pain.

His wife ran back and forth – hysterically, aimlessly.

'Water,' he yelled.

She grabbed the tin can.

He poured the trickle over his daughter's body and wiped the remaining gruel away. Her screams sank to whimpers.

'More water.'

'There is no more. The waterhole is far. We cannot go until morning.'

The two boys gazed in horror.

'Get *osuguru*,' he shouted.

He cradled his daughter in his arms. Every time she convulsed, his wife cried out.

The boys returned with bundles of aloe leaves and pounded them with rocks. He rubbed the sap over his daughter's blistering skin. It gave some relief but she continued to whimper.

Darkness fell.

His wife sent the boys to bed and came and sat beside him.

No one ate that night.

His wife drifted into fitful sleep, her head resting on his knee. When she woke in the morning, he still sat, watching, waiting, staring – their daughter in his arms.

Her breathing was now very shallow. He dare not move.

'I go for water,' his wife said.

He nodded.

She returned an hour later and woke the boys.

Dima told them to build a small shelter to protect him and his daughter from the sun.

Throughout the day he watched over her, plying her with sips of water, driving away the flies, cradling her in his arms, stroking her cheek.

Just before dawn on the second night, he rose stiffly and carried the tiny body into the bush. He came to a place among the rocks. Set his daughter down. Scooped out a shallow depression in the sun-baked ground, oblivious to the pain in his blistered hands. He laid her to rest and covered her body with rocks.

He wanted her spirit to join that of his father soaring with the vultures. He tried not to think of them tearing her tiny body apart. But he knew they would. He added more rocks. He tried not to think of flies laying their eggs. But he knew they would. He added yet more rocks. He tried not to think of hyenas ripping open the grave. But he knew they would. There was no point in adding more rocks. The spirits of the rocks weren't strong enough to protect her.

'Kwa heri, swara mdogo – goodbye, little gazelle.'

It was the first time since his childhood that he cried.

When his wife woke, he was still sitting. Now alone.

She wiped silent tears from her cheeks.

Later that day, he rose to his feet. 'I go,' he said. 'The food is nearly finished.'

She didn't look up from her milking.

He went into the hut, collected his bow and arrows, his hyrax-skin bag. He bade his sons, goodbye.

'I go now,' he repeated.

'Eeh.' His wife continued milking.

He walked away without looking back.

Before long the sun would reassert itself. The land would bake, rivers and frogs would retreat beneath the sand, leaves would shrivel, dust devils would resume their aimless roaming.

And his wife would wonder how the family would survive until the next rains.

Chapter 7

A taxi dropped Colette outside the Ministry of Environment and Conservation. She made her way to a suite of offices on the third floor, labelled: *Minister, Private.* She signed in at the reception desk and waited to be received. The portrait of Kenya's President gazed impassively over batik prints of Maasai cattle. A potted orchid stood on the window sill. Photographs of wildlife adorned the walls. A cockroach wandered around looking lost. And the young receptionist smiled whenever Colette looked in her direction.

An inner door opened and a woman about Colette's age, emerged. 'Dr Fraser? I'm Maria, the Minister's PA.'

The cockroach scuttled off.

'Sorry I'm early,' said Colette.

'You're not the first. Colonel Sinclair is already here.'

'Is that Ian Sinclair?'

'Yes, he's a counterpart on one of the task forces. Do you know him?'

'I, um…'

Maria held the door of a meeting room open for her. 'Can I get you tea or coffee?'

'Er – coffee, please; milk, no sugar.'

Ian was sitting on his own at the end of the room, reading a newspaper. He looked up as Colette entered, smiled and came over.

She was relieved he didn't try to kiss her.

'Hi, Colette. I saw your name on the programme.'

'Did you?'

'You're looking well.'

She applied a smile.

'It's been a long time.'

'Yes, hasn't it.'

'How are you keeping?'

She shrugged. 'Fine.'

'So how come you're involved in this?'

'That's what I keep asking myself.'

'So what have you been up to?'

She studied her hands. 'Work and things.'

'Right.' Ian looked round the room.

Other people were beginning to arrive. He waved to one of them then turned back to her. 'It's great to see you.'

'Is it?'

'Yes.' He paused. 'I was wondering if we could meet up for a drink.'

She was getting low on conversation.

'Could we?'

'Ian, it *has* been a long time. I'm not sure I want to—'

'Please.'

She lowered her eyes. 'All right.'

'Where are you staying?'

'The Fairview.'

'Six-thirty this evening?'

'I suppose so.'

Maria came in with Colette's coffee.

'See you then.' Ian moved across the room to join a tall girl in a smart police uniform.

'See you.' She screwed her eyes shut.

***

'It's Ian, isn't it?'

Ian hadn't noticed the distinguished-looking African who had come unannounced into the room to join him and Grace. 'Yes. Good morning, minister.'

'Good morning, Grace. What a splendid gathering,' said ole-Tomeno, beaming round and congratulating himself. 'Press as well.' He turned back to Ian. 'I see the High Commissioner has drafted you onto the programme to keep an eye on the funds.'

'Oh, er, no. No, not at all. I'm here as counterpart on the...'

'Quite so. I'm pleased Aubrey has released you. I think you and Grace will make a good team. I've asked her to lead the security task force.'

She smiled and shrugged.

Ole-Tomeno beckoned to a tanned fair-haired man who had just entered the room. 'Sean, good morning.'

'Morning, Daniel.'

'Can I introduce Ian Sinclair, military attaché at the British High Commission?'

Ian was aware of Colette watching them as he and Sean shook hands.

'Well, he was until recently,' continued ole-Tomeno, 'but I

41

persuaded the High Commissioner to release him to work on Condor with Grace here.'

'Sounds good,' said Sean. 'You must come and see our side of the programme, Ian, up in Samburu.'

'I will. Any excuse to get out of Nairobi.'

'And you, Grace, go and visit your old stamping ground,' said ole-Tomeno. 'It was good when you were keeping law and order in my constituency. Kept the men in order,' he added with a chuckle.

'We did our—'

'So, Sean, still peaceful up there? The usual cattle rustling, wife stealing and gun running, I suppose?'

'Pretty much.'

'Nothing changes.' Ole-Tomeno gave a shark smile then leaned forward and lowered his voice. 'Tell me, is it true that one can exchange a goat for a Kalashnikov?'

'So I'm told,' said Sean.

The Minister frowned. 'We must do something about that, Grace.'

'We're certainly aware of the problem, sir, the difficulty is...'

'Yes, yes, I know: resources. Nonetheless, it might be an idea to go and have a look. Wear your Condor hat so as not to tread on toes.'

'I'll see what I can do.'

'Take up Sean's offer. Ian as well. If we play our cards right, this Condor money might...' He waved to someone on the far side of the room. 'Otherwise, Sean, all quiet – no whisperings?'

'There are always whisperings, Daniel, as you know, but there could—'

Ole-Tomeno looked at his watch. 'Goodness, is that the time? I expect Jeff will want to get started soon. Excuse me.' He moved away to continue working the room: a wave here, a squeezed elbow there, a murmured pleasantry to a colleague – a stately stork among lesser waterfowl.

'He doesn't miss much,' said Sean.

'He doesn't miss anything.' Grace took Sean's arm and led him aside. 'Excuse us a moment, Ian.'

'Sure.' Ian wandered back to Colette who was talking animatedly to a young African wearing dark glasses and a name-badge which read: Richard Omar.

***

Colette came into the garden of the hotel. Ian was seated at a table in the shade. He had ordered two White Caps – what they used to drink. He rose as she approached. She made no attempt to kiss him.

'I've got you a beer,' he said. 'Hope that's okay.'

She resisted a perverse inclination to ask for fruit juice. 'Thanks.'

'Cheers, welcome back to Kenya.' He raised his glass.

'Cheers.'

'Nice place this. The garden's probably at its best now after the rains. Look, turaco!' A large green bird with scarlet wings swooped across the lawn and landed in a tree. It began a raucous call which was echoed by another bird on the other side of the road. 'It always amazes me that you can get such a variety of wildlife in the middle of—'

'You and the bloody army,' she snapped.

'Sorry?'

'You heard what I said.'

'Yes.' He paused. 'I'm sorry.'

'Is that it? I'm sorry.'

They waited tensely as a steward placed a bowl of crisps on the table.

'I've still got that picture in my office,' he said.

'What picture?'

'You with the baby cheetah.'

She said nothing.

'That was my introduction to Kenya's wildlife. On the Hopkins' ranch near Athi River.'

'He was called Toto,' she said in a flat voice.

'He's now fully grown – a fine male. Remember, you thought he wouldn't make it. They tell me he's—'

'Ian, stop!'

'Stop what?'

'Stop this bloody small talk.'

'Sorry.'

'And don't keep saying sorry, for Christ's sake.'

He sipped his drink and waited.

'Ian, we can't just pick up as though nothing has happened. You've moved on. I've moved on.'

He winced.

'All right, I know it wasn't only you. It was me as well: my PhD, my research, my ambitions. It all happened too soon. We both had careers. You in the army – I understand it's colonel now.'

He waved a dismissive hand. 'Perhaps we could have worked

43

things out.'

'Could we?' She twisted her glass and tried to restrain her emotions which threatened to wing off round the garden. 'There was no way I could have joined those women who meet each morning to play tennis, drink coffee, and grumble about house servants.'

He gave a slight smile.

'It wasn't me.'

'I never thought it was.'

'Why, for God's sake, didn't you say so?'

'We never talked about it.'

She rubbed distracted hands over her face.

'You okay?' he asked.

'Not really.' She put her hands in her lap and twisted her fingers together. The garden really was looking at its best: the bougainvilleas, the cannas, the poinsettias. Some of the tension eased. 'Those clouds are awfully black. I wonder if it's going to rain again.'

'Who's making small talk now?'

She turned towards him. 'Ian, what are we going to do?'

'We could make a fresh start.'

'With all the baggage?'

'We could leave it behind.'

'And what sort of relationship would that be; you here and me in London? Ian, be realistic.' She thought of her pathetic little house.

'You could work on Condor I'm sure if I had a word with Jeff...'

Colette turned white. 'I cannot believe what I'm hearing. Of all the conniving—'

'I shouldn't have said that.'

'Too bloody right.' She bit savagely into a crisp.

The look in his eyes softened. 'I know why I fell in love with you.'

'What the fuck's that supposed to mean?'

'The feistiness, the spirit.'

'Huh.' The anger subsided. She looked down at her hands and tried to stop her lower lip trembling. 'Ian, we can't simply wipe the slate clean. I couldn't – even if you could.'

He laid his hand on hers. 'I shouldn't have come – it wasn't fair.'

Emptiness replaced the anger in her eyes.

He slipped his hand away and stood up. 'I'll pay for the drinks on the way out.'

She stared at his unfinished beer.

Why the bloody hell did I come back?

Chapter 8

Dima had no idea how many days he'd been walking, subsisting on honeycomb and berries. He travelled south through the hills, crossing the great rivers – now drying up – crossing the deserts, crossing the savannahs, crossing more hills, and all the time searching. Searching the bush, searching the forests, searching the game trails he knew so well. Searching for kudu, for leopard, for rhino, even – the ultimate prize which could keep his family in food for many rains and allow him to send his sons to school.

Every day his daughter's smile haunted him. Every night her screams tormented him. He would wake sweating and panting, and would rise and continue his search. But his mind was not on hunting. His skills had become blunted. Success eluded him.

Until he reached the high hills.

He rarely hunted monkeys which, when they were they skinned, looked like small people. Their meat tasted sickly and their skins were valueless. Colobus monkeys, though, with their beautiful black and white fur, were different. These ones were feeding in a large podocarpus tree, its branches draped with lichens which emulated the monkeys' flowing manes.

Dima, the invisible hunter, slipped through the thick vegetation. Stopped near the tree. Unwrapped the binding covering one of his arrows. These monkeys were not alert like normal monkeys. No matter, it made hunting easier. He took no pleasure in killing animals but hunting was his only skill, the skill which kept him and his family from starvation.

Several females had babies, their tiny white-furred bodies clinging limpet-like to their mothers who ran fearlessly along the slender branches, heedless of the dizzy height.

A flock of wood hoopoes moved through the trees cackling to each other. It was a peaceful scene such as he had witnessed many times; the spirits of the forest in harmony.

The large male screamed as Dima's arrow thudded home. It rocked briefly on the branch where it was sitting then crashed to the ground.

The rest of the troop fled screeching. The cackles of the wood hoopoes became cries of alarm. Bats cowered in hollow trees. Even the butterflies paused. The harmony of the forest shattered.

Dima apologised to the monkey as he watched its gasping life ebb away and he offered a silent prayer of thanks to *Mungu* who had brought him this prize. If *Mungu* had chosen this beautiful animal to be his family's salvation, so be it. There would, though, be no salvation for his daughter.

He took the *simi* – the dagger – from his belt and began to cut off the skin. There was more blood than usual and it ran like water. Some splashed into his eye. The naked oozing body made him shudder. He covered it with leaves, not wanting a reminder of another body he had seen so recently.

Here the killing was easy, and over the next three days, he killed and skinned four more monkeys, two of which oozed watery blood. His heart began to lighten. The skins would bring a good price. His family would be well fed again. Next day he could kill more then he would return home. But perhaps he should wait until the heat in his body had cooled and the pain in his head had eased. He hid the skins in an old porcupine den and his weapons in the crevice among the branches of a large fig tree. He lay down to rest among the tree's great buttress roots.

The day advanced. The heat and pain worsened.

Next day: more heat, more pain. His throat had fire. Light blinded him. His eyes screamed.

He washed his face in the nearby stream and drank some water to kill the fire. It made him sick. He had to find *enyaru*. He tried to stand. Trees swirled before his eyes. He staggered and fell. *Mungu is angry with me for killing many monkeys. I was greedy and he has sent a great sickness. I have broken the hunters' code. I have killed without need.*

Find *enyaru*.

Thunder in his head. Burning in his eyes. Fire in his throat and body. He had to find *enyaru*.

He rose, using a stick to steady himself. He was now a *mzee* – an old man. His muscles had no strength. He leaned on the stick. Bushes came towards him. Went away. Lights flashed off them.

He stumbled along a game trail which kept appearing and disappearing.

Enyaru. Find *enyaru*. He tottered and fell.

A purple-flowered plant. It wasn't *enyaru*.

He struggled to his feet and staggered on.

Another plant with purple flowers. Also not *enyaru*.

He came to a track through the forest.

Enyaru!

He slumped down among purple flowers. A cloud of butterflies erupted.

Liquid poured from his mouth. Ran down his body. Formed a red pool which turned black on the ground.

He stuffed some of the leaves in his mouth and chewed, fighting the fire which wanted to throw them out.

More leaves.

The blinding light split his head. His family would starve. His sons would not go to school. The deaths of his parents would not be avenged. He was about to join his daughter.

He had failed for the last time.

Chapter 9

Colette struggled to shake off jetlag as she fumbled for the phone. 'Hello.'

'Sorry to wake you, Colette. Jeff here. I'm afraid something has come up. Nothing to worry about, but it means I won't be able to come to Tandala with you this morning.'

'Oh.'

'It's all right, Sean says he's happy to take you, and you can stay at the ranch. There are no tourists at the moment and the guest accommodation is free.'

She failed to think of anything sensible to say.

'Sorry about that. Plan's still the same. Sean will meet you in the foyer at eight o'clock. He'll take you to meet the Petes and you can check out the monkeys.'

'Jeff, what exactly am I supposed to—?'

'Enjoy your trip.'

'But I still don't—'

She stared at the buzzing receiver. Doubts trespassed into her thoughts. The receiver continued buzzing.

***

She'd packed her rucksack with things she'd need for the trip and left her suitcase in the hotel's lock-up store. Now, she sat in reception partially hidden from the entrance by a potted palm. She'd scarcely managed any breakfast and had failed to come up with a valid reason why she shouldn't travel to Tandala alone with Sean. She almost wished Ian was coming with them.

A Land Rover drove past the entrance.

There was still time to slip out through the other entrance. She leaned back and closed her eyes. When she opened them, he was there talking to the receptionist. She approached the desk. 'Hello.'

He turned and a smile lit up his face. 'Hi.' He held out his hand. 'Welcome to Kenya.'

'Thanks.'

'Sorry I didn't get a chance to talk to you at the meeting yesterday. It was all a bit of a rush.'

His eyebrows really were unusually fair.

'This is a bit different from London, then?' He waved a hand round Africa.

She pasted a smile over her nervousness.

'Sleep okay?'

'Fine thanks.' She had a brief flash of wondering what it would have been like if he'd been sleeping with her.

'You all set, hey?'

She nodded. 'Do you know why Jeff had to cry off?'

'He didn't say. Probably something ole-Tomeno wants tidied up after yesterday's meeting.'

'Yes, probably.' She fiddled with her rucksack. 'I'm afraid I've got rather a lot of stuff.' She indicated the large plastic box beside the palm. 'It's all my sampling stuff. My monkey tricks.'

He didn't seem to think the quip amusing. Nor did she. She wished she'd kept her mouth shut.

'No worries. Plenty of room in the Landy.' He picked up the box and headed for the door.

'Have a good safari, Dr Fraser,' called the receptionist.

'Thank you.' She shouldered her rucksack, stepped out into the sunshine and wondered about the meaning of life.

'Here, give me that.' Sean opened the passenger door and tossed the rucksack onto the middle seat. 'There you go. Hop in.' He loaded her box into the back then went round to the driver's side and climbed in. 'All set?'

She nodded.

He reached into the seat behind and passed her a copy of a local newspaper. 'Have you seen this?'

Colette read the headline. 'Marburg!'

'Isn't that something you deal with?'

She stared across the car park. 'It's something I dread whenever a monkey gets sick at the Zoo. There was a scare that day we met in the canteen.'

'I remember. Anyway, this happened a few thousand miles away and the Kenyan link seems pretty tenuous.'

'It's a most terrible disease,' she said, gazing ahead but seeing nothing. 'How that poor man would have suffered.'

'What's this Fort Detrick place?' he asked.

She gazed vacantly at him.

'Fort Detrick: do you know anything about it?'

'Sorry, Sean. I was miles away. It's where the Americans check out nasty tropical and emerging diseases, including those which could be

49

used in biological warfare.'

'And you deal with diseases like that?'

'God, no! I just worry about them.' She pulled a face. 'Can we go?'

'Sure.' He started the engine and drove out of the car park. After a while he turned to her. 'Tell me about yourself.'

'What?'

'Your life history.'

She laughed. 'Why?'

'A long drive ahead. Go on.'

'It's not very interesting.'

'I'll be the judge of that.'

He sounded like Jeff.

'Do you like classical music?'

'I, er… Educate me.'

He slipped a disc into the CD player.

She was grateful for the distraction, closed her eyes and let the music wash over her. She opened her eyes as the piece ended. 'What was it?'

'*Wachet auf.*'

'Sorry?'

'By Bach.'

'It was lovely.' She closed her eyes as the music continued.

***

She woke with a start, conscious of the rattling vehicle. They were now on a dirt road. 'Was I asleep?'

'If your snores were anything to go by.' He gave his lopsided grin.

'Oh, no. Where are we?'

'Just left the tarmac. About two hours to go. You can go back to sleep.'

'No chance.' She sat up, hoping he wouldn't quiz her about her life history.

They drove mostly in silence, punctuated by Sean's occasional remarks to point out a bird, a flower or some half-hidden animal. She was still trying to fathom this enigmatic man of the bush with his easy confident manner, the man into whose life she'd been thrown. Surely that hadn't been Jeff's motive for not coming with them.

She sighed as she tried to shuffle her emotions into a semblance of order.

'Cares of the world?'

'Sorry, Sean. Life's a bit complicated right now.'

May you live in interesting times. These were certainly that and a far cry from posers on London's Underground. For that she was grateful.

'Have you made any plans to meet the Petes?' she asked.

He chuckled. 'Arrangements and the Petes tend not to be compatible.'

'Jeff said he'd sent them a message.'

'I wouldn't hold your breath on that, but we'll drop by their camp, see if they're around.'

'Are they still as mad as ever?'

'I'll let you decide.'

'I'll take that as a yes.' She was looking forward to meeting them again. She'd been collaborating now for nearly three years and they'd sent her some excellent material from which she'd isolated a hitherto unknown virus which still awaited formal classification. They had also discovered the insect vector of two other viruses and the possible vector of a third.

'See that line of trees ahead,' said Sean, 'that's the sand river marking the ranch boundary. Look kudu.'

'Where?'

'Straight ahead, under that tree, standing very still.' He stopped the vehicle and passed her his binoculars.

'He's magnificent, those massive spiral horns. Greater kudu?'

'Those are the females behind – the ones without horns. They're how the ranch gets its name.'

'*Tandala* means kudu?'

He nodded.

It was all coming back: the excitement of the bush, the expectation, the beauty and... and the peace. A large turquoise and mauve bird swooped on something hidden in the grass.

'What's that?'

'Lilac-breasted roller.'

'It's beautiful.'

Perhaps returning wasn't so crazy.

Sean started the engine and moved off.

She made a pretence of searching out of the side window for further game.

'It looks as though we may be in luck,' he said a few minutes later. 'There.'

A battered Land Rover was parked in a sand river under the shade of an overhanging acacia tree. Two figures lay on their backs beside the vehicle, bush hats over their faces, bottles of beer beside them.

Sean followed the track down to the river bed, pulled up and switched off the engine.

'Bugger off,' said one of the hats. An arm waved them away.

'Pete,' called Colette, as she and Sean climbed out.

One of the figures sat up and grabbed his bottle. 'Dear lady. We are honoured.'

The one whom Colette knew as Pete-A scrambled to his feet and kicked his companion. 'We have company.'

The other Pete sat up. 'So much for the peace of the bush; vehicles and hordes of riff raff. Have a beer.'

'You old reprobates, how are you?' She embraced each of them in turn. 'Did you come to meet us?'

'Certainly not,' said Pete-A. 'We have more intellectual tasks to pursue than running a tour-guide service.'

'So I see.'

'Do not misinterpret what you see, dear lady. We are recharging the batteries before returning to the relentless pursuit of knowledge.'

'Bullshit,' murmured his colleague.

'Did you get Jeff's message?' she asked.

'Much as we would wish to sit around all day awaiting... No, we didn't. But no matter, our day has been lightened by your gracious presence.' He took Colette's hand and kissed it.

She laughed. These crazy bronzed guys were two of the best entomologists in Africa. Both had scruffy beards and were similarly clad in faded khaki shirts and shorts, and with tyre-sandals on their feet. But there, similarities ended: Peter Acheson was tall and languid, while Peter Barnsley was short, stocky and bustling. The Pete-A and Pete-B nicknames were inevitable. They lived permanently in the bush, subsisting, as far as she could tell, almost entirely on beer.

Pete-B, who had been rummaging in his vehicle, returned and thrust cold bottles into their hands. 'Cheers and welcome.'

They chinked bottles.

'So, how's life treating you?' she asked.

'Rarely, dear lady, rarely,' said Pete-A, 'but it is a cross we bear for the sake of science.'

'You two off somewhere?' asked Sean.

'Nairobi,' said Pete-B. 'There's only one disadvantage to our life-style.'

'What's that?' asked Colette.

'Absence of the fair sex.'

'Disgusting,' said his colleague. 'We are indeed heading for Nairobi, to spend time in the rarefied atmospheres of the museum and the university, consulting the literature and cataloguing our collections.'

'Bollocks. That's how he tries to justify it.'

Colette laughed. 'What about your camp?'

'Kimani, our faithful retainer, is acting as custodian of the hallowed premises,' said Pete-A. 'He would, I'm sure, be delighted to welcome you in our absence, and serve you victuals and ale, should you wish to visit the forest.'

'Is that where the colobus are?'

'Indeed.'

'Anything in the blood slides we sent Jeff?' asked Pete-B.

'Malaria parasites,' said Colette, 'probably *Hepatocystis* – almost certainly benign. But what's happening to the monkeys?'

'They're dying, dear lady, dying,' said Pete-A.

'What symptoms?'

'As far as one can tell through binoculars, they show lethargy, photophobia and nasal bleeding.'

'Sounds like you on the morning after,' murmured Pete-B.

Pete-A ignored the jibe. 'And two of those we darted showed haemorrhages in the mouth, and bleeding from the eyes.'

'Any deaths?' she asked.

'We found one body, but the troop is reduced in numbers.'

'What did you see on post mortem?'

Pete-A drew himself up. 'Dear lady, we are scientists, not butchers.'

'What do you think, Colette?' asked Sean.

Memory of the newspaper article flooded back. 'Let's say, I hope it doesn't get into man.'

'Would that be serious?' Pete-B tried to sound nonchalant.

'It could be fatal.'

'Right,' he said slowly.

She looked from one to the other. 'What?'

'Tell her, Pete.'

Pete-A took a thoughtful sip from his bottle. 'We've been camping for about six weeks in the forest where the colobus are, sampling mosquitoes and midges at different levels in the leaf canopy – some really interesting material. But my distinguished colleague contracted something a couple of weeks ago which made him sick, red-hot temperature, vomiting and purple blotches all over.'

'One hell of a hangover,' said Pete-B. 'Had to go round in dark glasses – and off the beer for a week.'

'Are you all right, now?' she asked.

'Apart from some blotches on my arse.' He started to undo his shorts.

'Okay, okay, I'll believe you. Anywhere else?'

'Here and here.' He showed her the backs of his knees and his elbows.'

'Was it you who prepared the blood smears?'

He nodded. 'Pete doesn't like the sight of blood.'

'True, true,' murmured his companion.

'Did you wear gloves?'

'In the bush? You've got to be joking.' Pete-B showed her his hands, covered in scratches and cuts. 'Goes with the job.'

'I think you might have caught something from the monkeys.'

'It's his simian ancestry,' said Pete-A. 'I've always said there was a likeness: the shambling gait, the low brow, the—'

'Piss off!'

'My guess would be contaminated blood in one of these cuts,' she said, turning his hands over.

The monkey at the Zoo had been a false alarm. But this? Or was it a knee-jerk reaction to that article?

She turned to Pete-A. 'You've been all right?'

'Yes. I let Pete do the messy bits.'

'Any thoughts?' asked Sean.

Thoughts? Plenty. Which one do you want? She took a deep breath. 'Possibly Marburg.'

'Shit a brick,' muttered Pete-A.

'Are you sure?' said Sean.

'Of course I'm not bloody sure but it looks like a haemorrhagic virus and that's the most likely.' She was conscious of her pounding heart and waited for it to settle.

'I need a beer.' Pete-B stumbled off towards the Land Rover.

Colette found him kneeling in the sand, retching. She put a hand on his shoulder. He looked up with watery eyes, then struggled to his feet, opened the door of the vehicle, retrieved a beer from a cool-box and removed the cap with his teeth.

She waited until he'd drained half the bottle. 'Pete, I'm sorry I alarmed you.'

'Alarmed me? You scared me shitless.' He finished his beer. 'So, which is it?'

'The only way we'll know is to isolate virus or specific antibodies.'

'How?'

'Virus from sick monkeys or antibody from recovered ones or… or I could collect some blood from you and get it tested.'

He winced. 'I guess so.'

'Come on.' She put an arm round his shoulder and led him back to the others.

She went to the vehicle, returned with her sampling kit and collected two tubes of his blood.

Pete-A stood by, averting his eyes. 'It is customary, after giving blood, to replace one's fluid level.' He handed his companion another beer.

'I'll get these tested as soon as possible,' said Colette, 'but they'll have to go back to the UK.'

'Will I live?'

'You are just so lucky. It's likely you had some previous low-level exposure – perhaps from mosquitoes – which gave you protection.'

'I didn't think they could transmit.'

'Probably not true vectors, but mechanical transmission is a possibility.'

'Infected blood on mosquito mouth-parts?'

'Something like that, resulting in a mild infection.'

'Mild!'

She winced. 'Sorry, Pete, but it could have been so much worse.'

'Okay, okay. So am I out of the woods?'

'I think so but you should get yourself checked when you're in Nairobi. Try and see Kelly Ryder.'

'Is that a he or a she?'

'Good question,' said Pete-A. 'You don't want a she tinkering with—'

'*She* is a specialist in tropical diseases,' said Colette. 'Mention my name.'

'How do I contact her?'

'I don't have a number, but her husband works in the US Embassy. Try them for starters.'

'Thanks.'

She gave him an impulsive hug.

'We should get going,' said Sean.

'Let us not delay you,' cried Pete-A. 'We would not wish to deprive this dear lady of the hedonistic pleasures of Tandala.'

Sean laughed. 'Take care, you two.'

'Parting is such sweet sorrow.' Pete-A wiped away a mock tear.

Colette kissed them both and climbed into the waiting vehicle. 'Behave yourselves in Nairobi.'

'No chance.'

Both Petes gave sweeping bows.

'Cheers, guys,' said Sean. 'We'll drop by Kimani, see if there's anything he needs.'

Colette put her head out of the window and waved. 'Remember to contact Kelly.'

***

Having been climbing steadily, they entered the forest where great podocarpus and juniper trees spanned the track and the heat of the open savannah was replaced by cooler moister air filled with the whistling and calling of birds which could only be glimpsed flitting through the trees and undergrowth.

They came round a bend in the track and three buffalo bulls looked up from their wallow. They flicked their tails and rolled back into the mud. Life was too agreeable to be bothered.

Sean carried on upwards. 'Look! Colobus.'

A large black and white monkey which had been feeding on the ground scampered up into the trees.

'He looked healthy enough,' said Colette. 'Let's hope whatever was killing them has run its course.'

They continued up the track and saw three more colobus – all apparently healthy.

'About another twenty minutes,' said Sean. 'I wonder if—' He slammed on the brakes.

'Why are we stopping?'

He didn't answer but jumped out and ran back down the track.

Chapter 10

Ian arrived at the Thorn Tree café for a meeting with Grace who looked fresh and invigorated in Kenyan tracksuit and trainers, a glass of fruit juice at her elbow. She smiled and gestured to a chair. 'Coffee?'

'Please. So why the early—?'

There was a scuffle at the entrance and a scruffy bare-foot boy eluded the clutches of a waiter and ran up to her. The waiter grabbed him.

'Leave him.'

'But, madam?'

'I said, leave him. Bring a Coke.'

The waiter reluctantly released the boy.

'Sit down, Amos.' Grace pushed the plate of biscuits towards him. 'This is a friend.' She indicated the bemused Ian.

The boy was too busy wolfing down biscuits to respond. 'I followed that man,' he said, showering the table with crumbs.

The waiter returned and plonked the Coke down.

A man in a suit came over to their table with Ian's coffee. 'Excuse me, madam, I wonder if I might have a... Grace Kiptagat?'

She nodded.

'Madam, we are most honoured to welcome an Olympic gold medallist. Please be our guest.' He looked doubtfully at the boy. 'And your friend, of course.'

'Thank you.'

'Is there anything I can get you?'

'More biscuits.'

'Of course, madam.' The manager clapped his hands and spoke sternly to the waiter, who hurried over with another plate of biscuits. The manager removed the bills. 'So pleased to welcome you, madam.'

'Thank you. Now, if you don't mind...'

'Of course, of course.' The man bowed and hurried away.

Ian watched the performance, still with bemusement. 'Such is fame.'

Grace shrugged and turned to the boy who had almost finished the second plate of biscuits. 'Tell me, Amos; that man?'

'He went to a big building near Kenyatta Avenue. It is called

57

Fedha Towers. Me and Njoroge waited, and he came out after some time with another man – not an African.'

'A *mzungu* – a European?'

'No he was a *mhindi* – an Asian. Tall with a beard. They got in a car and drove away. See.' Amos indicated a number scratched on his forearm.

Grace jotted it down. 'You've done well, Amos.'

The boy grinned. 'I talked to one of the askaris at the building – he is a friend – he thinks the *mhindi* man works for Blessed Flowers.'

Grace frowned. 'Who are they?'

'The askari doesn't know.'

'Now, Amos, you and your friends must watch for those men. You still have that special phone I gave you?'

He patted the pocket of his shorts.

'Keep it switched on.' Grace extracted from her bag what looked like lottery tickets and passed them over. 'For you and Njoroge. Off you go now.'

'Thanks.' The boy grabbed the remaining biscuits and ran off.

'Who was that?' asked Ian.

'A future Olympic champion.'

'I'm lost.'

'Could be, once his sponsorship comes through. Watch out for the name of Amos Chege.'

'Sure, but…'

'Have you heard of the Mlango Trust, Ian?'

'*Mlango*, as in door or gate?'

She nodded.

'Can't say I have.'

Grace focused on a spot somewhere above Ian's head. 'No one takes any notice of kids hanging around in the city – except to chase them off. They bring me valuable information which I could never get through official sources.'

'What do their parents think about it?'

'They don't have parents,' said Grace softly.

Ian's smile faded. 'Sorry.'

She shifted her focus to his eyes. 'Life can be hard in Nairobi when you have no one to support you. Lots of people turn to crime – kids as well.'

She toyed with her empty glass. 'Olympic medals can open doors.'

'The Mlango Trust?'

'A door opening into a new life, if you like. The Trust gives me meal vouchers for my helpers. In return, I've assisted the Trust in setting up training camps for young athletes.'

'And what does the Mlango Trust think of your... your unofficial police force?'

Grace's face relaxed into a smile. 'They don't know.'

The head waiter hurried over and replaced Grace's empty glass with a full one.

'Thanks.'

'Tell me, Grace,' said Ian, 'the man whom Amos followed was Omar?'

'Yes. And I'm presuming the tall Asian was this fellow Faizal Malik.'

'And Blessed Flowers?'

'Never heard of them but I doubt they're florists. Let me call Felix.'

As Grace made the call, Ian gazed at the bustling cosmopolitan throng in the street outside and wondered how many were terrorists.

Grace finished her call and Ian abandoned fruitless speculation.

'Felix's office at two,' she said. 'He'll see what he can dig out.'

***

Ian and Grace, who arrived together, barely had time to sit down, before Felix started.

'Email just come in. Pin your ears back.'

'Ears back,' said Grace, closing her eyes and switching on the choir-girl.

Felix glowered and began to read: '*Blessed Flowers is a flower-exporting company located in Sudan, but with its probable headquarters in Pakistan. They have several farms around Khartoum where they have set up laboratories for plant breeding and culture of orchids. However, intelligence suggests that the farms are a front for terrorist training and related activities We believe there are plans to establish similar centres in Kenya, possibly with support from a newly-formed terrorist organisation known as—*'

He struggled with the words. '— those Ninja guys based on the Kenya-Somali border.' Felix drew a breath. 'And while we're at it, you seen the Marburg article?' He gestured to the newspaper lying on his desk.

Ian nodded. 'Like Grace said, some sharp-eyed reporter getting ahead of the game.'

'Game? What game?' shot Felix, then sighed. 'Okay, okay. What's

59

the worst case scenario?'

'You asking me?' said Ian.

'Sure; if you got the answers.'

'Blessed Flowers have brought in Malik to set up a lab in Kenya to develop Marburg as a bio-weapon.'

'I wish I hadn't asked.' Felix sank his chin on his chest. 'And the best case?'

Ian stared out of the window. A line of wildebeest was wandering across his view; the migration must be reaching its northern limit. 'The best case?'

'Yeah, if there is one.'

'Marburg virus could be a hazard to orchid collectors who come into contact with monkeys in Kenyan forests.'

'Guess we'll stick with scenario one.' Felix got up and began prowling round the office. 'Anything else?'

Grace extracted a slim folder from her bag. 'That's a copy Omar's cv plus a photo. You may want to run them past your people.' She tossed the folder onto the desk.

'How did you get hold of it?'

'Through Maria, Ole-Tomeno's PA. I told her it was in connection with Condor.'

'That the new wildlife conservation thing the Ambassador's been talking about?'

She nodded. 'Ole-Tomeno is the patron and Omar is his link person on the programme.'

'Is that so?'

'For our sins, they've roped in Grace and me,' added Ian.

'They what?' Felix threw back his head and roared with laughter. 'Jesus, man, what you do, go round hugging hippos?'

Ian gave a tolerant smile. 'Not quite. We're involved with a task force responsible for security and anti-poaching.'

Felix's laughter evaporated. 'Security? Why in hell didn't you say?'

'You didn't ask.'

'Yeah, well.' Felix peered out of the window, folded his arms and brooded. 'This Maria person...'

'She and I share an apartment,' said Grace.

'That's handy.'

'Yes.'

'Is she likely to tell Omar about your interest?'

'No chance. She hates his guts.'

Felix raised his eyebrows.

'He wants her to sleep with him.'

'That could be kinda awkward.'

Grace sniffed. 'Maria can look after herself.'

Felix waved a placating hand. 'You know what, folks? This thing stinks: friend Malik rocks up, and gets met by some jerk—'

'Omar,' said Grace.

'Like I said: some jerk.' He swung round. 'Tell me, Grace, why's OT swimming in this crap?'

'Ole-Tomeno. He isn't.'

'Yeah, and my name's Mickey Mouse.'

'I'll remember that.'

'Piss off. Excuse my Swahili,' – added as an afterthought. 'My guess is Malik and Omar ain't running the show.' He paused. 'OT – not so sure.'

'No!' Grace glared.

'Okay, okay. But listen, guys, whoever is running this show, ain't going to put their top brass up front. Some other joker's calling the shots, pulling the strings – he's the one we've gotta find.' Felix resumed his game-viewing. 'Any suggestions?'

'We keep close to Malik and Omar. See where they lead us,' said Ian.

Felix grunted. 'It's a start.'

'Grace, your, um, special force,' said Ian, 'can they watch those two?'

'Only in Nairobi.'

'Special force?' said Felix.

'Street kids.'

'You what?'

'The system works.'

'Huh. I guess this ain't New York.'

Seraphic smile.

'Okay then,' said Felix doubtfully, 'soon as they find the vehicle, let me know and we'll fit a tracking bug. What kinda vehicle?'

'Toyota Land Cruiser.'

'You sure?'

Grace smiled. 'If there's one thing these kids know, it's the make of every vehicle in Nairobi.'

'Fair enough.' Felix returned to his chair, linked his hands behind his head and swung his feet onto the desk. 'Okay, if we go with the idea these jerks are into bio-weapons and setting up labs here, what they gonna need: buildings, equipment, staff – what else?'

'Money,' said Grace.

'Yeah. And we ain't talking candy bars. Something else to work on, I guess. What else?'

'Good communications, roads, security.'

'Okay, now we're cooking.'

'Somewhere off the beaten track?' said Ian.

'Go on.'

'Felix, those satellite pictures your Ambassador was getting twitchy about?'

'Let's see.' Felix swung his feet off the desk and began typing. A grainy image appeared on the screen.

The other two peered over his shoulder.

Felix flicked through a number of images. 'Not a lot to go on. That could be a new road.' He jabbed a finger at the screen.

'And that sort of irregular ring?' asked Ian.

'Could be where they've cleared some bush, I guess.'

'Those could be buildings inside the ring,' said Grace.

'Yeah. CIA says all the clearing's been done in the last six months – earlier pictures showed the ring and some buildings but there's a lot of new activity.'

'Where is it?' asked Ian.

'Place called Laisamis. Leastways, somewhere near there. You know it, Grace?'

'It's on the Isiolo to Marsabit road. Zoom out, Felix. There.' She indicated a straight line running north south on the image. 'And that's probably the township.'

'What's that?' asked Ian, indicating a regular outline some thirty miles to the south.

'Could be some sort of camp,' said Felix, 'and that looks like an airstrip. Any military up there, Grace?'

'I don't think so.' She peered more closely at the screen. 'I think that's Loloroi – Franco's place.'

'Who's Franco?' asked Ian.

She looked up and smiled. 'If you've not met Franco, you've got a treat coming. He's an Italian who runs an aid distribution programme for northern Kenya, linked to the World Food Programme, I believe.'

'Food aid, medicines, clean water, that sort of thing?' said Ian.

'He is one crazy baboon.' She chuckled.

'Could he be mixed up in this?' asked Ian. 'It would be the perfect cover: back of beyond, own airstrip, loads of gear coming in and out.'

'No. He may be crazy, but he's straight.'

'What do you think, Felix?' said Ian.

'Sure, drop in if you're passing. See what he has to say.'

Ian frowned. 'At least we eliminate him from our enquiries – isn't that what you people say?'

When neither of them responded he tried a different line. 'Where's Sean Paterson's place?'

'Somewhere to the west of... Probably around here.' Grace indicated the screen.

'Who's Paterson?' asked Felix.

'He's on one of the task forces on the Condor Programme,' said Ian. 'Manages a wildlife ranch in Samburu district, part of ole-Tomeno's constituency.'

'What did you say?' growled Felix.

Grace glared. 'We're not going there again. The answer's no.'

Felix gave a slow smile and stared at the ceiling. 'Now, wouldn't that be interesting? Wouldn't that be real cosy?'

'Felix, no way!' Ian joined forces with Grace. 'There's no way ole-Tomeno would be implicated.'

'Why?' Felix's expression was mild.

'Because, because, he bloody isn't. He's straight, he's... Besides, why would he bring Grace into the Condor Programme and... and suggest she and I go and have a look round his constituency?'

'Those things don't make him straight. They make him devious.'

'Felix, you're getting paranoid.'

Felix repeated his slow smile. 'Who suggested checking out this Franco guy?'

'That's different.'

'Bullshit!' Felix leaned across his desk, his eyes angry. 'Listen, Ian, I don't give a monkey's if I tread on a few toes or ruffle some feathers if it flushes these scumbags out of the woodwork.'

'I think you're barking up the wrong tree.'

'I don't give a shit what you think, Ian. I ain't prepared to see Nairobi blown up again – or whatever – leastways, not on my watch.'

Ian pursed his lips.

'What does someone like OT get paid?' shot Felix. 'Tell me that?'

'I don't know.'

'Grace?'

'More than me; that's for sure.'

'I'll tell you,' said Felix. 'He gets paid peanuts.' He rubbed his thumb and fingers together. 'What's a few million greenbacks between friends when you play in this crap? Except, sure as hell, they ain't *my* friends.'

'Felix, no!'

'Listen, Ian, I don't do Mr Nice Guy and I don't play cricket – all that fair play stuff. In my game, everyone's guilty unless proved otherwise.'

Words pinged off the walls as he and Ian glared at each other, then Felix threw his hands in the air and slumped back his chair. 'Aw sorry, guys. I guess I'm getting old. I still say we put a watch on OT. We'd soon learn who his friends were.'

Grace shook her head. 'No chance.'

'Why?'

'He has two security fellows who watch his back all the time. They're on the lookout for anything like that.'

Felix glowered. 'So?'

'So we wouldn't get near him and my career would be finished.' She held Felix's eyes then smiled. 'But there's also a copy of ole-Tomeno's cv in that folder.'

'Goddam it, Grace. You—'

Her mobile rang. She crossed to the window, her back to the other two. They exchanged glances but couldn't hear what she was saying.

She finished the call and turned. 'Omar and friend have just gone on safari.'

Felix swore. 'Who says?'

'Amos, one of my kids. He and his friends were following the vehicle – not hard in Nairobi's traffic. It went into the underground car park at Fedha Towers and came out loaded with boxes and a stacked roof-rack covered with a tarpaulin.'

'And I don't suppose it was camping gear,' observed Ian.

'Probably not.' Grace, returned to her mobile. 'I'll see if Maria knows anything.'

Felix leaned back and closed his eyes. Ian studied the floor.

Grace finished her call and regarded the two of them.

'Anything?' asked Ian.

She nodded. 'Omar applied for leave, but Maria doesn't know for how long.'

Felix snorted.

'But before he left, he had a meeting with the Minister. Two others also attended: one was an Asian man, Dr Faisal Malik, whom Maria had not met before. The other was Professor Carter, Coordinator of the Condor Programme.'

Chapter 11

Ian and Grace left the American Embassy and walked towards where their respective cars were parked outside the compound. Their drivers, who were lounging against the police car, hastily stubbed out cigarettes.

Ian laid a hand on Grace's arm. 'Are we over-reacting, building a house of cards?'

'Meaning what?'

'About ole-Tomeno being implicated. Jeff, even?'

'No.'

'But you said…'

She shook his hand off. 'I know what I said, Ian. Of course I want to believe ole-Tomeno isn't involved – and Carter for that matter – but we can't ignore things because they're uncomfortable.' She gestured at the Embassy and regarded him with an expression he found unsettling. 'Perhaps we could learn something from the ninety-eight attack.'

'How do you mean?'

'Go back and re-read the report.'

'I know the bloody thing backwards. What new is there to learn?'

'*Nakuja* – I'm coming,' she called to her driver, then rounded on Ian. 'You want to take this thing forward. So do I.'

Ian held up his hands. 'Okay, okay.'

'Right. We start by making a few assumptions.'

'Like what?'

'Listen.'

Ian pursed his lips.

'One: some of the people involved in ninety-eight are still out there.'

'We know that.'

'Just listen! Point two: they reckon they have unfinished business to complete.'

'Like what?'

She ignored the question. 'Point three: the target is the same. Point four: the planning approach and execution – assuming it's the same people involved – will be similar; even if the weapon to be used is different.'

'That's a lot of assumptions.'

'Have you any better ideas?'

'No.'

'So we go back to the report of the ninety-eight bombing and read the small print. Okay?'

Ian shrugged. 'I suppose so.'

'Right, we pass by my office and I'll give you a copy. *Tuende* – let's go.'

Ian told his driver to follow and joined a tight-lipped Grace in the back of the police car. Some thoughts, though, he didn't share with her: how does Colette, who works for Jeff Carter, know Omar and how is she caught up in this mess?

They turned onto the main road and headed past the Football Stadium towards town.

'I wonder what—'

The car rocked and Ian's eardrums exploded.

He spun round to see the High Commission Land Rover engulfed in flames. It careered off the road. Smashed into a tree. A second explosion blew the doors off.

People screamed.

Vehicles swerved round the wreckage, stopped in the middle of the road.

Occupants jumped out. Ran back to the carnage.

Grace grabbed the microphone off the car's radio and called police HQ.

She and Ian scrambled out.

Grace waved her police badge. Shouted in vain for people to keep back.

There was nothing anyone could do for the driver, as well as a dozen or so other people – including two children – who lay mangled and inert beside the wreckage. Others, with clothes ripped off and blood pouring from faces and bodies, reeled in confusion, shock and terror. Some lay moaning. Some lay still. Blood and gobbets of flesh and fruit were spattered on the wall behind.

A piece of brightly-coloured cloth fluttered in a tree.

A child's doll lay near a small heap which didn't move.

Traffic on the opposite carriageway stopped. Horns honked. Engines revved. People shouted. Both lanes became grid-locked. The stench of burnt car, burnt rubber, burnt flesh mixed with that of exhaust fumes and the scent of frangipani trees.

A man started searching bodies.

'Get away.' Grace brandished the pistol from her backpack.

'That was meant for me.' Ian staggered to the side of the road and leaned his head against the trunk of a shattered tree. 'Bastards!'

Grace put a hand on his shoulder. 'You okay?'

'Sorry.' He spat out the taste of fear and wiped his mouth. 'I'm okay but some of these poor sods aren't.' He went and knelt beside a girl – no more than ten or eleven – who lay moaning in a pool of blood. Shards of glass had ripped open her arm which was pumping blood. Ian yanked off his tie and used it as a tourniquet.

The girl tried to sit up.

'*Lala tu* – just lie there,' he said gently. 'We'll get you to hospital as soon as we can.'

'Thank you, sir. My arm is really paining.' She tried to smile through her tears. 'My name is Charity.'

'You're going to be all right, Charity, but you must lie still.'

'How is my mama?' She turned her head in the direction of a figure lying closer to the remains of the Land Rover.

'Don't worry, Charity, we'll take care of her.'

Christ! Who imagines hardened soldiers don't cry? He wiped a savage hand across his eyes.

In the distance, a siren.

A police car, lights flashing and siren blaring, forced its way along the pavement through the rapidly gathering crowd. Behind, a lorry full of riot police who jumped down and drove the onlookers aside, clearing a way for two ambulances.

'Over here,' shouted Ian.

A paramedic ran across with his emergency bag.

'This little girl is called Charity. I think she'll be okay, but the mother…'

'I'll see.' The man ran to the inert figure and knelt down. He looked up and shook his head.

Another ambulance arrived. Two more police cars.

Someone touched Ian's shoulder.

'Nothing more we can do here,' said Grace softly.

He didn't care she could see his tears. 'Good luck, Charity,' he croaked and stumbled back to the police car.

This was no house of cards.

***

Ian, his ears still ringing, sat in Grace's office in Police Headquarters clutching a mug of steaming tea and staring into space. All he could see was a lifeless body. All he could hear were the words: *"How is my mama?"*

He closed his eyes. The nightmare, remained. What lay ahead for that little girl? Was there a grandmother, older sister, aunt who would care for her? Or would she finish up on the streets, scavenging, sleeping rough, and – as so many kids in Nairobi – depending on charity? He winced at the irony.

He'd seen horror before but this: a child's life torn apart as someone pressed a button in furtherance of some twisted and grotesque cause. A cause which left a young girl pumping blood and lying near her dead mother in a roadway in Africa.

Oh, God. Was there one?

He gazed bleakly at the activity in the outer office. Plain-clothes and uniformed officers rushed in and out, shouted down phones, bustled back and forth clutching files, peering at computer screens, tapping at keyboards. Grace was in the middle of the turmoil, conferring with senior colleagues, issuing orders, talking on her mobile. Finally, she came back to her office and slumped into a chair.

'Just like ninety-eight,' she muttered, fiddling with the pen on her desk. She gazed unseeing at Ian. 'Cry, my beloved country – again.'

Her mobile rang. She threw the pen down.

Ian listened to the one-sided conversation. 'Yes, put him through. Good morning, sir. Yes, terrible. Not yet.' Grace shot a glance at Ian. 'I'm afraid he died. I'll do that. Yes, a good friend. Thank you, sir. I will. Goodbye.'

She finished the call and gazed at Ian for what seemed like an uncomfortably long time. 'I've just killed you off.'

'You what?'

'That was ole-Tomeno. I told him you died in the bombing.'

'Why?'

'I don't know. I suppose I was thinking back to our earlier conversation.'

'I see,' said Ian slowly. 'Bit quick off the mark, wasn't he?'

She shrugged, rose to her feet, opened a filing cabinet and pulled out a document which she tossed onto the desk. 'Some light reading at Tandala Ranch. Report of the Embassy bombing.'

'Tandala?'

'Sean Paterson's place. We follow up the Minister's suggestion and get out of Nairobi for a while.'

'Now I'm dead, you mean?'

She began doodling on a pad in front of her. 'I'm having your Land Rover – what's left of it – brought in for forensics and I've asked for some of Felix's people to help us.'

'And my body?.'

'We write your obituary and issue it as a press statement. I've got a contact on the Daily Nation who can arrange it.'

'You've worked it all out, then?'

'I had to think fast.'

'As long as this doesn't become a habit.'

She gave a humourless smile. 'If the people who did this think they succeeded, it may give us some breathing space. And no harm in including ole-Tomeno until we know otherwise.'

'But if they – whoever they are – know I wasn't in the vehicle?'

'It doesn't change things. It's worth a try.'

Ian sighed. 'Nothing to lose, I suppose, but I'll have to get the High Commissioner on board.'

She pushed the phone across the desk.

'Writing my own obituary. I'm not sure I want to do this too often.' He called the direct number.

'High Commissioner's office.'

'Helen, it's Ian.'

'Ian! I heard… We've had a most terrible message.' A sob.

'Helen, I'm okay. It was a High Commission vehicle but I wasn't in it. But I'm afraid Mwangi wasn't so lucky, nor quite a few others.'

'Oh, God. What happened? Who was it? Where are you?'

'I'm in Police HQ. It's a long story but— Helen, can I speak to the High Commissioner?'

'I'm afraid he's not here. He's with the Foreign Minister. Are you sure you're all right?'

'Yes. But listen, Helen, I want whoever did this to think they succeeded and I want the High Commission to arrange a press release reporting my death.'

She gave another sob. 'Ian, this is so awful.'

'I know. Can we organise that?'

'I suppose so, but I'll have to clear it with Sir Aubrey.'

'When's he due back?'

'In about— Hold on, I've got another call coming in.'

He could hear a phone ringing in the background and Helen's voice answering. She came back on the line. 'Are you still there, Ian?'

'Yes.'

'It's Sir Aubrey on his mobile. He's just heard the news. He says can you meet him in the High Commission in an hour – around three o'clock?'

'No. If this thing's going to work, I'll need to keep out of sight. I can't risk coming into the High Commission.'

'Wait a second.'

He stared into space.

'Ian. Where exactly are you?'

'I'm in Police HQ: Inspector Grace Kiptagat's office.'

'Can we find you there?'

He covered the mouthpiece while he had a whispered conversation with Grace.

'Helen, that's fine. Who's coming?'

'Sir Aubrey has asked me to get Mr Melhuish.'

'That twit.'

'I didn't hear that, Ian. I'll get him there as soon as possible.'

'Thanks. One other thing: the police are getting the Land Rover in for forensic examination – we're asking the Americans to help – could you ask Tim Hollis to join them? Tell him to contact Felix Rossi, head of security at the US Embassy, about the arrangements. Otherwise, we keep the lid on this. No one else should know.'

'Right, I've got that.'

'One other thing, Helen. I'm getting out of town for a while, would you keep an eye on my mail?'

'Yes, of course.'

'Thanks.'

'Ian, about your mail; your pills have come.'

'Pills? What pills?'

'I think they could be vitamin capsules. The label has your name on, and you have to take one morning and evening. They're probably a pick-me-up.'

'I haven't… Wait. You didn't order them?'

'Of course not. Why me?'

'What was it you said about me needing a break, office work getting me down?'

'Ian, I promise I didn't order them.'

'It doesn't matter.'

'That's strange.'

'What is?'

'There was a hiss when I unscrewed the top.'

'Perhaps the capsules have gone off – the heat or something.'

'They don't smell like vitamins.'

'Helen, I'll sort it out when I get back. You're okay holding the fort while I'm away?'

'I suppose so.' There was a pause. 'Are you sure you're all right?'

'I'm okay. I'll expect Melhuish shortly. And, Helen...'

'Yes?'

'Thanks.' He cut the line.

'Who's Tim Hollis?' asked Grace.

'My deputy; he's covering for me while I'm on the Condor Programme. You don't mind if he joins the forensic team?'

Grace pulled the phone back across the desk. 'I'll tell Felix.'

Once again, Ian listened to a one-sided conversation. Grace then passed him the phone.

After some choice expletives, Felix asked: 'Are you okay, Ian?'

'I'm bloody lucky.'

'We heard the explosion. People here pissing their pants. One of my guys went and took some pictures. I'm downloading them now.' There was a pause followed by more expletives. 'Looks like the scumbags are back in town.'

'Felix, I need your help.' Ian explained about his obituary. 'But listen, Felix, we don't know whether we'll fool them. If I was the target it's possible they'll have set up something at my house or booby-trapped my personal vehicle. High Commission's not geared up for this sort of thing. Any chance your people could help?'

'Sure.'

'I'm here in Grace's office, can someone come and collect my keys?'

'Yeah. Hold on a moment.'

Ian waited and wondered about life – and death.

'All fixed. Guy's name's Hank. He's on his way.'

'Hank who?'

'That's all you need to know, Ian. You've met him.'

Chapter 12

Colette jumped out of the Land Rover and ran after Sean.

As he knelt down beside the track a cloud of butterflies erupted. 'What is…?' She reeled. 'Is it Kimani?'

'No, this chap's really skinny. Some hunter, I guess.' He reached down to turn over the body.

She knocked his arm away. 'Don't touch.'

She ran back to the vehicle and returned with the plastic box. 'It could be the same thing as Pete.' She pointed to the blackened earth beside the man's head. Butterflies, attracted to the moisture, were already returning.

She wriggled into a protective boiler suit and fitted a facemask. 'This may be over the top but I'm not risking it.'

'Were you serious about Marburg infection in the monkeys?'

'Completely.' She struggled to put disposable gloves onto trembling hands, then reached down to the body clad in threadbare shorts and a grubby T-shirt. She took a deep breath and turned it over. 'Shit. I never thought I'd see the real thing.'

'Marburg?'

'Almost certainly. Keep well away.'

The man's eyelids fluttered.

'Thank God. He's alive – just.'

'I guess these people are hard as nails.'

The man gave a convulsive heave. A mass of leaves and black liquid shot out of his mouth.

Colette snatched her hands away and just managed to avoid being covered. 'See what I mean?'

The man moaned and murmured something incomprehensible.

'He's coming round. Get some water.'

Sean ran back to the vehicle and returned with a bottle.

She forced herself to look at the vomit. 'Looks as though he's been chewing leaves.'

'Could be – some sort of bush medicine, I guess.' Sean kicked at a purple-flowered plant. 'This looks like a *Vernonia*. Some of them have anti-emetic properties.'

The man's eyes were now open, but what should have been the whites were bright red. She slipped an arm under his shoulders, sat

73

him up and placed the bottle against his lips. She allowed him a few sips then took the bottle away. Waited.

The man closed his eyes and slumped forward. A few moments later he sat up and gestured to the bottle.

She allowed him to drink a little more.

A sudden crack from somewhere in the forest.

'What was that?'

'That was a shot,' said Sean slowly. 'And not that far away.'

They waited. The sound wasn't repeated.

'Who would it have been?' she whispered, looking up.

It was a moment before he replied. 'Poachers, possibly?'

'Poachers!'

He nodded.

Further thoughts were banished as the man moaned. Colette laid him back and felt his pulse. 'He's not out of the wood but he's hanging on. Any chance we could get the Flying Doctor?'

'Not today. We'll take him with us and I'll call them first thing tomorrow.'

She looked up. 'Thanks, Sean.'

He backed the Land Rover down and held the rear door open. She placed some plastic sheeting on the floor then lifted the man – no heavier than a child – and laid him down. She climbed in the back beside him.

'Well done, you,' said Sean.

She gave a faint smile beneath her facemask.

***

It was dark when they reached the house. A security light snapped on. A door opened and a small terrier rushed out, barking. A man and a woman followed.

Sean stopped the vehicle and switched off the engine. '*Jambo*, Jotham. *Jambo*, Leah.'

'Warn them to keep clear,' said Colette.

Sean called out and they checked.

'It's okay, as long as they don't try and help,' she said.

'What about Suni?'

Before Colette could respond, Sean opened his door and the terrier leaped in panting and grinning, and covering him with her slobbery tongue. She would have leaped over the seats to the back and given Colette the same treatment if Sean hadn't grabbed her.

'Meet, Suni,' said Sean.

'Suni, nice to meet you.' Colette waved.

'Let's get this guy sorted,' said Sean. He climbed out, passed Suni to Jotham and went to the rear door. 'How is he?'

'He seems a little better.' Colette slipped an arm under the man's back and sat him up.

Suni watched with great interest. Jotham and Leah hovered.

'Who is this person?' asked Leah.

'We found him in the forest,' said Sean. 'Do you know him?'

She shook her head.

Jotham peered more closely. 'It could be Dima.'

The man perked up and nodded. 'Dima. *Mimi* Dima.'

'Where's he from, Jotham?' asked Sean.

'He's a *Ndorobo* from Turkana – a poacher.'

'Long way from home, then,' said Sean.

'He travels far.'

Dima continued nodding.

Colette gave him some more water, waited, checked his pulse. 'Seems a bit stronger. He may be okay.'

'Will we need the Flying Doctor?'

'Let's see what he's like in the morning. Is there somewhere he can stay? Somewhere isolated.'

Sean pointed into the darkness. 'There's an old hut over there. We can lock the door so he doesn't wander off in the night.'

'Can it be disinfected afterwards?'

'We can burn it. I've been meaning to get rid of it.'

'Is there a bed?'

'Of sorts. Anything else?'

Colette offered Dima another drink. 'Sean, his salt balance will be all screwed up after that vomiting. We need to sort that and start restoring his energy level.'

'We should have the necessary'

'Energy drink, salt tablets, that sort of thing?'

'Sure. He's not the first visitor we've had to treat. Normally sunstroke or heat exhaustion.'

'Let's hope this is the first and last case of Marburg.' Colette eased herself out of the Land Rover, still supporting Dima. 'Sean, if you organise the hut I'll carry him there.'

'You'll be okay?'

'I'm ignoring that.'

He grinned and hurried off with Jotham and Leah. Colette

followed carrying the sick man, a puzzled Suni at her heels.

***

What a luxury in the bush. Colette closed her eyes as the water from the shower streamed over her body washing away the dust and heat of the day – and, she hoped, any of the residual virus she thought she'd never encounter. What was it Pete-A had said: "*the hedonistic pleasures of Tandala*"? For a while, she shut out the world and immersed her mind and body in hedonism. Reluctantly, she turned off the water and emerged from the shower. She wiped the mirror and examined her reflection. They *were* wrinkles but she had to look quite hard. She hastily dried and put on fresh clothes. Those she had been wearing were now sealed inside a plastic bag which would be burned along with the boiler suit, facemask and gloves. It would deplete her wardrobe but she couldn't risk it. Besides, the T-shirt had been a present from Paul. Good riddance.

Now what? She sat on the bed wondering. What do I do until Jeff arrives? What do I do when he does? What do I do if, if...? She sighed, picked up the torch from beside the bed and ventured into the dark unknown. A log fire was burning. Sean sat beside it, his back to her. Suni lay near his feet.

Colette stood absorbing the night sounds of Africa: cicadas, an owl, and surely that was a lion grunting in the distance? And that? It took her a moment to place it: guitar music – out here? Not from the house; from the direction of the fire. She stood listening to the mellow tones blending with the other night sounds.

Sean put the guitar down and moved to tend the fire.

She gathered her courage and approached. 'That was beautiful.'

He started and turned round.

'Sorry, I didn't mean to startle you. I didn't want to interrupt.'

Suni trotted up wagging her tail. Colette bent down and stroked her.

'Feeling better?'

'Mm.' She sat down in the vacant chair beside the fire and Suni came and lay on her feet.

'Sorry about that,' said Sean.

'What?'

'Suni on your feet.'

'It's lovely.' Colette stroked Suni's ears.

'Beer?'

'Please.'

76

He handed her a bottle from the cool-box beside his chair; the same brand she and Ian had been drinking the previous evening all those years ago. She shut out the memory.

'How's Dima?' she asked.

'Seems to be getting stronger. He's kept the drink down and eaten a banana. Leah used to be a nurse. He's in good hands.'

'I have a good feeling about him.' She stared into the fire. How distant London seemed. 'Can you play some more?'

'No.'

'Why?'

'Because...' He shrugged. 'I guess I'm not very good with an audience.'

She took a sip from her bottle. 'Wasn't that what I heard yesterday on the CD?'

He nodded. 'Bach seems to work quite well out here.'

'What's it called?'

'*Wachet auf.*'

'Which means?'

'Wake up, but the piece is usually called: "Sleepers Awake".'

'Sleepers awake; that's strange.'

'Why?'

She stared into the darkness, sipping her beer. 'What are those lights?'

'Fireflies. We see lots at this time of year.'

'They're magical.' She watched them through half-closed eyes. 'Is it always this beautiful out here?'

'Mostly.'

'Even when it rains?'

'Particularly then.'

'Why?'

'The promise of new beginnings.'

New beginnings, new pastures, new life?

'Are you married?' she blurted.

He got up and put another log on the fire. A fountain of sparks rose into the night.

'Sean, I'm sorry. That sounds so rude.' She studied her bottle, conscious of her crassness. 'I didn't mean to...'

'You don't have to apologise.' He studied the sparks. 'Yes, I am married. Her name is Helen. But she has a job in Nairobi and doesn't get out here very often.'

'Oh.'

'She works as PA to the British High Commissioner.'

'That must be interesting.'

'I suppose so. Another beer?'

'I haven't finished this one.' She got to her feet.

Suni looked up reproachfully.

'Sean, do you mind if I go to bed? It's been a long day and I'm really tired.'

'Don't you want some supper?'

'No. No thanks. I'm not hungry. All the excitement.'

She stumbled off into the heart of darkness.

Chapter 13

There was a knock on the door and a policewoman entered. 'Inspector, I have a Mr Brown outside. He says he has an appointment to see you.'

'Show him in,' said Grace.

The marine, whom Ian and Grace had met briefly in Felix's office, entered. He was wearing jeans and a T-shirt, and just managed to stop himself saluting.

Ian rose and held out his hand. 'Hank, isn't it?'

'Yes, sir.' The man braced his shoulders.

'I'm Ian. This is my colleague, Grace.'

'Ma'am.'

'Have a seat, Hank.' Ian pulled a chair forward. 'Let's keep this informal.'

'Yes, sir.' Hank sat upright on the edge of the chair.

Ian studied him. 'Feli— Major Rossi has told you what this is about?'

'Yes, sir.' His eyes lit up. 'We've been wanting something like this to happen. Gets kinda boring sitting on your ass all day.'

'Yes, I'm sure,' – dryly.

Hank took a notepad from the breast pocket of his shirt, and flicked the lid open. 'We check out your house, your vehicle, your garage—'

'I don't have a garage. The vehicle – a Land Rover – is parked in the driveway. Here are the keys. The house-servant's name is Lawrence. He's expecting you. I've told him some men are coming to set up a new telephone link to the High Commission.'

'The address, sir?'

Ian gave him the details.

'Anything else, sir?'

'No, I think that's everything.'

The man snapped the notepad shut and stood up. 'We'll report back to Major Rossi, sir.'

'Right.' Ian held out his hand. 'Thanks.'

Hank shook his hand and turned to Grace. 'Ma'am.' He nodded and left the room.

Grace sank back in her chair, chuckling. 'I don't believe it.'

Ian gave a wry smile. 'He's probably trained to the eyeballs and has all the latest gizmos – let's hope so.' He crossed to the window, and saw Hank approaching a nondescript Toyota four-wheel-drive against which a man, also wearing jeans and a T-shirt, was leaning. The only things which set him apart from other Africans lounging nearby were the set of his shoulders and the haircut.

'They seem to have got most things right,' murmured Ian, as he watched the Toyota drive off.

'Good afternoon – *hamjambo*,' boomed a voice in the outer office. 'I have an appointment to see Inspector Kiptagat.' It sounded like an airport announcement.

Ian groaned as the policewoman led in his High Commission colleague, who looked hot and flustered in tartan Bermuda shorts and a blue polo top, with dampness showing under the arms. Unruly dark hair flopped over his face. Quentin shook Ian vigorously by the hand. 'Ian, old chap, terrible business. Can't say how sorry we are. Frightful rumpus, all this nonsense. You can't imagine. HC called me on my mobile. Always keep it with me for emergencies like this. Lucky to hear it – just about to tee off.'

Ian winced. The priorities of the privileged contrasted harshly with the needs of the destitute – Charity and a million like her. He drew a breath. 'You weren't followed?'

'Great Scott. You think I might have been followed?'

Ian shrugged.

Quentin turned pale and looked around. 'I thought we'd left all this behind in Pakistan.'

'Pakistan?'

'My previous posting. Always blowing each other up: letter bombs, car bombs, suicide bombs. National pastime. Hell on wheels. Never imagined—'

'Have you met my colleague, Inspector Kiptagat?' asked Ian.

'Who?'

'Grace Kiptagat.'

'Good Lord, not the… How do you do? Quentin Melhuish, First Secretary. So pleased to meet you.' He shook Grace's hand almost reverently then sank into a chair and ran a trembling hand over his damp face. 'Tell me the score.'

'The thing is, Quentin, we want these people to think they succeeded in their attempt.'

'Rather – call their bluff, as it were?'

'Something like that.'

'Good idea. Splendid.'

'This is where you come in.'

'Ah, yes, the press release, obituary – clever idea that. The usual thing, I imagine: tragic loss, distinguished service, next of kin informed, sadly missed by colleagues, bright future ahead of him, played cricket for Oxford. Or were you at the other place?'

'I went to Sandhurst.'

'Oh, right. I think I've got the picture, though.' He nodded again. 'Then, something about leaving no stone unturned, perpetrators to be brought to justice, Kenya and Britain standing shoulder-to-shoulder, and—'

'Quentin, to save you the trouble, we've already drafted something.' Ian handed over the wording he and Grace had agreed.

He scanned the note. 'Could I add the shoulder-to-shoulder bit? Good for diplomatic relations, that sort of thing.'

'I should leave that for the interviews.'

'Interviews?'

'Yes, I'm sure the press will want to interview the High Commissioner. You as well, perhaps.'

'You think so?'

Grace was nodding. 'We can arrange that.'

'Could you? I say, that would be rather splendid.'

'We must be careful not to overdo it, though,' said Ian.

'Rather. Leave it to me, old boy. I've handled the press before. Now, anything else before I go? Is Dodgy Dan in on this?'

'Who?'

'Daniel ole-Tomeno. Can't think why the donors are giving him all that money for this Condor thing. I wouldn't trust him with the petty cash for the Christmas raffle.'

The temperature in the room plummeted.

'Sorry, inspector, spoke out of turn there.'

'Yes,' – tone venomous. 'The Minister was informed that Ian died in the bombing.'

'Ah, yes. Right. Splendid. Probably best that way.' He turned to Ian. 'You've organised a safe house, I presume?'

A safe house? Quentin, who seemed to go through life serving double faults, had at last got one in court.

'No, I, um, thought I'd check into a hotel for the night rather than go back to my place, just in case.'

'Come and stay with us, old boy. Moments like this we have to stand shoulder-to—' He noticed Ian's expression. '—pull together.'

'I wouldn't want to put you to any trouble,' said Ian. 'I'll find somewhere low-key and then leave first thing in the morning.'

'Nonsense. I insist. Least we can do. Fiona keeps our guesthouse ready for things like this.'

'Like this?'

'Well, we've not had a bombing before but you know what I mean.'

'It makes sense, Ian,' said Grace. 'I'll pick you up from there tomorrow.'

Quentin glanced at his watch. 'Good Lord, is that the time? I'm due at rehearsals in an hour.'

'Don't let us hold you up then.'

'No, rather.' He took out his wallet. 'Here's my card, inspector, with my address in Muthaiga. I live opposite the Settlers Club.'

'Thank you. I'll be there at seven tomorrow morning.'

'Splendid.'

Ian shrugged. 'Seems I don't have a say in the matter.'

'Well, I must get things moving.' Quentin rubbed his hands and rose to his feet. 'I'll send a car here for you at five o'clock.'

Ian shook his head. 'Thanks, Quentin, but that could undo all the good work.'

'How do you mean?'

'Let's say, I'm getting a bit nervous about travelling in vehicles with British CD plates.'

'My vehicle has those.' Quentin paled. 'You don't think I might be a, er, possible target?'

'Not a chance. Just make sure no one follows you.'

***

Ian took a taxi from Police Headquarters and stopped briefly to buy some supplies and spare clothes for his trip to Tandala. He arrived at Quentin's bungalow as it was getting dark. He rang the bell by the gate, setting off a chain-reaction of barking dogs in the neighbourhood. Two mean-looking askaris, wearing army great-coats, scowls and pick-axe handles, escorted him to the front door and knocked. The door opened as far as the security chain would allow and Quentin peered out.

'Oh, it's you.' He released the chain, glanced round the garden then dragged Ian inside.

'Ian, darling.' Quentin's wife, Fiona, dressed in a floral sweet-wrapper, rushed forward, threw her arms round his neck and gave a theatrical sob. 'We've been watching the news on television – it was ghastly.'

'Sorry you missed it,' said Quentin.

'I'm not.'

'No, well… They reported the shoulder-to-shoulder bit – went down rather well, I thought.'

'You poor poppet.' Fiona steered him into the sitting room where a steward wearing a white jacket and a lugubrious expression greeted him from behind a well-stocked bar. 'Good evening, *bwana*.'

'*Jambo*, Stanley,' said Ian. 'How are you?'

'Not bad, sir, but my head is—'

'Don't take any notice of him,' boomed Quentin. 'Always something the matter. That right, Stanley?'

The man gave a watery smile.

'Colonel Sinclair will have a large G and T.'

Ian held up his hand. 'Only the tonic, please.'

'Right,' said Quentin. 'Same as me. Watching the weight, you know.' He patted his stomach. 'You can give me a top-up, Stanley.'

'Yes, sir.'

'And the *memsahu*, plenty of gin for her.' He turned to Ian. 'Usually knocks off a few before dinner.'

'Quentin, really!'

'Well you know you—'

'How was the rehearsal?' asked Ian.

'Rehearsal? Oh, yes. Splendid. Going well. Sure you won't have something a bit stronger?'

'No thanks, this is fine.'

It was a surreal evening. Quentin, who was at his most loquacious when he had nothing to say, rabbited on about a range of things, none of which Ian could remember. Fiona kept accidentally brushing his foot under the table. And Stanley shuffled round like the butler from a Dracula movie.

Ian was only too ready to make his excuses after dinner. 'If you wouldn't mind, perhaps I could…' He set down his coffee cup and rose to his feet.

'Of course.' Fiona took his hand. 'Come on, darling. I'll show you to your room. You won't mind being on your own in the guesthouse?'

'No, it's most kind of you to have me.'

'Hmm.' She guided Ian across the lawn to the separate guesthouse, opened the door, turned on the light and led him into the bedroom. She felt the double bed. 'It's lovely and soft, I do hope you'll manage.'

'This looks absolutely fine. Thanks.'

'I've had your bag brought across.' She lingered in the doorway.

'Great.'

'Is there anything, I can get you? Another blanket perhaps?'

'No, this is fine.'

'Are you sure? Nights can be a bit chilly at this time of year.'

'I'm sure.'

'Don't forget to use the mosquito net.'

'No.'

Still she lingered. 'Ian…'

'Yes?'

'It's… it's nothing.'

He raised his eyebrows.

She gave a wistful smile. 'Sweet dreams, Ian.'

'Thanks.'

'You will let me know if there's anything you need?'

'Goodnight.'

'Goodnight, Ian.' She blew him a kiss. The wistful expression remained as her hand strayed to a bruise on the side of her face. But perhaps he imagined that.

He locked the door.

***

An explosion tore into Ian's sleep. Shouts and breaking glass. Something was thrust over his face. He struggled to break free, to escape from the nightmare. Couldn't move. Tried to cry out. Bands of steel clamped his arms. He was frogmarched across the lawn. Couldn't see. Another explosion. He was thrust into a vehicle and driven off.

Chapter 14

Dima sat up. His head was clear. Pain was leaving his body. He swung his feet off the bed onto the hard earth floor and stood up swaying slightly as he looked round the hut. A plate of food on the floor and some bananas. A bottle of that special water. These are good people. The taste of the maize-meal porridge reminded him of home. He peered through the small window. The surrounding bush shone clear in the starlit night. An askari sat on the veranda steps of the big house, his head nodding forward.

The door of the hut was bolted from outside. If he tried to break it the askari would hear. He poked at the wooden frame which served as a window and some of the frame crumbled away. The rustle of termites reminded him of his childhood. First, though, he would rest some more to recover his strength.

He woke at the darkest part of the night, sat up, ate a banana and drank some of the special water. He worked quickly and quietly. Removed the crumbling window frame and wriggled out, taking with him the bottle and the bananas.

He stood for a moment in the shadow of the hut. No sign of the askari. He listened to the spirits of the night. Reassured, he turned towards the distant forest and merged with the darkness.

He reached the edge of the forest just as it was getting light. He stopped to admire the beauty he never expected to see again, ate the remaining bananas and finished the water.

A vulture sailed overhead. Then another. Then two more. He hurried forward. Perhaps he would find some meat.

He approached the kill, conscious he had no weapons should there be a leopard – lion, even. He parted some bushes. The squabbling vultures were reaching forward with their long necks at something hidden in the grass, tearing flesh and entrails. Their heads covered in blood. No acrid smell of lion or leopard. No tawny or dappled bodies hiding.

Dima thrust the bushes aside. Ran at the carcass. The vultures exploded in a cloud of confusion, feathers and raucous cries.

He reeled. Not a bushbuck, duiker, bush-pig. A man. The remains of a man.

Dima waited for his breathing to settle, his head to clear.

The tracks were so obvious – and he had missed them. He knelt down, studied the disturbed soil, sniffed the crushed grass, noticed the way the stems had been brushed aside. Three men coming out of the forest: one running with fear, two running with purpose. Two men, walking back into the forest.

The vultures were making indignant cackles and hopping back to their meal. A jackal approached, its nose raised and sniffing. The undertakers of the bush would take care of everything.

He returned to the man's remains. The vultures backed away and watched with beady eyes. He wasn't afraid to look at death. The man was an African, but not a hunter like him. This man was fat. Had lived an easy life. Impossible to recognise him. Most of the face ripped away. The eyes torn out. But that? He peered more closely. That was the hole of a bullet.

Something bit his foot. Another. Several more. Both feet. He leaped back and brushed off the *siafu*: a solid line of numberless ants – mini-undertakers – attracted to the meal.

Avoiding the *siafu*, he followed the trail of the two men back into the forest. Were they watching him? Waiting to shoot? He hid. Sniffed smells and scents of morning air. Listened. Looked with restless eyes. These men were skilled and knew how to move quickly and confidently through the undergrowth. Here, their tracks were obliterated by bush-pigs rooting in the soil. There, covered by the print of a leopard. There, the crushed stems of the grass were beginning to wither. Signs that the men had passed the previous day.

Smoke. Not the smoke of a campfire. Not the smell of acacia wood and roasting meat. This was acrid and pungent, the smell of burning cloth.

He came to the edge of a clearing. Only his eyes moved. The remains of a tent still smouldered. Bottles, books and bedding lay scattered – some burning. A body covered in black and white hair lay in the grass. There, another. The colobus were cold and stiff. These men had killed the monkeys and left them for the hyenas. Why? They were both females, which had been feeding babies. These men were not hunters. He knew the hunters' code. He had broken that code and nearly paid with his life. These men had broken the code. Perhaps they would pay.

He left their trail, reached a small stream and followed it downhill. A swish in the branches overhead. He looked up at the colobus monkeys feeding. 'I have promised *Mungu* that I will hunt you no

86

more,' he murmured.

He came to the big fig tree and climbed into the lower branches. His *simi*, and his bow and arrows were as he had left them. He climbed back down, repeated his thanks to *Mungu* and continued downstream to the old porcupine den. But hyenas had been there. The only remains of the colobus skins were tufts of black and white hair.

I have learned a lesson.

He continued downhill. Before long the forest thinned and gave way to thorn scrub. Here progress was faster. He came to the bank of a large river where elephants – his favourite animals – were drinking.

The older elephants seemed to recognise him as he waded through the shallow water, but the younger ones flapped their ears and trumpeted. He laughed, called to them in the language his father had taught him and they settled.

The area on the far bank was greatly disturbed by the elephants and it was nearly dark before Dima, casting ever widening circles, picked up the trail of the two men. No sense in trying to follow in the dark. He cut fire sticks and a throwing stick, and slipped off into the twilight.

He sat over the fire roasting a hare. This was how it should have been all that time ago: the day he and his father hunted a hare, the day he watched his father die, the day he found his mother dead, the day he became a man. The great scorpion in the sky was once again clear above him. That man with one ear – was he also looking at it?

Chapter 15

Colette slept well, despite the traumas of the previous day, and woke feeling refreshed. After a quick shower, she dressed in shorts and a T-shirt, and made her way to the veranda. Sean, who was already eating breakfast, pulled out a chair.

'Sleep okay?' He passed her some coffee.

'Mm.' She nodded.

The bush was coming to life. Birds were beginning to sing. The sun, having cleared the horizon, was splashing flamingo colours on the landscape. 'What a magical place,' she said.

He smiled. 'It can have its—'

There was a shout. Jotham was waving. 'That man, *ametoka* – he's gone.'

She ran after Sean, and the three of them examined the remains of the hut's window frame.

'I guess we don't need Sherlock Holmes to solve this one,' said Sean.

'Where do you think he's gone?' she asked.

'Home, probably.'

'He's going to walk all that way?'

'Take him a couple of weeks. What's the hurry?'

'You know, I sometimes wish my life could be like that.'

He shrugged.

She wondered what he was thinking.

'*Hapa* – here,' called Jotham.

Even she could see the footprints in the soft sand, heading towards the forest in the distance.

'No point in following,' said Sean.

'I do hope he'll be all right,' said Colette.

'He will. These guys are tough.' Sean checked his watch. 'I was planning to fly over to Franco's with his mail. Do you want to come?'

'Is that fly, as in flying?'

He pointed to a light aircraft parked some distance away which she hadn't noticed in the dark.

'Don't people pay thousands of pounds for safaris like this?'

'So is that a yes?'

'Of course. I'll just grab a couple of bananas.'

'You don't want Leah to cook you something?'

She shook her head. 'Too excited.'

'Right. Leave in five minutes.'

***

'Who's Franco?' she asked, shouting above the noise of the engine.

'Someone who keeps his ear close to the ground.' Sean grinned. 'A one-off.' He pointed into the hazy distance. 'About twenty minutes to go.'

Colette peered through the windscreen and could make out a collection of buildings arranged haphazardly with a few grass huts around their periphery. But it was almost ten minutes before the patch of sand, marked out by white-painted rocks and a forlorn windsock, revealed itself to be an airstrip. Further rocks, which had also once been white, spelled out the word Loloroi.

'Franco's office,' shouted Sean, pointing to a lone hut with a lean-to attached. It was set in the shade of an umbrella acacia, with other similar trees scattered around.

She opened her mouth to shout something else but he was concentrating on landing. The ground came racing towards them. At the last minute, Sean eased the controls back, the nose lifted and the plane seemed to float above the sandy strip.

The bump of wheels. She looked out of the side window to see them rattling over the rough surface. The plane coasted to a gentle halt. Sean swung it round and taxied towards the corrugated iron hut which was Franco's office. He stopped some fifty metres short and the propeller came to a stuttering halt as he switched off the engine.

'Welcome to Loloroi.' He leaned across her and released the door catch.

She noticed the sun-bleached hairs on his arm as it passed close to her chest. For God's sake, girl, get a grip!

She pushed open the door and scrambled down onto the baked sandy soil, dragging her emotions after her.

Sean followed. 'Come and meet Franco.'

She was reluctant to tear her eyes away from the view. Some hills away to their left were hazy in the shimmering heat, wisps of cloud on their summits. 'Is that where the Petes have their camp?'

'We'll fly over on the way back.'

Her eyes swept round the panoramic vista. The only signs of life were a lone goat which had climbed a stunted tree and was nibbling the few remaining leaves at the top, and a man in the distance leading

89

two camels further into the distance.

She became aware of an increasing noise coming from the office. 'What's that?'

Sean laughed. 'I guess it's Italy's ambassador in Isiolo District. Let's go and see.'

A stocky man with a mass of wavy black hair and a lined face the colour of mahogany was seated behind a desk yelling down a phone with a volume which made the instrument seem superfluous. He wore faded beach shorts, a bush jacket and open sandals. A lion's claw hung from a leather tie round his neck. He beckoned them in and continued his harangue.

Colette gazed round the office. The fan on the desk struggled against the heat, barely rustling the papers and miscellaneous catalogues held down by rocks, brake shoes, and a skull – possibly a leopard. A radio, on which various lights were winking, stood between two heaps of papers. On a shelf, between more catalogues, was a glass dome containing a stuffed owl which stared cross-eyed at her. She hastily looked away. Most of the floor space was taken up with half-opened boxes spewing out milk powder, blankets, drugs, and vehicle spares. A shape, covered with a brightly-coloured cloth, lay in a gap between some sacks. Colette's eyes widened as the shape gave a moan. She was about to draw it to Sean's attention when Franco's tirade increased in volume.

'What you send me that rubbish for, *bwana*? Is full of *dudus*. How you expect people to eat when is full of beetles?' There was a pause. '*Bwana* is *bure* – useless.'

He put his hand over the mouthpiece and turned to Colette. 'Arse-hole.'

She raised her eyebrows.

'He send me useless rubbish.' He turned back to the phone. 'I no pay until—' The radio sprang to life. A muffled voice. Franco snatched up a microphone. '*Ciao*, Larry. You brought my whisky this time, you bugger?'

More muffled voice.

'Clear to land, Larry.'

Franco returned to the phone. '*Bwana*, I need twelve tonnes, and don't send me rubbish next time.' He slammed the phone down. It immediately rang again. '*Pronto.*' He started gabbling in Italian.

'We'll wait outside,' mouthed Sean, gesturing to Colette.

Franco heaved some boxes off the chairs and motioned them to sit down. The shape moaned again. Another phone rang. Franco scrabbled in the pocket of his jacket and pulled out a mobile. He said something down the other phone then yelled into the mobile. 'Yes. No, I don't speak Swedish. German, French, English, Swahili, Italian, Spanish – which you want?' He finished the conversation on his mobile and reverted to French on the other phone.

'Good trip?'

Colette realised Franco was looking at her. 'Er, yes, fine.'

'You like?' He gestured to a calendar on the wall bearing an improbably proportioned girl who seemed to be wearing nothing but a bunch of bananas. She was advertising tractors.

Colette gave a hesitant smile. 'Very tasteful.'

The French conversation ended and Franco put the phone down. It rang again. This time he ignored it. 'Come.'

He led Colette and Sean outside and a broad grin lit up his face. 'Hey, Sean my friend, *karibu*, welcome, *benvenuto*.' He shook his hand and clapped him on the back, then turned to Colette. 'Franco.' He took her outstretched hand and put it to his lips. '*Signora*, welcome, *karibu*.' He gave a mischievous grin.

She returned the grin. 'They seem to keep you pretty busy.'

'Too bloody right. Fixer Franco, that's me.'

His mobile rang again. 'Yes, what? Speak up. What... x-ray machines? I no hear you. What you say? No. I no want bloody x-ray machines. What? No. No way! I want generators. You send me in x-ray machines, I tell you where I shove the plugs. What? I no care. I no want for half price. I no even want for Christmas. Generators. I need generators. Pah!'

He switched off the mobile. 'You see the sons of bitches I have to deal with.'

The radio cut in again. Franco ran back to his office.

Colette turned at the sound of a low-flying aircraft to see a twin-engine plane coming in to land.

'Looks like the Flying Doctor,' said Sean.

The plane landed, taxied towards them and stopped besides Sean's Cessna. The engines died, a door opened and two smartly dressed nurses climbed out carrying a stretcher. They were followed by the pilot, a tall languid individual dressed in khaki shirt and shorts, and wearing cowboy boots.

'*Jambo*,' said the nurses brightly, as they hurried into the office on an apparently everyday mission.

'How you folks a doing?' The pilot sauntered up to Colette and Sean and held out a hand. 'Larry Stopolski.'

'Pleased to meet you,' said Colette.

'You from these parts?'

'I manage a wildlife ranch over there,' said Sean, pointing. 'Colette's from London.'

'That so?' Larry gave a lazy grin.

'Good flight?' asked Sean.

'No, it fucking wasn't.'

Colette started.

'Begging your pardon, ma'am. Some mother-fucking nutter, took a fucking pot-shot.'

'What do you mean?'

'See here.' Larry led them to the plane and pointed to a hole in one of the wings. 'Goddamned, cotton-picking ass-hole.'

'Where was this?' asked Sean.

'Shortly before we landed at Laisamis. You know it?'

Sean nodded.

'We do a clinic once a month. While we were there, Franco gave us a call to pick up some woman – been in labour three days.'

Colette winced.

'Hey, Larry!' Franco came hurrying out of his office.

'Here you are, you old coyote.' Larry handed over the bag he was holding.

'*Salute.*' Franco embraced Larry, took his arm and looked furtively around. 'You got anything for clap? Is no for me, is for friend, you understand. I no like to ask the girls.'

Colette pretended not to hear.

'Well, I guess you're a going to have to ask them.' Larry gave his lazy smile. 'They don't get to do the flying, and I don't get to do the doctoring. You tell your friend that.'

Franco shrugged. 'Is no *problema.* I got the whisky now.'

'You had any more trouble with those ass-holes round Laisamis?' asked Larry.

Franco swore. 'Those sons of bitches. What this time?'

'Some motherfucker took a pot-shot.'

'*Bastardo.*'

'Why I got out of Iraq,' said Larry.

'We're ready, Mr Larry.' The two nurses emerged from the office carrying the stretcher on which lay the inert shape still covered with

92

the brightly coloured cloth.

'How is she?' asked Colette.

'She is not good but she will live,' said one of the nurses, who looked to Colette to be about fifteen.

'These people are very strong,' said the other nurse. 'But the baby – I fear for him.'

'Okay, ladies, let's move it.' Larry hurried back to the plane and opened a door on the side.

Colette helped them manoeuvre the stretcher into the aircraft.

Larry strapped it to the floor; then held out his hand. 'Nice meeting you folks. You take care now.'

'Thanks,' said Colette. 'I hope the patient is all right.'

'Mr Larry is a very good pilot,' said the fifteen-year-old. She gestured to the mound on the stretcher. 'This is her first baby. The doctor must cut this one open. Then who knows? God is kind.'

'Yes,' said Colette. 'Yes, I suppose He is.'

Larry climbed into the doorway of the plane. 'You folks, have a nice day. Be seeing you.' He gave a perfunctory wave and disappeared inside.

Colette waved as the plane took off: a hole in one wing and two lives in the balance.

Chapter 16

Franco clapped Sean on the back. 'So why you no come see your old friend since many days, eh? Where you been all this time?'

'I was here last month,' said Sean, laughing. 'Here. I picked up your mail while I was in Nairobi.'

Franco glanced through the bundle of letters. 'Pah! Bills. Anyway, why worry? I no pay. If they want their money they have to come and see me.' He winked at Colette. 'Tell me, Sean, what news of my friend Grace?'

'Grace Kiptagat?'

'*Si, si* Grace.'

'She's now a desk *fundi* in Nairobi.'

'Why she want to waste her time there?'

'She's on this Condor Programme I told you about. Ole-Tomeno appointed her.'

'Wildlife conservation?'

Sean nodded.

Franco looked around and lowered his voice. 'We need Grace back here.'

'Why?'

'We no have trouble when Grace in charge at Isiolo. Now...' He spat in the dust.

'What sort of trouble?' asked Sean.

Franco put his fingers in his mouth and gave a piercing whistle. A young man, wearing a pair of shorts and pouring sweat, emerged from a nearby building.

'Hey, Khalif, why you so hot? What you doing? You got woman in there?'

The man grinned.

'I go for lunch now. You look after the office.'

'Okay, chief.'

'And no using telephone, okay?'

'Okay.'

'And keep your sticky fingers off my calendar.'

The man grinned again.

'Come.' Franco jerked his head and led Sean and Colette to a dilapidated Land Rover without doors, roof or windows, which was parked in a lean-to out of the sun. 'We eat first. You come with me.' He climbed into the driver's seat. 'Your plane okay there, Sean. *Signora*, please, you sit next to me.'

Colette scrambled into the middle seat and found herself wedged between Franco and Sean.

'Is bit of squeeze,' said Franco, 'but you no mind?'

'I'm fine,' she said, trying to keep her legs out of the way of the gear lever and of Sean's legs. 'This is great.'

'Is like your Metro, I think,' shouted Franco, above the noise of the engine, the rattling of the bodywork and the wind.

'This is nothing like our Metro.' She had a brief vision of Poser Paul but immediately shut it out. 'Give me this any day.'

Franco pulled into a shaded oasis of thorn trees within which was a small bungalow with a thatched roof. A sprinkler turned lazily on a pocket-handkerchief-sized lawn and weaverbirds bathed in the dribble of water.

Franco led Colette and Sean into the cool interior of the bungalow and called out. A tall Somali girl appeared. 'You are most welcome,' she murmured.

'Samira is very good cook,' said Franco. 'You like goat? Is only thing we have. First day is roast goat, then cold goat, day-three stewed goat. Today curried goat.'

'Sounds good,' said Colette.

The girl smiled, left the room and returned a few minutes later with three cold beers.

'Sit, sit.' Franco gestured to some chairs. '*Salute.*' He raised his bottle, sat back and studied Colette and Sean.

'So, Franco,' said Sean.

'*Che cosa?* Why you say, so?'

'This trouble, what is it?'

'What trouble?'

'What you and Larry talked about, and you wanting Grace back.'

Franco took a long draught from his bottle. 'Sure we got trouble,' he muttered. 'How they expect me to run aid programme when vehicles get shot up, when food get stolen, when lorries get hi-jacked, when…? You saw what happened to Larry's plane. Somebody get themselves killed if someone don't sort out those fuckers.'

'Which people, Franco?' asked Sean.

'How the hell I know?' Franco flapped his hands.

Samira entered with a tray and set down plates of curried goat, rice and chapattis. '*Karibuni* – you are welcome.' She moved silently out of the room.

'Eat, eat,' said Franco, tearing off a piece of chapatti and scooping up curry. 'Is good.'

'Who's causing the trouble?' asked Sean.

Franco shrugged. 'Who knows? Some people say they come from Somalia to make trouble. Others say they from Sudan. Others say they local *ngorokos* – *banditos*.'

'What do you think?'

Franco leaned forward. 'What I think is something going on, something these people no want us to find out about.'

'What sort of thing, Franco?'

Franco sat back and threw up his arms. 'No one take any notice of old Franco. Too long living in the bush, they say. The sun get to Franco's head, they say. And they do nothing.'

'Who does nothing?' asked Sean.

'The police. Those useless wankers, they sit on their arses all day. They take no notice of what Franco say.' He stuffed more curry into his mouth. 'We need Grace to come back and sort out this *maneno*.'

Sean studied him. 'I could have a word with her.'

Franco nodded. 'Is good.' He scooped up the remaining curry and wiped his finger round the plate. 'What you do here?' He gestured at Colette with his chin.

'I, I'm a virologist.'

'*Che?*'

'I work with monkeys.'

'So, with monkeys? You must go and see the Petes. You know the Petes?'

She chuckled. 'Sure. I know the Petes.'

'They come here last month and we have party. He was good party.' He gazed wistfully round the room. 'They drink all my beer.'

'Franco,' said Sean.

'*Sì?*'

'What can I tell Grace?'

Franco gave a loud sniff and wiped his hand over his mouth. 'Curry was good, no?'

'Very good. Franco, what sort of trouble?'

Franco sighed. 'You know a place called Lokinang?'

'Near Laisamis?'

'*Sì.*'

'Isn't that where a missionary and his wife were killed, ages ago?'

Franco nodded. 'I had just started working here. Big *maneno* at the time.'

'And that's where Larry was shot-up?'

'You no go there. Is no safe. My drivers, I tell them you no go or you get your arses shot off. If those people want food aid, they have to come to Laisamis. I tell drivers keep on main road. Come, I show.' Franco led them to the next room which was set up as an office. A large-scale map of the area was pinned to one wall. He jabbed a finger onto it. 'Lokinang Mountain.'

Sean studied the map. 'This is you, Franco where the cross is?'

'*Si, si.*'

'So, what can I tell Grace about Lokinang?'

'Is just talk, you understand. Just the local people.'

'But what are they saying?'

'They say some big *bwana* is building place inside great *boma*. Many askaris.' Franco stared morosely out of the window. 'Many tourists now coming through Isiolo. They say they go Samburu Park.'

'But they've always done that, Franco. It's a great park.'

'*Si, si.* But some now come through back door.'

'Back door? What back door?'

'From Somalia. Is leaky back door?'

'And these people are going to the Park?'

'No way. They not have cameras, binoculars and sensible shoes. Since when Somalis come to Kenya to watch birds?'

'So where are they going?'

Felix shrugged. 'Lokinang, perhaps.'

'Why?'

'I not know.'

'Have the police been there?' asked Sean.

Franco threw his hands in the air. 'They paid not to go.'

'The police are being paid?'

'Big *chai*. That inspector at Isiolo he now drive Mercedes. You tell me where he get that money.'

'So who's paying him?'

Franco spread his hands. 'Who knows? Mlala, perhaps.'

'Mlala? Who's that?'

'Is only a name. I don't know.'

'But you must know something. Who is this person?'

'Sean, my friend, I only tell you what I hear. Is just talk.'

'But there must be—'

Franco's mobile rang. *'Pronto.'*

While Franco was talking to the caller, Colette studied the map. Apart from the hills to the west, most of the area seemed featureless, except for the occasional mountain like Lokinang in the north, and a main road running from Isiolo towards the Ethiopian border, with the town of Laisamis – hardly more than a dot – about midway. She stared at Lokinang Mountain. The contours suggested it was an extinct volcano; not that large, probably no more than ten miles circumference. She'd seen it from the air; the day she flew in from London. A sudden memory was triggered. Before she could retrieve it, Franco finished his call.

'I have to go,' he said. 'Delivery of supplies coming in. You stay, be Franco's guest. Samira, she look after you.'

'No thanks, Franco,' said Sean. 'We'll come back with you.'

'No problema. Momento.' He opened the door of a metal cabinet which was stuffed with folders, boxes and papers. 'Is here somewhere.' He heaved some folders off a shelf. *'Si*, this one.' He dragged out a faded box-file, blew the dust off and passed it to Sean.

'What's this, Franco?'

'Is probably rubbish but who knows?' He shrugged. 'That missionary – I forget his name.'

'The one from Lokinang?'

'Si, si. They say he write a book about Lokinang. These his notes and photos.'

'So, how come you've got them?'

'Sean, my friend, it was terrible. District Officer, he took me there with police soon after that one killed. His wife also; she was nurse. Local people, they show us the house and the bullet holes. House was empty, everything taken, but people there know nothing – what you expect? Only things left were few books and this.'

'Why do you want me to have it?'

'Police say those *banditos* looking for money. Who want books?'

'So they let you take them?'

Franco smiled. 'In those days I was – how you say? – wet behind ears. I want to learn all about new place so I keep.'

'What did you find?'

Franco glanced round as though expecting to be overheard. 'There is big compound near Lokinang.' He gave a mischievous grin. 'Italian prisoners of war shut away there when America and Britain kicking the shit out of Italy in Second World War.'

Colette held up her hands in protest. 'I wasn't involved.'

Franco's eyes twinkled. '*Signora*, even old Franco not involved.' He sank his voice to a whisper. 'No one knows what went on in that place, but I think missionary discovered something.'

'And that's why he was murdered?' said Sean.

Franco shrugged. 'See what you can find.' He gestured to the box-file.

'But haven't you looked through it?'

'*Si, si*. Is notebooks and photographs, but my English no so good. You look.'

'Okay. I'll let you know if we find anything.'

'Is good. Come – *tuende*.'

They called their thanks to Samira, squeezed into Franco's Land Rover and drove back to Sean's plane. 'Good to see you guys. Not many people come to see old Franco these days.'

Sean smiled. 'You take care, hey.'

Franco lifted the hem of his jacket. 'No one mess with Franco.' He patted the revolver strapped to his waist.

'Have you got a licence for that?'

'Sure. Sure, I got licence. I issue licence.'

'I won't tell Grace.' Sean gave Franco a hug. 'Look after yourself, man, and thanks for lunch. I'll be in touch.'

'*Ciao*. You tell Grace, we need her back here.'

'I'll see what she says.' Sean climbed into the plane and began pre-flight checks.

'Thanks, Franco,' said Colette, kissing him on the cheek. 'And thank Samira for a lovely meal.'

As she turned to climb into the plane, he caught her arm and dropped his voice. 'Don't hurt him.'

'Who? What do you mean?'

'Sean. I see the way he look at you.'

'What? But his wife?'

'She no like living in bush, not after…'

'After what?'

'After, after… Is no for me to say. Perhaps Sean tell you?'

'All he's told me is that his wife works for the British High Commissioner.'

Franco's voice sank even lower. 'He should—'

'Stop chatting up the birds, Franco,' called Sean. 'We need to get going.'

'She coming.' He took Colette's hand and kissed it. 'You no forget what Franco say, eh? Trust me.'

She gave him an impulsive hug. 'I won't forget, and thank you. Thank you so much. Thank you for everything.' She turned and scrambled in beside Sean.

'What was all that about?' he asked.

'Nothing.' She closed the door.

'Nothing?'

She kissed his cheek. 'Nothing.'

Sean gave a quizzical smile and started the engine.

Franco waved as the plane took off. She waved back. What did he mean? Perhaps she'd never know. She'd intruded enough into Sean's life and wasn't going to delve further. She sat back to bask in the joy of a flying safari across unspoiled Africa.

'See that?' shouted Sean, above the noise of the engine.

She peered through the cabin windscreen at the approaching hills. 'Is it smoke?'

'Looks like it.'

'A forest fire?'

He didn't respond, but his jaw clenched.

She turned to gaze out of the side window at the vastness of Africa. Far below, the tiny shadow of their plane moved at a snail's pace over the unending landscape. Gradually the hills came nearer then rushed beneath them. The plane passed over a clearing in the forest and she had a glimpse of a smouldering something.

Sean banked round in a tight turn and passed again over the site.

She had a better view but still couldn't make out any detail. 'What is it?'

It was a moment before he replied. 'That's the Petes' camp – what's left of it.'

Chapter 17

Dima resumed his journey next morning as soon as it was light. He followed the trail of the two men round the great table mountain of Ololokwe and reached the place where they'd spent their second night.

He was now near the *manyatta* – the homestead – of his friend Emunyu. Dogs barked. Some women and children, who were seated on the ground, looked up.

'*Hodi* – may I approach?'

'You are welcome,' called a woman, who was scraping the pegged-out skin of goat.

A large man emerged from one of the huts rubbing sleep out of his eyes. He wore Wellington boots, a woolly hat and a pinstriped waistcoat buttoned crookedly across an ample stomach. Round his waist was a red and white-checked cloth held in place by a beaded belt from which hung a sheath containing his *simi*.

A smile lit up his face. 'Dima, my friend, how are you?'

'I am well, Emunyu.'

'Come, come.' He ushered Dima to a log in the shade of an acacia tree.

An older woman emerged from one of the huts carrying a gourd. 'You are welcome, Dima,' she said with a toothless smile, offering him frothy fermenting beer.

'This is very good beer.' He passed the gourd to Emunyu.

She smiled her thanks and left.

A pregnant bitch covered in ticks wandered over, sniffing towards the gourd. Emunyu threw a stick and it ran off with a yelp.

'It is good to see you, Dima, after many days. We have killed a goat. You must join us in a feast.'

'Thank you, Emunyu, you are kind but I cannot stay.'

'You are not looking well.'

'I am well, Emunyu,' – dismissively. 'But how are things here? How are your sons?'

'They are well, but one is sick.'

'How is this?'

'Yesterday, two men passed this place. Namunak, my son, was looking after the sheep and goats by the hill there.' He indicated with

101

his chin. 'The men tried to steal a goat but my son chased them with his spear,' he said proudly. 'They shot him and ran off, but the sheep and goats are all well.'

'I have been following those men.'

'Why is that?'

'I will kill them.' Dima explained the purpose of his journey.

Emunyu nodded and remained silent.

'Those men, where were they going?'

Emunyu shrugged. 'Perhaps to the place of the monkeys.'

'What is that?'

He glanced at Dima. 'It is a bad place. They have askaris with guns. They shoot anyone who goes near. We don't go there.'

'I will go.'

Emunyu passed the gourd. 'Take care, my friend.'

Dima took a sip and passed the gourd back. 'How is your son?'

'Namunak is well, but I fear he will die.'

'Die!'

Emunyu gazed into the distance and nodded.

'May I see him?'

Emunyu called out.

One of the women came across and led Dima to her hut. She stooped and went into the gloomy interior filled with buzzing flies.

A young boy, about ten years old – the same age as Dima's elder son – lay unconscious on a rough bed of sticks covered with a cow skin. The boy's breathing was laboured, a wound in his chest covered in flies. With each breath, pink froth bubbled from the wound, attracting yet more flies.

'This boy is very sick,' he said.

The mother nodded, tears on her face as she stroked her son's forehead.

Dima called two other women. Between them, they lifted the cow skin and carried the boy outside. One of the dogs came and started to lick the blood. Dima kicked it away. He turned the boy over. A larger wound on his back. Flies poured into the fresh meal. Dima ignored them and put his nostrils to the wound. No bad smell. That was good.

He spoke to the women, who hurried off and returned with a variety of leaves, some berries and fresh cow dung.

He pounded the leaves with a rock and mixed them with the dung. He smeared the paste over the wounds, then bound the boy's chest with the skin from the freshly-killed goat. He called for the beer gourd, chewed the berries and spat them into the beer. He swirled the mixture, and trickled some into the boy's mouth.

The boy swallowed and opened his eyes. He was already breathing more easily. He smiled then closed his eyes again.

Dima stood up, gave further instructions to the women and returned to Emunyu who was sitting under the tree brooding. 'Your son will live.'

Emunyu nodded, still staring into the distance. 'You are a good man, Dima.'

The two men sat.

Eventually Emunyu broke the silence. 'It is good you go to kill those men.'

'*Eeh*,' replied Dima. A few minutes later, he got to his feet. 'I go now.'

'Go in peace, my friend. *Kwa heri* – to happiness.'

'To happiness.' Dima walked away.

Chapter 18

Ian found himself lying across the back seat of a Land Rover being driven at speed, surprised he wasn't tied or gagged.

'How you doing buddy?' said a well-known voice.

'Bloody hell.' Ian struggled to sit up.

'Recognise your vehicle?' asked Grace, who was driving.

'Hank gave it the all-clear,' said Felix. 'And your house.'

'What's going on? Why the—?'

'Too many people getting to know about your survival.' Felix turned in the front seat. 'We thought we'd better kill you off again.'

'I hope this isn't going to become a habit.'

'Man, you should take out life insurance. Your dependents could make a fortune.'

'Ha bloody ha.'

'We wanted to give that ass-hole Melhuish something to think about,' said Felix. 'All that crap on the television about shoulder-to-shoulder, Britain leaving no stone unturned, poor security at the Embassy.'

'He said that!'

'Yeah, said you'd been at the US Embassy and that's when the bomb was planted. Ambassador's spitting bullets.'

'I'm not surprised.' Ian lapsed into silence; then began to chuckle. 'I'd love to see his face right now.'

'Guess he's shitting bricks.'

'Let's hope so.'

'Thunder flashes can be quite noisy,' observed Grace.

'You buggers.' Ian checked his watch. 'Hell, it's three in the morning.'

'Early morning call,' she said. 'Nothing more I can do in Nairobi, so we make an early start. We take Felix to his place. You can change there. Your bag's in the back. Then on to Isiolo.'

'Like we agreed; you drop in because you happen to be passing,' said Felix. 'And Grace can check out her old pals.'

***

Ian's Land Rover had been on enough rugged safaris to have acquired the dents and scratches which allowed it to blend in with the disparate vehicles in Isiolo: a dusty township which had hardly changed since colonial times. He parked under an acacia tree in one of the few patches of shade available. Then he and Grace – barely disguised by dark glasses – threaded their way between over-loaded minibuses belching smoke and reggae music, lorries bearing Somali or Ethiopian number plates, around goats resting in the road, and handcarts laden with suspicious-looking sacks. They passed what Ian took to be a garage: a small boy filling a vehicle with fuel from a watering can, a Samburu warrior in traditional dress bashing a gearbox with a rock and a six-inch nail, and a man welding a chassis – the hot sparks cascading round his bare feet. They skirted a circle of boys crouched in the dust passing a cigarette among themselves. 'Nice girl,' said one of them.

Ian scowled.

They moved into the shade of an awning outside a rundown building claiming to be the New Paradise Bar and Hotel.

'Let's watch for a while,' said Grace. 'See what's going on.'

'What are we looking for?'

'As Felix would say: any joker who doesn't look right.'

'Like that fellow who's lost an ear and seems to be watching us?'

'He's probably thinking, what's the British army doing here?'

'Is it that obvious?'

'At least you've removed your tie but you don't look like the average backpacker.'

'I'm working on it.' Ian rubbed the stubble on his chin.

The man lost interest and sauntered off to talk to another man who was leaning against a Toyota Land Cruiser, its roof-rack piled high.

A Land Cruiser with a piled roof-rack?

Before it fully registered, Grace grabbed Ian's arm and whisked him inside the bar. 'Did you see who that was?'

'No.'

'It was Omar. I'm sure it was.'

A bus pulled up, blocking their view. When it moved on, there was no sign of Omar, the one-eared man or the Land Cruiser.

'Let's get some breakfast.' She led the way to the bar.

The proprietor looked up from his newspaper and his face lit up in a huge grin exposing brown and broken teeth. 'Grace, my friend, how are you since many days?' He hurried round the counter to welcome her.

'Solomon, good to see you. How are you?'

'I am well, but—'

'I know; the cows are sick, your wife has run off, the roof is broken, the children have—'

Solomon gave a shout of laughter and clapped Grace on the back. 'I don't complain.'

'Much.'

The man shrugged. 'Not much.'

'This is my friend John,' said Grace. 'He's visiting from England.'

'You are welcome.' Solomon, shook Ian's hand and gestured to the paper. 'Things are not good in Nairobi.'

Ian struggled to keep his composure as he saw the headline and photos of the bombed vehicle.

'They're bad,' said Grace. 'And here?'

Solomon turned to a rusting fridge behind the bar, took out two beers and flipped the caps off. '*Karibuni* – welcome.'

'You know I don't drink beer,' she said.

The man scowled, opened a Coke and took the second beer for himself.

Grace and Ian pulled up bar stools and sat sipping their drinks.

While Grace and Solomon chatted about old times, Ian studied the seedy décor. On one wall was a portrait of the President gazing in puzzlement at a calendar on the opposite wall, showing people punting on the Cam with Cambridge colleges in the background – hardly Solomon's scene. Alongside fly-blown posters announcing political rallies, was a framed newspaper cutting showing Grace on the Olympic rostrum flanked by the silver and bronze medallists from Ethiopia.

'I see you've got your fans,' observed Ian.

'Oh that.' Grace smiled. 'Solomon put that up ages ago, probably to keep me off his back.'

The proprietor nodded. 'That one is a good person,' he said, addressing Ian. 'She did not interfere with my business, not like some of the—'

'What is it these days, Solomon: smuggling, cattle theft, gun-running, poaching, or some new *maneno?*'

He seemed to think the question hugely funny. 'We were always good friends though, Grace.' He gave the bar a perfunctory wipe with a grubby cloth. 'I'm too old for that sort of thing now.'

'But you still keep your eyes and ears open?'

'I run a hotel.'

'So what's new?'

'How should I know?' He avoided her eyes and continued wiping the bar.

Grace's expression hardened. 'Who's Mlala?'

Solomon's wiping barely faltered. 'No idea.'

She sighed, reached into her bag and laid her police ID on the bar. 'Can I see your licence?'

Solomon glared; then laughed. 'I'll fix breakfast for you.' He disappeared through a door at the back, shouting instructions.

'Do you think he can help?' asked Ian.

'Maybe. He's scared, and that's interesting.' Grace gazed at the view outside the dusty windows. 'And he's heard of Mlala.'

Ian waited but she was lost in thought. He glanced at the paper and wished he hadn't. Fortunately, the photo of a man in military uniform could have been anyone.

Grace looked up. 'You think it's strange that ole-Tomeno appointed a woman to be your counterpart, don't you?'

Ian recoiled. 'No.' Lie.

She took a sip from her Coke and studied him. 'Do you know anything about running?'

'Why do you ask?'

'Do you?'

'Well, it hurts. I learned that at military academy.'

She gave a faint smile. 'It hurts, but you learn to forget that. What else?'

'I guess you need talent and commitment.'

'Talent and commitment,' she repeated. 'And?'

'The will to win?'

'I have all those. That's why I'm a good runner,' said without arrogance. She pointed to the framed cutting. 'Those Ethiopian girls, Makeda and Fetiya, are also good runners, some might say better than me, but they didn't win. Why?'

'You tell me.'

'Because I cheated.'

'Cheated! How? Drugs?'

'Not really cheating, I suppose. I applied my police training.'

'How?'

'My coach knew those two would be my main rivals and he made me study every race in which they ran, including when Makeda broke the world record. I studied those races as though I was investigating

107

crime scenes or studying CCTV footage. I noted their times for every lap of every race, including races they didn't win. I studied when they pushed and when they coasted – I could tell those things from the tension in their shoulders. I studied where in the field they felt comfortable and where not. I learned that Makeda likes to lead from the front, but Fetiya stays with the leaders and kicks just before the last bend. I went into the final with all that knowledge and knew I couldn't lose.' She gave a self-deprecating smile and took another sip from her bottle.

'Tell me about the race.'

She kept her eyes on the photo. 'The three of us broke from the rest of the field with four laps to go. Makeda leading as usual, and Fetiya tucked in behind. They probably expected me to break in the last lap, which I usually did. Instead, I shut out the pain, gained five metres and held that lead for the next lap. I then eased off and we returned to our previous positions.'

'Weren't you exhausted?'

'Yes. But I'd unsettled Makeda and that boosted my confidence – the plan was working.'

'And the other girl?'

'Fetiya kicked fifty metres sooner than usual.' She turned back to Ian. 'And the rest you know.' She began drawing random patterns on the bar surface. 'I unsettled them and they cracked.'

Ian studied her, at a loss for words. 'I'm really impressed,' he said eventually. He felt strangely moved; the first time she'd revealed to him the real person beneath the professional exterior.

'It also explains why I'm good at my job and why ole-Tomeno appointed me.'

The awkwardness was broken by Solomon bustling in with two plates piled with food. '*Karibuni*,' he said, setting them on the bar.

'You're a good man,' said Grace. She passed him a hand-written note. 'That's my mobile number.'

Solomon sniffed and put it in his pocket.

'In case you remember anything,' she added.

They continued their breakfast in silence waiting for him to speak.

'That news is very bad.' He gestured to the newspaper.

Grace nodded.

Solomon leaned forward. 'You know Lokinang?'

She shook her head. 'No.'

'Near Laisamis.'

'Right.'

'Much *maneno*.'

'What sort of *maneno*?'

Solomon shrugged. 'No one can go there.'

'Why?'

'The monkeys.'

'Monkeys? What monkeys?'

'They keep monkeys and no one can go near.'

'Who keeps monkeys?' She frowned. 'What do they do with them?'

'How would I know?'

'It's probably not important.' She cleaned up her plate with a piece of bread. 'What news of ole-Tomeno?'

'That one?'

'Yes.'

'He was here last month, some big *baraza*, many people went to the meeting.'

'Did you go?'

Solomon gave his expansive grin. 'It was very good for business. Ole-Tomeno bought many beers for people.'

'What was the meeting about?'

'I don't know.' He glowered. 'You stop asking questions and go now.'

Grace laid some money on the bar. 'Good food,' she said, finishing her Coke. 'One more question: what do you know about Njia Mpya?'

'You go.' Solomon pushed the money back and hustled them out through the kitchen.

They turned to say their thanks but Solomon had returned inside.

'What now?' said Ian.

'We see if he cracks. In the meantime…' She tossed Ian the keys of his vehicle. 'Go and be a tourist in Samburu Park. I need to do some more chatting. Meet back here at six.'

Chapter 19

Dima picked up the trail of the two men and continued northwards. The terrain here was featureless except for the few hills which poked out of an otherwise flat landscape – a seemingly barren wasteland. To Dima, a wilderness of space, beauty and plenty. He knew where the waterholes were, knew the network of elephant trails – some of them hundreds of years old – knew the berries and leaves to eat and the ones to avoid, and understood the tracks of mammals, reptiles and birds.

He noticed disturbed soil. Crushed vegetation. A patch of dried blood in the sand. He knelt down and smelled it. This was not blood from killing an animal. This was blood from the stomach. As he continued, the men's tracks became more distinct. Another patch of vomited blood. Further on, another; this one with flies buzzing round.

Someone shouting, the speech slurred like someone drunk. A pause; then retching. A longer silence. The man shouted again.

Dima crept nearer.

The man was sitting at the base of a tree, his head lolling forward. Vomited blood stained his ragged T-shirt.

As Dima watched, the man rolled to the ground. Black liquid poured from his mouth. His face lay in the vomit surrounded by a cloud of flies.

'Hello, friend,' said Dima.

The man's eyes snapped open. They were muddy red. 'Who are you? Where's Nelamis?'

'He's gone.'

'Who are—?' Another bout of retching – the blood bright red this time.

Dima felt no pity.

The man lapsed into rambling abuse.

'Nelamis has gone to the place of the monkeys?' suggested Dima, remembering his conversation with Emunyu.

'Place of monkeys,' muttered the man.

The call of a hyena sounded in the still evening air. The man shuddered.

Dima watched dispassionately. 'I go now.'

The man raised his head. 'Don't, don't leave…' A rattling gurgle in his throat and he lay still.

The hyena called again – nearer this time.

Dima walked towards the darkening evening.

The bush was the bush. In life and in death; it was simply the bush. It was the same for all who lived there.

He continued his journey.

Wood smoke.

He crept forward. The smell of smoke mixed with that of roast meat. He felt hungry, drew nearer. The faint glow of a fire. The silhouette of a man. Nelamis?

Dima settled behind a tree and ate some berries he'd collected earlier. His strength was returning all the time.

Shadows lengthened. Darkness fell. Stars appeared. A spiny mouse emerged from its burrow, blinked at him, trotted off in search of supper. A camel spider scurried across the warm sand, its feelers dangling like ghostly arms. A nightjar began its monotonous churring call. The moon rose rinsing the landscape clean.

The man was now asleep by the fire; two bags and a rifle beside him. Dima edged closer and removed them. The smaller bag contained dried meat and stale bread. The other was tied at the neck. He opened it and recoiled at the smell. Dead monkeys. Why would a hunter – if that's what this man was – keep dead monkeys?

He re-tied the bag. Replaced both bags beside the sleeping man but kept the rifle.

A slight movement near his foot. He drew a sharp breath. One of the few things in the bush that he truly feared. In the cool of the night air, the saw-scaled viper was drowsy but still deadly.

He crept back to the sleeping man and retrieved the smaller bag. He tipped out the food, grabbed the snake at the back of its head and dropped it in. He returned the bag to the fireside.

He ate the man's food and settled down for the night. The spirits of the night settled with him.

Chapter 20

The first thing Colette knew the next morning was someone shaking her shoulder.

'Sorry to wake you,' said Sean, 'but you said you wanted to come.'

'What?' she murmured. 'Where?'

'The Petes' camp.'

She sat up, her mind instantly clear. 'Of course I want to come.'

'I've no idea what we'll find.'

'So?'

Despite the lop-sided smile, his face was tense. 'I've brought you some tea.'

'Thanks. What's the time?'

'Just after six. Soon be light.'

***

Jotham drove with Suni sitting next to him. Colette and Sean stood on the backseat with the roof-hatch open. A slight chemical smell came from inside following Sean's disinfection of the Land Rover.

They began to climb. The dusty bush track became rougher and rockier. The forest closed in and the trees shut out the sun. A bushbuck bounded across the track and disappeared into the undergrowth. She glanced at Sean and smiled.

They continued in silence until Jotham stopped and pointed.

Sean looked through his binoculars then handed them to her.

Indistinct shapes moving in the grass in a clearing. 'Are they vultures?'

'I'll go and see,' said Jotham. He slipped out of the vehicle, took the *simi* from his belt and crept off.

Sean picked up Suni to stop her whining.

Jotham reappeared, beckoned and melted back into the trees.

'Do you want to stay here?' asked Sean. 'It may not be pretty.'

'I'm coming,' she said.

He ducked down inside the vehicle, slipped out of the door and set Suni down.

Colette followed.

Squawks and cackles. A flapping of wings.

Jotham was studying something hidden in the grass. Suni beside him questing forward, her tail between her legs. The vultures watched

112

from the surrounding trees, their wings hunched like ghouls from a horror film.

Cold sweat formed on the palms of Colette's hands.

'Mind where you stand.' Sean pointed to a line of black treacle in the grass. Safari ants. Millions of them.

It wasn't pretty – what could be seen through the blanket of voracious ants. The rustling sound of numerous tiny jaws. The mutilation wreaked by the vultures made it even more horrendous.

'Is it Kimani?'

Sean nodded. 'Poor bugger.'

'A leopard?'

'No.' Sean pointed to the skull with a stick. 'He's been shot.'

'Shot! Why? When? Who by?'

'What we heard yesterday, I guess.'

She made herself look again at the remains: a mutilated body, a few scraps of clothing, a blood-stained belt. And this was Kimani, the Petes' faithful retainer, the custodian of the hallowed premises. The Kimani who would serve them victuals and ale. The Kimani who was being rapidly stripped of his flesh and tissues. The Kimani whom she was destined to meet only in his appalling death. Despite the heat of the day, she shivered.

Sean put an arm round her shoulders. 'You okay?'

She nodded.

He released his arm. 'Nothing we can do. Let's press on.'

'Surely, we should take him back?' she cried. 'At least bury him.'

'Tell her, Jotham.'

Jotham pointed to the vultures, which glared back. 'Those ones carry the spirits of dead people into the sky.' He gave an expansive gesture with his hands. 'This man does not want to be shut in a box inside the earth. See.' He pointed across the forest to where the snow-covered twin peaks of Mount Kenya were faintly visible in the far distance. 'Is this not a very fine place?'

'Huh,' was all she could manage.

'When it is my time,' said Jotham, 'this is where I will want to stay.'

'Me too,' said Sean.

She gazed at the distant peaks, serene and beautiful in the morning light. Looked back at the devastation. 'You're right.' She stared at her feet. And if the ants took my soul into the soil, I would still want to stay.

'Come.' Sean gave her arm a squeeze. 'We need to check the

camp.'

'I go by footing,' said Jotham.

'Take Suni,' said Sean. 'We'll see you there.'

Colette followed him to the Land Rover, trying to shut out the rustling of insatiable mouths administering Kimani's last rites.

Sean drove fast, savagely, his jaw clamped, his hands gripping white on the steering wheel.

She kept glancing at him but he ignored her until they reached a clearing. He pulled up. 'Sorry.' He switched off the engine. 'I had to get that out of my system.'

She rested her hand on his arm. 'That's okay. That poor man.'

'Thanks for understanding.' He gave a rueful smile. Then he was kissing her.

She found herself resisting.

He tore himself away. 'Sorry.'

'Don't apologise.' She took his hand and held it to her lips. 'It was nice.'

'You're so beautiful,' he whispered.

She laughed. 'Come on.' She jumped out of the vehicle and ran to join Jotham.

Suni was barking at something hidden in the grass.

The black and white colobus had been dead for a while and part of its body had been eaten.

'Also shot.' Sean pointed to a hole in its chest.

'Sean, what's going on?'

'I wish I knew.'

She picked up a stick and gently rolled the body over. 'See that?'

'The blood?'

'Yes. This monkey's obviously been dead for a while but the blood still hasn't clotted. And look: that rash on its abdomen.'

'Marburg?'

'Or similar.'

'Another here,' called Jotham.

This corpse was stiff and also partially eaten, but the blood round the bullet wound had dried and there was no sign of a rash.

A swish in the branches overhead. They looked up. A large male colobus glared at them. Sean focused his binoculars. 'He looks okay.' He handed the binoculars to Colette. 'Which means what?'

She watched the monkey, placidly chewing leaves. 'The infection could have moved on, or it's still active and some monkeys are still to go down, or some have been infected and recovered. Hell, I don't know.'

She handed the binoculars back and began wandering through the remains of the camp. It was like being in a ransacked house and seeing someone's private life strewn around: pathetic belongings, worthless and banal – a torn paperback, a smashed radio, a broken chair, a ripped sleeping bag, a cheap shoe, a mobile phone – totally dead.

Why, why, why? And why were the monkeys shot?

The clear liquid call of some bird rang through the clearing. She looked up.

Sean came and joined her, passed her the binoculars and pointed to the top of a tree. 'Black-headed oriole.'

She could just make out the brilliant golden plumage almost hidden among the leaves. 'That is so beautiful. But this...' She kicked savagely at a broken mug.

'Let's see if we can sort this place,' he said.

An hour later, they had heaped the remains of the camp onto a revived fire. There was very little worth salvaging except some note books and numerous specimen bottles which seemed undamaged, their contents unharmed. They collected these things into a box to give the Petes. Finally, Sean took a spade from the Land Rover and placed the bodies of the two monkeys on the funeral pyre.

They stood and watched the two beautiful animals being reduced to charred remains.

She linked her arm through his. 'That is so sad. How are we going to break this to the Petes?'

For a moment he didn't reply. 'I'm afraid communication with the Petes tends to be a one-way system. They contact me if they need something. Otherwise...' He shrugged.

'There's no way we can get in touch?'

'No.'

'That's so awful, us seeing this and them not knowing.'

Suni gave a woof.

Colette looked up to see Jotham returning out of the forest.

'Three men,' he said, 'I followed their tracks, but they are now far. One I think is Dima. He goes after the other two.' He pointed in a northerly direction.

'I guess that's it, then,' said Sean.

***

115

Colette emerged from the shower and gazed into the mirror as she dried her hair. The wrinkles had gone. Perhaps it was simply that the lighting was poor. You're so beautiful. Was he talking to her or to Helen? She joined him on the veranda. He was sitting, a beer at his elbow, gazing into the hazy distance and listening to the radio. She sat down beside him.

'You okay?'

She nodded.

'Here.' He passed her a beer.

'Thanks.' She sipped thoughtfully. 'I still can't—'

'Sh.' He turned up the radio.

'...*police are no nearer to finding the perpetrators and are appealing for witnesses who were in the area of the Nairobi Football Stadium when the explosion occurred. Fifteen people are confirmed dead, including the driver and passenger of the British High Commission Land Rover which was believed to have been...*'

She clutched the edge of the table.

'... *High Commissioner, Sir Aubrey Gilmore confirmed... Colonel Ian Sinclair, military attaché killed... the President... message of condolence... link to US Embassy bombing...*'

She slumped across the table, heedless of bottles crashing to the ground. She became aware of a dripping sound. She opened her eyes to see a pool of beer trickling off the table onto the floor of the veranda.

'Ian?' she whispered.

Sean had his hand on her shoulder. 'God, you scared me.'

She sat up. 'Is he dead?'

He didn't reply.

She watched the beer: drip, drip, drip. What a waste. It was the same brand she and Ian used to drink.

'How well did you know him?'

She looked up, her eyes unable to focus. 'What?'

'How well did you know Ian?'

Drip, drip, drip.

Suni came and nuzzled her hand.

'What happened?' Colette asked in a flat voice.

'I don't know any more than you. Only that his vehicle was blown up by a bomb.'

'Was it meant for him?'

'Seems like it. But who would want to do that?'

'Ian would never talk about his work. Probably why he was so good... Christ!' She scrambled to her feet, ran off the veranda and back to her room. She sat on the bed and stared out of the window.

She'd no idea how long she sat there staring, thinking.

There was a knock on the door.

'Come in.'

'I thought you could use this.' Sean placed a mug of coffee on the bedside table.

'Thanks.'

'No sweat.' He closed the door behind him.

Still she sat, thinking. Not thinking. Thinking about what? She couldn't remember.

She reached for the coffee. It was cold. She poured it down the sink. Rinsed the mug. Splashed some water over her face, ran a comb through her hair, returned to the veranda.

Sean was seated at the table eating a late lunch. He looked up as she approached. 'Are you all right?'

She gave a nervous smile. 'Sorry, I fell asleep.'

He indicated the seat beside him.

She sat down and stroked Suni, who then sat on her feet.

'I'm afraid it's only cold.' Sean moved a plate of food towards her.

She took a lettuce leaf, conscious of him watching her. 'What?'

'Are you on a diet?'

'Why do you—?'

'There's a vehicle coming.' He pointed at a dust cloud approaching through the bush. A vehicle was making its way along the bumpy track.

'Who is it?'

'I've no idea.'

Suni ran to the edge of the veranda and pricked her ears.

The vehicle drew nearer.

Stopped.

Two people got out.

Chapter 21

Daylight was shaking off darkness as Dima woke. He could just make out the shape of the sleeping man. As he watched, the man stirred and rubbed his eyes. He stood up, stretched and went to gather some sticks. Poked them into the embers of the fire. When they caught light he reached for his bag.

Dima watched with interest.

The man screamed.

Leaped to his feet, the snake attached to his thumb.

He seized a rock and pounded the snake against the ground.

He fell, screaming, clutching his rapidly swelling hand.

Rolled into the fire. His T-shirt caught light.

He continued thrashing. The charred T-shirt fell away.

The swelling spread up his arm.

Sweat streamed off his body.

He began retching.

Dima had once seen a boy die of a bite from this snake. That was why he feared it. But he felt no remorse for the man. The thrashing weakened.

Dima walked over to him. 'You are Nelamis?'

The man looked up. 'Help me,' he implored.

Dima tore a strip off the charred T-shirt and bound it round the man's hand in a show of helpfulness.

The pain appeared to ease but the man's breathing became shallow and irregular.

'I can take the monkeys for you,' said Dima.

The man was probably past caring as he drifted in and out of consciousness. 'Go to…'

Dima knelt down to hear the faint words.

'Go to… place… dead monkeys… pay money…'

'Where?'

'Place… Molito…'

'Where's that?'

'He will… water… I need… Molito.'

Dima shook him. 'Where is Molito?'

'Water… I…' His eyes fell shut.

Dima stood up. Molito? Was this a person or a place?

A hornbill called from a nearby tree.

The jumbled words of the dying man made little sense: Molito, go to Molito, money, place of monkeys, pay money. Pay money for monkeys? He knew there were traders who paid for live monkeys, but this Molito seemed to pay for dead ones. It made no sense. He untied the bag. The stench had intensified overnight. Why would anyone buy dead monkeys?

Then he knew. *Uchawi!*

These monkeys were to be used for *uchawi* – witchcraft. He threw the bag down. Recoiled from it. Fearful that he would become bewitched.

Uchawi explained everything.

The hornbill was still calling. It flew to another tree and joined its mate. The two began a frenzied duet.

Dima turned and walked away. He stuffed the useless rifle down a chimney of a termite mound – much to the consternation of the resident mongooses. He wanted nothing more to do with dead monkeys, hunters who broke the code, hunters involved in *uchawi*.

But my family needs money.

He stopped and looked back at the foul bag. If I can take it to someone who is mad enough – evil enough – to pay for dead monkeys, I can get the money my family needs.

He shut his mind, shouldered the grisly bundle and continued northwards. In the far distance he could see Lokinang – one of the few landmarks in the huge landscape. He thought of home.

Vultures circled overhead.

The morning advanced and Lokinang came gradually nearer.

He heard the sound of sheep and goat bells. Two boys, playing a game in the dust, looked up in alarm.

'Where is Molito?' he called.

One boy ran off. The other pointed with his stick and followed. Despite Dima's calling, they refused to come back.

He continued on and heard the sound of chopping. A woman with a baby strapped to her back, was hacking at a tree for firewood.

'I'm looking for Molito,' he called.

She whirled round, startled. Tried to run off, but was hampered by the weight of her child.

Dima easily caught up with her. 'Where can I find Molito?'

She gave a sharp cry and tried to flee.

He grasped her arm. 'Molito. Where is Molito?'

She whimpered, indicated a path and broke free.

Soon a dilapidated *manyatta* came into view. A place of gloom and melancholy – a stark contrast to the tidy and homely *manyatta* of his friend Emunyu. Two marabou storks pecked at the remains of a goat.

Dima called out and waited. A mangy dog came and sniffed him then wandered away. Still he waited. He was about to call again when a fat bleary-eyed man appeared and stood swaying on his feet.

'What do you want?'

'I am looking for Molito.'

The man glared through blood-shot eyes. 'I am Molito. Why have you come?'

'I have monkeys.' Dima indicated the bag at his feet.

A spasm flickered across the man's face.

'You can pay me for—'

The man gave a shout. A youth appeared from one of the rundown huts. He was almost naked and very dirty.

Molito turned and went back to his hut.

The youth came up to Dima, a crazed look in his eyes. He plucked at his arm, grinning and gibbering. He turned and set off at a run. Waved for Dima to follow.

Dima, with his load, struggled to keep up.

They continued at this pace for what seemed a great distance. Then the youth stopped and gave a shrill whistle.

A rattle of stones on the path ahead. An askari, dressed in a camouflage jacket and trousers, appeared carrying a rifle.

The youth pushed the reluctant Dima forward and ran off.

'Who are you?' asked the askari.

'I have monkeys,' said Dima.

'Follow me.'

They came to a small road with a gate across it. A hut at the side. A large wire fence stretched in both directions from the gate. It seemed to go round some sort of *boma* or compound set at the base of a cliff beyond the trees.

The askari called out. A second man emerged from the hut, dressed and armed in the same way.

'*Jambo*,' said Dima. '*Habari yako?*'

The man ignored the greeting. Looked at him.

Dima began to feel uneasy. He shouldn't have come. But if he tried to run away the men could shoot him with their special guns called Kalashnikov and probably would. He smiled but got no response. Instead, one of the askaris went into the hut and talked in a muffled voice on a radio.

The askari came out. 'Wait.'

Dima sat under a tree and waited.

The men weren't unfriendly – simply indifferent. They stood by the gate smoking, ignoring him.

The sound of a vehicle inside the compound. The askaris stubbed out their cigarettes. A battered Suzuki four-wheel-drive drew up. The askaris saluted. One of them opened the gate. The vehicle turned round and stopped. An African, wearing a white coat, got out.

One of the askaris beckoned Dima. 'You, come.'

Dima picked up the bag.

'Who are you?' asked the man.

'I am the brother of Nelamis,' said Dima.

'Where is Nelamis?'

'He is sick. A snake bit him.'

The man ignored the statement. 'You have brought monkeys?'

Dima gestured at the bag with his foot.

'Wait.' The man went back to his vehicle and started talking on a radio.

Dima returned to the shade of his tree. He was beginning to doze off when another vehicle appeared. A tall man got out. He was a *mzungu* but not a *mzungu*. Dima supposed he was a *nusu-nusu* – a half-half. Round his neck were special glasses for watching birds. He spoke briefly to the man in the white coat, then the two of them came to Dima.

'Where are the monkeys from?' asked the tall man.

'From the forest.'

'Which forest?'

Dima pointed vaguely. 'Where the monkeys are dying.'

'Dying?'

'Yes. I fear these monkeys are dead, but you can pay—'

'Why are the monkeys dying?'

He shrugged. 'Their blood goes like water.'

The two men exchanged glances. The taller one led his companion aside and started talking rapidly to him. The latter nodded then drove off.

The tall man ignored Dima and wandered off searching for birds with his special glasses.

Dima returned to the shade of his tree.

121

The askaris lit fresh cigarettes.

The man in the white coat returned in the Suzuki. He pulled up and opened the door at the back. The taller man returned from his bird-watching and gestured Dima to bring the bag with the dead monkeys. The man in the white coat got out a knapsack sprayer – like the ones Dima had seen people use to spray cattle against ticks – and doused the bag in chemical. When the tall man was satisfied, Dima had to lift up the bag and put it inside a second bag, then get into the Suzuki and hold the bag.

After a bumpy ride, the vehicles came to a set of low buildings hidden among thorn trees. More armed askaris. Cages containing screeching monkeys.

The vehicles stopped at a small stone building. The tall man got out of his vehicle and disappeared inside. The driver of the Suzuki climbed out and waited. Another man – tall and with a beard, perhaps a *mhindi* – came out of a building and spoke to the driver.

Dima couldn't hear what they were saying. He wriggled round and peered out. The compound was like some sort of school or hospital, but no children or patients. The only people he could see wore white coats. Perhaps they were nurses or doctors. Perhaps warders and this was a prison.

But why monkeys? – which were now quiet.

A pair of double doors opened at the end of the building, and the bearded man emerged, clothed completely in green and his face covered by glass.

This was *uchawi* but *uchawi* far more powerful than Dima could have imagined. If he'd not been locked in the vehicle, he would have fled – despite the askaris.

The Suzuki's driver unlocked the rear door. 'Bring the bag.'

Dima looked fearfully at the green man, who gestured impatiently. Could he run?

An askari approached.

The green man gestured again.

Once inside the building there would be no escape. He might make it to the trees if—

The butt of a rifle slammed into his back. He slumped to the ground.

'*Haraka* – hurry!' The askari kicked him in the ribs. 'Get up.'

The rifle butt crashed down again before Dima noticed the ragged scar where the man's ear should have been.

***

Dima's head was pounding. Lights kept flashing and there was a stabbing pain in his leg. He opened his eyes. Bushes, sand, dead grass.

Stab.

A swishing sound. A croak.

Stab.

He sat up.

Two vultures flapped off in confusion.

He inspected his leg. The bird hadn't broken the skin. He looked around. Nothing but bush. He listened. The buzzing of flies and the cackle of vultures. He hobbled to the nearest cover and waited for his pounding head to settle.

He was on the edge of a clearing surrounded by thorn trees. A vehicle track led into it. Whitened bones lay nearby. Over there, more. He hissed; that was a human skull and that was a… a hand, a person's hand.

There was a swish of wings and a vulture settled.

He began to sway: monkeys, death, pain, exhaustion and… and *uchawi*. His knees buckled and… and strong hands caught him.

He was carried. Carried far. Carried where?

His eyes refused to open.

He was laid down.

Water trickled into his mouth. Fresh cool water.

Still his eyes refused.

A voice spoke to him from far away. A man's voice. A man beside him but speaking from afar.

Another drink.

Sight and hearing returned in time to see the man leaving.

A tall man. A *nusu-nusu* man with special glasses for seeing birds.

Chapter 22

Ian? It couldn't be. He was dead. She'd heard it on the news.

He waved.

Colette stared. It was him. But who was the woman with him?

'Ian?'

'Sorry to come unannounced,' he said.

'But the... the... bomb?'

'Oh.' He checked. 'You've heard, then?'

'It was on the radio,' said Sean. 'We heard it at lunchtime.'

'I see.'

'Was the report was wrong?' she asked.

'No. Only some of the, er, detail.' He sat down in a chair and studied his hands.

Colette felt unsettled by the woman who chose the chair beside him. She had said nothing but was listening with her eyes.

Ian looked up and seemed to focus on Colette. 'There was a bomb – two in fact. It's just that I wasn't in the vehicle. It was my... my driver who bought it.'

'But it was meant for you?' Her voice sounded like someone else's.

'Probably.'

She stared bleakly at nothing. 'It's not ninety-eight all over again, is it?'

'We hope not.'

'What more can you tell us?' asked Sean.

Colette continued to stare at nothing.

'Are you going to join us?'

She glanced up to see Sean studying her. Was this what Franco meant: "*I see the way he look at you*"? She scrambled to her feet. 'What?'

'We're going to sit over there in the shade. You coming?' He was holding a whisky bottle and some glasses.

'Yes. Yes, of course.'

'Bring your chair.'

Colette shrank into her seat and peered from her cloak of confusion at the other three. Then she remembered. That was the policewoman whom she'd seen in uniform at the Condor meeting. It wasn't until she asked Sean for a soft drink that Colette learned her name was Grace. Hadn't she been an athlete or something?

124

Colette half listened to the others discussing the bombing. What would happen to her life now that Ian had returned from the dead? His too, for that matter? She stroked Suni lying on her feet.

'Where've you come from?' asked Sean.

'Isiolo,' said Grace. 'We spent the night at the New Paradise.'

'That dump.'

Ian pulled a face. 'Shall we say it wasn't exactly paradise. All in the line of duty, though.'

The line of duty. Colette winced.

'You should have come and stayed here,' said Sean.

'Tonight if we may,' said Grace. She studied Sean. 'Do you know a fellow called Franco? He runs a—'

Sean laughed. 'I doubt there's anyone within a hundred miles of here who doesn't know Franco. We saw him yesterday.'

'He came here?'

'No we flew over. He gave us lunch.'

'So, a social call?'

'Partly. I took his mail.'

'Did he have any news?'

'Plenty.'

'Like what?'

'Like people trying to sell him x-ray machines, sending him dodgy maize meal, a party he'd held at—'

'Sean, you know what I mean.'

'You guys eaten?' he asked.

'We had breakfast,' said Grace tersely.

'So you can either have a late lunch or an early supper.'

'Sounds good,' said Ian.

'I'll talk to Leah.' Colette scrambled to her feet and ran back to the house, Suni at her heels.

When she and Leah returned carrying trays of food, the others had moved their chairs beside the campfire which had been revived from the previous night. Some of the tension seemed to have dissipated and Sean was identifying the calls of birds for the other two.

'I hope you're hungry,' said Colette, setting a grill over the hot ashes. She applied herself to cooking steaks while trying to muzzle her emotions and listen in on their conversation.

'I guess we'd better give that bit to Suni,' said a voice.

'What? Oh no.' She looked in horror at the charred cinder. 'Sean, I'm so sorry.'

'Here, let me help.' He squatted beside her and began flipping over steaks with a practised hand.

She noticed Ian watching and hastily stood up. 'Can I get anyone another drink?'

They shook their heads.

'Food's ready,' called Sean. 'I've eaten but you guys come and help yourselves.'

'Ladies first,' said Ian.

Colette gave a forced smile and picked up a plate. Damn you. Having collected her food, she chose a chair away from his and was grateful to Grace for coming and sitting next to her.

'I don't think we've met,' said Grace, holding out her hand.

'No.' Colette juggled cutlery, plate and glass and extracted a hand. 'Pleased to meet you.'

'This looks good.'

'Yes, doesn't it?' Colette applied herself to the meal.

'Franco's an interesting fellow.'

'Yes, very.' Colette was conscious of Sean watching them.

'Have you met him before?'

'No, first time.'

'Did he tell you about his work?'

'A bit. He seems to keep pretty busy.'

'Yes.' Grace turned to concentrate on her food, apparently oblivious of the others watching her. 'We plan to go and visit him tomorrow.'

'Have you heard he wants you to come back here?' said Sean.

'Why?'

'To sort things out.'

'What things?'

Sean pushed a log into the fire with his foot. 'You know how hard it is to pin Franco down, but he did mention a name... something like Mlala – presumably a nickname.'

'Mlala?'

'Some sort of background figure, I imagine. Do you know who he means?'

'Did he tell you anything about this person?'

Sean shook his head. 'He'd jumped onto the next topic before we could follow up.'

'Which was?'

'A place called Lokinang.'

Grace glanced briefly at Ian. 'We know Lokinang.'

'Have you heard of any trouble there?' asked Sean.

Grace, again, side-stepped the question. 'What did Franco say about Lokinang?'

'He said quite a few outsiders are coming through Isiolo just now, ostensibly to go to Samburu Park but he thought they might be heading to Lokinang instead.'

'Did he say why?'

'No. But he inferred they didn't look like tourists.'

'I've been there,' blurted Colette.

'Excuse me?' said Grace.

'I'm sorry to butt in,' she said, 'it's just that when Franco mentioned the name, it triggered a faint memory. Now I remember what it was.'

'Go on.'

'It must be five or six years ago when I was here before, working at the Primate Research Centre. I was looking for somewhere remote where I could do virus studies without risking local monkey populations if any bugs escaped. Jeff suggested—'

'Jeff? Is that Jeff Carter?' asked Ian.

'He was my boss. He had a link with this place at Lokinang. Something about physiological studies on primates in arid conditions. I think he said the Americans. They wanted to see if findings in primates could be relevant to troops engaged in desert warfare.'

'So you worked there?' said Grace.

'No.' Colette shook her head. 'Jeff arranged for me to fly up there with Richard to—'

'Richard?'

'Sorry, Richard Omar. He was a sort of PR assistant to Jeff at the time. You may have seen him at the Condor meeting. He now works for ole-Tomeno. Do you know him?'

'No. No, I don't know him,' said Grace.

'So what stopped you working there, Colette?' asked Ian.

'It was a non-starter. My grant would never have supported the costs. So I decided to—'

'What sort of place was it?' asked Grace.

'It was ages ago. I don't remember much except a massive security fence and a few buildings.' She gave an apologetic smile. 'Sorry, that doesn't help much.'

'Did you see any of the work being done?'

'A bit of building work. I think that was all.'

'What about the research?'

'I wasn't shown any. I seem to recall I was pretty hacked off.'

'Why?'

'Jeff sending me all that way simply to look at some buildings in the middle of nowhere.'

'You lot carry on,' said Sean. 'Be back in a moment.' He got up and ran into the house. Suni followed.

'You say you flew up? Where did you land?' asked Grace.

'There was an airstrip of sorts nearby and a driver came to meet us.'

'This, um, this Richard fellow? How well do you know him?'

'I knew him a bit socially, but soon after I joined the Research Centre he went off on an overseas training scholarship somewhere.'

'Do you know where?'

Colette shook her head. 'I think Jeff—'

'Here we are.' Sean returned from the house with a box-file. 'See what you make of this. Franco gave it to us.'

'What is it?' asked Ian.

'I haven't had a chance to look but he says it's a collection of notes and photographs taken by a missionary from Lokinang who was killed by bandits soon after Franco arrived in Kenya about twenty years ago. The chap's wife, a nurse, was also killed.'

'How did Franco acquire it?'

'The police said he could have it.'

Grace stared into the fire.

'I see.' Ian took the box and began to examine the contents. He blew the dust off a notebook. 'This looks like some sort of journal. Very neat writing. Seems almost intrusive delving into this poor chap's past.' He slowly turned the pages. 'Hmm. Listen to this: *Some men brought a sick boy to the mission today. He was strapped to the back of a donkey and suffering from a terrible rash, fever and bleeding in his eyes; a disease that the men said he contracted in caves on the mountain. My wife had never seen the like before and was unable to save him. That night we committed his soul to the Lord.*' He looked up. 'Sounds rather nasty.'

'It sounds horrendous,' said Sean.

'It sounds like Marburg,' said Colette, conscious of the others watching her.

Chapter 23

Colette lay in bed drifting in and out of sleep. Her life, having moved on, had been suddenly wrenched back. She felt like a marionette under the whim of some maniacal puppeteer who took malicious delight in jerking the strings when she least expected. Why did everything have to be so bloody complicated? And Sean? No one had ever kissed her like that before. And all she could say was: *It was nice.* Nice!

The moon was shining through the mosquito net onto her face. She sighed and turned over.

And then there was...

She lay still, listening, straining her ears against the call of an owl, cicadas, and the other night sounds.

Nothing.

Her body relaxed, her normal breathing resumed, her alarm subsided. Considering the two men and the policewoman nearby, she could hardly be better protected. Where were they sleeping? Where did Sean sleep? What would it be like if he...?

No doubt this time.

The owl was still calling but the cicadas had momentarily fallen silent.

She pulled the mosquito net aside, slipped off the bed, peered through the bars of the open window.

The askari lay at the top of the veranda steps, his blanket over his head. That wasn't where the sound came from.

The cicadas started again in full voice – as though someone had thrown a switch.

Colette swore and tried to accustom her eyes to the two-dimensional landscape.

Was that a shape near the fire. Some animal looking for scraps left over from their dinner?

A cloud came over the moon.

She reached for the table beside her bed and fumbled for her binoculars. Their extra light-gathering properties helped, but it was still only a shape.

The cloud passed.

Colette gave an involuntary gasp as everything was thrown into sharp relief. But was it a man or a woman?

She didn't dare call out. Didn't dare put on the light.

The whimper which had woken her was repeated.

She felt for her flip-flops under the bed and moved to the door. Unlocked it. Winced as it creaked open. Waited, trying to will her rapid breathing and pounding heart to settle. She moved along the passage and tried the next door. Not locked. Whose was it? It didn't matter. She crossed to the bed, moved the mosquito net aside and shook the occupant.

Ian was awake in an instant. Had he been waiting?

'Ian, there's someone outside. I think they're hurt.'

He sat up. 'What?'

Moonlight streamed onto his bare chest and shoulders, still as toned as she remembered.

'There's someone by the fire. Come.' She beckoned him to the window and pointed. 'Ian, he or she needs help.'

'I'll call the others.' He was gone before she could respond.

She ran back to her room for a sweater and glanced out of the window to see Ian and Grace hurrying across to the fire. Sean appeared and kicked the sleeping askari, who sprang to his feet, grabbed his spear and gave a shout of alarm.

She hurried outside to where Sean was kneeling beside a woman – more a girl, really. Her arms, covered in blood, were wrapped round her head.

'What's happened?' whispered Colette.

'Don't know,' said Sean. 'I think it's Samira.'

'Samira? Who works for Franco?'

Sean spoke softly to the girl and she released her arms, allowing him to sit her up. Apart from her eyes, her whole face was wrapped in a blood-stained cloth.

'She's been attacked?' whispered Colette.

'Probably a *panga* – machete.' Sean lifted Samira into his arms. Carried her up the steps of the veranda. Into the house. The others followed.

He laid her on the sofa and turned her head to the light. 'Jesus,' he whispered, as he unwound the head-cloth.

The girl couldn't help whimpering.

The cloth came away and Colette recoiled. The right side of the beautiful face she had seen only yesterday, was hanging off and dripping blood.

She became aware that Sean was speaking to her. 'What?'

'Could you do that?'

'Do what?'

'Put her back together?'

'Me?'

'You're a vet.'

'Yes, but…'

'Listen, she needs urgent treatment. There's no way we can get her to a hospital for a good twelve hours, and the chances are the local places won't have the necessary. Flying Doctor couldn't get here until midday tomorrow at the earliest – always assuming they have a spare plane.'

'But, Sean, I…'

'I keep all the gear here. It wouldn't be the first time I've had to use it.'

She drew a breath, knelt down beside the girl and examined the injuries. She'd dealt with things like this in dogs – road accidents, fights and similar – but to operate on a person? She could be struck off. Did she have a choice? She turned back to Sean and nodded.

'I'll be as quick as I can.' He gave her shoulder a squeeze and hurried off.

Colette examined the girl's face more closely. The cheekbone was exposed – possibly chipped. The cheek was hanging loose giving the face an appalling grimace with all the teeth showing on that side. She felt Samira's jaw. The girl moaned but, mercifully, it seemed undamaged. There was plenty of blood, but it was oozing rather than pumping. The ear was partly cut away but still attached. That would be tricky. The hardest part would be reconstructing the mouth. And there was no knowing what nerve damage might have been inflicted. She tried to remember the enervation of the face in the dog – people couldn't be that different.

She sat back on her heels.

'You okay?' asked Ian.

She nodded and waited for Sean's return. She'd not been in this room before. A zebra skin on one the wall. Lots of books. His guitar propped against the bookcase. Framed photos on top. That one? Sean with an attractive fair-haired woman holding a baby – his sister, possibly. She wondered who—

Sean returned, followed by Leah, carrying a basin of hot water and some towels. 'Oh, my Lord,' she whispered.

'Bring the light closer.' Colette indicated a table lamp.

'Hope you can manage with what I've got,' said Sean.

She looked over syringes, surgical instruments, suture materials, dressings. She checked through the bottles. 'Looks fine.' She glanced round the others standing in a circle.

Ian gave her a reassuring smile.

Leah, the former nurse, offered to help.

Colette felt a surge of confidence and filled a syringe with local anaesthetic. This was small-animal practice back in England. I can do this. I can bloody do it. Apart from a few details such as... She quickly blanked them from her mind.

'Hold her head, Sean. Ian and Grace, hold her body, please – just in case.'

She sprayed local over the ravaged flesh then gently inserted the needle into the skin and tissue around the wound. The girl's eyes were closed. She didn't move, didn't even flinch.

Colette washed and dried her hands, opened a packet of sterile gloves and a facemask. She checked everything was ready and to hand; then, kneeling on the sitting room floor of a house in the African bush in the middle of the night, shut out all the what-ifs.

For the next two hours, no one spoke, other than Colette, giving the occasional instruction, and Leah who was passing instruments back and forth.

Suni had given up wondering what was going on and lay with her nose on her paws watching with a bored expression.

Samira's face began to resume its natural form and the girl's beauty, bisected by a line of sutures, started to return. Finally, Colette cleaned the face, stood up stiffly, removed her facemask, peeled off her gloves.

Leah cleared the instruments and debris away.

The girl's eyelids fluttered. She opened her eyes. Seemed to have problems focusing. She held Colette's eyes momentarily. One corner of her mouth twitched in the semblance of a smile.

'Here.'

Sean stood beside her, glass in hand. Colette gratefully accepted. Sat down on the nearest chair. Closed her eyes. Felt a comforting arm round her shoulder. Didn't look to see whose it was. She sipped whisky, which made her cough, vaguely aware of those around her talking in low voices. The arm was removed. She was oblivious to the passage of time. Someone spoke her name. She opened her eyes.

Sean was studying her face.

She gave a tentative smile 'Do you know who did this?'

He shook his head. 'But we intend to find out. Will you be okay?'

'What do you mean?'

'Leah and Suni will be here, and the askari. Jotham has called in some of the Samburu men who help on the ranch. Some will stay here and some will come with us.'

Suni thrust a wet nose into her hand.

'We're going to Franco's place,' he said. 'We'll take Ian's vehicle.'

She and Sean were the only ones in the room. He'd changed into jeans and bush shirt.

'Where's Samira?' she asked.

'Leah's put her to bed. She's going to be fine. You did a brilliant job.'

She gave a faint smile. 'She needs to see a professional, though.'

'I'll call the Flying Doctor first thing in the morning.'

A Land Rover drew up below the veranda; Ian at the wheel, Grace beside him. Jotham and three other men crammed in the back.

'Sure you'll be okay?'

She nodded.

He picked up a rifle which was leaning against a chair, and turned to go.

'Sean.'

'Yes?' It was that look again.

'Come back safely.'

Chapter 24

Ian concentrated on the driving. Other than an occasional instruction from Sean, there was silence in the cramped vehicle. So much to think about. So much to take on board. Colette had been bloody brilliant. He tried to shut out the past – the past past, and the present past – bombs and a girl bleeding beside her dead mother. Now, another girl bleeding. He focused on the track ahead. It was going to be a long night.

The headlights picked out nightjars flying up from the sandy tracks – barely avoiding being run over – then twisting and swooping to snatch moths out of the cone of light. Spring hares, their large eyes glowing pinkish, hopped kangaroo-like out of the path of the oncoming vehicle. A honey-badger was caught fleetingly in the lights as the track led through a patch of woodland. Beyond, a herd of buffaloes. Slowly, reluctantly, they moved aside. One brushed against the vehicle. Back up through the gears. No one complained about the bumping and jolting.

'Left beyond that tree,' said Sean.

'How much further?'

'About an hour.'

Ian glanced across. Sean was holding his rifle and staring fixedly ahead, the line of his jaw visible in the glow from the dashboard. What was he thinking?

The track and the night carried on.

And on. And on. And—

'Look out!'

Ian swerved back onto the track. 'Sorry, folks.'

'Shall I drive?' asked Grace, who was sitting beside him.

'I'll be fine. Sorry about that.' He banished thoughts of bed, sleep – and bombs. Still the seemingly endless track leading into darkness.

'We're getting close,' said Sean.

Jotham murmured something from the back.

'Stop,' said Sean. 'Switch off. And the lights.'

They sat in the silence of the night. The only sound the ticking of the cooling engine.

'There is a fire,' said Jotham. 'We will go and see.' He and the other three men slipped out of the back.

'Carry on slowly without your lights,' said Sean.

Ian started the engine and moved off.

Jotham appeared and waved them down. 'Come. It is Franco's house.'

The thatched roof was nearly burned out. It collapsed as they watched and a fountain of sparks rose into the night air.

'God, I hope there was no one inside,' muttered Sean.

'We saw no one,' said Jotham.

'We'll come back and check when it's light.'

'That won't be long.' Grace indicated the glow on the horizon.

***

They found Franco lying on the floor of his office, his jacket soaked with blood. The place was ransacked, the contents of drawers and cupboards vomited onto the floor. Catalogues and books strewn around, boxes ripped open, a book shelf upended. An owl inside a glass dome stared cross-eyed at the chaos.

Sean dropped to his knees beside Franco. 'He's alive. Get some water. There, on the desk.'

Ian passed the bottle.

Grace stuck her head out of the door. 'Jotham, take the men and search the buildings and stores. Be careful.'

Sean raised Franco's head and trickled some water into his mouth. His eyes fluttered open. 'Grace?'

'Franco, it's okay.' She knelt down and took one of his hands. 'What happened?'

'So you come back?' He started to cough. 'You come back to, to see your old *rafiki*... your...'

'Yes, I've come. Franco, don't talk. We'll get you treated as soon as we can.' She sat him up. 'Take over, Ian. I'll try and call the Flying Doctor.'

Ian found himself kneeling beside Sean. The last time he'd applied his military first aid was the little girl Charity. Had she survived? Would Franco survive?

'He's stopped coughing,' he said. 'Let's lie him down again.'

Sean put the cushion from the office chair under Franco's head and they laid him back.

There was a screech from the radio. 'It seems to be working,' said Grace. 'How is he?'

'Shoulder's a mess,' said Ian. 'That's where most of the blood's come from.'

'How bad?'

'Seemingly, a very lucky man.'

Grace nodded and turned back to the radio.

'Lie still and let's see if we can slip this off.' Ian unbuttoned Franco's safari jacket.

'*Mamma mia*,' he gasped.

Ian patted the good shoulder. 'Not here, I'm afraid. You'll have to make do with us.'

'Tell me what I can do,' said Sean.

Ian indicated the medical supplies strewn around. 'No shortage of materials. See what you can dig out.'

They worked in silence; Ian conscious of the awkwardness between him and Sean. He was relieved when some radio-speak interrupted his thoughts.

'They reckon they could leave in half an hour,' said Grace. 'Pilot's called Larry something or other.'

'Be good if it is,' said Sean. 'Ask them if he could stop at my place on the way back to pick up Samira.'

'Will do.'

Grace finished her call and removed the headphones. 'About two hours. They'll tell the pilot about the other patient.' She knelt down. 'How is he?'

'That you, Grace?' asked Franco faintly.

'Yes.'

'I want you…'

Grace had to lean down to hear. She raised her head, a wry smile on her face. 'Let's see.' She crossed to the calendar of the busty girl with the bananas and moved it aside to display a safe with a combination lock. She twirled the dials, opened the door and drew out two whisky bottles.

'I see he's got his priorities right,' observed Sean.

'Anyone bring the cards?' said Ian.

The atmosphere in the room lightened.

'Franco told us he could look after himself,' muttered Sean. 'But where's his…' He began searching.

'What are you looking for?'

'His revolver. Franco carried a revolver in his belt.'

'Can't see it anywhere.'

The office door opened and Jotham appeared.

'What did you find?' asked Grace.

'Not much. Some people in a store but all they could say was men came with guns last night and locked them in. Then they heard shooting. That one, Khalif, though, he is missing and Franco's Land Rover is gone.'

'Who's Khalif?' asked Ian.

'Franco's right-hand man,' said Sean. 'Holds the fort when he's away.'

'I'll go and talk to them,' said Grace. She was about to leave when the radio sprang to life. She grabbed the microphone. 'Go ahead, caller.'

'Say, that you, Grace?' said a well-known voice.

'Felix!'

'How's life in the bush?'

'Interesting. How did you know where we were?'

'My old drinking buddy, guy called Larry Stopolski... That don't matter. Listen, you folks had any recent contact with Nairobi?'

'No. We can't get a signal.'

'Right. Anyway, you and Ian need to get your asses back soonest.'

'Why?'

'Something's come up. Larry says he'll have space.'

Grace glanced at Ian, who nodded. 'That should be fine, Felix.' She checked her watch. 'We're expecting the plane around eight. Anything you can tell us?'

There was a brief pause before he replied. 'I guess it'll come out soon enough.'

'What?'

'The Daily Nation newspaper received some flowers yesterday with a note saying: "*In memory of Colonel Ian Sinclair, who liked orchids.*" Same Mlala guy signed it.'

Chapter 25

Colette woke with a start. The sun was beating into her room which was becoming uncomfortably hot. She had a quick shower, threw on some clothes and hurried over to the veranda. Four places laid for breakfast but no sign of anyone, or of Ian's Land Rover.

She went into the house, calling.

'In here, *memsabu*,' came a voice.

Colette pushed open a door. Leah was seated on a bed talking to Samira who was propped up with pillows. Colette took Samira's hand. 'How are you?'

Samira tried to smile.

'She is paining very much,' said Leah.

The right side of Samira's face was badly swollen and the eye was closed.

Colette felt round the swelling and along the suture line, Samira gave a slight whimper. Despite the swelling, neither the wound nor her forehead were hot – yet. But she needed antibiotic, otherwise infection was almost inevitable. She hoped Sean had some.

'Leah, is she able she drink?'

'A little, *memsabu*. I found her this.' She indicated a drinking straw in the mug by the bed. 'It helps but the pain is very bad.'

'I can give her something.' Colette hurried back to her room and found some soluble aspirin. It was pretty crude but would help.

Samira grimaced at the taste as she sucked through the straw.

'Have you any milk, Leah?' asked Colette.

'I will fetch.'

As soon as she was gone, Samira caught Colette's arm.

'What is it?'

Colette could just make out the words: '*Baya sana* – very bad.'

'I know, Samira, but it will take time to heal.'

Samira shook her head and gripped Colette's arm. '*Watu wabaya* – bad people.'

'What bad people?'

Samira indicated her face.

'They certainly were bad.'

Leah returned with two mugs.

Samira released Colette's arm but the imploring look remained.

'For you, *memsabu*,' said Leah, handing Colette a mug of coffee.

'Thank you, that's really kind.'

Leah passed Samira the milk and she sucked it slowly through the straw. When she finished, she drew Leah closer and began whispering.

Colette recognised the odd word but couldn't follow what was being said. 'While you were out of the room, Leah, I think Samira was trying to tell me what happened, but I'm afraid my Swahili's not very good.'

Leah didn't appear to hear but continued to listen to Samira. She gave the occasional nod, and when Samira finished, she turned to Colette. 'She says, no police. She fears the police.'

'Why no police?'

'*Memsabu*, Samira has no papers. Police will say that is very bad and will send her to prison or back to Somalia.'

Samira's eyes were now closed but she nodded.

Colette frowned. 'I'm not sure I—'

'Please, *memsabu*.'

'I suppose so.'

'It is best.'

'I can't promise, though. That policewoman who was here last night; she may come back.'

'No police,' mumbled Samira, through her swollen mouth.

Colette gave a gesture of helplessness. She was conscious of Leah studying her. 'Leah, I'm only trying to help.'

Leah made a pretence of adjusting Samira's pillows then began addressing them. 'Samira sometimes comes here to talk to me. Her home is at a place called Kismaayo, in Somalia. She was a teacher there but there has been much fighting in that place and some children from the school were killed. Samira was frightened she might be killed also, so she came to Kenya. It was very hard because she had no papers. She had to hide many days in the bush. A driver said he could take her but she would have to help him.'

'Help him? How?'

Leah looked down at her hands. 'He would tell the police she was his wife but if, if she didn't…'

'It's all right, Leah, I understand.'

'But this man was not good and he beat her. He also said, if she tried to run away, he would tell the police she had no papers.'

'So what happened?'

'That driver came here to Isiolo for loading maize to take to Somalia. He made her stay in the lorry, but while she waited she saw a Somali man coming out of a place called New Paradise bar. Do you know?'

Colette shook her head.

'She says she managed to call to the man without the driver hearing. She didn't know if she could trust the man but she told him her problem. He was also afraid but he said he might get her work with his uncle who owned a *duka* – a store – near Laisamis. But she feared very much.'

Colette glanced at Samira who seemed to have fallen asleep. 'Leah, do you know the man who helped her?'

'His name is called Khalif. You have seen him, I think?'

'The one who works for Franco?'

'He is the one. He is a good man.'

Colette gave a brief smile. 'What did Khalif do?'

'He pretended to argue with that driver, saying he should be paying him money to help unload his lorry. While they were shouting, Samira ran from that lorry and hid in the bush and Khalif found her when it was dark.'

'And took her to his uncle?'

'No. He took her to *Bwana* Franco who said the *duka* was far and Laisamis was a bad place. I need someone to work in my house, so you can stay here.'

'What happened then, Leah?'

'There are some men in Somalia who call themselves Njia Mpya.'

'Who are they?'

'I don't know, *memsahu*. But they cause much trouble there. And some, I think, now stay in Isiolo. This driver, who brought Samira to Kenya, he didn't go to the police. She thinks he told those Njia Mpya people about her and where she came from.'

'Why does she think that?'

'One day, Khalif brought her a letter, a letter from her father. She thinks that driver brought it.'

'Her father? But how did *he* know where she was?'

Leah turned to address the wall. 'Those Njia Mpya people caught her father and held him in Kismaayo. They made him write this letter to her saying if she didn't work with them, they would kill him.'

Colette wondered why she hadn't stayed in London. Her coffee was cold. 'What sort of work?'

'To watch and listen but mostly to sleep.'

'To sleep?'

'That was what Samira said, but I think she means wait.'

'For what?'

'Wait for instructions.'

'Is Khalif also involved with these, these Njia Mpya people?'

'Samira doesn't think so but they don't talk about it. Sometimes, though, she knows Franco gives Khalif letters to take.'

'Take where? Who to?'

'She doesn't know,' – still studying the wall.

'Surely not to Njia Mpya.'

'Only God knows.' Leah turned, her face impassive.

'God?' Colette twisted her hands together. If only Sean or Ian or Grace were here, they might know better than God. She looked out of the window in forlorn expectation of seeing the Land Rover returning. All she could see were two distant giraffe nibbling the top of an acacia tree.

'Leah, why this?' She indicated Samira's ravaged face.

Leah stared ahead. 'Those Njia Mpya people are saying Samira is not helping them. A man like *Bwana* Franco must know many things, they say. Must hear many things. Why is she not telling them? And they send her a picture.'

'A picture?'

'A picture of an old man who was beaten. They said next picture would be of dead man.'

'Her father?'

'Yes, I think.' Leah paused. 'The other day, when you and Sean went to that place, Samira gave you lunch.'

'It was very good – curry.'

'And there was much talking. Samira cannot speak English very well but she understands and she heard many things and she wrote a letter for Njia Mpya. She wanted to give to Khalif to take to Isiolo – to those Njia Mpya people – but *Bwana* Franco came and said they all had to go to Isiolo.'

'Why?'

'He said there was much trouble. He would talk to police and she and Khalif must talk to Somali people to find out what happening.'

'And the letter?'

'Samira came back with it. She was fearing very much.'

'Who was the letter for?'

'She says she has to tell what she hears to someone called Mlala, but that is not his real name.'

'Does she know this person?'

'No.'

'Does Khalif know this person?'

Leah shrugged.

Colette was content to wait.

Anger suddenly flared on Leah's face. 'Samira says she should not have written that letter. She was wrong to tell all those things she heard in *Bwana* Franco's house. If it is God's will, her father will die, but she has to tell about Njia Mpya and what those men did to her and at her school so they can be killed.'

'She has to tell the police.'

'No. She will tell you and God will decide.'

Colette pursed her lips. God's going to be pretty busy. 'These men who came, Leah, what did they do? What happened?'

'They came at night to the house. She thinks *Bwana* Franco was at his office. She doesn't know what happened to him, but she heard shooting—'

'Sean and the others! They've fallen into a trap.'

Leah stared at her hands. 'Perhaps.'

Colette chewed her knuckles. 'I'm sorry, Leah, I interrupted.'

'These men came to the house. They broke the door and caught Samira and said she must tell them more. Then, then one of them tried to, to…'

Colette laid a hand on Leah's arm. 'It's all right, you don't have to go on.'

Leah took a gasping breath. 'She fought that one. She fought him so hard. But he was strong and cut her – she thinks with his *simi*. She fell and the letter also fell—'

'That man found the letter?'

Leah nodded. 'Then another man came who was very angry. Samira didn't see him, but he made that one to stop and to give him the letter. Then they all went in a car.'

'Did she see the car or this other man?'

Samira flapped a hand to attract their attention. Leah leaned forward to hear what she was saying and frowned.

'What is it, Leah?' asked Colette.

'Samira says her face was paining so much and she couldn't see, but she thinks the other man was a *mzungu*.'

'A *mzungu* – a white person?'

Leah nodded.

'Why does she think that?'

'His Swahili was good but the way he spoke was not like an African.'

'Does she know him?'

Leah turned to Samira but she was already shaking her head.

'Could it have been this, this Mlala person?'

Leah shrugged. 'Only God—'

'Yes, okay.' Colette got off the bed and went to the window. The giraffes had moved on but a herd of zebras had come into view. She vaguely noted they were the larger Grevy's with narrow stripes. She turned back to the bed. 'Leah, we have to tell someone about this.'

'Not the police.'

'Okay, who then?'

'Sean he will know.'

Colette took a deep breath. 'He will know. I hope.' And God, if we can get in touch. She checked her watch. Nearly eight o'clock. Should she have breakfast or wait for Sean and the others?

Leah raised her head. 'I think he comes.'

'I'll go and see.' Colette hurried out onto the veranda where Suni, who had been dozing in the sun, was delighted to see her. Colette knelt down and stroked her. They both looked up at the sound of an approaching vehicle.

Colette frowned. She wasn't good on engines but this didn't sound like Ian's Land Rover. A Toyota Land Cruiser came into view. As it drew nearer, the zebras trotted off and Colette could see the occupants.

She rushed down the steps and ran to greet them.

'Hi, Colette, good to see you,' called Jeff, climbing down from the passenger's seat and coming towards her.

She ran up and kissed his cheek then waved to Richard, who waved back. 'So, you finally made it. Would you like some breakfast?'

Chapter 26

'Felix sounded a bit up tight,' said Ian.

No one responded.

Grace, who was sitting on Franco's desk, continued swinging her legs and drawing random patterns in the dust. Sean leaned against the wall, his eyelids drooping. Franco appeared to be asleep.

Ian tried again. 'What did Felix say the pilot's name was?'

'He's called Larry,' said Sean. 'Good guy; knows this area well.'

Grace swivelled round on the desk. 'You also know the area well, Sean.'

'So?'

'Tell us what's going on. Who did this?' She waved an arm round the ransacked office. 'Who is Mlala? Who shot Franco? Who beat up that girl – what's her name?'

'Samira.'

'What the matter with Samira?' asked Franco, looking up from the floor.

'She was... was dusted up by people who set... who went to your house,' said Sean. 'But she's okay. She's going on the plane with you to Nairobi.'

'Is good.' Franco let his head fall forward and closed his eyes again.

Grace flapped an impatient hand. 'Yes her. Also, find out why ole-Tomeno buys beers for everyone in Isiolo. And that boy who works for Franco – what's happened to him? I need some answers, Sean, not more questions.'

'I'd better get going, then.'

Grace sighed and rubbed her hands across her face. 'Sorry, Sean, it's been a long night.'

'I guess that applies to all of us.'

'I know, I know.' Grace got off the desk and stood peering out of the window, her back to the others.

The only one oblivious to the tension in the cramped room was Franco, who sat with his back against the wall, his eyes shut and whisky glass in hand.

Ian glanced at Grace's back then turned to Sean. 'You okay looking after my vehicle for a while?'

'Sure.'

'I'll be in touch about getting it back.'

'No rush. When you're ready.'

Grace spun round. 'I said I was sorry, okay?'

'Here.' Ian offered her a glass of whisky.

'I don't drink alcohol.'

'It might help.'

'No.' She seemed lost in thought for a moment then looked up, her face drawn. 'Sorry, Sean.'

'No sweat.'

'Could some of your people look after this place while Franco's away?' she asked. 'If we don't put guards here, people might think Christmas has come early.'

'Sure. I'll set that up.'

'You've got my mobile number?'

Sean nodded and checked his watch. 'I'll go and warn Samira.'

'Keys are in the ignition,' said Ian.

Franco opened his eyes. 'Sean, my friend, you tell Coletta, she remember what old Franco say?'

'Sure. I'll do that.' He patted Franco's good shoulder. 'You get better, hey.'

'I already better,' said Franco, raising his glass. 'How you say? One for the road?'

'At seven in the morning?'

Franco's chuckle ended in a bout of coughing.

'Take it easy, you crazy baboon.'

'What is "take it easy"? I not know this expression.' He grinned and gestured at Ian with his chin. 'What your name?'

'Ian. My name's Ian.'

'Sean say I crazy baboon. He probably right, Ian, but even baboons need to drink.'

'Like Sean said, you'd better go easy.'

'Bullshit,' said Franco affably.

'See you guys.' said Sean. 'Good luck, Franco.'

'*Salute.*' Franco waved his glass.

'I'll be in touch,' called Ian. 'Leave the door open. It's getting like an oven in here.'

'Is good whisky, no?' said Franco. Apart from the red stain seeping through his shoulder bandage, he appeared to have recovered much of his spirit.

'Yes, very good,' said Ian.

'There is still other bottle.' Franco began to chuckle then winced with the pain.

Ian studied him for a moment. 'Franco, Sean said you had a revolver. What happened to it?'

'I not know. Perhaps someone take.'

'Who? The people who beat up this place?'

Franco held up his empty glass.

Ian poured him a small measure and made a pretence of pouring himself some.

Grace went and sat beside Franco on the floor. 'Who did this, Franco? Who took the revolver? What can you tell us?'

Franco peered into his glass and swirled the contents round. 'Is good you come back, Grace.'

She glanced at Ian and waited.

Franco took a sip of whisky and looked between the two of them. 'You know Lokinang?'

'I've heard of it,' she said.

'I give Sean some notes about that place, from missionary. You read those.'

'We've read bits,' said Ian.

'You meet Samira, I think?'

'Er, yes, we've met her – sort of.'

'She is good person, but she is fearing.'

Grace' eyes flicked up to Ian. 'What's she fearing?'

'She has no papers. I tell police, they must get papers for Samira as she work for me now. They say yeah, yeah, but do nothing.' Franco winced and eased his shoulder. 'We need you back, Grace.'

'What else can you tell us, Franco?'

'Khalif, who work for me, he Somali. He also fearing.'

'Fearing what?'

'You know Njia Mpya?'

'I know them.'

'They just boys, Grace.'

'That's not what I heard.'

Franco flapped a dismissive hand. 'For sure, they cause few problems. But how you say: is small beer?'

'What sort of problems, Franco?'

'Just messing, but I think they lean on Samira and Khalif.'

'What do you mean?'

Franco spread his hands. 'What does it matter what Franco think?'

'Come on. Of course, it matters. Why do you think you were nearly killed?'

Franco looked up. 'John, is it?'

'Ian.'

'*Sì, sì*. I have empty glass, Ian.'

Franco smiled as his glass was replenished. 'You know Solomon, who runs New Paradise?'

'I know him,' said Grace. 'What about him?'

'He shit-scared.'

'Why?'

'He hear many things, like old Franco.' Franco gazed morosely into his glass.

'You think he's—?'

'No more questions, Grace.'

She patted Franco's knee. 'Just one. Where's Khalif?'

Franco glowered. 'Ask Solomon.' He finished his whisky, his head fell forward and the glass slipped from his hand.

For one dreadful moment, Ian thought he might have died, but a loud snore reassured him. He reached out a hand and pulled Grace to her feet. 'I think I hear a plane.'

Chapter 27

'Some breakfast'd be good,' said Jeff.

'Come on, then. I'll tell Leah.' Colette took his hand. 'Where've you come from?'

'Up that way.' Jeff waved an arm in a vague northerly direction.

'Doing what?'

'Checking things out.'

There was no sense in pursuing it. He would tell her if he thought it was important.

'It's so good to see you,' she said, as they made their way towards the house.

'You've settled in, then?' said Jeff.

'It's such a lovely place. I'm so glad you suggested I came.'

'Is Sean around?'

Her face clouded. 'No he... he had to go off. Some, er, local trouble. A girl beaten up. He should be back soon. He can tell you the details.'

Jeff and Richard exchanged glances.

'Have you heard about it?' she asked.

'No.'

'Right.' She paused, confused. 'I'll call Leah.' She let go his hand and ran to the house, calling.

Suni greeted her but no one appeared.

'Where is she, Suni?'

Suni cocked her head and wagged her tail.

Colette frowned as she entered the house and made her way to Samira's room.

Empty.

'What's happened, Suni? Both of them gone.' She rushed through the house calling and checking the rooms. Suni trotted along behind.

Nothing.

'Suni, where are they?'

The little dog seemed to shrug.

'You're useless.' She couldn't help smiling as Suni wagged her tail.

Colette went back to the veranda. 'There's no one around,' she said. 'I don't know where they've gone but I should be able to fix you something.'

'That'd be great,' said Jeff.

'Grab some seats. I'll see what I can find.'

'Do you want some help?' asked Richard.

'No, I'll be fine.'

'I hope you didn't come all this way to check on me,' said Colette, some twenty minutes later, setting down her coffee mug.

'No,' said Jeff. 'I was wondering if—'

Suni sat up and pricked her ears.

'That must be Sean,' said Colette. 'Tell me in a minute, Jeff.'

'Right.' He nodded curtly.

Suni scampered down the steps, Colette close behind.

Ian's Land Rover came into view, Sean at the wheel. But where were Ian and Grace? Where were Jotham and the other men?

He switched off the engine and climbed out. 'Whose vehicle's that?'

'It's Jeff and Richard. They finally made it. Sean, where are the others?'

'Franco's been shot—'

'No!'

'Not too serious, we hope. The Flying Doctor plane's picking him up—' Sean checked his watch. '—about now. Ian and Grace are going with him. That's why I've got Ian's Landy.' He bent down to stroke Suni. 'Larry, whom we met a couple of days—'

'The pilot?'

'Yes. He's on his way here to pick-up Samira and take her to hospital.'

'Oh.'

'What?'

Colette scuffed her shoe in the sand. 'It's just that she's, she's disappeared.'

'She's what?'

'Samira's gone. I can't find her anywhere. So's Leah.'

'Leah's disappeared as well?'

'All right, I know. It was the only thing I had to do and I screwed up.'

'Where have you looked?'

'Everywhere. I don't know where they bloody are.' She challenged him with her eyes.

He studied her briefly then kicked one of the tyres. 'Come on.' He strode off towards the house, Colette and Suni following. 'Hi, guys,'

149

he called, as he approached the veranda.

Jeff raised his coffee mug.

'Be with you in a moment.' Sean turned towards the back of the house and Colette ran to catch him up.

'Sean, I just want to say…'

He stopped. 'Say what?'

'To say I… I…' She turned. 'Nothing. I'll go and join the others.'

He caught her arm. 'Sorry I lost it back there.'

She pulled herself free. 'When's the plane due?'

'Very soon. You're sure you've looked everywhere for Samira?'

'What have I just said?'

He pursed his lips. 'Too late now.' He rushed into the sitting room. 'The file. Where's the bloody file? The missionary's papers. It's here somewhere.'

'Is this it?' She picked up the box-file from a chair.

'Thanks. I'd better go. Won't be long.'

'Sean, no.'

He stopped. 'What?'

'Give me the Landy keys and I'll go to the airstrip. I need Ian to send off those samples in the diplomatic bag – the ones we collected from Pete. They're still in the fridge.' She pulled a face. 'It'll also give me a chance to unwind.'

'Sure.' He smiled and tossed her the keys.

***

Colette sat on the ground in the shade of an acacia tree, her back against a Land Rover tyre, Suni beside her. Noisy weavers were building untidy nests in the branches overhead, chattering away unbothered by her or Suni. Some gazelles wandered onto the airstrip and became distorted in a mirage of heat. The dot she had been watching grew into a plane and the gazelles trotted off.

The plane touched down and a cloud of dust billowed up in the draught from the twin propellers. Larry taxied towards the Land Rover, stopped and switched off the engines.

The door opened. 'Morning, ma'am.'

'Good to see you, Larry.'

'How's the patient?' he asked, as the side-door opened and the same two teenage nurses jumped down with their stretcher.

'I'm afraid she's done a runner.'

'She's what?'

'She's disappeared, Larry. We don't know where she's gone.'

He shrugged. 'Oh well, I guess she didn't fancy flying.'

'That one has gone?' said one of the nurses.

'I'm afraid so,' said Colette.

'That is a pity,' said the other nurse. 'Mr Larry is a very good pilot.'

'I'm sure,' said Colette. 'But you collected Franco all right?'

The nurse tutted. 'That one. He is singing very rude songs.'

'Taught me a few new ones.' Larry chuckled.

'But now he is sleeping,' said the other nurse.

Colette smiled at their primness. 'Are Ian and Grace with you?'

'Yeah,' said Larry. 'I think that's their names.'

'Can you give Ian a bag to take back?'

'Sure.'

Colette ran to the Land Rover and found a notebook and pencil under the dash board. She scribbled Ian a note giving instructions for sending the samples to Alan Davies. She paused at the end of the message and felt only a twinge of guilt before writing: "*Thanks, Colette*". She put the box-file into the bag with the samples, together with Alan's business card, and ran back to the plane.

'Thanks, Larry.'

'No problem, ma'am.'

She reached up and kissed his cheek.

He gave his slow grin. 'Well, you have a nice day. Come on, ladies.'

'*Kwa heri*.' The nurses turned back to the plane with their empty stretcher.

'Bye,' said Colette. '*Kwa heri*.'

Larry started the engines and waved from the cockpit, She waved back. He taxied to the end of the airstrip and turned. The plane began to roll forward, picked up speed and was airborne in a great cloud of dust.

Larry waggled the wings as he flew past.

Colette waved.

Was it Ian who waved back?

'Have a nice day,' she murmured.

Chapter 28

Colette returned to the house to find the three men poring over a map spread out on the table.

Sean looked up. 'All okay?'

'Fine.'

'Coffee's there on the side.'

'Thanks.' She helped herself and joined them.

Jeff took a sip from the mug at his elbow. 'Do you remember this place?' He jabbed at the map.

Colette peered at the name. 'Lokinang?' She shot a quick glance at Sean. 'I think so.'

'I sent you there to check it out for your research.'

'I went with you,' said Richard. 'Surely you remember?'

'Vaguely.' She looked up and tried to smile. When it didn't work she hastily bent forward again. 'Oh yes, a possible location for my virology project.'

'Exactly. We've just been there. We think it could work this time.'

'What could?'

'You working there.'

'What? Why?'

'Because of your expertise.'

'But, but I… Didn't Franco say something about some trouble in the area?'

'It's not linked.'

Something snapped. 'Jeff, what the bloody hell's going on? You get me out to Kenya on some pretext about the Petes needing my help. That was a load of bollocks. Now you want me to go to some God-forsaken place in the middle of a tribal war because of my expertise. No! You can stuff that.' She caught a breath. 'Oh, God.' She turned and fled to her room and buried her face in the pillow.

A few moments later, there was a knock on the door.

'Go away!'

Someone entered.

'I said, go away!'

'You were bloody brilliant,' said Sean. He came and sat on the bed and began stroking her hair.

'Don't touch me!'

He raised her to a sitting position.

'Sorry, Sean.'

'Why are you sorry?'

'Making a fool of myself.' She gave a rueful smile. 'Why does it always have to be like this?'

'Like what?'

'Me screwing up all the time. Putting my bloody great clod-hopping boots into everything. Jeff's going to hate me.'

'No. He respects you.'

'Huh.'

'I don't know him well but I do know he respects people who fight their corner.'

'You're such a kind person.'

'Come on, we must go back and join the others.'

She kissed his cheek and gently pushed him away. 'Go on. I'll be out in a moment.'

When he'd gone she peered at herself in the mirror which reflected her image without flattery or malice. 'Mirror, mirror, on the wall, who is...? Forget what you've seen in recent days. Okay?' She rinsed her face, tidied her hair, stuck her tongue out at the image and went back to the veranda.

'Sorry to catch you by surprise,' said Jeff.

She shrugged.

'Are you okay?'

'As long as you don't patronise me.'

'Sure.'

She slumped into a chair. 'So what is all this?'

'Not quite what it seems, I think.'

She reached out for her coffee mug. 'In what way?'

'The centre at Lokinang is being used for vaccine research.'

She recalled Franco's phrase, something about people getting their arses shot off if they went there. 'So why all the... the security?'

'Commercial confidentiality.'

'But why such a remote region – and here in Kenya? The logistic costs must be enormous.'

'They are.'

'Jeff, just tell me, okay?' She took a sip of cold coffee.

'Okay. But this goes no further than the four of us. Richard knows, but can I have your assurances?' He looked at Sean and Colette in turn.

153

Sean nodded.

'Colette?'

'I suppose so.'

He regarded her through hooded brows. 'Apart from those involved in the programme, the only other one who knows is ole-Tomeno, who sanctioned the work.'

She was about to say something, thought better of it and lowered her eyes.

'I'm going to tell you a story,' he said. 'Part may be myth, part may be untrue, but part is undoubtedly true.'

Get on with it.

He sat back in his chair and steepled his fingers. 'Around the turn of the twentieth century – give or take a few years – a hunter somewhere in a West African rain forest killed a chimpanzee and skinned it for bush meat. Unbeknown to the hunter, the chimpanzee was infected with a virus: a simian immuno-deficiency virus. The hunter became infected with that virus but didn't become sick. However, the virus changed within his body – mutated, if you like – to one which was readily transmissible to other humans through sexual contact.' Jeff looked up as though anticipating some comment; when none was forthcoming he continued.

'A little later, we have a similar scenario, also in West Africa, but this time involving sooty mangabeys. Colette will appreciate the difference.' He glanced at her, inviting comment.

She stared at the table. 'Mangabeys are classified as monkeys but chimpanzees are apes and more closely related to man.'

'Exactly.'

Damn you, Jeff.

'The virus which originated from the chimpanzee is now called human immuno-deficiency virus one – HIV-1 – and that from the mangabey is HIV-2.'

'And HIV-1 is the cause of the AIDS pandemic currently sweeping the world,' she intoned, still staring at the table. She looked up, challenging him. 'Jeff, all this is well documented. Why are you telling—?'

He held up his hand. 'Fast forward to the present day, but this time we're in East Africa. Again, the same scenario, but now we're talking about colobus monkeys in Kenyan forests.' He paused. 'We are provisionally calling the new strain HIV-3.'

Again he waited. Again no one responded. 'Preliminary studies in experimental monkeys here in Kenya – Lokinang to be precise – suggest HIV-3 causes sub-clinical infection, but more importantly, recovered monkeys are then resistant to the virulent HIV-1. If these results hold up in man, it is no exaggeration to say that we have a potential vaccine for AIDS.'

Jeff turned to Richard. 'Tell Colette.'

'Ole-Tomeno wants you to help with the vaccine development programme.' Expression deadpan.

Chapter 29

The propellers of the Flying Doctor plane had barely stopped at Nairobi's Wilson Airport, before a nondescript ambulance drew up and two muscular paramedics, in shades and hospital whites, jumped from the back and wheeled out a stretcher. The driver, similarly well-built, remained in the ambulance, its engine running.

One of the paramedics hammered on the side of the plane. The door opened and a startled nurse peered out.

'It's okay, ma'am, we'll take over.' The man climbed into the plane.

'Do you need some help?'

'No thanks, ma'am.'

The nurse and her colleague retreated back inside and twittered to each other.

'This one Franco?' The man gestured to the snoring patient.

The nurse nodded. 'Be careful the poor man is—'

'The Major says can you guys join him in the cab?' said the man, addressing Ian and Grace.

'You folks having a nice day?' asked a laconic voice from the front of the plane.

'Hi there, Larry,' said the paramedic. He undid the seatbelt, lifted the still-sleeping Franco into his arms and passed him to his waiting companion.

The nurses stared in disbelief as the man carried the stocky Franco and laid him on the stretcher with no more apparent effort than if he'd been a child.

'*Dove sono?*' muttered Franco, trying to sit up.

'What d'he say?' asked one of the paramedics, pushing him down.

'No idea,' said the other, securing him in place with straps.

They wheeled him to the back of the ambulance, climbed in with the stretcher and closed the doors behind them. The whole operation was over in less than a minute.

'Guess we'd better follow.' Ian held out his hand. 'Thanks, Larry. Thank you, ladies.'

'You take care now,' said Larry.

'And you.'

The nurses twittered their goodbyes.

'*Asanteni.*' Grace followed Ian out of the plane.

'Why the theatricals, Felix?' asked Ian, as he climbed into the cab of the ambulance.

'Put those on.' Felix handed Ian some dark glasses. 'You're dead. Remember?'

Ian glared and fitted the glasses.

Grace closed the door beside her. 'You haven't answered Ian's question, Felix.'

'Yeah, well.' Felix turned to the two paramedics behind. 'How is he?'

'We've given him something to knock him out for a while, sir.'

'Good.' Felix put the ambulance in gear and moved off.

Some five minutes later, they approached the American Embassy. Felix drove to the back of the building, down a ramp and through a security gate. He raised a hand to the corporal on duty, who saluted and closed the gate after them.

'Now what?' said Ian, as Felix drew up beside an elevator.

'You guys had breakfast?'

'No. Felix, just what is going on?'

'Tell you over breakfast.' He jumped out of the cab and watched the paramedics wheel Franco to the elevator. 'Give me a shout when he wakes up.'

'Sir.'

***

Ian and Grace sat in Felix's office with trays of food on their laps. Felix studied his computer, his back to them.

'More coffee?' he asked, without looking round.

'No thanks,' said Ian.

'Tea,' said Grace tersely.

Felix made a brief call on his phone and went back to his computer.

A few minutes later, Felix's secretary came in with a mug of tea. Grace accepted it with a nod.

Felix spun his chair round. 'Beard's coming on well.'

'I hope that remark's addressed to Ian,' said Grace.

Felix ignored the comment. 'So how's it going?'

'You tell us,' said Ian. 'And why the urgency to get us back?'

'What you make of that orchid thing I mentioned?' asked Felix.

'What do *you* make of it?' said Ian.

'Not a lot. Could you get your people onto the paper, Grace, see if they can find who sent the note.'

She nodded.

Felix studied her briefly. 'That friend of yours, Maria, is one smart lady.'

Grace glowered. 'Why do you say that?'

'We happened to bump into each other in town over coffee.'

'Felix, that's going too far! There's no way we drag Maria into this.'

'Correct. We don't drag her in; she's already in.'

'Meaning what?'

'She contacted me.'

'Why?'

'Because you folks were out of town and she was worried.'

'About what?'

'She was very sorry to hear about Ian's death – didn't know you well, but you seemed—'

'Cut that out!' snapped Ian.

'Sure, sure.' Felix flapped a placatory hand. 'She wanted to ask me about this guy.' He passed Ian a business card.

'Viktor Levkov. Who's he?'

'A reporter for the Russian newspaper Izvestia. Speaks good English.'

'What's this got to do with Maria?' asked Grace.

'He visited her office with a local reporter from the Daily Nation to try and see OT.'

'Why?'

'They said they wanted to ask him about that Condor thing you guys are in.'

'So?'

'Sure, nothing unusual about that, except Russia ain't great on conservation in Africa – anywhere for that matter.'

'Did they see ole-Tomeno?' asked Grace.

'No. He was out of town, seemingly. So these reporters started quizzing Maria: had she heard of the Marburg virus link to Kenya, was Condor investigating, could the Minister assure the public there was no risk to health from Kenyan monkeys, was tourism likely to be affected? The usual horse-shit.'

'What did she tell them?'

'Yes, she'd heard about the possible link with Kenya – who hadn't? It was all over the papers. But she thought it was far-fetched.' Felix chuckled. 'That didn't go down too well with the Kenyan guy, seeing as he was the one who'd written the article in the Daily

Nation. When the reporters left, Maria got to thinking and wondering why these people seemed to be more interested in Marburg than conservation, so she started doing some online searches – not least to learn about Marburg.'

'What did she find?' asked Grace.

'Pretty much what we did, plus some. That's when she contacted me.' He gestured to their trays. 'You guys want any more?'

'Get on with it, Felix,' said Ian.

'Okay, okay. Then the name Olga Levkova came up – same as it did when we searched.'

'Remind us,' said Ian.

'She's the researcher who's thought to have died of Marburg, a while back in an accident at that Russian lab working on biological weapons.' He paused. 'Maria reckons she could've been Viktor's wife and that's why he's digging.'

'No kidding?'

'Anyway, the other thing you'll remember about the lab is that the former director – Boris something-or-other – was the guy who defected to the US at the end of the Cold War and gave them the low-down on the Soviet Union's bio-weapons programme. Then died of Marburg.'

Ian sniffed. 'Are you saying this Viktor person killed Boris… Borishenkov; wasn't that his name?'

Felix shrugged. 'I guess he was pretty hacked off about his wife's death.'

'Let's ask him.'

'Ask him what?'

'About Borishenkov's death – and his wife's. Good opportunity while he's in Kenya.'

Felix sat back and blinked. 'Hi, Viktor, nice meeting you. Say, is it true you rubbed out Boris?'

'Not quite in those terms.'

'What then?'

Ian set his tray on the floor.

'Listen, Felix, I imagine quite a number of people in Russia would have been pretty hacked off about Borishenkov passing details of their bio-weapons programme to the States, even if it was supposed to be the end of the Cold War. Let's get Viktor's side of the story.'

'Right, so we pull him in and see what he can tell us?'

'No,' said Grace.

'Why?'

'Because the American Embassy is the last place a Russian reporter wants to be seen visiting.'

'What then?'

'Did you get the name of the Kenyan reporter?' she asked.

'Guy called Cheriyot, I think Maria said.'

'Walter Cheriyot?'

'Could be.'

'That might be useful. He's the one I sent Ian's obituary to after the bombing.' Grace took out her mobile and moved to the window. 'Now it's his turn to— Walter? *Jambo*. It's Grace, Grace Kiptagat... I'm fine. How are you? Listen, Walter, that story of yours in the *Nation*... The one about the virus in monkeys... Can we meet...? The Serena would be fine. And, Walter, bring your friend Viktor with you... You know perfectly well who I mean. See you tomorrow around nine.'

'What do I do?' asked Ian. 'Stay in my grave?'

'No,' said Grace, 'you come with me. Just keep your sunglasses on. You're my friend John who's a wildlife specialist advising Condor.'

Ian glared and said nothing.

'I thought we could take Walter and Viktor to the Nairobi Game Park.' She gave Felix her cherubic smile. 'Any chance you could lend us a vehicle?'

'Bugger off.'

'One without diplomatic plates.'

Felix sighed and reached for his phone. He glowered at Grace when he'd finished. 'All fixed.'

She repeated the smile.

'Could I use the phone?' asked Ian. 'I guess I shouldn't use my mobile while I'm dead.'

Felix pushed the instrument across the desk.

Ian hummed tunelessly, ignoring Felix's scowl.

'High Commissioner's office.' An unfamiliar voice.

'Er...'

'High Commissioner's office. Can I help you?'

Ian grabbed his handkerchief and thrust it over the mouth piece. 'Could I speak to Helen Paterson, please?'

'I'm afraid Helen's not in today. May I know who's calling?'

'I'll, er, call back later.' He replaced the receiver. 'Damn.'

'Problem?' said Felix.

'It seems it's her day off. I'll try tomorrow. Anyway, moving on: tell me, Felix, my deputy Tim Hollis, he's working with your people on the remains of the Land Rover?'

'Yeah. They reckon the explosive was the same as that used on the Embassy in ninety-eight.'

'That's a result, then.'

'Sure is, and the device was probably detonated from a mobile-phone signal from a nearby car or van. My guys reckon your Land Rover was spotted soon after you and Grace left the Embassy, and then followed. Probably hit-men?'

'Why hit-men?' asked Grace.

'I guess because their instructions were to target a British High Commission Land Rover – such-and-such number - and give it the works.'

'Without checking who was in it.'

Felix shrugged. 'There's a turning off the carriageway just beyond the Stadium. The vehicle could have hightailed it down there as soon as the driver, or whoever, pressed the button.'

'And virtually no chance of being picked up or even noticed,' added Grace.

'Correct.'

'So a dead-end,' said Ian, staring at his feet.

'I guess so.' Felix tapped his fingers on the desk and glanced between the two of them. 'Anyway, Ian, what was it you were asking about Hollis?'

'Another bloody dead-end!'

'Ian: Hollis.'

'Sorry.' Ian placed the package from Colette on the desk. 'Could you get Tim to send this in the diplomatic bag to UK. Tell him it's from me and it needs to be kept cool.'

'What is it?'

'Blood samples from someone who recovered from a monkey-transmitted disease – probably Marburg.'

'Holy shit.' Felix extracted a large envelope from a drawer in his desk and used a pen to push the package inside; then sealed it.

'Staple that to the envelope,' said Ian, passing across the business card. 'That's where the samples have to go.'

Felix read the card, glanced at Ian then rose to his feet. 'Now let's go see if Franco's awake.'

Chapter 30

'After the ninety-eight bombing, Ambassador insisted we improve our medical set-up,' said Felix, as he, Ian and Grace travelled up in the elevator. They arrived in an area reminiscent of a hospital wing, except that several of the staff wore military fatigues and some carried discreet weapons.

The orderly, on duty at a desk, saluted when they arrived. 'In here, major.' He unlocked a door and showed them into a small room with bars on the windows.

Franco was sitting up in the only bed, a pristine white bandage round his shoulder. He gave a despondent wave as they entered.

'*Come va?*' asked Felix.

Franco shrugged, winced in pain and began gabbling away in Italian.

A knock on the door. The orderly returned and whispered in Felix's ear. 'Won't be a moment,' he said. 'Doc wants to see me.'

Ian and Grace drew up chairs on either side of the bed. 'So how is it, Franco?' she asked, patting his hand.

'Why they shut me in a locked room with bars? Is like prison.'

'You're safe here, Franco. I expect they want to keep an eye on you.'

The door opened, Felix returned and stood at the end of the bed studying Franco. 'Must've hurt like hell.'

'I not know what you mean.' Franco focused on his bed covers.

'What happened to the revolver?'

'What revolver?'

'Your revolver,' – as though addressing a small child.

Franco scowled.

'Why d'you do it?'

'Do what?'

'Franco, one thing military doctors get used to dealing with is gunshot wounds. I've been speaking to the doc who treated you and he reckons you shot yourself – scorch marks on your clothing, nature of the wound and suchlike.'

Franco continued his study of the bed clothes then looked up and grinned. 'You right, Felix, it did hurt like hell. At least they no find my whisky.'

'Listen, ass-hole! Stop friggin' about. It's time for straight talking.'

Franco didn't seem in the least fazed by Felix's outburst. 'They okay?' He nodded towards Ian and Grace. 'I can tell?'

'Sure. Go ahead.'

'How long is it, Felix?'

'I guess about five years.'

'What's about five years?' asked Ian.

'Since we took on this crazy coyote to work for us,' said Felix. 'Like you said, Ian, back at our first meeting, something about the perfect front, back of beyond, own airstrip, plenty of—'

'Is, how you say, part-time job?' said Franco. 'They no pay very much, though.'

'You'll have to talk to the Ambassador,' said Felix.

'You can tell him—'

'Her.'

'*Che cosa?*'

'The Ambassador's a she.'

'So, you tell her come and see me and we discuss.'

'Piss off.'

Franco turned to Ian. 'What you find in missionary papers?'

'I've only had a brief look. Haven't had a chance to study them.'

'See what you can find. That probably when things started.'

'So when I was at Isiolo, you were working for the Embassy?' said Grace.

'*Si, si.*'

'Why wasn't I told?'

'Hell, Grace, it was no big deal,' said Felix, smoothing feathers. 'You folks had enough on your plate. We just wanted to keep an eye on Somalis coming and going.'

'Why?'

'Let's say we haven't been the best of buddies since the dust-up in Mogadishu in ninety-two, ninety-three – Operation Restore Hope.'

Grace sniffed.

'Is, how you say, leaky border?' said Franco. 'Eastern side of Kenya where meets Somalia. And main road from there comes through Isiolo. So Embassy they say to Franco you listen and watch and tell us what you hear and see. They say people using Isiolo as back door to come to Kenya. Although I see and hear things early on and tell them, they no able to prevent ninety-eight attack on Embassy. They say all rumours, and too vague. Now they know several of those involved in attack, were coming and going through back door.'

'And people are using the back door again?' said Felix.

'Including some posing as tourists?' said Ian.

Franco nodded morosely. 'I think.'

'They going to Lokinang?' asked Felix.

'Perhaps.' Franco rubbed his shoulder and winced. 'This Njia Mpya – the new path thing – is no so good.'

'But you told me they were boys messing about,' said Grace.

'I no want you, how you say, stir up hornets' nest?'

'Seems a bit late for that,' said Felix.

'*Si*. They now stirred.'

'So what happened, Franco?' asked Grace.

'You know Khalif and Samira, I think?'

'The two who work for you?'

'*Si*. They also work with Njia Mpya. They hunt with the hyenas and with the lions – is very dangerous for them.' Franco stared at a fly crawling across his bed covers and seemed oblivious of the others. 'They good people, they tell me many things they hear and I tell Embassy. But is risky game. Others get suspicious and smelling rats. They say why Khalif and Samira always asking about Lokinang and about Mlala? Perhaps they double-crossing Njia Mpya. But my friend Solomon – you know Solomon at New Paradise bar?'

'We know him,' said Grace.

'He warn me.'

'Tell us what happened, Franco.'

'I need drink. Is thirsty work all this talking.'

'Sure. Tea or coffee?' said Felix.

'Whisky?'

'No chance.'

'Is *no problema*,' said Franco. 'I have tea.'

'Same for you folks?'

Grace and Ian nodded.

Felix stuck his head out of the door and spoke to the orderly. 'On its way.' He returned and sat on the end of the bed. 'So what happened?'

'My friend Sean he come with this lady who work with monkeys. Coletta, she very nice lady. She very nice legs and—'

'Get on with it,' growled Felix.

'*Si, si*. Soon after lunch I get call to say new supplies coming in. Is

164

call from Solomon and I know is to warn me something bad. So I tell Sean and Coletta— You know Coletta?'

Ian tried to keep his expression neutral.

'I tell them Franco has work to do but you can stay. Sean he say, no we go. Then I call Khalif and we drive to house to see Samira and I say to them, what going on, what you been saying, why Solomon send me warning?'

'What did they say?' asked Grace.

'They say, is no problem. Solomon he imagining. But I say, no; that one shit-scared. We go talk to him and you come. They not pleased and I know they worried too.'

'So you drove to Isiolo?' said Grace. 'What then?'

'We go to Solomon's place and have afternoon tea. Like you British, I think.' He winked at Ian. 'We go to New Paradise for tea but Khalif and Samira they refuse to come in because they see other people also having afternoon tea. I say is *no problema*, but they say we no want afternoon tea and they bugger off. So I go in and I say good afternoon to other people, same like in Britain. Those ones ignore me. They no even look at me.'

'What sort of people?'

'Two African men and a *mzungu*. I think he *mzungu* but I no see his face, but I see reflection in window and I see he watch me.'

'Can you describe him?' asked Grace.

'Black hair.'

'Short, long?'

'A bit long, I think.'

'And white skin?'

'Not white white, but tan white.'

'Anything else?'

'Wearing safari jacket like mine.'

'Tall, short; fat, thin?'

'Quite tall. Not fat.'

'Would you recognise him if you saw him again?'

Franco sighed. 'Probably not.'

'And the other two men?' asked Ian.

'Somalis, quite young. I see they scared of the *mzungu*. I think they – how you say? – arse-lickers. There now many Somalis in Isiolo. Some not so good.'

'So you reckon these were Ninja guys?' said Felix.

'Is possible.'

'Why you say that?'

'Because Solomon, he frighted. He pretend not to know me, but when I go pay bill he give me note so others can't see.'

'What was in the note, Franco?' asked Grace.

'Note say be careful of tall one. He bad news.'

'Did the note say who he was?'

'No.'

'Who do you think it might have been?' asked Ian.

Franco sank back on his pillows. 'I too tired to think. Perhaps Mlala.'

There was a knock on the door and the orderly entered carrying a try with tea and biscuits, which he set down on the bedside table.

'Thanks,' said Felix, handing the mugs round. 'There you go, folks.'

'Franco, why do you think that *mzungu* could have been Mlala?' asked Grace.

Franco waved a dismissive hand. 'Is just a name.'

'But you must have a reason for suggesting it.'

'In note, Solomon also say you, Grace, visit previous day with *mzungu* called John, and ask about ole-Tomeno and about Mlala. I think Solomon has wind put up him.'

'We also asked him about Njia Mpya,' said Grace.

'No wonder he shit-scared.'

'What happened after you left that place?' asked Felix.

'I go to see police. Those useless wankers; they know nothing, they say get lost, old man, and when... Grace, why you no come back to Isiolo?'

She ignored the question. 'Then you met up with Khalif and Samira?'

Franco nodded and stared at several flies attracted by the biscuit crumbs on the bed clothes. 'They come back to Land Rover, where I wait, and say no one will talk to them. So I know is trouble big time, but I not know what sort of trouble and Khalif and Samira not know.'

'So what did you do?' asked Grace.

'We go back. Is dark when we arrive and I take Samira to house and I say you lock doors. Then I tell Khalif we go back to office and I say to warn other men who work at mission. But before we warn them, vehicle arrive—'

'What sort of vehicle?'

'Is dark. I not know. All I know is show time.' Franco sipped his tea, lost in thought.

Felix got up and stared out of the window. 'Then what?'

'Khalif, he wetting himself. He say they out to get him. I say why? He say they think I not working for Njia Mpya. I traitor. Then Franco he have brainwave. I say to Khalif we make big mess in office. He no understand but he help me empty boxes and drawers and throw stuff around. Then I give Khalif my gun and hold to here and I say you shoot. He say, no. He can no shoot me. I say. bullshit. You shoot, and these *ngorokos*, these *banditos* they think you try to kill me so you must be on their side. You shoot and take my Land Rover. Go with Samira and tell Sean big bust-up at Franco's place.'

'Why didn't you go?' said Ian.

'We not have time. Because, how you say, shit hit fan?' He rubbed his bandage thoughtfully. 'Everyone say Franco he one crazy bastard, so I shoot. And is like kick from zebra. Then I yell at Khalif: take my gun and get the fuck out. So he yell back to fuck off, but he go and I hear vehicle drive away.'

'Did those people find you?' asked Felix.

'I pretend to be very bad, and all I say is Khalif is bastard. So they go.'

'But they might have killed you,' said Grace.

'Is possible.'

'Then what?' said Felix.

'Then I think, you the crazy baboon, Franco, you going to die if you bleed like this, like stuck pig. Then I go to sleep and you people come and wake me. So I think, what the hell?'

Felix crossed to the door and gestured Grace and Ian to follow. 'Back in a moment.'

Franco flapped a hand and helped himself to another biscuit.

'Do we believe him?' said Felix, when he'd closed the door.

'Sounds unlikely enough to be true,' said Ian.

'Probably the only person who can confirm it is Khalif – wherever he is,' said Grace.

'Should we get this Solomon guy in and lean on him?' said Felix.

She shook her head. 'He's probably the only person in Isiolo who can help us.'

Felix shrugged. 'I guess so. And Franco?'

'Let him go when the doctor agrees. I'm sure he has friends in Nairobi where he can stay.'

Chapter 31

'Ole-Tomeno wants me to help with the vaccine development programme?' Colette was incredulous. 'Why me? I don't know anything about vaccines.'

'But you know about simian viruses,' said Jeff.

'I know a bit about simian viruses.'

He regarded her over his coffee mug. 'There're probably less than ten other people in the world who know more.'

She shrugged. 'That doesn't mean I can contribute to a vaccine programme.'

'I think you can. So does ole-Tomeno.'

Colette pulled a face. 'I'm not sure, Jeff. I've never worked in industry. I know nothing about efficacy and safety testing. Nothing about—'

'Listen, Colette.' He leaned across the table. 'This is probably the biggest thing in AIDS research since Robert Gallo and Luc Montagnier identified the causative virus. We're giving you a chance to be part of the team.'

'What about my work in UK?'

'Is that more important?'

She dropped her eyes 'Probably not.' She was vaguely aware of someone speaking on the radio in Sean's office and of his hurrying through to answer it. 'Can I think about it? There's so much happening at the—'

'Richard and I are going back to the centre. Why not come with us and see the set-up, then decide?'

'It's all so—'

'Colette,' called Sean, 'can you come?'

'Excuse me, Jeff,' she said, getting up. 'Who is it?' she whispered.

'Someone called Kelly Ryder,' said Sean.

'Kelly! How did she know I was here?'

'She didn't say.'

Colette reached out a hesitant hand for the microphone. 'Kelly?'

'Colette, hi. How you doing?'

'I'm fine.'

'Long time, no see.'

'Yes, isn't it?'

'Listen, Colette, your friend Peter Barnsley.'

'Pete, what about him?'

'Couple of crazy fellows.' There was a chuckle over the airwaves. 'I checked him out. Seems fine. A bit of a close call, I guess.'

'I think it was.' Colette glanced at Sean. 'Kelly, do you know where they're staying?'

'No, afraid not. Why?'

'We need to contact them urgently, their camp's been… The details don't matter, we just need to talk to them. Some bad news, I'm afraid.'

'Sorry, Colette, the only contact detail he gave was a PO-box number.'

'A mobile number?'

'Pete says he forgot his phone, left it at the camp.'

'Not to worry then. They'll find out in time but it would have been good to warn them.'

'Sure.'

'Sorry, Kelly, I interrupted you.'

'That's okay. Thing is, any chance you could get down here?'

'When?'

'Soon as possible.'

'What's the urgency?'

There was a slight pause. 'It's just I think we've gotten one of those things that's up your street.'

'What do you mean?'

'White. Female. Early thirties. No apparent contact with monkeys but it looks like one of those nasty haemorrhagic viruses you deal with.'

'For God's sake, Kelly. I don't deal with them. I know about them and have nightmares about them.'

'Sure, sure. But I'd really appreciate it if you could get here.'

'Hang on.' She turned to Sean. 'Kelly wants me in Nairobi. Could I take Ian's Landy? Be a way of getting it back to him.'

He thought for a moment. 'Sure. You'll be okay on your own?'

'I didn't hear that.' She turned back to the microphone. 'Kelly, listen, I'm coming to Nairobi but it's a long drive so I won't make it until—'

'Stay overnight at Naro Moru,' whispered Sean. 'No way you're driving that road in the dark.'

She nodded. 'Kelly, I won't be able to make it until tomorrow morning. I'll be there as soon as I can.'

'That's great, Colette.'

'Where shall I meet you?'

'I'll give you my mobile number. Give me a call when you get here.'

'Hang on.' Colette scrabbled on Sean's desk for a pen and paper. 'Go ahead. Yes, I've got that.'

'Look forward to seeing you.'

'Thanks, Kelly. That's got me out of a hole.'

'Excuse me?'

'Tell you later.'

'Really appreciate it, Colette. Travel well.'

'Thanks. See you.' She replaced the microphone and turned to Sean. 'Can you do me a favour?'

'Sure.'

'Explain to Jeff, while I go and pack?'

He gave his lop-sided smile. 'I guess he won't be best pleased.'

She stuck out her chin. 'That's tough.'

Chapter 32

Ian tried to stop his imagination working overtime as he sat next morning, still unshaven and in dark glasses, in the driver's seat of a nondescript Toyota four-wheel-drive.

A security guard from the hotel was wandering past the parked vehicles.

Ian shrank into his seat as the man came up to his window.

'How are you, sir?'

'Fine.'

'Are you from England?'

'Yes.' Ian tensed, waiting for the inevitable question.

'Do you know Gary Lineker?'

'Sorry?'

'He play football.'

Ian relaxed. 'No. No, I don't know him.'

'He play very good. He play for England.'

'We've not met.'

'Before this job, I play for AFC Leopards. You know AFC Leopards?'

'No.'

'I play like Lineker. I play striker.'

'Really?'

'Now I am too old to—'

Ian was rescued by the return of Grace accompanied by two unlikely-looking figures. Walter Cheriyot was younger than Ian expected and his rimless glasses gave him the air of an academic. Viktor Levkov was built like a wrestler and sported a large straggly moustache, giving him the appearance of a dyspeptic walrus.

Introductions were hardly necessary, but Grace went through the formalities as she ushered the two of them into the rear seats. She then came and sat beside Ian in the front.

'Have you been to Nairobi Park before?' Grace turned in her seat.

'Yes.' Walter didn't look up from his laptop.

'In Moscow many parks,' said Viktor.

'Are they wildlife parks?'

'Yes. Many parks.'

Ian and Grace exchanged glances. It looked like being a long day.

171

Thirty minutes later, they arrived at the entrance of the Park, and Grace paid their entrance fees from the dollars she had persuaded Felix to contribute to the trip.

Ian felt the familiar sense of anticipation as he drove through the high archway and into what was almost unspoiled Africa. After no more than a few hundred yards, they came upon a herd of reddish brown antelopes standing in the shade of croton trees.

'Those are impala, Viktor,' said Ian.

'In Russia, we have many.'

'I don't think they occur outside Africa,' said Ian, offering his binoculars.

Viktor ignored the offer. 'In Russia, plenty.'

'I see.'

As the morning wore on, it was apparent that most of the birds and mammals they saw in the Park, despite their restriction to the African continent, were also common in Russia. Ian decided to write the day off and enjoy the wildlife. He continued out into the open plains and stopped to allow a family of warthogs to trot across the road, tails held vertical like the pennants of Japanese tour guides.

'Do these occur in Russia, Viktor?' he asked, tongue firmly in cheek.

'They are ugly. We don't have.'

Ian moved off.

'We'll soon be at the Hippo Pools,' said Grace. 'We can stop there and have some tea.'

Neither of the reporters responded as they studied something on Walter's laptop.

'Looks like just you and me then, Grace,' murmured Ian.

The track led down a slight hill and into an open dusty area where a number of cars were parked. Two Park wardens, rifles across their knees, sat on a log in the shade of a small tree, playing cards. They looked up without interest when Ian pulled up, then returned to their game.

Also watching the vehicle was a group of baboons, sitting and grooming each other in the grass at the edge of the parking area.

'We can get out here,' said Ian, 'but make sure you close the windows otherwise the baboons will get in looking for food.'

'I'll stay here,' said Walter.

'Would you like some tea?' asked Grace.

'Coffee, please.'

172

'I'm afraid we didn't bring coffee.' She indicated the thermos in the basket at her feet. 'Would you like some tea, Viktor?'

'I bring own drink.' Viktor took a hip flask from his pocket. 'Is Russian drink. Very good. It put hairs on your chest.' He laughed uproariously and poked Grace in the back.

'Let's go,' – through gritted teeth. Grace grabbed the basket at her feet.

She and Ian climbed out, went to the front of the vehicle and sat on the bumper.

'I'm sorry I suggested this,' she said.

Ian smiled. 'Do we give up or keep trying?'

'Let's see how we get on with them on their own.' She poured him a cup of tea. 'You take Viktor for a walk. I'll see what I can learn from Walter.'

'Seems I've drawn the short straw?'

She shrugged.

Ian closed his eyes and leaned back against the warm radiator. Colette had brought him to this place all those years ago, on his first visit in his brand new Land Rover. He'd been enthralled to see hippos in the wild. Later that day, they'd driven to a remote part of the Park to look for wild dogs which Colette had seen on a previous visit. They made love for the first time but never saw the dogs. It was almost dark when they left and were reprimanded by the wardens for being late.

The slamming of a door brought him out of his reverie.

'I go for pissing,' announced Viktor.

Ian pointed to a discreet building behind some trees.

'I'll talk to Walter,' said Grace, picking up her tea. 'Good luck.'

'I need it.'

Viktor returned, ostentatiously adjusting himself and zipping up his fly. He came and sat by Ian and offered his hip flask. 'You like vodka?'

'Not now thanks.'

'Vodka is Russian drink. Very good.' Viktor took a swig from his flask and gestured towards some vervet monkeys watching them from a nearby tree. 'They have Marburg disease?'

Ian turned, startled. 'No. No, I don't think so.'

'You know about Marburg disease?'

'A bit.'

'Marburg disease very bad. It kill my wife.'

'Your wife? That's awful. How did she, er, catch the disease?' Ian tried to keep his expression neutral.

'What you call those?' said Viktor, whose gaze was elsewhere.

'Baboons.'

'In Russia, we don't have.'

'Right.' Quick glance. 'You were telling me about your wife.'

Viktor leaned forward, rested his elbows on his knees, chin on hands, and gazed morosely into the distance. 'Is many years since she die. She work on Biopreparat programme at Progress, Scientific and Production Association in Stepnogorsk. You know this place?'

'No.'

'They work to make vaccines. Very fine Russian vaccines, they say. But is bullshit.' He rounded on Ian, a squall sweeping through his walrus moustache. 'They make disease weapons. They kill my wife. They bloody bastards. They not tell her is dangerous. Ass-holes!'

Ian slopped his tea. The Park wardens looked up from their cards. The vervet monkeys scampered higher into the trees.

Viktor took some more vodka and the storm in his moustache subsided. 'Comrade Alexei Borishenkov, director of institute, was good man. He very sorry about my wife die. He say to me, Viktor, is not so good this work. Next month I go with Comrade President Gorbachev on Test-ban Treaty talks to United States, I want you, Viktor my friend, come to United States as reporter. I arrange your papers. So I say, sure, I come with you. My newspaper say, sure, you go there as reporter for Izvestia.'

He lapsed into silence and Ian waited.

Viktor smoothed his moustache. 'United States they say, welcome, Comrade Boris – they always call Borishenkov, Comrade Boris – you stay with us now. And he say sure. They say to me, welcome, Viktor Levkov. Have a nice day. We all friends now after *glasnost*. You come live with us and tell us about Biopreparat programme at Stepnogorsk. I say, I not know. All I know is my wife die, you have to ask Comrade Boris.' Viktor sipped from his flask.

'Shall we go and find the hippos?' asked Ian.

Viktor peered in the direction of the baboons. 'They not safe. We not walk. In Russia, we don't have.'

'Sure. What did you think of the States?'

'Is good but not so good like Russia, but food better, I think. I decide to stay and learn English.'

Ian smiled.

'I like very much McDonalds and Kentucky Fried Chicken.'

'Yes, I can see that.'

Viktor nodded. 'I like very much. Also I find here in Nairobi. My friend Walter, he take me to—'

'What was Borishenkov able to tell the Americans?' Voice casual.

'Why you want to know?' Viktor's moustache bristled like an angry ferret.

'It's only that I'm, er, interested. There's been some talk of Marburg recently in Kenya. I wondered if there was a, um, link.'

'You read Walter's article?'

'I didn't think his ideas sounded very likely.'

'You wrong. He get his ideas from my article when some bloody bastard kill my friend Alexei.'

'Borishenkov was killed?'

'Same disease what killed my wife.'

'Marburg?'

'Many people in Russia not so pleased that Alexei go to States and tell about Biopreparat programme. He say me many times, Viktor my friend, those ones out to get me. I say, bullshit. You safe here. Uncle Sam he take care of you. He say, no. He very sad. He say, when I die you promise me you tell the world. I say, you not going to die. He shake his head. You promise? So I promise. Then every week Alexei and me we meet for McDonalds and I laugh and say, you not dying. But he say, they still going to get me. I say, bullshit. But he say, perhaps a car accident, perhaps a bullet, perhaps some nerve poison.'

Viktor paused to scratch himself in an intimate place.

'One day, Alexei show me pills his doctor send him. They vitamin pills. I supposed to take one each day, he say. But he sniff bottle and say, I know they not vitamins. Perhaps a poisoned dagger hidden in shoe – like in James Bond. I say and I laugh. Alexei say, perhaps. He not laugh.'

Something triggered in Ian's mind but was lost as Viktor continued.

'One day, Alexei not come for Big Mac. So I call his phone and there no answer and I leave message on answerphone, but he no phone back. So I call place where he work and they say, he no work here. I say bullshit, he my brother.' He turned to Ian. 'He was like brother to me, you understand, we drink vodka together, we eat Big Mac together, we go watch baseball—'

'When you said you were his brother, what did his work place say?'

'They say, you lie. He not have brother and they stop my call. And I think, you bastards are like KGB. I know all about KGB and I know about KGB successor. You understand, John, KGB always changing name, but bastards they still the same. They not change. I know how those bastards work. So I start to dig. Is not so easy for Russian to dig in USA. CIA they watch me but I know many tricks and I keep digging.'

'What did you find?' Innocent question – hopefully.

'I remember my promise to Alexei. I tell the world about he die. I write article for Izvestia and send copy to local newspaper, Frederick News-Post. You know?'

Ian shook his head.

Viktor grinned. 'I make guess-work and make up big story Some I know is true, but most... most is made up, but sounds true. We journalists, we good like that.' He chuckled and took a generous sip from his flask. 'What those?' he asked, indicating some animals which had wandered into view.

'Waterbuck. Another kind of antelope.'

'Plenty in Russia. You know Fort Detrick?'

'No.' Deadpan expression – wasted, as Viktor was watching the waterbuck.

'Is like Stepnogorsk, I think. Much research on bad diseases.'

'And Borishenkov worked there?'

'He say he adviser to Americans but he not tell me about work. He very good to keep buttoned up, but one day he bring another man to eat Big Mac with us.'

'Who was that?'

'His name Sayed Farouk, he worked at Stepnogorsk as visiting scientist. My wife, Olga, she not like that one. She say he very clever but he fanatic about work, about many things. Americans, they like because he speak good their language. His mother American, I think. So they say, you welcome, Sayed. You come work at Fort Detrick now Stepnogorsk close down after Test-ban Treaty. You know about viruses and molecular stuff. You help us. But I say to Alexei, I not sure about that one. He say, bullshit, he like orchids.'

'Orchids?' Ian couldn't keep the astonishment out of his voice.

Viktor nodded. 'Russia not so good for orchids, but many in America so Alexei tell me. He like very much. I think Farouk send orchids to Frederick News-Post when Alexei die. He say he good friend of Alexei but I not believe.'

Raise binoculars. Pretend to study the waterbuck.

'Do you want to look, Viktor?'

The man shook his head. 'In Russia, plenty.'

'Does this, er, Sayed Farouk still work in the States?' asked Ian.

Viktor grabbed his arm, put his face only inches away from Ian's, his blue eyes piercing and his breath reeking of vodka. 'He come to Kenya, I think. That why I come here.' His voice sank to a conspiratorial whisper. 'Is John, yes?'

Ian nodded and tried to retreat from the alcoholic haze but Viktor's grip tightened.

'You know what I think, John? I think Farouk he kill my wife?'

'But why?'

'Because she find out what he doing in Stepnogorsk. This work is not good, Viktor, she say to me. Then she get sick and die.' Two tears ran down his cheeks. 'That one kill her.'

Ian dared not move from the sobbing man or the alcoholic miasma for fear of breaking a delicate thread. He patted Viktor's arm. 'Did he kill Borishenkov as well?'

Viktor nodded and gave a thunderous sniff. 'I think.' He released Ian's arm. 'Is still very upsetting for me, you understand.'

'Yes, of course.'

Viktor blew his nose on a voluminous purple handkerchief, gave a final sniff and drained his flask. He turned to Ian. 'You heard of man called Colonel Ian Sinclair?'

Bolt from the blue. 'Ian Sinclair? Er, no, I don't think so. Why?'

'He killed by bomb here in Nairobi.' Viktor frowned. 'You must hear. Is in all papers.'

'I've been out in the bush for the last week or so. We don't get much news out there.' Conscious he was walking on egg-shells, Ian said: 'This, er, Sinclair person, what about him?'

'Someone send him orchids.'

'What do you mean?'

'I think that Sayed Farouk send this Sinclair man orchids.'

'Sayed Farouk is here in Kenya?'

'I think.' Viktor blew through his moustache and stood up. 'I go for pissing again. Is only bad thing about vodka.'

As he made his way toward the toilet one of the baboons, a big male, began to follow. Viktor broke into a shambling run and the baboon scampered after him. The wardens shouted. The baboon stopped, glared at them and ambled back to the others. Viktor returned to Ian.

'I not need go pissing after all.' He settled himself back on the bumper.

The vehicle door opened and Grace climbed out accompanied by Walter, who came and stood studying Ian and Viktor, a slight smile on his lips.

'What for you smile like that?' muttered Viktor.

'Have you been playing the stupid Russian again?'

Viktor scowled and looked away.

'What lies has he been telling you, Colonel Sinclair?'

'We had a good…' Ian's voice trailed off. 'What did you say?'

'It's all right. We won't say – or write – anything, provided…' He left the sentence hanging.

'Provided what?'

Walter smiled. 'Provided our respective newspapers have exclusive access to any material you're prepared to make public relating to Condor, Marburg and terrorist threats in Kenya.'

'I see.' Ian glanced at Grace who shrugged. 'And if we don't?'

Walter's expression was mild as he took off his glasses and polished them on his shirt.

'You blow my cover?'

'What a quaint phrase.' Walter's expression became almost avuncular. 'It seems we understand each other.'

'Is, how you say, we have you over barrel.' Viktor's eyes were twinkling.

'You bugger,' said Ian. 'So have you been telling me a pack of lies?'

'Only about the animals we have in Russia. The rest was true.' Viktor nudged him. 'Mostly.'

'I see.' It was Ian's turn to scowl. 'So how did you find out about me?'

'The Minister's briefing meeting on Condor when all the task force leaders were introduced,' said Walter. 'The press was invited and I maintained a low profile. It's my style. Viktor, on the other hand, has a different style.'

'So I've noticed.'

Viktor gave a dismissive gesture. 'It works, particularly in the States.'

'Despite your, er, somewhat changed appearance, Colonel Sinclair,' said Walter, 'it was not hard to recognise you.'

'So what now? Now that everyone's put their cards on the table.'

'All their cards?'

Ian regarded the shrewd reporter. 'I think we understand one another.'

'Walter, you and I have already talked,' said Grace. 'I was able to help you over that bombing and—'

'I believe the help was mutual.'

'—and I see no reason why we can't collaborate again.'

'Good.'

'Ian and I need to confer with a colleague and then we'll get back to you.'

'That Major Rossi?' asked Viktor.

'As Grace said, we'll get back to you,' said Ian.

'Time to leave,' she said. 'So you didn't go and see the hippos?'

'No,' said Viktor. 'In Russia plenty.'

***

Ian drove back to the hotel. While Grace took Viktor and Walter inside, he called Felix.

'How was the Park, Ian?'

'Interesting. Listen, Felix, we need to come and brief you but in the meantime, I've got a name.'

'Who?'

'Sayed Farouk.'

'Never heard of him.'

'The Russian journalist, Viktor, believes this Farouk guy killed not only his wife but also Borishenkov.'

'No kidding?'

'See if your people have anything on Farouk. Also, Viktor thinks he's now in Kenya.'

'Jeez.'

'I can't stop, Felix. You've got that name?'

'Yeah. I'll get onto it. Call you back.'

'Cheers.'

Ian closed the phone and stared through the windscreen.

A scuffle in the gateway of the hotel car park. The security guard, who had waylaid him with talk of football, was grappling with a child who had been begging from some tourists.

Ian leaped out of the vehicle just as Grace arrived. 'Quick. Grab that girl.'

'What? Which girl?'

'There. Just do it. I'll explain.'

179

Grace hesitated briefly, by which time the girl had broken free of the guard and was racing away.

Grace set off brandishing her police ID.

Ian jumped back into the vehicle and followed them down the road. The girl could run but she'd not won any Olympic medals and the chase could have only one outcome.

Ian drew up beside them and Grace bundled the screaming, scratching, biting girl into the vehicle. Startled bystanders shouted at Ian as he drove off.

'Grace, meet Charity,' said Ian, over his shoulder. 'Charity, meet Grace.'

The girl stopped struggling and Grace relaxed the neck-lock.

'Sir?' said the girl.

'You were injured in that bomb,' said Ian.

'You saw that thing?'

'Yes. I saw it. How is your arm?'

'My arm is paining me, sir.' She indicated the grubby bandage, through which fresh blood was seeping.

Grace released the girl. 'I also was there. I remember you.'

'My mama was killed. Now it is only me.'

Ian winced. 'What shall we do, Grace?'

She thought for a moment. 'Go to my place. I'll show you the way.'

Chapter 33

Colette failed to be uplifted by the beauty around her as she sat toying with her breakfast on the lawn of the Naro Moru River Lodge: the sunlight sparkling on the river, the snow-covered summit of Mount Kenya above the treetops, the colourful gardens, and turacos calling from the forest. A pair of paradise flycatchers flitted through the trees, chestnut tails streaming.

The chance to work on a pioneering programme to develop an AIDS vaccine. Was she stupid to be so reticent? She'd always been ambitious. Perhaps the big break was there waiting for her. At least, she'd learned the real reason why Jeff had summoned her from London. If he'd told her at the time, she wouldn't have come – probably wouldn't have believed him. Was he being straight with her now? Why had he ducked out of going to Tandala with her and Sean? And Sean: what did he actually do? He had some role on Condor and ran the ranch – but mostly other people seemed to do the work, leaving him with plenty of time on his hands.

Questions swirled in her head, too erratically for her to catch one to examine. Why did Sean agree so readily she should return to Nairobi rather than go with Jeff to the centre? Was it really his concern about her welfare, or was this a convenient excuse to get her out of the way, to stop her cluttering up his life? Perhaps even now, he'd forgotten her as he returned to the problems of the ranch: the disappearance of Leah and Samira, the fire at Franco's house, the outbreak of Marburg in the forest monkeys.

Get real, girl. Sean is married. With his wife in Nairobi, he may fancy a bit on the side, but anything more? Forget it.

She closed her eyes and a tune tumbled her back to a log-fire in the bush and a man playing a guitar, a man playing Bach. Why did it have to be that? Something about sleepers? Sleepers awake. Was it to waken something in her?

Stop! Stop deluding yourself.

She gathered her resolve and her things from the room, paid her bill and went to collect Ian's Land Rover from the car park. Ian's Land Rover; that didn't help.

A woman in Samburu dress accosted her. 'See, *memsabu*, lucky bracelet, only five hundred shillings.'

Colette laughed. 'You think it will bring me luck?'

'Yes, *memsahu*, very lucky, very beautiful.'

'Okay, I'll give it a try.' She allowed the woman to fix the bead bracelet round her wrist. 'I know it's not worth five hundred shillings, but I'm prepared to pay for luck.'

'*Asante, memsahu.*' The woman was surprised to be paid the full amount. '*Asante sana.*'

'*Asante* – thank you,' said Colette. Smiling, she climbed into the Land Rover and waved as she drove off. Was she totally stupid?

The woman waved back. 'Very beautiful,' she called.

Was this to be her lucky charm as she navigated uncharted waters ahead?

When she reached the outskirts of Nairobi, she pulled into a garage and filled up the tank. Then called Kelly.

'Colette! You've made good time.'

'The road was pretty clear. Where do you want me to come?'

'You know the Nairobi Hospital?'

'Yes.'

'I'll meet you in the car park in half an hour.'

'Fine. How's the patient?'

There was a pause. 'See you around eleven. Bye.'

Colette needed all of half an hour to negotiate Nairobi's traffic and when she arrived she found Kelly waiting.

'Good to see you.' She gave Colette a hug. 'You look great.'

'You too.'

'Really appreciate your coming. This way.' She led Colette through a door which read: *Staff Only*, along a corridor, down some steps, then further steps.

'Where are we going?'

'You'll see.'

They came to a solid metal door with a phone and keypad to one side and a glowing red light above.

Kelly spoke briefly into the phone. The light went out. She entered a code on the keypad and opened the door to reveal a spotless waiting area of gleaming tiles, shiny metal work and the prospect of scary viruses.

'In here.'

Colette slipped into the hospital clothing and was reminded of the Zoo, but this time it wasn't a colobus monkey. The need to wear a Perspex visor, instead of a facemask, heightened her apprehension.

'Let's go,' said Kelly.

Colette drew a breath. Despite the clothing, she felt naked.

'Follow me.'

They entered another room of tiles. Subdued lighting. A faint hum from the air system and various pieces of equipment. At one end a sealed observation window. A single bed. A mass of blonde hair tumbled over the pillow. An array of tubes, pipes and wires from the equipment to the patient. One nurse tending. Another watching dials and screens on the monitors.

'This is Dr Fraser,' said Kelly.

The nurses nodded and smiled.

The patient's eyes were closed and most of her face was obscured by an oxygen mask. Her skin was flushed. A rash on her neck.

'How you feeling?' called Kelly softly.

The woman opened her eyes – the whites angry red.

'We need to look at your tummy.' Kelly turned back the sheet and gently lifted the hospital gown. The whole abdomen was inflamed with a red nettle-rash.

Colette drew a sharp breath.

Kelly replaced the covers. 'Any change?' she asked the nurse.

'That one is still very bad, doctor,' she whispered.

'Temperature?'

'Very high. And bad headache.'

Kelly took a stethoscope and listened to the patient's chest. She'd closed her eyes again and seemed unaware of things around her.

Kelly patted the covers. 'You're doing great. You're in good hands.'

The woman's eyelids fluttered briefly.

'Carry on as we are,' said Kelly to the nurse. 'I'll be back again this evening.'

'Yes, doctor.'

Kelly signalled to Colette and they left the room. It wasn't until they were outside the building that either spoke.

'Am I being alarmist?' asked Kelly.

'No.' Colette slowly shook her head.

'Is it Marburg?'

'Almost certainly a viral haemorrhagic infection. Whether or not it's Marburg, I wouldn't like to say.'

'But it could be?'

'Yes.'

183

'What are her chances?'

'I'm not a clinician.'

Kelly briefly studied some brightly-coloured birds squabbling over a piece of discarded bread. 'Right, put that on hold for a moment. You got anywhere to stay?'

Colette hesitated. 'I was staying in the Fairview. I thought I'd check in there again.'

'No way. We've so much to talk about, come back to my place.'

'Are you sure?'

'I'm sure. Felix would love to meet you.'

'Felix?'

'My hubby. He also works at the Embassy.'

'Well, if you're sure he wouldn't—'

'You hungry?'

'Starving. All I've had is some fruit.'

'Right, follow me. There's a nice little Japanese place nearby.' Kelly extracted car keys from her bag.

***

Kelly and Colette sat at a secluded corner table, trying to make small talk as they sipped *sake* and nibbled *sushi* and prawns *tempura*.

'Tell me the history,' said Colette finally.

Kelly laid down her chopsticks. 'Sudden onset, collapsed at work, high temperature, nausea, dizziness, severe headache. Soon after, acute conjunctivitis and a maculopapular rash as you saw.'

'Any association with monkeys?'

'Not as far as we know but she's been too sick to tell us.'

Colette pulled a face. 'I'm pretty sure it was Marburg that was killing monkeys in the forest where I was recently. Could the patient have been there – north of Mount Kenya?'

'It's possible but I doubt it.'

'It's the place where the Petes were working.'

'Peter Barnsley?'

'Yes, and his crazy colleague Peter Acheson. Soon after leaving them, we found an African hunter who'd also been infected – probably with the same thing – but we think he recovered.' For a moment she was back in the forest bending over an emaciated man whom Sean described as hard as nails.

'Previous sub-clinical exposure?' asked Kelly.

'Could be – in both cases, I imagine, and hence some acquired immunity. Presumably that doesn't apply in this case?'

Kelly didn't respond.

'Marburg seems the most likely,' said Colette, 'but there are other possibilities.'

'Make my day.'

'I've no first-hand experience but Lassa fever, Ebola, Machupo, and even some of the nasties from bats, are similar and hard to differentiate clinically.'

'And that chances of recovery from any of them are not great?'

'As I said, I've no direct experience.' Colette toyed with her glass. 'Lab tests?'

'I'm expecting the results tomorrow.'

For a while they ate in silence.

'This is delicious, I wish I could enjoy it more.' Colette pushed her plate away. 'Tell me how you got involved.'

'You've had enough to eat?'

'And to drink. That was great.'

Kelly wiped her mouth with her napkin. 'Mostly, I'm based in the Embassy but the hospital lends me an office as I've helped them out over similar cases, all of which turned out to be false alarms. Acute malarias, things like that. But there've been a few cases of Marburg in the past – before my time – most notably a Ugandan physician who treated a French tourist who'd been visiting caves somewhere in northern Kenya. The patient died but the physician survived thanks to the treatment he received here. Following that he persuaded the authorities to establish the unit I took you to this morning.'

'And this case?'

'The hospital contacted me as soon as she was brought in.'

'What do you know about her?'

'She's thirty-two, works at the British High Commission. Been there for—'

'The High Commission?'

'Yes.'

'Surname?' Somehow, she already knew.

'Paterson. Helen Paterson. Colette, are you okay?'

She gulped. 'I, er, I've met her husband. He runs a ranch in the Samburu area. I was staying there when you—'

'Thank goodness. We've been wondering how to contact him. All the High Commission could tell us was that he worked in the bush.'

Colette was conscious of fiddling with the bracelet on her wrist. Right now, her lucky charm didn't seem to be working too well.

Chapter 34

Ian drove to Grace's apartment and dropped her and Charity. Before leaving, he called Quentin, his colleague from the High Commission.

'Ian, old chap. Are you calling from the other side? How's life on the gossamer cloud? Harp playing coming on well?'

'Quentin, I can do without your wisecracks.'

'So you're back in harness?'

'Just about.'

'Glossy coat, sound in wind and limb, raring to go, champing at the—'

'Quentin!'

'Sorry, old boy, I jest.'

'Good. Listen, I need somewhere to stay, somewhere low-key.'

'Come back to our place.'

'Sorry, Quentin, better not.'

'I say that was a bit of a rumpus the other night. Mind you, I guessed it was some sort of diversion. Clever those chaps in, in... What are they in?'

'It doesn't matter. The thing is I can't risk staying with you. People may be watching.'

'Good Lord. You think I should move?'

'Better not. Keep them guessing.'

'Good thinking. Don't let them know we know. Eh?'

'Something like that. Quentin, I was wondering if you could get me into the Settlers Club for a few nights.'

'Ian, who are "*they*" – the ones who've rumbled me?'

'I think it's best you don't know.'

There was a pause and Ian could hear heavy breathing. 'What I don't know, I can't reveal under... under duress or... or torture. Is that it?'

'It probably won't come to that.'

'Perhaps I should apply for that posting to Reykjavik.'

'Sorry?'

'Reykjavik. Sir Aubrey has suggested I might need a change of scenery – the strain you know. One can only take the stress of being at the sharp end for so long.'

'I see. Does Fiona like raw fish?'

'Raw fish?'

'Isn't that what they eat in Iceland?' Ian studied the closed door of Grace's apartment. Charity could hardly be in better hands. 'Quentin, about the Settlers, can you fix that? I believe the High Commission has a standing arrangement.'

'Consider it done, old boy. On my way to the club now as it happens. Just finished my round when you called – perfect timing. I'll be there in a couple of minutes. *Weka ndani ya gari huko.*'

'What was that?'

'Sorry, telling the caddie to put my golf bag in the Range Rover. Can we offer you a spot of dinner beforehand?'

'Better not. We want to keep "them" thinking.'

'Oh Lord, this won't do my nerves any— What about Barbados?'

'What about it?'

'That's the other possible posting. What do they eat in that part of the world?'

'Burgers, probably. Very fattening.'

'Good golf, though. Perhaps I'll apply there.'

'Good idea. In the meantime, Quentin, I—'

'Sorry, old boy. I'm on the case. By the way, I've had your desk cleared.'

'My desk?'

'Yes. Clever that: pretending the bomb killed you off.' Quentin chuckled. 'Need to keep up the pretence, if you know what I mean.'

'I see.'

'Don't worry. All your stuff is packed into boxes for when you come back from the dead.' Another chuckle. 'Is Dodgy Dan in the—'

'Quentin, you must stop calling him that.'

'Sorry, *lapsus linguae.*'

'What?'

'You probably didn't have a classical education.'

Ian drew a breath. 'As far as I'm aware, ole-Tomeno still believes I was killed in the attack.'

'Right. Good to be kept in the picture. Now, can I give you a lift to the club?'

'Your car has British CD plates?'

'Yes, I…' The line went quiet.

'It's all right, Quentin, I've— Are you still there?'

The First Secretary sounded as though he was emerging from a barrel. 'Yes. Sorry about that. Still here.'

187

'I'll make my own way to the Club.'

'Should I get the plates on my car changed?'

'Your vehicle's quite distinctive.'

'Right. Yes, I'll er, get onto it.'

'Quentin, the Club.'

'All under control, old boy. I'll have the red carpet laid out for you.'

'I think I'd prefer to go in unannounced.'

'Rather. I speak in metaphors, you understand?'

'Of course. Thanks for your help, Quentin.'

'No problem, old boy. I say, can I send you a ticket for *The Mousetrap*? Not many left. You know the play?'

'Yes, the detective did it.'

'Exactly, clever twist that. The only one no one suspects. You'd like a ticket, then?'

'No thanks. Knowing the ending would spoil it for me. Besides, I'm supposed to be dead. I think it's best if—'

'I'm playing the lead.'

'Quentin, no!'

'Oh well.' His voice sank to a Churchillian rumble. 'We shall fight them on the beaches. We shall fight them—'

Ian cut the call and raised his eyes to the heavens.

***

Ian allowed himself to indulge in the anachronistic colonialism of the Settlers Club on the High Commission's expense account. After an agreeable dinner of sailfish followed by chicken à la something-or-other and his second glass of wine he called Felix and Grace who agreed to meet him later that evening. He found a quiet corner in the lounge bar and settled into a leather armchair which could well have seated the likes of Lord Delamere or Karen Blixen in former times. He began examining the material in the box-file from Franco and soon found himself immersed in missionary life in northern Kenya as lived by one Huw Williams, some twenty years ago. Ian had travelled once to that region, his vehicle laden with extra fuel, extra water, extra food, extra vehicle spares, extra everything. And yet the people who lived there – and people did – had nothing. Was it faith that drew missionaries like Williams, and his wife with her nursing background, to share in drought, poverty and deprivation in the hope of saving souls – whatever that entailed? Or was it bloody-mindedness, delusion, or some lofty aspiration which eluded Ian?

Perhaps it was the desire to escape the rat-race and embrace the remoteness of endless barren hills, thorn scrub, sun-scorched rocks, wilderness, and mirage-permeated vistas where sun, sky and sand merged imperceptibly into a haze of heat and hell. A place of sun-scrubbed beauty, solitude, peace and hardship. What drove people like Williams and his wife to forsake the comfort of their Welsh homeland to help others in such places? And what drove people to kill them? For that matter, what drove people to forsake the laws of common man and plant bombs to shatter the lives of children like Charity?

Ian gazed in the direction of an elderly man in a soup-stained waistcoat who was slumped in an armchair in the far corner of the room. He'd probably been there for the last fifty years, being cleaned round and dusted periodically.

What had Huw Williams done or discovered to deserve death? And was it relevant to the present trouble?

He began flicking through the pages of a journal and re-read the entry he'd noticed earlier: *Some men brought a sick boy to the mission today. He was strapped to the back of a donkey and suffering from a terrible rash, fever and bleeding in his eyes; a disease that the men said he contracted in caves on the mountain. My wife had never seen the like before and was unable to save him. That night we committed his soul to the Lord.* Could it really be Marburg, as Colette suggested? If so, what were the implications? Marburg was a disease of monkeys – wasn't it? And people caught it from monkeys. Monkeys didn't go into caves and yet the assertion was the boy had become infected in some caves – presumably in Lokinang mountain.

He called for another glass of wine, and signed the chit with an illegible signature.

Why was Huw Williams killed? Even in that lawless part of the world, there had to be a reason. Or did there? Was it so lawless that life was insignificant, trivial, of no consequence? The one with the AK47 was king.

He found another entry: *Should these random jottings come to your attention, dear reader, I trust you will not think unkindly of this poor sinner. God moves in a mysterious way his wonders to perform.*

I am that "*dear reader*". Ian felt profoundly moved. I have been entrusted with this journal. Fate has chosen me.

Perhaps it was the wine talking.

Don't be so bloody melodramatic. He glanced round the sepia prints of past presidents of the Club displayed on the wall of the lounge bar. The men – and they were all men – regarded him sternly.

Bet Huw Williams never came here.

Why was he killed?

My guide says the mountain is a bad place and I should not go there. But a man of God does not shirk his calling.

Good for you.

The Lord has called me to investigate that poor boy's death and, with torch and bible in hand, I ventured into the caves of the mountain. I feared the world of Dante or of Hieronymus Bosch. Instead, I encountered a world of laboratories, of white coats, of science, albeit within the bowels of the earth.

Good grief.

I fear my presence was detected, if the ringing of alarm bells was anything to go by, but the Lord saw fit to lead me to safety and to blind my pursuers to my presence. I regret that in my hasty departure I mislaid my bible.

What the hell does all that add up to: some clandestine scientific or medical operation being conducted inside a mountain? Our intrepid missionary stumbles across it, loses his bible on the way out, gets tracked down and killed as a result. Seems a bit far-fetched. Stumbles across what?

Shouts of raucous laughter erupted and a group of men, waving beer bottles and competing in piggy-back races, cantered past in the corridor.

The elderly resident remained lifeless.

Ian leafed through the file: pictures of donkeys, children herding sheep and goats, bare-breasted local women, a herd of oryx, camels browsing acacia trees, more bare breasts, a corrugated iron hut that could have been a chapel, a vehicle stranded in a swollen river, yet more breasts – this time in close-up. Ian paused. Was this why Huw Williams was sent to the after-life: the locals thinking he was taking a prurient interest in their women? Was this why the "poor sinner" sought absolution from his "dear reader"?

He was grateful to be taken out of his ramblings by the arrival of Grace and Felix.

'This is a strange place.' Grace glanced round the portrait gallery of white colonials. 'I have not been here before.'

'Sorry to inflict this on you,' said Ian, 'but it's a place where I can keep a low profile.'

'That one okay?' asked Felix, indicating the only other occupant of the room.

'He's been stuffed.'

190

'They go in for that sort of thing here?'

'Club tradition – deceased members.'

As if stung by the remarks, the man sat up and looked around. '*Simba? Wapi?* – Lion? Where?' He slumped back to unconsciousness.

Ian reached for the bell-push. 'This is on the High Commission,' he said, when a steward appeared to take orders for drinks.

'In that case, I'll have orange juice,' said Grace.

'Coke,' said Felix, eyeing the other occupant warily.

The steward departed with their order.

'Sorry we're late,' said Grace. 'I was getting Charity settled.'

'How is she?'

'Fine.' She began pushing a beer mat aimlessly round the table. 'Nairobi can be a difficult place for people on their own, particularly girls. I wish I could get them all off the streets but it's not that simple.'

'What'll happen to her?'

Grace relinquished the beer mat. 'After you dropped us, Maria and I cleaned her up, dressed her arm and I found some old clothes of mine which had shrunk.' She smiled. 'Charity is very proud to be wearing a Commonwealth Games tracksuit.'

'Could be appropriate,' said Ian.

'She can certainly run. I'll try to get her into my training camp.'

'She's that good?'

'We'll see. In the meantime, I managed to find her a place in a hostel where she can have a bed and a meal. The same place where Amos stays.'

'Your other Olympic hopeful?'

'At least she'll be off the streets at night.'

They paused while the steward served drinks.

'Now, folks,' said Felix, 'bring me up to speed on the other things.'

'These are the papers from a missionary who was killed somewhere up near Lokinang around twenty years ago,' said Ian, indicating the box-file. 'Franco gave them to Sean and said we might learn something.'

'Did you?'

'Possibly. Firstly, it appears the missionary – name of Huw Williams – got to roaming the hills for material for the memoirs he planned to write, and stumbled on some sort of laboratory operation based inside a mountain.'

'Like hell he did?' said Felix. 'Why they want to work inside a mountain?'

'Presumably to keep the work secret.'

'He say which mountain?'

'No, but my guess would be Lokinang, the one the village takes its name from. Seems that alarms went off while he was inside but he escaped – he thinks undetected. He did, though, lose his bible which I suppose could have been used to track him down.' Ian took a sip of wine. 'The second point is pure speculation, but another reason for his death could be an unhealthy interest in local women.'

Grace frowned. 'What do you mean?'

'I know it's the custom for women there not to wear anything on their top half, but there do seem to be quite a few pictures of them. It's possible their menfolk got fed up.'

'And rubbed him out?' said Felix.

Ian shrugged.

'And the third point?'

'There's mention of a sick boy who'd been brought in for the missionary's wife to treat – seems she was a nurse. But he was too far gone and died. From the symptoms described, Colette reckons it could have been Marburg.'

'No kidding?' said Felix.

'Apparently the boy contracted it in the caves on this mountain. That's why the missionary went to investigate.' He pushed the box-file across to Felix. 'Anyway, see if your people can get any more out of it.'

'Sure.' Felix extracted the straw from his Coke and drank from the bottle. 'Tell me a bit more about your trip to the Park. Grace says she didn't learn anything new from that Walter guy but I gather friend Viktor was a bit more talkative.'

'It seems he enjoys playing the stupid Russian,' said Ian. 'He certainly fooled me. I'm just not sure whether I can believe what he says.'

'Walter seemed to think we could trust him,' said Grace.

'Can you trust Walter?'

'Probably.'

'We'll see,' said Ian. 'Anything on that name – Sayed Farouk?'

'We're still checking,' said Felix.

'So are my people,' added Grace.

'You reckon it was because of Farouk that friend Viktor came hotfooting it to Kenya?' said Felix.

'Seems so,' said Ian. 'I'm not sure, though, whether he was chasing a story or whether he was looking to avenge his wife's death and that of his friend Borishenkov.'

'Where's Viktor now?'

'He's staying in the Six-Eighty Hotel,' said Grace. 'I've had a watch put on the place.' She sniffed. 'I'm told he's interested in Nairobi's night-life.'

'I reckon we need to chat to our Russian friend again,' said Felix. 'Find out what really—' He broke off as a woman came staggering into room. 'She pissed?'

'Fiona!' Ian jumped up from his armchair and hurried over.

'Oh, Ian. Thank God.' She collapsed into his arms.

Chapter 35

'Sleep all right?' asked Kelly, looking up from her laptop as Colette came and joined her and Felix for a late breakfast next morning.

'I crashed out. What time was it when we finally went to bed?'

'I went at midnight,' said Felix. 'Left you guys still shootin' the breeze.'

'Well after two, I guess,' said Kelly. 'Help yourself, Colette. I'll go make some fresh coffee.'

'Any chance you could drop by the Embassy some time, Colette?' asked Felix.

'Yes, of course. Why?'

'Pick your brains about this and that.'

'Sure.'

Kelly came back into the room. 'There you go, Colette. Hope it's not too strong.'

'Thanks.'

'Excuse me, folks,' said Felix, rising from the table. 'I should get going. Be in touch, Colette.'

She waved. 'Bye, Felix. Thanks for lending me Kelly.'

'My pleasure.'

Kelly joined her at the table. 'I've been in touch with the hospital.'

'And?'

'The lab has confirmed Marburg.'

'And the patient?'

Kelly wiped a hand over tired eyes. 'I'm about to go see. You want to come?'

'Yes, all right.'

'You don't have to.'

'I'll come. I owe it to Sean.' Colette concentrated on her coffee. 'You don't have to look at me like that. It's complicated. Okay?'

'Whoa there.' Kelly held up her hands.

Colette took a deep breath and subconsciously fiddled with her bracelet. 'Sorry.'

'I don't need to know. But I do need to contact him.'

Colette stared down at the table. 'He's the one you spoke to when you first contacted me.'

'That was Helen's husband?'

'Yes, but I don't have his mobile number or his radio-contact details.'

'The Embassy found him for me. I'll call Felix.' She picked up her mobile from the table.

Colette waited and wondered.

'Felix will call me back if they can track him down.'

'And if they can't?'

'Figure it out on the way. Come on, we should go.'

Colette was grateful they travelled in their separate vehicles. Figure it out on the way. Trouble was, there was so much to figure out.

'Right. Same procedure as yesterday,' said Kelly, when they met again outside the hospital.

Different nurses were on duty today. As they relayed the latest news about the patient, Kelly's expression grew more resigned.

To Colette, the woman fighting for her life was no longer a patient. She was Sean's wife, Helen. That photo on his bookcase. With the distraction over the Samira, she'd only glimpsed it. Now she realised. The woman holding the baby was his wife. His wife, Helen. She and Sean looked so happy. Their daughter? Where was she now? A relative or friend – or perhaps the *ayah*. She was conscious of Kelly talking. 'Sorry?'

'What do you make of that?' Kelly had raised Helen's covers.

Colette grimaced. The nettle-like rash had become multiple ecchymotic haemorrhages – the classic terminal stages.

'I'll put her onto procoagulants to try and control the bleeding,' said Kelly. She replaced the bed covers and lifted one of Helen's eyelids. 'Sub-corneal haemorrhaging. Classic, I guess.'

Colette nodded. Suddenly she cared. If there was anything she could do to save Helen, she would. She owed it to Sean – and herself – to see Helen recover. To see her reunited with her daughter – and with Sean. The present was here and now. The future could take care of itself.

'Pete,' she blurted.

'Excuse me?' said Kelly.

Colette was conscious of babbling. 'Peter Barnsley recovered from probable Marburg. He must be hooching with antibodies. Could we use some of his serum to treat Helen? That is if—'

'Goddam it, yes!'

'I've had Pete's blood sent to Porton for confirmation but I doubt they've received it yet.'

'We can't wait.'

'I suppose if it wasn't Marburg, it couldn't do much harm.'

'I'll take that responsibility.' Kelly gestured to the bed. 'See that face – that beautiful face. Now look at it. Look at that body ravaged with haemorrhages. We're losing her, Colette. We're losing her.'

The lump in Colette's throat prevented her responding.

'Where can we find Pete?'

'Oh, God. I… I don't know. Somewhere in Nairobi. That's all I—'

'Right. We pull out all the stops.' She spoke briefly to the nurse about the new treatment then led Colette out.

Now, they were seated at a quiet table in the staff canteen, mugs of coffee ignored as Kelly fired questions.

'Did Pete give you the name of a hotel or contact in Nairobi?'

'No, but I think he said they would be working in the museum and the university library.'

'That's a start, then. They're close to each other. Who might they know in Nairobi?'

Colette shook her head. 'They know Sean and Jeff Carter, my boss. But he's also up at Tandala Ranch – or was a day or so ago. But I don't have contact details for them.'

'Not even your boss?'

'He does the contacting if he thinks it's necessary.'

'A control freak, then?'

'I'm used to it.'

Kelly drummed her fingers on the table. 'Who else?'

'Other people on Condor, I suppose.'

'Come on, Colette: names.'

'There's ole-Tomeno the Minister, Maria his PA… Then there's Ian.'

'Who's he?'

'My ex.'

'Part of the complication, then?'

'Kelly, that doesn't matter. What matters is—' She snatched her mobile from her pocket.

'Sinclair.'

'Ian, it's Colette.'

'Colette? Are you okay?'

'I'm fine, but listen—'

'Where are you?'

'Just listen! Do you know someone from the High Commission

196

called Helen, Helen Paterson?'

A pause. 'Yes. I know Helen. Why?'

'She's most dreadfully ill.'

'How ill? How do you know?'

'It's a long story but I came back to Nairobi in your Landy. A medic friend contacted me because of my experience with... with Marburg.'

'Helen has Marburg?'

'Yes.'

'Are you sure?'

'We've had laboratory confirmation.'

'Oh, my God. But how? Where from?'

'We don't know.'

'Can I see her?'

'No. She's in strict isolation and in very good hands.' She glanced up at Kelly. 'Ian, we need to contact someone called Pete Barnsley. He recovered from the disease and his serum could help Helen. He's somewhere in Nairobi but we don't know where and don't have contact details.'

'I can't help. I've never heard of him.'

'Sean knows him, though.'

'Does Sean know about Helen?'

'No. We've tried various numbers but we're getting no response.'

'Where are you?'

'At the Nairobi Hospital.'

'Right. I'll grab a taxi. Be about ten minutes. Keep your mobile switched on.'

Chapter 36

Dima woke. He was not aware of having crept into this refuge. Then he remembered. That man carried me. He gave me water. He saved my life. And he... He felt in his pocket. He gave me one thousand shillings. One thousand shillings payment for dead monkeys. He knelt in the dust, touched his forehead to the ground and blessed the man. The man who had special glasses for seeing birds.

Dima still had pain in head and muscles, but no longer agonising pounding pain. Better to be alive with pain than dead without pain. He hoped his daughter was... He shut out the thought and rose stiffly to his feet.

Apart from his restless eyes, he stood without moving waiting for his senses to fully waken. Waiting for the spirits of the bush to reassure him.

The birds started singing. A ground squirrel scrabbled at something in the leaves. A lizard scuttled across the sand. A scrub-robin hopped onto a nearby branch and peered at him.

He drew a deep breath. I am at peace.

The bird cocked its head and flew off.

Mungu has spared my life yet again, and he has sent me money. I could go to my family and rest, and the money will enable my wife to buy food for many days. He looked up at the sun. But that will not help avenge the death of my parents. I will go to the man who can help me. He set off at a loping run.

He travelled all that day subsisting off berries, grubs and honey. The pain he'd suffered from his beating was lessening and he was feeling stronger. He could not, though, become the hunter again until he had a new bow and fresh arrows. To fashion these he needed a knife or a *simi*. Then he would find that man, the man he had first seen all those years ago on that night when he himself became a man. The task would not be easy.

Next morning, he once again approached the familiar *manyatta*. 'Hodi – may I come in?'

'Dima, my friend,' cried a voice. Emunyu came hurrying out of one of the huts. 'You have returned? Tell me about your journey.' He led him to the log where they had previously sat and, with much tutting and head-shaking, listened to his story. 'That Lokinang is a bad place, a very bad place.'

'It is bad.' Dima stared at his feet. 'Now, tell me, how is your son?'

The man shouted. A boy looked up from a group of calves he was tending and came running over. He bowed his head, first to his father and then to Dima.

'How are you, Namunak?'

'I am well, sir. And see these places will also soon be well.' He turned to show the wounds on his back and chest.

Dima smiled. 'You are strong, Namunak.'

'I am strong.'

'Go now,' said Emunyu, and the boy ran off. 'You are a clever man, Dima, you know about medicines.'

'I know.'

'Now there is another person who needs your medicine.'

'Another one?'

Emunyu called to some women who were tending a pot of maize meal over a fire. One of them stood up and Dima recognised Namunak's mother. She went into a hut and led out a tall slender woman who had to lean on her for support. The woman's face was badly swollen and a cut extended from her jaw to her ear.

Dima took her arm and led her to the log-seat.

She sank down breathing heavily.

'I can feel you have much heat in your body,' he said.

The woman pointed to her face.

He peered closely. '*Aieeh*! Some person has sewn you.'

'A *mzungu* lady,' she mumbled through swollen lips.

'A *daktari* – a doctor?'

'I suppose.' The woman raised her chin towards the forested hills in the distance. 'She stays beyond that place.'

Dima frowned. Could it really be? Was this possible? 'Tell me, does this person stay with a *mzungu* man who lives in the bush and speaks like us Africans?'

'He is called Sean. He is the one.'

'I know that one. His woman also treated me for sickness.'

She tried to smile with her distorted face. 'They are good people.'

'They are good. Now, tell me about this thing.'

The woman held her head high and her hand strayed to her face. 'A man attacked me but I fought him. I fought him so hard and he cut me.' She paused and closed her eyes briefly. 'And that *mzungu* she was the one to sew me.'

He carefully felt the woman's face. The swelling was hot and liquid was seeping from the line of the cut. 'You have poison.'

She continued to stare ahead.

'Can you kill the poison?' asked Emunyu.

'I can kill it.' Dima turned to Namunak's mother. 'That medicine I made for your son, do you have some remaining?'

She nodded, departed to one of the huts and returned with a gourd.

He swirled the contents round and sniffed it. He turned to the seated woman. 'This medicine has a bad taste, but is very strong. It made that boy to get better and it will make you better.'

The woman took the gourd and grimaced as she drank.

'It is enough,' he said. 'You will drink more tonight.'

She handed the gourd back without a word.

'How are you called?' he asked.

'My name is Samira.'

'Tell me, why did you come to this place? Did not that *mzungu* lady say you should stay?'

'She said that, but then she said I must tell the police.' She briefly lapsed into silence. 'I have no papers and I fear the police.'

'I also fear the police,' he said.

'I can have some milk?' she asked.

Dima nodded to Namunak's mother.

They waited in silence, which was broken only by the monotonous calls of emerald-spotted wood-doves.

'I ran so far from that place,' said Samira, 'and then I could run no more and I lay down. I was thinking to die.'

Namunak's mother returned with a chipped mug.

Samira smiled her thanks. 'But some men found me and brought me to this place. Here is a good place.'

'Tell Dima why you left your home in Somalia,' said Emunyu.

Samira sipped the milk. 'In Somalia now is not good.' She looked up. 'You know Njia Mpya?'

Emunyu spat in the dust.

'I hear they are very bad,' said Dima.

Samira handed back the mug. 'The one who made this cut, I think he works with them.'

Dima and Emunyu exchanged glances.

'If ever I see that one,' said Samira, 'I will know him. He has lost an ear.'

Dima hissed. 'You have seen that one?'

She touched her suture line and nodded.

'That one killed my parents,' he said. '*Mungu* has sent me to kill him.'

'You must take care,' said Emunyu.

'I will be careful but I must do this thing. Can you help me, Emunyu?'

'Help you, how?'

'Can you lend me a *simi*?'

'No, my friend, I can *give* you a *simi*.' He unbuckled the weapon strapped to his waist.

Dima felt the blade. '*Aieeh*, this one is *kali sana* – very sharp. My thanks, Emunyu.' He strapped it to his own waist. 'Now I can make a very fine bow and arrows.' He turned to Samira. 'Do you know where I can find that man – the one who has lost an ear?'

Samira drew herself up. '*Bwana* Sean will know. I will take you to him.'

Chapter 37

Colette and Kelly remained in the hospital canteen, neither interested in their coffee nor in the other's attempts to make polite conversation.

Finally, Colette's mobile rang.

'Colette, Ian. Where can I find you?'

'I'm in the hospital canteen. Do you know it?'

'I'll find it. See you in a couple of minutes.'

She put her phone away. 'Here in a moment.'

'I'm interested to meet this Ian,' said Kelly.

Colette studied her colleague. 'Can I tell you something about him in confidence?'

Kelly smiled. 'You don't have to.'

'This is nothing about relationships. It's… it's different.'

'I'm intrigued.'

Colette wished she hadn't taken a sip of cold coffee. 'You remember that bomb blast last week?'

'I'm not likely to forget it. I was called in to help with some of the casualties.' Kelly grimaced. 'I particularly remember a girl – about ten or eleven. She was so brave and uncomplaining.'

'Did she survive?'

'Her injuries weren't life-threatening.'

Colette spoke in a flat voice. 'Ian was the target.'

'He's *that* Ian? But I thought the papers said—'

'I don't really know what's going on, but the Kenyan police told the press he was killed, presumably in the hope that those responsible will think they succeeded.'

'I see.'

Colette heard her name called and looked up to see an unshaven Ian wearing dark glasses and standing in the doorway with that policewoman, Grace. She waved them over.

'What news of Helen?' he asked.

'Not good, I'm afraid.'

'Ian told me it's Sean's wife,' said Grace.

'You know her?'

'I've met her, but— I understand it's Marburg.'

Kelly nodded.

202

'What are her chances?' asked Ian.

Kelly paused. 'If we can get recovered serum into her she may have a chance.'

'Who is it you need to find?' asked Grace.

Colette remembered the hostile questioning she'd received from Grace that evening at Tandala Ranch, and trod carefully. 'His name's Peter Barnsley. All I know is that he and a colleague, Peter Acheson, were planning to spend some time in the museum and the university library. They didn't say where they were staying.'

'Can you describe them?' Grace took out a notepad.

Colette felt her descriptions were very inadequate. How could they possibly find two *mzungus* who looked hardly different from any of the other hundreds – thousands even – of similar-looking backpackers, tourists and locals in Nairobi?

'Vehicle?' asked Grace, scribbling away.

'It's a Land Rover, quite an old one.'

'Short or long wheelbase?'

'Er, short, I think.'

'Colour?'

Colette wrinkled her brow. 'Faded greenish.'

'Registration number?'

'Sorry, I've no idea.'

'Right, that's a start.' Grace closed her notepad, looked up and smiled for the first time. 'It won't be easy but I may be able to call on some help.' She took out her mobile and moved out of earshot.

While they waited, Colette avoided Ian's eyes.

Grace returned. 'All arranged. We're meeting in fifteen minutes. Could you take me, Ian?'

'I, um… Can I make a suggestion? If Colette hangs onto my vehicle for the moment, she could take you. Would that be okay?'

'Sure, if she doesn't mind.'

'Fine by me,' said Colette.

'Thing is I need to see someone here at the hospital.'

'I'm afraid I can't allow that,' said Kelly.

'No, it's not Helen.' Ian gave an awkward smile. 'Someone else. Kelly, if you're free, I'd really appreciate your coming with me.'

***

As soon as they were in Ian's vehicle, Grace slipped out of her police role and became quite chatty as she directed Colette beyond the railway station to one of the poorer parts of the city.

203

'Who are we meeting?' asked Colette.

'You'll see. Pull in here.'

Colette turned into the forecourt of a rundown warehouse. A hostile-looking guard appeared then recognised Grace. He gave a grin of brown broken teeth and made some wisecrack. Grace responded with a tolerant smile.

Colette looked on with mild amusement which turned to puzzlement as two scruffy children appeared. They ran up to Grace's window and started enquiring after her health. Then the same to Colette. She smiled and responded in the same Swahili, becoming even more puzzled when the guard opened the rear door of the Land Rover and the two children scrambled in.

'This lady is Colette,' said Grace.

'*Jambo sana,*' chorused the children.

'*Jambo.*' Colette turned in her seat.

'This is part of my, shall we say, unofficial police force,' said Grace.

'Unofficial police force,' echoed the boy. 'My name is Amos.'

'Pleased to meet you, Amos,' said Colette.

'And I am called Charity,' said the girl.

'Pleased to meet you, Charity. You have injured yourself? How did that...?' She recalled her conversation with Kelly only a few minutes earlier.

'It was a bomb. My mama was killed.'

'I'm so sorry.' Mumbled response. Colette felt mortified.

'Let's go,' said Grace. 'I'll tell you the way.'

Colette was grateful of the driving to distract her from the raw emotion gnawing her insides.

'We need your help to find a *mzungu* man called Peter Barnsley,' Grace was saying.

'Pita Baanesli.' The boy struggled with the unfamiliar name.

Grace then repeated the details Colette had given her.

'He will probably be with another *mzungu* called Peter Acheson,' said Colette.

Amos repeated another difficult name. 'We will find those ones. Where do they stay?'

'Somewhere near the museum, we think,' said Grace.

'My mama used to work in a hotel near there,' said Charity. 'It is called Hotel Bulivadi.'

'Hotel Boulevard?'

'Yes, that one. I know all places near that hotel.'

'Let's go,' said Grace. 'Left at the traffic lights.'

As she forced the vehicle along the crowded streets, Colette began to feel their previously impossible task beginning to seem feasible.

'Stop!' cried Amos.

'Where? Why?' Colette was startled.

'Pull onto the pavement,' said Grace.

The vehicle had barely stopped before Amos leaped out and darted off between the cars and *matatus*.

'Now what?' said Colette.

'We wait,' said Grace, an amused expression on her face.

'What for?'

'I'm not sure.'

The owner of a shop came out to complain that Colette was blocking his pavement. Grace showed her police ID and the man returned to his shop grumbling.

The back door of the Land Rover was flung open and Amos scrambled back in with five other boys and a girl, all chattering and laughing.

'Now we can go,' called Amos.

'Reinforcements?' said Colette.

'Looks like it,' said Grace.

Colette glanced over her shoulder at the children, chattering away like excited puppies let out of their pen.

This is going to work. It bloody is.

She pulled back onto the road, wondering what Ian would make of the lingering smell of unwashed bodies in his vehicle.

After some fifteen minutes spent weaving through the backstreets of Nairobi, Colette drove onto a patch of waste ground beneath some eucalyptus trees. Grace then turned to the children and spoke in rapid Swahili – too fast for Colette to follow. They listened attentively, asking the occasional question. Finally, Amos cried: '*Tuende* – let's go.' The puppies tumbled out and scampered off in different directions.

'What's the plan?' asked Colette.

'Amos and Charity will wait over there.' Grace pointed with her chin to the two children playing among the fallen leaves of the largest eucalyptus. 'The others have gone to check out the local hotels and boarding houses.'

'How can they do that? They'd never be allowed in.'

'They talk to the guards – many of whom will know them – also to gardeners, sweepers, people like that. Those people often know as much about their guests as the staff on reception.'

'Then they report back to Amos?'

'And he reports back to me. The system works.' Grace smiled. 'Now, we go and learn something about volcanoes.'

'Volcanoes?'

'Yes, in the museum. Follow this road round and you'll see the car park.'

Ten minutes later, the two of them were peering into a glass case at a relief model of Kenya's Rift Valley, its lakes and surrounding areas.

'That's Lokinang,' said Grace. 'Tell me: why would someone build a laboratory inside it?'

'Inside?'

'Yes. Ian says the missionary's papers he got from Franco—'

'How is Franco?'

'He'll be fine.'

'Sorry, I interrupted you.'

'The missionary describes coming across a laboratory inside a mountain. Soon after; he was killed.'

'Where was this?'

'Probably Lokinang – it's the only mountain in the area.'

'That's where my boss, Jeff Carter, wanted me to go,' said Colette.

'You were telling us that night at Sean's place.'

'No, this was more recent.' Colette tried to clear her head. 'So much has happened it's hard to remember. While you lot went to Franco's place late the other night, I stayed with the Somali girl who'd been attacked. Jeff arrived next morning.'

'At Tandala?'

'Yes. With Richard Omar. The two of them were on their way to Lokinang.'

'And Jeff suggested you should go and work there?'

'Yes. He was quite insistent. Wanted me to go with them. Richard said ole-Tomeno also supported the idea.'

Their conversation was interrupted as a class of excited schoolchildren came and clustered round the case, and a teacher started explaining the features of rift valleys.

Grace drew Colette to a bench by the wall. 'Let me get this straight. Jeff Carter, Richard Omar and the Minister all want you to

206

go and work at Lokinang?'

Colette nodded.

'Why?'

'Jeff said because of my expertise in virus diseases of monkeys.'

'Like Marburg?'

'I know about Marburg, but I certainly don't work on it – far too dangerous. Jeff said there was a highly confidential laboratory in Lokinang doing advanced vaccine research. He didn't say anything about being inside a mountain.'

'What did you say?'

'I said I wasn't keen. Then I got the call about Helen. It was a good chance to postpone a decision on Lokinang.'

Grace got up from the bench and went to stare out of the window.

Geology wasn't Colette's thing, but she turned to the display on the wall and studied the write-up.

Lava caves and lava tubes are formed when a low viscosity lava flow develops a hard crust which thickens and forms a shell around the still-flowing lava stream. When the lava ceases flowing and the volcano cools it can be left honeycombed with tunnels and caves – some of which can be massive.

Well, well. Could be the perfect place: out of sight, stable environment. Problems with water and electricity, I imagine. She was about to call Grace over but she was on her mobile.

Grace beckoned. 'It's Amos. He thinks they've found them.'

'Great! Where?'

'They're in three different places – all at the same time.'

'Ah.'

'He says that all *mzungus* look the same, but he hopes one of the places is correct. Let's go.'

Colette almost had to run to keep up. 'What are we doing?'

'We'll collect Amos and Charity, then go and check the hotel registers.'

Chapter 38

Kelly took Ian to the second floor, opened a door and led the way in.

A nurse, who was tidying the bedside table, looked up. 'Good morning, doctor.'

'How's the patient?'

'She slept well, doctor.'

Fiona Melhuish was sitting up in bed, looking pale and with a turban-like bandage round her head. 'Ian, darling. To what do I owe this pleasure?'

'I came to see how you were.'

'I'm a bit woozy. No, not alcohol – something they've given me here.'

Ian forced a smile. 'This is Kelly, a friend of a friend. I brought her along in case you—'

'In case I what?'

'In case my expertise in infectious tropical diseases was needed,' said Kelly. 'Do you mind?' She indicated the patient's notes at the end of the bed.

Fiona waved a languid hand. 'Be my guest.'

Kelly scanned the notes. 'You seem to be doing fine.'

'I wonder.'

Kelly raised her eyebrows. 'Leastways, tell the nurse if you have any concerns. Now, if you'll excuse me.'

Fiona gave another languid wave.

'Thanks for coming, Kelly,' said Ian. 'Good luck with the other patient.'

'Sure.' Kelly nodded to the nurse and slipped out of the door.

Fiona regarded Ian thoughtfully. 'So, you beautiful man, how did you know I was here?'

'I brought you.'

'Oh.' She toyed with her covers. 'So you know about last night?'

'Some of it.'

'I see.'

'Has Quentin been to see you?'

'No!' Fiona's face clouded. 'Nurse, would you mind leaving us?'

When it was just the two of them, Fiona seemed to cast off the mantle of flippancy and replace it with a more thoughtful and perceptive demeanour which Ian found vaguely unsettling.

'I hope I didn't say anything too indiscreet,' she said.

'No, no.'

'I seem to remember some others with you last night.'

'Two professional colleagues.'

'And what did you think?'

'My first thought was that you'd had one too many.'

'Typical Fiona?'

'No, not at all.'

'You're not a very good liar, darling.'

He hurried on. 'Then I realised you'd been hit, mugged or something.'

'Yes, I suppose it was something like that.'

'Did you see who it was?'

'Yes. I saw him.' She lapsed into silence and took a sip of orange juice. 'It was Quentin.'

'Quentin! Why?'

'That's a bit more difficult to answer.'

'Where is he now?'

'On a plane out of the country if he's got any sense.'

'I hope so for his sake.'

'Ah, ever the man of action, Ian. Probably why I'm in love with you.' She smiled. 'You don't have to look so alarmed, it would never work.'

'I, I don't know what to say.'

'You don't have to say anything.'

'I will, though. Why Quentin? Did you have a row?'

After a few moments thought, she seemed to make up her mind. 'Let me tell you my life history.'

'Sure.' He glanced at his watch.

'Don't worry, darling, only the interesting bits.'

'Sorry. I'm not in any hurry.'

Fiona leaned back against the pillows and closed her eyes. 'When I was born my parents christened me Fiona: Fiona Amelia Gilmore to be precise.' She gave a faint smile. 'The acronym was the bane of my life at boarding school.'

'Did you say Gilmore? Your father?'

'You didn't know?'

'I'd no idea.'

'It's good to know there are still some secrets in the High

Commission.' She gave a wistful smile. 'The High Commissioner's daughter married to a senior member of staff; you can imagine the mutterings about nepotism and suchlike if it became known.'

'Does anyone else in the High Commission know?'

'Only Helen. Tell me, Ian, how is she?'

'You've heard about her, then?'

'Quentin told me. Collapsed at work or something?'

'Kelly – the doctor who was here – is looking after her. She's quite worried.'

Fiona's voice hardened. 'I hope *he* didn't have anything to do with it.'

'He?'

'Quentin, of course.'

'I can't see how.'

She sighed and sank back against the pillow. 'Nor can I.'

'You were telling me your life history.'

'Ah, yes. Fast forward a few years and Daddy was posted as Chargé d'Affaires at the High Commission in Islamabad. Soon after, Quentin arrived as Third Secretary. I was an undergraduate at Cambridge but used to go out to Pakistan during the summer vacations. Typical colonial, I suppose. It wasn't a very big ex-pat community and we had to make most of our own entertainment.' She paused. 'I'm not boring you?'

'Not in the least.'

'Quentin and I were both keen on amateur dramatics – we were good actors – and one summer we put on a production of Oscar Wilde's *The Importance of Being Ernest* in which he and I played the leads. It was pretty dreadful but it made a change from endless tennis and cocktail parties. Anyway, the audiences seemed to enjoy the productions.' She paused to regain her breath.

'Somehow, Quentin and I carried on the relationship afterwards and then drifted into marriage. Soon, it became a way of life and we became trapped in it.' She opened her eyes and studied him. 'Fortunately, there are no children.'

He avoided her gaze. 'This was, what, ten years ago?'

'More like twelve. Then things started hotting up politically.'

'How?'

'Pakistan backed the Taliban which was becoming established in Afghanistan and the Brits didn't approve.'

'How did that affect you?'

'It didn't affect *me* but Daddy became embroiled in all sorts of diplomatic activities. Quentin also had some involvement. Daddy then got his knighthood and Quentin got nothing, not even an OBE.'

'Was he bitter?'

'Very. Not only the Brits; the west in general – particularly the US. Always meddling in things they knew nothing about – so he said.'

'How did he show this bitterness?'

'He tried to hide it. Daddy never knew but things sometimes boiled over.'

'How?'

'He took it out on me.' She seemed to be confiding in the bedclothes.

'Fiona, I'm sorry.'

She shrugged. 'Anyway soon after, he and Daddy both got posted here. I don't know who wangled what but I think it was supposed to be a sort of pre-retirement post for Daddy, a nice peaceful posting after Pakistan.'

'Then someone blew up the American Embassy.'

'Yes.' She picked at the bed covers. 'I know it sounds terribly trivial in the context, but that's when things between Quentin and me started to unravel.'

'You don't have to tell me.'

'I have to tell someone.' Her voice sank to a whisper. 'I so wanted to confide in you that night you came and stayed with us, Ian, to hold you close and... ' She gave a sob and a tear trickled down her face.

'Here.' He offered his handkerchief.

'Quentin was furious, asking why I'd been so long taking you to your room. He thought we'd been...'

Ian found himself with his arm round her shoulder but she pushed him gently away. 'Darling Ian; you're very kind. But things have moved on.'

'I'm so sorry.'

'Don't be. I've often wondered if fate had led us down a different road how things might have turned out. But it was not to be.' She wiped away her tears and handed the handkerchief back. 'It was the bomb that blew up your vehicle.'

'What about it?'

'It was the final straw.'

'What do you mean?'

'I'm so glad you were all right, Ian.' She impatiently brushed away another tear. 'That's when things really changed. Quentin changed. Most of the time previously he was superficial and frivolous – I could live with that. And he could be very amusing. Afterwards, he became hurtful and vindictive. On the surface he remained the same, but...' A hand strayed to her bandage. Ian took the hand and kissed it then stood up and turned away to gaze out of the window.

'Do you hate me?'

Still with his back to her, he shook his head.

'After last night, I couldn't stay with... I managed to drag myself across the road to the Club. Quentin had told me you were staying there.'

Ian remained staring out of the window.

'I haven't told anyone else,' she said.

The mobile in his pocket vibrated.

'Sinclair.'

'Ian, Felix. Get your ass down here. We've gotten a match on Farouk.'

Chapter 39

Colette's optimism began to falter when they drew a blank at the first hotel. But as they drove into the car park of the second, Amos was convinced they'd be successful.

'See Land Rover like you said.' He pointed to a faded green vehicle. This one, though, had *Tembo Safaris* painted on the side.

'Sorry, Amos, it's not the one,' said Colette.

'Another there,' cried Charity.

'I'll go and talk to the guard,' said Grace.

It certainly looked like the Petes' vehicle – what Colette remembered of it – but then a woman climbed in and drove off with three small children.

Grace returned. 'The guard hasn't seen anyone who matches their descriptions. What's the third place, Amos?'

'It is called New Hibiscus Hotel.'

'Show us.'

Colette's hopes fell further as they drew into the hotel car park, which contained no Land Rovers of any description. Perhaps this was another dead end, or perhaps the Petes had gone to the university, or out to do some shopping, or to visit friends. Perhaps they'd simply gone – gone back to the bush. When she tried to rationalise the search, it seemed hopeless. Okay, Nairobi wasn't London but still… She pulled into a parking space, increasingly disillusioned about Grace's unofficial police force. Then she noticed a hotel guard remonstrating with a small boy at the entrance gate.

'That is Njoroge,' cried Amos.

'Come!' Grace jumped out of the vehicle. She and Amos ran over to the guard who pointed to a side gate that led to the hotel garden.

Grace waved Colette and Charity over. 'We could be in luck,' she said.

They passed through the gate and into an oasis of hibiscus, frangipani, poinsettia and manicured lawns.

'This is a very grand place,' whispered Charity.

Chairs and tables were set beneath cheerful umbrellas where guests sat sipping drinks, nibbling snacks and writing postcards. On the far side, a swimming pool of turquoise water was surrounded by sun loungers bearing cooked bodies. Smart waiters hurried back and forth with trays of more drinks and snacks, while pool attendants plied the bodies with bath robes, towels and bowls of nuts. The scent of sun cream mingled with frangipani and barbecued sausage.

Charity's grip tightened on Colette's hand.

A man wearing a suit hurried towards them but was stopped in his tracks by a booming voice.

'Dear lady.'

Guests, waiters, pool attendants, and even the suited man, turned towards Pete-A, waving a bottle of beer. He was dressed in floral swimming trunks and a T-shirt which bore the caption: *Save the mosquitoes* beneath a lurid picture of a gorging mosquito.

'Pete!' cried Colette, running across and embracing him. 'Thank God, we've found you.'

'Search and ye shall find.'

A number of guests applauded.

He released himself from the embrace and gave a gracious bow.

The suited man hesitated, but when confronted with Grace's ID, retreated indoors and peered at proceedings from the safety of the dining room.

'This is Charity,' said Colette, trying to introduce the girl hiding behind her back.

Pete peered round. 'Boo.'

'This is a bit different from our last meeting place, Pete.'

'This, dear lady, is close to the university and the museum.'

'That's handy, then.'

Pete drew himself up. 'Do not be deceived by the veneer of decadence.'

'Hi, Colette.' Pete-B sauntered up wearing faded shorts and a T-shirt with the caption: *Save the ticks.*

'Pete. Are you all right now?'

'Absolutely. Lovely person that Kelly bird.'

Pete-A clapped his hands and called out in an imperious voice: 'My guests wish to swim, please bring towels.'

The pool attendants looked uncertainly at the two ragged children. The suited man came out of the dining room, thought better of it and scurried back inside.

Charity ran to Grace, who was still holding Amos's hand.

'Grace Kiptagat?' said Pete-B, peering at the tall policewoman.

She smiled.

'Grace Kiptagat,' whispered the nearest guest to his partner.

'Grace Kiptagat, Grace Kiptagat.' The whisperings went round the garden like surf on shingle.

Pete-A took Grace's hand and put it to his lips.

She tried to hide her embarrassment as guests once more applauded.

'Hell, we must move it,' muttered Colette. 'Guys we need your help.'

'Anything, dear lady, anything,' cried Pete-A. 'Cold beers, a massage, ice creams for the *watoto*, a tour of the—'

'No.' She explained their mission.

'Bloody hell,' muttered Pete-B. 'Hang on, I'll go and grab some things.'

'How bad is Helen?' asked Pete-A.

Colette pulled a face. 'I just hope we're not too late.'

'Jesus.'

Grace finished a call on her mobile as Pete-B came running back.

A police siren could be heard in the distance.

'*Tuende* – let's go,' said Grace.

'I'm coming as well,' cried Pete-A, scooping Charity into his arms. Her initial alarm turned to delight when he trumpeted like an elephant and charged out of the garden gate. A police car – its blue light flashing – pulled up.

'I'll take Pete and call the hospital on the way,' shouted Grace. 'Colette, you bring the others.' She and Pete-B piled into the car, which sped off, blue light flashing, siren blaring.

Colette drew a deep breath when she got back into the Land Rover.

'You okay?' asked Pete-A.

'God, I so hope we're in time.' She turned in her seat. 'Well done, Amos. Well done, Charity.'

'Unofficial police force very good,' cried Amos.

'Very good indeed.'

'We can give Njoroge a ride?' said Amos. 'He is over there.'

'Sure.' She waited for the boy to scramble aboard.

'How are you?' he asked.

'Fine,' she replied and eased into the traffic.

'You were lucky to find us,' said Pete. 'This time tomorrow and we'd be gone.'

'I nearly panicked when I didn't see your Land Rover.'

'It's being serviced. We're picking it up first thing tomorrow. Then back to the luxury of corned beef and canvas.'

Colette caught her breath. 'Pete, you've not heard?'

'Heard what, dear lady?'

'Your camp, has… has been plundered and Kimani is… is dead.'

'Tell me it's not true,' he whispered.

'I wish I could. Pete, we so wanted to let you know but—'

'When was this?'

'Four or five days ago. Sean and I went there and—'

'What happened?'

'We're not sure, but it seems two men came – poachers, we think. They ransacked the place but most of your notes and specimens are okay. Sean's got them.'

'And Kimani?'

'He'd been shot.'

'Why the fuck did someone do that? He was such a good guy, never hurt anyone.' He sank his head in his hands.

'Pete, I'm so sorry.' Colette pulled up at some traffic lights. 'What will you do, now?' She put a hand on his shoulder.

He looked up, his face bleak. 'How the hell do I know? Sorry,' he said, a few moments later. 'Did Sean notify the police?'

'He called them but… Pete, there was nothing they could do. By the time they got there, nature would have—'

'Okay, you don't have to spell it out.' He gave a fierce sniff. 'I suppose it had to end one day.'

'What do you mean?'

'Running away from reality.'

'Pete, no! Science needs people like you and Pete.'

'You're too kind, dear lady. As to what we do now…' He gazed forlornly out of the windscreen. 'I suppose we'll go back – at least for a while. We need to make our peace with Kimani and contact his family. Then…' He shrugged. 'I need to discuss with Pete. Who knows? Academia, perhaps.'

'We can stop here?' cried a voice from the back.

'Are you sure, Amos?'

'Here is good.'

She pulled up behind a bus, which was disgorging its passengers. 'Thank you so much for your help.'

'That police lady helped me and now I help her,' said Charity.

'I know she'll want to speak to you again.'

Amos proudly waved his phone. 'Unofficial police force very

okay.' He opened the rear door and the three of them scrambled out and ran off.

'Very okay,' echoed Colette. A few minutes later she turned into the hospital car park.

'Come on, Pete. I'll see if I can buy you a beer.'

He shook his head. 'Not beer. Coffee would be good, though.'

Chapter 40

Dima and Samira left Emunyu's *manyatta* soon after sunrise. He carried a bag containing dried meat, cooked maize meal and her medicine. He was concerned she would still be weak but she seemed to be regaining strength as the morning progressed. Also, the heat was leaving her body and the swelling on her face was going down.

He chose the elephant highways; him in front and her following a few paces behind. The sun rose and the day became hotter but she still kept pace with him, never slowing, never complaining. They came to a sand river and Dima followed it until they reached a waterhole dug out by elephants. They drank the fresh water; then while she rested concealed by bushes, he began making a new bow and arrows using the resources of the bush. He'd just finished stringing his new bow, when he detected something. Sound? Scent? He couldn't be sure.

He slipped back to Samira and they lay concealed watching the waterhole and the surrounding area.

'Is it animals?' she whispered.

'People, I think.'

A face appeared within some bushes on the far bank. Almost before he could register, it disappeared.

He withdrew the *simi* from its sheath.

The face reappeared. Then another. Watching and waiting.

A sharp *ah-ooh* cry. Some baboons scampered across the hard sand of the riverbed down to the waterhole.

Still the two watchers on the far bank. Now a third.

The baboons clustered round the waterhole, jostling and squabbling as they drank.

The wind changed direction.

The baboons looked up in alarm.

A shot rang out.

A baboon screamed.

The troop screeched and fled to the nearest trees.

The wounded one tried to drag itself after them.

Another shot. A spurt of sand.

The baboon ceased crying but continued to twitch.

A watcher came into the open. He wore a grubby T-shirt and

ragged camouflage trousers. On his feet, army boots without laces. A boy – perhaps fifteen, sixteen – a thin-faced boy. But a thin-faced boy with one of those special guns called Kalashnikov.

The boy sauntered up to the still-twitching baboon, rolled it over with his boot and fired a volley of shots, a look of glee on his face. The baboon's body jerked as the bullets tore into it. The boy punched the air, pointed his gun at the sky and fired more shots.

Samira was shaking. Dima laid a hand on her shoulder and whispered. 'We must be very still.'

'That one, that… He is… is Somali like me.'

An older, boy appeared. He was similarly dressed and also carried a gun. Two belts of bullets were draped round his neck. He came up to the still-laughing boy, swung his gun and smashed the butt into the boy's face.

The boy crumpled to the ground and lay still.

The older boy poked him with his boot then signalled to the bank where three more boys appeared, pushing ahead of them a man carrying two buckets.

Samira tensed beside Dima and a whimper escaped from her lips.

He shushed her.

'That one,' she whispered, through her tears. 'He is my friend Khalif.'

The older boy pointed at the waterhole ordering Khalif to fill the buckets.

The rumbling noise of a lorry. They must be closer to the big road than Dima realised.

The older boy urged Khalif to hurry. Having used one bucket to fill the first, Khalif tried to fill the second by scooping water with his hands. The boys stood watching and mocking his efforts.

As Khalif struggled out of the soft sand, he slipped. One of the buckets fell over. The older boy shouted. The others laughed.

Khalif bent once again to his task. This time he took more care climbing out.

The older boy gave an order and they pushed Khalif, struggling with the weight of the two buckets, ahead of them.

They ignored the boy lying on the sand and passed close by where Dima and Samira lay hidden. They crossed the sand river and disappeared into the bush. Then one of the boys came running back. He took his unconscious companion by a foot, picked up his gun, and dragged him across the sand. One of his boots fell off.

Dima and Samira waited.

A few minutes later, another movement on the opposite bank: the blunt muzzle of a hyena testing the air. Then several, followed by a chilling *ooh wuup* cry.

'We must move,' whispered Dima. 'The hyenas are coming for the baboon. Soon it will not be safe.' He led Samira deeper into the bush until they came to a huge baobab tree with its greatly swollen trunk. Honey hunters had hammered wooden pegs into the soft bark. Using these, Dima climbed up to investigate. Scraps of honey comb and the absence of bees showed the hunters had gathered their harvest.

He scrambled down. 'It is a good place to hide. The bees have gone and no animals can reach you.'

'What will *you* do?' Fear crept into her eyes.

'I have to go and find those people.'

Another *ooh wuup*.

Samira whimpered.

'Hurry,' he urged.

She reached tentatively for the pegs and began to climb, her ragged breathing betraying her fear.

He followed close behind guiding her feet onto the pegs.

One came loose. She cried out.

He grabbed her foot and held it against the tree. 'Go slowly, slowly.'

She reached a safe place among the branches and slumped down.

'Here is a good place,' he said.

'The ground is very far.'

'You must not look. Here you are safe.'

She tried to make herself comfortable.

'I will be quick.' He scrambled down the trunk without waiting for a reply.

Collecting his things from the base of the tree, he set off. It was good to be free again and not worry about another person. He avoided the hyenas squabbling over the luckless baboon, crossed the sand river and made his way to the track where the boy had been dragged through the bush.

The rumble of another lorry reminded him of the proximity of the road. He hid while the lorry lumbered past, its tyres pounding on the wind-blown corrugations of impacted sand. When it was out of sight, Dima stepped onto the deserted road and headed towards a lone building in the distance: a *duka* – a store made of sun-dried mud bricks, with rough holes for windows and a corrugated iron roof. A place he recognised. He had once brought some skins here and the owner had given him good money. Perhaps this man could help him now.

A vehicle was parked beside the building – an open Land Rover with its cab removed. A man was loading things into the back.

'You!' A boy holding a gun stepped out of the bush.

'*Jambo*,' called Dima, trying to appear relaxed.

'Where are you going?'

'Home.' He indicated the vague direction ahead.

The boy seemed uneasy but waved him on.

The man loading the Land Rover retreated inside the building but emerged a few minutes later carrying a watering can. Khalif! A boy with a gun followed. The two went in among some trees where Dima could just make out a metal drum propped up on rocks. Khalif opened a tap on the drum and filled the watering can; then, under the watchful eye of his guard, filled the vehicle with petrol.

Two more boys appeared, also holding guns. 'What do you want?' said one, in a strong Somali accent.

'I want to buy maize meal,' said Duma.

The older one, the leader at the sand river, said: 'The store is closed.'

A mean-looking man, wearing a baseball cap, emerged from the dark interior of the building. 'Who are you?'

'*Jambo*. How are you?'

The man ignored his question and joined the boys watching Dima as he tried to maintain his relaxed walk.

The man shouted at Khalif who scurried into the building. The man turned back and Dima's knees nearly gave way when the side of the man's head was revealed.

'What are you doing here?' called One-Ear.

'I came to buy food.' Dima tried to keep the terror out of his voice. 'But the *duka* is closed. So now I go to my home.'

'You just go.'

'*Kwa heri* – to happiness.'

'To happiness.' One-Ear snatched a gun from one of the boys and fired into the ground round Dima's feet.

The sharp sand stung his legs. He fled, shouts of laughter ringing in his ears.

Chapter 41

Colette and Pete-A had long exhausted small talk by the time Kelly and Pete-B found them in the hospital canteen.

'Come,' said Kelly.

The Petes exchanged glances but no one spoke as they followed her along corridors and down several staircases. Finally, she reached a door with a notice which read: *Strictly no admittance*. She punched in a key-code, opened the door and turned on a low-intensity light.

One of the Petes – Colette didn't notice which – squeezed her hand.

Hell, he's more nervous than me.

Kelly ushered them inside and indicated the window ahead. Colette knew what to expect peering into the aquarium, but the Petes were clearly taken aback. Pete-A caught his breath, grabbed a chair and sat down.

'God, she's beautiful,' whispered Pete-B.

Helen lay in the same position as when Colette had last seen her. Most of her features were still covered by a facemask. Her blonde hair still tumbled over the pillow and what little Colette could see of her skin was now covered in angry red and purple blotches.

'Jesus,' whispered Pete-A. 'Is she, is she…?'

'Too early to say,' said Kelly. 'She's no worse than when Colette and I saw her this morning. We've started the infusion of Pete's serum but now we have to watch for signs of anaphylaxis – reaction to the foreign proteins.'

One of the two nurses tending the patient looked up and waved at the window. Colette waved back. She doubted she could be seen. The nurses seemed no more flustered than if they'd been dealing with a minor accident – their calm demeanour a sharp contrast to the tension of those looking in.

Despite physical separation, Colette was down there with the nurses, with Helen, willing her to get better. She twisted her good-luck bracelet.

Kelly touched her arm. 'Let's go.' She ushered them out of the cramped room and led them back to her office. 'Can I get you folks anything?'

The slumped figures shook their heads.

'That could have been me,' muttered Pete-B. 'That could so easily have been me stretched out there with tubes and bits going in and out of my body.' He looked up. 'Except it would probably have been the bush and there wouldn't have been any tubes.'

'I guess you got lucky,' said Kelly.

He stared morosely at the floor. 'Anything else I can do?'

'Pray.'

Colette was conscious of a ticking clock on the wall behind her.

Kelly studied the three of them then seemed to make up her mind. 'Listen, guys, I'll give it you straight. If Helen survives the night, she'll live.'

'I won't bloody sleep.' Pete-B rose to his feet and stuck out his hand. 'Thanks, doc. Come on, Pete.'

'Can I give you a lift?' asked Colette, as the two of them stumbled out of the door.

'We'll get a taxi,' he called over his shoulder.

'How can we contact you?' asked Colette, running after them.

'The hotel.'

'Pete, are you sure you're okay?'

He continued striding down the corridor.

She stared after them.

They were about to turn the corner when Pete-A came hurrying back. He gave Colette an impulsive hug. 'Thanks, thanks for every—' He broke free and ran after his colleague.

'Take care, guys.' She took a deep breath and went back to Kelly. 'They're taking it quite badly.'

Kelly gave a slight smile. 'The hard men from the bush; they're always the soft ones.'

'Sean! Has anyone made contact?'

'Not as far as I know. Let me call Felix.'

Colette stared at the framed certificate testifying to Kelly's graduation from Harvard Medical School.

Kelly replaced the phone. 'Sean's flying down today.' She looked up at the clock above Colette's head. 'Probably be dark by the time he arrives.'

'Oh.'

'One other thing.'

'What?'

'You're in no fit state to be on your own. Felix is dropping by shortly. He'll take you back to our place and you can stay there until this thing sorts itself out.'

'Thanks, Kelly.' Colette drew random patterns on the desk. 'What *are* Helen's chances?'

'In a word: good.'

'Good? But you told the Petes…'

'I know what I told them. We're by no means out of the wood but I'm cautiously optimistic.'

'You're not just saying that?'

'Bullshitting isn't my style. Don't say anything to the Petes, though, in case there's a relapse. I wouldn't want—'

There was a knock on the door.

'Come in.'

A nurse entered carrying a pot-plant. She might have been the one who waved from the aquarium.

'Sorry to trouble you, doctor, but someone left this for the patient.'

'How kind.'

'What shall I do with it?'

'I'll look after it. Just put it on the desk. Anything to report?'

'Nothing new, doctor.'

'You will let me know – day or night.'

'Yes, doctor.' The nurse placed the plant on the desk and left the room.

'What a beautiful thing,' said Kelly, turning it round.

'Does it say who it's from?' asked Colette.

Kelly picked up a card. 'All it says is: *To Helen Paterson, who liked orchids.* No name or signature. I guess it'll be from the Petes.'

'Or Ian.'

The phone rang. 'Dr Ryder, speaking.'

Colette watched in alarm as Kelly's expression crumpled. 'Helen?'

Kelly replaced the receiver and slowly shook her head. 'No. This one's male.'

Chapter 42

It was almost dark by the time Ian reached the American Embassy. Most of the staff had gone home, but judging from the papers strewn across Felix's desk, it would be some time before he would get away. He gestured Ian to a seat. 'How's it going?'

'Not sure.'

'Coffee?'

'No thanks.'

Felix yawned. 'Not keeping you up, I hope?'

Ian scowled.

Felix didn't bother to smile. 'Ian, that Russian reporter—'

'Viktor.'

'Remind me. What did he tell you about this Sayed Farouk guy.'

'Your people have come up with the goods, then?'

'Just tell me, and I'll say if it squares.'

Ian extracted a notepad from the folder he had brought and flicked over some pages.

'That Sandhurst?'

'Is what Sandhurst?'

'This note-taking and stuff. That the training?'

'Bugger off, Felix. Viktor had so much to tell me that if I hadn't written it down, I'd have forgotten half of it.' He sniffed. 'There happens to be quite a lot going on at the moment, in case you hadn't noticed.'

'Sure, sure.' Felix waved a placatory hand. 'Go ahead.'

'Okay, but no wisecracks.'

'Shoot.' Felix leaned back in his chair, swung his feet onto the desk and closed his eyes.

'Firstly, I think we have to treat what Viktor says with a degree of scepticism. We're going back quite a few years, and because of his personal involvement he may be biased. Also, his style of operation is a bit off the wall.'

'Also, we don't know whose side he's on.' Felix still had his eyes closed.

'In view of what happened to his wife, I think we can be fairly certain.'

Felix grunted.

'Anyway, as you know, Viktor's wife worked at this lab in Stepnogorsk in Kazakhstan, and according to him, died of Marburg disease – something the lab was working on as part of Russia's Biopreparat weapons programme. When Olga died—'

'That the wife?'

'Yes. Viktor claims that this Sayed Farouk killed her – at least, was responsible for her death. Seems Farouk worked as a visiting scientist in the same lab and didn't get on with Olga. All we have from official reports, though, is that she died in a laboratory accident.'

'Could be true.'

'An accident, you mean?'

'Go on.'

'Whatever the background to Olga's death, it seems the boss there, Borishenkov, felt some sort of conscience and when the opportunity came for him to go to the States – something connected to *glasnost* talks – he defected and became an adviser to—'

'Adviser?'

'That's what Viktor said. According to him Borishenkov became an adviser to the Fort Detrick people. He then invited Viktor to join him. With his wife dead and little to keep him in Russia, friend Viktor ups sticks and heads for the great US of A – apparently attracted by the food.'

Felix opened one eye and closed it again.

'Worked as a reporter for Izvestia. Next thing Viktor knows is that Farouk shows up and becomes Borishenkov's bosom pal because they both like orchids.'

'No kidding?'

'And because Farouk speaks fluent English – his mother was American, seemingly – he gets welcomed by Fort Detrick and your people start pumping him about Stepnogorsk and the Biopreparat programme. Viktor, meanwhile, wasn't best pleased to be rubbing shoulders with Farouk, the guy who killed his wife.'

'And Boris? What's Viktor say happened to him?'

'He says the Russians got pissed off with Borishenkov for spilling the beans and—'

'— slipped Marburg virus into his Big Mac?'

'I guess so, although Viktor muttered something about vitamin pills.'

'That it?'

'Pretty much, except for the orchid thing. According to Viktor,

Farouk starts calling himself Mlala and showering orchids on the deceased Borishenkov and—' Ian drew a breath. '— and the deceased Colonel Sinclair. And that about wraps it up.'

Felix opened his eyes and swung his legs off the desk. 'That ties in with what I've learned, except for a few details.'

'Which are?'

'Boris worked for KGB, or whatever they call themselves these days.'

'But... I...'

'Like I said, we also don't know whose side Viktor's on. So I guess we don't know whether he was spinning you a line or whether he believes his version to be true. That's possible. What we do know, though, is that Boris was recruited by the KGB soon after he defected to the States.' Felix chuckled. 'I don't know what the Russians made of all the garbage, Fort Detrick fed him.'

'If Borishenkov worked for the KGB, or whoever, why did they have him killed?'

'Dunno. Perhaps they twigged he was being used by Fort Detrick – leastways by CIA. Also, I guess he probably gave away a few secrets about the Russian bio-weapons programme and they weren't best pleased.'

'Perhaps what Borishenkov fed Fort Detrick, was also garbage.'

'Who knows? Some may have been, but apparently some goodies were in there.' Felix shuffled papers on his desk. 'Right, let's move on. You wanna hear about Farouk?'

'I thought that was why you got me here.'

'Sure.' Felix selected a sheet from among the papers. 'CIA was quite cagey 'bout him. In the end I had to get the Ambassador to lean on the Secretary of State before they would cough up.'

'Which was?'

'This picture for starters.' Felix held up an enlarged black-and-white passport-type photograph showing a bearded man of uncertain ethnicity who was probably in his thirties or early forties. 'D'ya know him?'

Ian peered at the photo. 'No.'

'Taken a few years back so I guess he'll have changed a bit.'

'Still, no. What's his background?'

'Like Viktor says, Farouk has, or had – she's dead now – an American mother, white Caucasian. Father was Egyptian and Dean of Medicine at the Kasr Al Ainy School of Medicine in Cairo. You

227

heard of it?'

'Nope.'

'Nor me. Anyway, dad's also dead. Seems Junior was a bright guy and graduated top student from the school. I guess having your old man as dean was kinda handy.'

'Don't be cynical, Felix.'

'No, well. Next we know is that Farouk rocks up with a Fulbright scholarship to Johns Hopkins University in Baltimore to do research: something about viruses in monkeys. You following this, Ian?'

'I'm all ears.'

'You what?'

'Doesn't matter.'

'Okay. Put that lot on the back-burner a moment.' Felix retrieved another sheet from the file. 'Next bit is from a *fatwa*... What's that?'

'Isn't it some sort of pronouncement on Islamic doctrine?'

'That fits. This one says: *The United States has been occupying the lands of Islam in the holiest of places – the Arabian peninsula – plundering its riches, dictating to its rulers, humiliating its people, terrorising its neighbours, and turning its bases on the peninsula into a spearhead through which to fight the Muslim peoples. Brothers of Islam, rise up. Nothing is more sacred than belief, except repulsing an enemy who is attacking religion and life.* It's signed by our old buddy Osama bin Laden.'

'Hmm. So what's the significance?'

'Seems our people started getting jittery – that Brothers-of-Islam bit – and anyone in the States with Arab connections got put on the CIA radar. And in Farouk's case recruited – American mother obviously helped.'

'Farouk is CIA?'

'Right. Code name Prairie Dog'

Ian slumped in his chair. 'I've heard it all now.'

'Not quite. CIA's a bit cagey on the details, but it seems when Comrade Boris rocks up at some scientific conference on monkey diseases held in Maryland, Farouk gets wheeled in to chat to him – I guess they talked the same language.'

'This was before Borishenkov defected?'

'Coupla years or so. Let's see.' Felix scanned through the document. 'Next thing reported is that Farouk "defected" – that bit's in inverted commas – to go and work at Stepnogorsk.'

'Having been recruited – also in inverted commas, I suppose – by Borishenkov and his mates?'

'Probably. And when Boris does finally come to the States, friend Farouk is called back by CIA to keep an eye on him.'

'And Farouk is now in Kenya?'

'I guess so, together with our bearded friend Malik.'

'Formerly Qasim Chaudhry, head of the bio-weapons programme at Stepnogorsk?'

'Correct.' Felix began prowling round the office. 'Seems like Kenya's becoming a bit of a holiday camp for people from Stepnogorsk. Did Viktor mention Malik?'

Ian shook his head.

'My people reckon he was also recruited by friend Boris around the time of the Maryland conference and invited to run the lab where Viktor's wife worked.'

'Could Farouk and Malik be in cahoots?'

'Dunno. Leastways, the folks at HQ in Langley think Farouk's on our side.' Felix scooped the folder off his desk. 'Let's go get a beer.'

He led Ian to the elevator outside his office. 'Great view from the top.' He pressed a button and the doors closed with a hiss. The elevator whizzed upwards and stopped. The doors whispered open and Felix led Ian into an open-air bistro-like setting on the roof of the Embassy. A number of tables and chairs were set out under umbrellas.

'Gets kinda hot up here in the daytime.' Felix chose a secluded table at one side. 'Like I said: great view.'

Ian gazed round the panoramic view of the city, Nairobi Park, and in the distance, the airport.

'Major?' A steward came to take their order.

'Coupla Buds'd be good.'

'Yes, sir. Some chips?'

'Sure,' said Felix. 'Sorry, Ian; only American beers.'

'Fine.' Ian sat back in his chair and watched the lights of a small plane coming in to land at Wilson Airport on the far side of the Game Park.

The steward returned with the beers and a bowl of crisps. Felix signed the chit then raised his glass: 'Cheers.'

'Cheers.' Ian regarded Felix over the rim of his glass. 'Tell me something. Our Farouk friend.'

'What about him?'

'He killed Viktor's wife, Olga. Right?'

'Wrong. That's may be what Viktor believes. CIA, though, reckon it was more likely an accident; faulty containment, virus escaping – something like that. Seems the Russians didn't mind cutting a few corners and accepted lab accidents as a price worth paying in their bio-weapons programme.'

'So who killed Borishenkov?'

'His Russian buddies. I guess Viktor was right on that one. Like we said: spiked his vitamin pills.'

Ian checked. 'Did you say vitamin pills?'

'Hell, I dunno. Vitamin pills, Big Mac, vodka, whatever.'

Ian slumped back in his chair. 'Felix, tell me I'm stupid.'

'You're stupid. So what's new?'

'Someone sent *me* some vitamin pills?'

Felix sat up. 'Like hell they did. When?'

'Around the time of the bombing. Sort of belt and braces, I imagine. If the bomb didn't finish me off, the pills would. Or perhaps this person knew I'd survived the bomb attack. Only problem was a colleague picked them up and...' Ian took a hasty sip of beer.

'Holy cow. Who?'

'Her name's Helen Paterson. She's the High Commissioner's PA. She agreed to keep an eye on my mail while I went away – that night you pulled me out of Melhuish's place. She... God, I'll never forgive myself if she, if she—'

'What happened?'

'She's in isolation at Nairobi hospital. Confirmed Marburg.'

'Jesus Christ.'

'Wait! The doctor who's treating her is American – Kelly something or other. You may know her.'

Felix chuckled. 'Sure, I know Kelly. She's my wife.'

'Your wife! So you know about Helen?'

'Nope. We have a professional truce.'

'Meaning?'

'I don't talk security and she don't talk medicine. Means we can get on with life back home.'

They lapsed into silence as a plane, bound for Nairobi airport, thundered overhead. Ian watched its lights edge towards the runway.

'What happened to the pills you reckon infected this Helen person?' asked Felix.

'Don't know. My colleague, Quentin—'

'That ass-hole.'

Ian gave a slight smile. 'He had my office cleared out. The bottle

230

could be among that stuff. I'll check.'

'Excuse me, major.' A marine arrived with a bemused Colette.

'Hi, Ian,' she said, giving a slight wave. 'How are—'

He scrambled to his feet. 'How's Helen?'

'Kelly's cautiously optimistic – her words, not mine.'

'Thank God.'

'Thanks for coming by, Colette,' said Felix. 'Grab a seat. Beer?'

'Please.'

Felix signalled to a steward then rummaged once more through his papers. 'I just need some help on folks researching monkey viruses.'

'What sort of help?'

'This guy?' He passed her the photo. 'You know him?'

She nodded. 'He's shaved his beard off now, though.'

Felix glanced sharply at her.

'It's Jeff. Jeff Carter, my boss.'

Chapter 43

Dima had almost recovered from his ordeal by the time he reached the baobab tree. He scrambled up and found Samira clinging terrified to one of the tree's great branches.

'I heard those shots and I feared,' she whimpered.

'We must go,' he said. 'We go to find *Bwana* Sean. Come. I will guide you.'

'I can't. The ground is far.'

'Just come.'

She struggled to turn in the awkward space then lowered a foot. He grasped it and placed it on the first peg. Slowly, gradually, they crept down the tree. He ignored her whimpers and protestations.

'Now we must eat.' He retrieved his bag from a crevice in the trunk. They sat in the gathering darkness and ate the remains of his sparse rations.

He told her about his encounter at the *duka*. 'That man with one ear; he is in charge.'

'That one!' Her hand strayed to her face.

'I think those people have stolen the food from the *duka* to take in the car.'

'And Khalif?'

'He is not one of them. They make him work for them.'

'We must save him.'

'Save him? How?'

'You are a clever man, Dima, you will think of a way.'

'Those people have many guns. They will kill me.'

'No. I can help you.'

'How?'

'I… I don't know.'

'It is not possible.'

'It *is* possible.'

He sighed. 'We will save him.'

But how?

He had not had time to prepare that poison for his arrows. His bow was untested and he had made only two arrows. Otherwise, all he had was his *simi* and his fire sticks.

An owl hooted in the branches above their heads.

Samira started. 'I fear this place.'

'Stay here.' Without waiting for a reply, he slipped off into the dark.

With so many elephants in the area, it didn't take him long to find what he was looking for. He ran back to Samira. 'Now we go.'

She looked with bewilderment at the ball of elephant dung but made no comment.

He led the way back to the waterhole and made Samira drink the remaining medicine. Then he rinsed out the gourd and filled it with fresh water. 'Are you ready?'

She nodded.

'*Tuende* – let's go.' Without looking round, he set off.

With the advancing night, the warm air rose and cooler air blew down off the neighbouring mountains. So it was every night. The impatient wind roused the spirits of the trees whose whisperings became mutterings, became hissings, became squalls of anger. He thanked the tree spirits for masking the sounds he and Samira made.

Another baobab tree grew beside the deserted road. They stopped in the shadow of its trunk and peered ahead. There was no moon but the brilliance of the stars gave a faint radiance to the night. He pointed out the silhouette of the lonely *duka* and the faint square of light – probably from a candle – coming from one of its windows.

'That is the place. Wait here.'

He'd gone no more than a twenty paces when he realised she was still with him.

'I said, wait!'

'No. You cannot speak the language of those people. You need me to come.'

He drew a deep breath. '*Tuende.*'

They reached the clump of trees beside the *duka* and stopped, watched, listened. The wind clattered the branches overhead. Voices came from inside the building. The Land Rover was parked nearby. A glint of starlight reflected off the metal fuel drum.

She pointed. 'That Land Rover; that is Franco's,' she whispered.

'I don't know that one.'

'He is the one I work for.'

He made no comment. Guards. Have they put out guards? No sign. Guards, though, keep still and can hide. Also guards can sleep, but they usually snore and sometimes cough.

No movement, no snoring, no coughing.

233

He turned to Samira. 'This time, you wait.'

He was gone. A phantom of the night. A wraith through the trees. A whisper round the building.

She started as he reappeared by her side. He took her hand. Led her towards the faint square of light.

They crouched in the shadow of the dried-mud wall beneath the window. Mostly it was mumbled voices from inside. The occasional shout, as in an argument, and once or twice laughter.

He dare not risk looking in. He recognised One-Ear's voice. So near – again.

Samira touched Dima's arm and they returned to the shelter of the trees.

'I think those ones will leave tonight,' she whispered. 'They said a man came past this place earlier. One said he was a honey hunter. Another said we should have killed him.'

'I was the one.'

'We cannot trust that one, they said. Perhaps he will tell the police we killed the owner of this place.'

'Killed him?'

'The man in charge says they have to go to a place called Lokinang. Do you know it?'

'I know. It is my home. And Khalif?'

'I am fearing for him. But I think he is the only one who knows how to drive Franco's car.'

'That is good. That is very good. It makes my plan easier. Now you must go.'

'Go? Go where?'

'To that big tree beside the road. Go and wait there.'

'I cannot go. I am fearing so much.'

'You must go. It will not be safe here.'

'I will stay with you.' She was almost crying. 'I will help you.'

'You cannot help me. It will be very dangerous.'

'I do not fear danger.'

He sighed. 'You are very brave, but I have to work alone. Come. Leave everything.' He dumped his things on the ground, took her arm and hurried her out of the trees. The time for caution had passed. Still holding her arm, he ran down the middle of the road through the blusterous night.

Apart from the occasional gasp when she stumbled, she kept running without complaining.

Some lights appeared ahead, bouncing up and down. A vehicle approached grinding its way over the unrelenting corrugations in the road.

'Hurry!'

The baobab tree came into view, illuminated by the bouncing lights.

They reached the tree. She collapsed into its shadow.

The ponderous lorry drew alongside and trundled past.

'Wait!' he cried. 'I will come back for you.' He ran after the lorry, grabbed the tailgate and clung on, his feet scrabbling for a foothold on the cradle holding the spare wheel. He was past caring whether she obeyed his instructions.

The lorry continued its laboured progress without pausing at the *duka*.

Dima waited until it was well beyond then dropped off. He landed heavily and for a moment lay winded. Time was slipping by. He sat up and grimaced. Shutting out pain, doubt and fear, he ran back to the trees for his things.

Wind whistled through the darkness. Branches overhead clattered against each other. The light from the window of the *duka* flickered.

Still the voices from inside.

He ran to the fuel drum and turned the tap. The sound of running liquid and the sharp smell of petrol. He grabbed his fire sticks, placed them against the ball of dried elephant dung. Checked.

Someone came out of the house. Hummed a tune as he relieved himself. A door banged as the man went back inside.

Dima drew a breath. Took the long stick of hard wood between the palms of his hands and began to spin it in a depression in the other stick.

A wisp of smoke. Flecks of glowing sawdust. He moved the elephant dung closer. Spin faster.

A flame appeared. Went out.

Faster, faster.

The flame crept into the ball which began to glow. He blew gently. Lifted the ball. Threw.

Nothing. The fire had gone out.

A flicker. A small flame.

Darkness erupted into light.

Shouts from the building. People rushed out. Flung themselves down as an explosion shredded the night. The fuel drum flew into the air. Crashed onto the corrugated iron roof. Flames poured down.

The drum rolled off. Landed near the Land Rover.

Panic.

Shouts.

Guns firing into nothingness.

Dima shrank behind a tree trunk.

One-Ear yelling orders.

Screams as a boy was doused in flames.

Dima peered round the tree. The boy thrashing on the ground. Khalif running to the Land Rover. Another boy prodding him with his gun. Fear showing on their faces in the light from the flames.

Branches crackled and caught light.

Khalif scrambled into the driver's seat. The boy into the passenger's seat – yelling, waving his gun.

More shouts from One-Ear.

The vehicle shot clear of the flames. Slowed as it weaved through the trees.

Dima was ready. His *simi* between his teeth.

The vehicle came alongside.

He jumped into the back. Put the *simi* against the boy's throat.

The boy screamed.

'Throw your gun.'

The vehicle slowed.

'Just go!' – yelled at Khalif.

The boy's screaming became wordless terror.

'Your gun!'

The boy tossed it out.

'Open your door.' Dima pressed the *simi*. 'Your door!'

The door flew open. Hit a tree. Bounced back. Swung open.

Dima heaved the boy out. Scrambled into the seat beside Khalif. '*Jambo*. My name is Dima. Go that way.'

He smiled and settled back in his seat. 'Now we go to find Samira.'

Chapter 44

'Jeff Carter? That's Jeff Carter?' said Felix.

'Yes, no question. He had that beard when I first met him, five or six years ago,' said Colette. 'Where did the photo come from?'

'Quite a few folks quizzing me just now 'bout monkeys and things – all to do with this Marburg scare – it was among that stuff. No big deal.' Felix gave a dismissive gesture.

'Oh, right.'

'You seen him recently?'

'Yes. Only a few days ago.'

'Ole-Tomeno's press do?' said Ian.

'No, he came by Sean's place, Tandala, shortly before I left.'

'Is he likely to still be there? We need to contact him.'

'I doubt it. He said he was on his way up north.'

'Did he say where?'

'A place called Lokinang.'

'What the hell's he doing up there?' said Felix.

'Something about a hush-hush vaccine programme. I was sworn to secrecy.'

'Why?'

'He wanted me to go and work on it.'

'Did he just?' Felix studied her for a moment. 'Can I ask you something else, Colette?'

'Depends what it is.'

He extracted another sheet of paper from his folder. 'This note: all kinda technical stuff – not my thing.'

She started to read and, despite the warmth of the evening, the temperature plummeted. Marburg was bad enough, but this. She stared out at the lights of the city. 'I hope to God, it wouldn't work.'

'What wouldn't?' asked Felix.

'It's possible the genome's too small.'

'The what?'

'Sorry, Felix. The genome, it's the virus's genetic blueprint, its RNA. Where did this come from?'

'Just something about Marburg. Loads of stuff getting chucked my way right now.'

'Fill us in, Colette,' said Ian.

She gazed at Felix for a moment. 'I won't enquire further.' She gave a brief smile and read the document more carefully. 'It seems to be some sort of internal memo – the sort of thing a friend of mine, Alan Davies, might have written.'

'Who's he?'

'He works in the UK at a place called Porton Down. It's a bit like Fort Detrick in the States?'

'Go on.'

'The two places are both concerned with national bio-security: viruses and bacteria of potential danger to the public, that sort of thing—' She paused. '—or which could be used in biological warfare.'

'What's the memo say?' asked Ian.

She tried to keep her voice neutral. '*The current agents under consideration as biological weapons are becoming obsolete. They have to be produced in bulk and have limited shelf life. There are vaccines and antibiotics which can be used to counter them, and with the exception of smallpox, they are not readily contagious. They are not effective as bio-weapons, except perhaps locally. Weapons which have to be delivered in bombs or sprayed as aerosols are wasteful, inefficient and indiscriminate – satisfactory as psychological weapons, perhaps – but useless as true biological weapons.* That seems pretty clear.'

'Sure. It's the next bit I had problems with,' said Felix.

Colette continued. '*Consideration should be given to applying molecular techniques to some of the emerging virus diseases such as Marburg, Ebola, Lassa, Machupo; diseases which are poorly understood but which are highly pathogenic and usually fatal, and against which there are no vaccines or therapeutic drugs. Technology is now available to engineer a virus as contagious as influenza, as virulent as Ebola, and as feared as smallpox. Delivery systems would not be needed to spread such an agent; it would spread itself through contagion. For example, myxomatosis killed over ninety-nine per cent of rabbits when first introduced into Australia. A similar scenario could be envisaged with, say, Marburg if the haemagglutinin and neuraminidase genes from human influenza – a highly contagious disease of man – could be inserted into the Marburg genome, a category-A bioterrorism agent. Such an agent would have considerable potential as a human bio-weapon, but steps would need to be taken to ensure laboratory and other personnel were appropriately protected by vaccination. The two approaches would need to be developed simultaneously.*'

She passed the paper back. 'Pretty scary, eh?'

'Does the science add up?' asked Felix.

'The premise is sound. It's whether, in practice, the various genes could be stitched in and whether they'd be expressed in the new construct.'

'If someone did succeed, what then?'

'Are sure you want to know?'

Felix nodded.

'As this memo – or whatever it is – says, Marburg isn't readily contagious. It's normally spread through direct contact with body fluids, not through aerosols. If someone could develop this new construct, he's got a strain of Marburg which is as contagious as flu or the common cold.'

Felix leaned forward. 'Let me get this right. If I'm sitting on the Metro next to some guy who's gotten this strain and he sneezes, I could get infected?'

'And all the others in the carriage.'

'Wish I hadn't asked.' Felix swirled his beer and peered into the glass.

'It's speculation, though, and assumes the theory could be put into practice.'

'What are the chances of developing a vaccine against such a strain?' asked Ian.

'Pretty good, I imagine. The only problem is time – like months, at the earliest. More likely years. Then there has to be safety and efficacy testing.'

They all looked up as Felix's name was called.

'Kelly,' cried Colette, seeing her friend approaching. 'What news?'

Kelly came and slumped into the chair beside her husband, then looked up gratefully as the steward brought her a beer. She took a long draught and wiped her mouth. 'Thanks. I needed that. The good news is that Helen's going to be fine. Her temperature's—'

'That's wonderful,' cried Colette.

'Her temperature's come down and she's off the respirator. It'll take a while for the rash to clear, but I see no reason why she shouldn't make a full recovery.'

Colette reached out and squeezed Kelly's hand. 'Thank you. Thank you so much. And the bad news?'

'The other patient died. I used some of Pete's serum but the infection was too far advanced.' She stared bleakly at the floor. 'Some you win. Some you don't.'

'What can you tell us about him?' asked Colette.

'An African male, forty to fifty. Brought in by *matatu* to Kenyatta

Hospital, collapsed in the waiting area vomiting blood, taken to intensive care, where some switched-on doctor recognised the symptoms and called me. We transferred him to our special facility at Nairobi Hospital but he died soon after.'

'Shit,' whispered Colette.

'That about sums it up.'

'How many contacts?'

'One doctor and three nurses at Kenyatta, plus patients in the waiting area, most of whom decided they didn't feel quite so ill and left after the man threw up. Other passengers in the *matatu* and the driver. Family of the deceased. Hell, I don't know how many. And probably me. I guess we'll need to bleed Pete dry to get enough antiserum.' She gave a hysterical laugh and burst into tears.

'Hey, honey.' Felix put his arm round her.

She buried her head in his neck. Eventually, she looked up with a wan smile. 'Sorry, folks, it's been a long day.'

'Here.' Colette offered a tissue.

'Thanks.' Kelly wiped her eyes and took a sip from her glass. 'Let me fill you in. We've contacted the police to try and trace the contacts. All we said is some possible risk of infectious disease, nothing to worry about. Like hell. We've given the doctor and the three nurses, some of Pete's antiserum, but that's now finished.'

'What about you?' cried Colette.

'I know what symptoms to look out for.'

'No way! I'll get hold of Pete first thing in the morning. We make sure we get some antiserum into you *before* you develop symptoms.'

'I'll be okay.'

'Yes. When we've treated you. Talk to her, Felix.'

'You ain't going nowhere, babe, until we get you treated. Like Colette says.'

'Okay, okay. It's no big deal.'

'Damn well is. You'll have to reckon with me if you don't do what these folks say,' he growled.

'I guess I don't have a choice.' Kelly shrugged. 'Provided you get some as well, Colette.'

'Why me? I've not had anything like the exposure level that you have.'

'Listen, girl, you know better than most that too little is known about this virus and its mode of transmission to run unnecessary risks.'

'It makes sense,' said Ian.

'Okay.' She glanced round the group. 'I said okay, right?'

A plane thundered overhead, cloaking an awkward silence.

'Do you mind if I, er, change the subject?' said Ian.

Felix waved a hand. 'Go ahead.'

'I think we should get our friend Walter on board.'

'Remind me,' said Felix.

'Walter Cheriyot. He's a local reporter who owes us one.'

'How d'ya reckon he can help?'

Ian turned to Kelly. 'What are the chances of some of those contacts going down with Marburg?'

'In a word: high.'

'Right. So others start getting sick and dying, and to coin a phrase: the shit hits the fan. The press go ballistic, and start spewing out hyperbole: killer bug hits Nairobi, death toll rising, millions at risk – garbage like that – and crackpots start predicting the end of the world and God's judgement.'

'You done?' asked Felix.

'That's the worst case scenario.'

'That's a comfort, then.'

'But it's possible.'

Felix glared. 'So where does this Walter guy fit in?'

'We contact him and give him the true story. Play it down a bit, but get him to print the factual account, and say people who develop such-and-such symptoms to contact a doctor or one of the hospitals. In that way we get ahead of the game.'

'You reckon he'd play ball?'

'We have to take the risk. Much better that, than the story breaking when someone gets hold of the wrong end of the stick.'

Felix grunted.

'Are you happy?' asked Ian.

'No, but I guess we don't have a choice.'

'Kelly, what do you think?'

'I think we should clear it with the authorities.'

'No,' said Ian. 'They'll just shuffle their feet and hope the thing blows over. When it doesn't, the fans will grind to a halt. Better we grab the initiative and give Walter the story straight. We insist, though, he doesn't mention any names.'

'I'm not sure,' said Kelly.

'Nor am I. But do we have a choice?'

'I guess not. The devil you know and all that.'

'We also need to tell the local medics and hospitals in advance. Can you get that set up, Kelly?'

'I need to alert them to the recent case, anyway.'

Ian checked his watch. 'I'll call my colleague Grace and get her to organise a meeting with Walter. Would you be happy to be there, Kelly?'

'Sure.' She studied her hands then looked up. 'Colette, it'd be good to have you there as well, in case he wants to get technical.'

'Fine. Whenever.'

'Only don't get into any of that doomsday stuff we talked about earlier,' said Felix.

'Don't worry.' Colette paused while another plane thundered over. 'Kelly, any possibility these two cases could be connected: Helen and this man?'

'I can't see how.'

'Anything more you can tell us about him?'

'The man who died worked in the house of a European couple. The one who brought him in was their gardener. We're getting the police to follow up and trace the couple. The man's name was Stanley. I don't remember the surname.'

'Could it have been Wambugu?' asked Ian.

Kelly frowned. 'Do you know him?'

It was a moment before he replied. 'I know a Stanley Wambugu who works for Fiona and Quentin Melhuish. Quentin is a colleague of mine in the British High Commission.'

Chapter 45

Dima woke feeling stiff and sore. He lay for a while listening to the murmurings of the bush spirits welcoming the dawn. He sat up, thankful to be breathing in a new day. Elephants were spraying themselves in the nearby river, a faint scent of muddy water drifting on the morning air. On the opposite bank, waterbuck were making their way down to the shallows. A group of hippos, having returned to the river after their nocturnal foraging, grunted to each other, their bodies largely submerged. Doves began calling. In a nearby tree, weaverbirds resumed nest-building with noisy chattering. A kingfisher perched on a branch overhead. Iridescent dragonflies shimmered by.

Samira and Khalif, still asleep, lay beside each other next to the Land Rover.

Dima took a sip of water from the gourd and studied them. Her face had lost the angry swelling, and although she would always have a scar, her beauty would soon return.

She murmured something in her sleep and nestled closer to Khalif.

Dima smiled. His thoughts went back to his family. So long since he had seen them. The last time was when his daughter, his daughter... He pushed her memory to the back of his mind. Did it always have to be this way? Him away from home, hunting, searching, seeking to avenge the death of his parents and trying to forget his daughter? But he would never, could never, rest until he knew that man was dead. Perhaps he could have killed him when he saw him at the *duka*. His bow and arrows, though, were untried and it would not have been possible with only his *simi*. Those boys with their guns had been with One-Ear all the time. *Mungu* had decided the time was not right.

Now there would be plenty of time to make fresh weapons and to prepare that special paste for the arrowheads. *Mungu* would decide and Dima would be ready.

Samira stirred and sat up.

'How are you?' he asked.

She smiled and her hand strayed to the scar on her face. 'This will soon be better. You are a good man, Dima.' She stood up and stretched. 'This is a very beautiful place.'

243

They stood silent, taking in the majestic scenery of mountains, the wide river curving away into the distance between sandy banks set with stands of doum palms and acacias, the sun lighting up the river and the countryside in the colours of dawn. A myriad of scents, from acacia blossom to elephants, hung in the air.

'How is this river called?' she asked.

'It is called Ewaso Nyiro.'

'That one goes to Somalia, to my country.' Her expression saddened. 'Things there are so bad, Dima. Those Njia Mpya are very bad.' She scuffed a foot in the sand. 'You know *khat*?'

'That one I don't know.'

'Those Njia Mpya boys, they chew it all the time. At first it makes them happy, but then they get wild. It is so bad. Then they get mad. All the time, they are like that.'

'My people call that *miraa*,' said Dima. 'Sometimes, I chew to keep me awake. But never to get angry.'

She went to the back of the Land Rover. 'There is much food here.'

Khalif, woken by their voices, scrambled to his feet.

'Are you well?' asked Dima.

'Very fine. It is so good to be away from those people.' He spat in the dust.

'Come.' Samira reached out her hand to him. 'Come and get food. We can eat.'

They rummaged among the boxes, tins and packets in the back of the Land Rover then sat with their backs against the vehicle munching biscuits and bread.

'Always I was thinking those ones would kill me as they killed my uncle,' said Khalif.

'Tell us what happened,' she said.

Khalif gazed at the elephants, which had finished their morning drink and were now ambling out of the river and into the bush. 'That night when those people came to our place, Franco shouted at me—'

'Who is Franco?' asked Dima.

'This is his Land Rover. He is the one we work for, Samira and me.' Khalif glanced at her but her eyes were closed. 'Franco said to take the Land Rover and go to Sean.'

'Did you see Sean?'

Khalif shook his head. 'Those ones caught me and made me drive. All the time they are shouting like they are mad. I think someone took their vehicle. That's why they were so mad – that and they chew *khat*. That man with one ear; he is the only one they listen to. He said I should take them to Lokinang. But I don't know Lokinang. You just drive he said, but the fuel runs out and the vehicle stops and they get mad again. Then that man with one ear says he knows this place and there is a *duka* near to get petrol. I pretend not to understand, but I know the *duka* is owned by my uncle and I want to warn him. But it is not possible. They catch that one and take him in the bush and I hear shots and my uncle doesn't come back.' Khalif paused as though lost in thought.

Samira rested a hand on his arm.

'I am thinking: Khalif, you are next. So I do what they say and I hope. We wait at that place, but I don't know why we wait and they won't say. I think even those boys don't know. All they say is you must load all the food from this *duka*. That night we prepare to leave but then you come.' He grinned. 'You come and scare the shit out of me.'

Dima laughed and stood up. 'Now we go to *Bwana* Sean.'

Khalif began drawing random patterns in the sand. 'No. First, we see Solomon then go to Franco.'

'Where do those people live?' asked Dima.

'Solomon stays in Isiolo at a place called New Paradise and Franco is not far. We must pass that way before we go to Sean but we must be careful.' Khalif got to his feet. '*Tuende* – let's go.'

Before they reached the dusty township, Khalif pulled off the road and they climbed out.

'It is possible someone will recognise us,' he said. 'I will drive to the back door of that place and we will go quickly inside.' He rummaged in the compartment below the passenger seat and found an old bush hat of Franco's. 'Samira, you must keep covered.'

She climbed in beside him and drew her shawl over her head and face.

Dima scrambled into the back,

Khalif grinned. 'Now I am safari driver taking my clients on game drive.' He pulled the hat over his eyes, returned to the road and drove into Isiolo.

They passed a ramshackle garage, squeezed between two buildings and continued along a dusty back street scattering chickens.

Khalif stopped outside a shabby building.

'Follow me.' He hurried them through a door and into a kitchen.

Two women, who were busy cooking, looked up startled.

'*Wapi* Solomon – where's Solomon?'

'I will find him.' One of the women hurried out.

A few moments later, the proprietor arrived. 'Khalif!' He hustled the three of them out of the kitchen, up some stairs and into an untidy office. He leaned against the closed door and studied them. 'Samira! Your face?'

She pulled her shawl closer. 'It was those Njia Mpya people. They were the ones. This man, Dima, helped me.'

Solomon turned to him. 'Who are you?'

'I am called Dima, *bwana*.'

'He is a good man,' said Khalif. 'He also helped me after those Njia Mpya killed my uncle.'

Solomon hissed. 'They killed that one?'

'And they stole all the food from the *duka*.'

'Where are those people now?'

'I think they are far,' said Khalif. 'I think they go to Lokinang. Perhaps they will hijack a lorry.'

'So, to that place?' Solomon stood lost in thought for a moment. 'Do you want food?'

'We have eaten,' said Khalif. 'But tea would be good.'

'Wait.' Solomon left the room.

Some five minutes later, one of the women from downstairs brought them tea and departed without speaking. Still they waited. Solomon finally returned.

'This way.'

They followed him along a passage and into a smartly-furnished sitting room where a tall man dressed as a tribal elder, was talking on a mobile phone. He looked up as they entered, finished his call and smiled.

'How are you, my friends?' he asked, extending his hand. 'My name is Daniel ole-Tomeno. Solomon tells me that one of the ladies kindly brought you tea.'

Chapter 46

Ian peered bleary-eyed into a new day. Fifteen minutes later, showered and dressed, he made his way to the dining room of the Settlers Club where all the tables were laid for breakfast but only one was occupied. The elderly resident, whom Ian had previously encountered in the lounge bar, had apparently been wound up, and was now spooning porridge with metronomic regularity, presumably until his spring ran down.

Ian selected a corner table and accepted orange juice from a hovering waiter, who indicated the buffet. Ian approached an impressive array of chafing dishes, tureens and dish covers of tarnished silver. He located a single fried egg and two pieces of toast. The porridge had presumably been finished and cleared away.

He returned to his table with the Club's offering. The coffee which was waiting tasted surprisingly good. He was about to start his breakfast, when someone approached his table.

He scrambled to his feet. 'Sir Aubrey.'

'Good morning, Ian. On my way to the office. Quentin told me I'd find you here.'

'Quentin?'

'Yes, poor fellow. May I?'

'Yes, of course.' Ian pulled out a chair and signalled to a waiter. 'Coffee?'

'Yes please.' The High Commissioner slumped down.

He seemed to have aged ten years since their last meeting. His tie was awry, his shoulders sagged, and even his normally prominent ears seemed to droop. He probably hadn't shaved.

'*Asante*,' said the High Commissioner, as the waiter placed a coffee at his elbow. 'Hardly recognise you with that beard.'

Ian shrugged. 'If you don't mind my saying so, sir, you don't look too well.'

'Hmm.' The High Commissioner sipped his coffee and his expression slipped further down the mast.

Ian decided to let him do the talking and see where it led. He returned to his egg on toast and waited.

'It's Fiona.'

'Your daughter?'

'Worried stiff about her. But she won't let me or her mother, visit her. Or Quentin, for that matter.'

'Why Quentin?'

'Come, come, man.' Some of his former asperity returned. 'You surely knew my daughter was married to him.'

'Good heavens.'

The shoulders slumped again. 'I thought everyone in the High Commission knew.'

Ian gave a non-committal gesture. 'Something to eat, sir? I'll see what they can rustle up.'

The High Commissioner batted the suggestion aside then leaned forward. 'Would you visit her? I'm sure she'd see you. Find out what's going on.'

'Well I—'

'She's in hospital.'

'In hospital? Good heavens.' He'd have to find a different expression of surprise. The High Commissioner didn't appear to notice.

'Quentin says some fellows beat her up.'

'Beat her up?'

'Yes, beat her up. Don't keep repeating me.'

Ian winced and chose his words more carefully. 'Does Quentin know what happened?'

'Probably burglars. House-boy – fellow by the name of Stanley – has disappeared. Quentin thinks he was in on it.'

'Good hea— That's terrible.'

'Quentin's worried sick. Been having a hard time recently—'

'He's not the only one.'

The High Commissioner didn't appear to hear but pulled himself up and braced his shoulders. 'Times like this, we Brits have to pull together, stand shoulder to shoulder.'

'Yes, of course.'

'Good man. I knew I could rely on you.'

'What is it exactly that you would, er, like me to do?'

'Visit Fiona. Find out how she is, why she won't see us. My wife's terribly upset.'

'Fiona is… is where?'

'In the Nairobi Hospital, one of the women's wards.'

'Right,' he said slowly. 'By the way, I hear that Helen is going to be all right.'

'Helen?'

'Your PA.'

'Oh, yes. Sounded quite nasty that.'

'Yes, it was quite nasty.' Was the High Commissioner really in the dark? Disparate thoughts of subterfuge, complicity and deviousness whirled through Ian's head.

'Quentin's been staying at the residence. I've arranged for him to fly out tonight?' said Sir Aubrey.

'Where to?'

'London, of course.'

'Whatever for?'

'Poor fellow's in a most frightful state. Just not coping. Fiona can follow when she's better.'

He studied the High Commissioner. Was this some complicated game? Was he being strung along, being used? By whom? How?

'Quentin's a stout fellow, a good egg,' said the High Commissioner. 'He showed that in Pakistan. Very good at handling those chaps, learned to speak their lingo. Plenty of bombs there.' As though reminded: 'The Nairobi bomb must have been the straw that broke the... Yes, well.'

Ian checked the anger that threatened to erupt. The straw? Fiona had used the same phrase with reference to the bomb. Just what was going on?

'You chaps getting anywhere with that bomb thing?'

Ian drew a breath. 'I presume you mean the bomb thing which was meant for me and killed God knows how many innocent bystanders.'

The High Commissioner recoiled like a startled rabbit. 'Er, yes. That one.'

'We're making some progress.'

'Good, good, splendid. Good show. Now, where was I?'

'Quentin.'

'Oh, yes. You sure you're all right?' He peered myopically at Ian. 'You seem a bit, a bit unsettled.'

'Bombs tend to do that to people.'

'Yes. I suppose they do. But you probably know more about these things than I do.'

'Probably.'

'Quite so.' The High Commissioner addressed his coffee cup. 'Quite so.'

Ian allowed his anger to subside. Let the old duffer stew for a bit.

The High Commissioner continued to address his cup. 'I'll have a quiet word with Halliwell.'

'Halliwell?'

'The Perm Sec. We were at Cambridge together.'

'Ah.'

'Get Quentin a head of mission post in some quiet location: Vanuatu, Gambia, Montserrat...'

'Reykjavik?'

'What?'

'Nothing.'

The High Commissioner gave him a sideways look. 'He deserves something like that.'

Ian sniffed. 'Very appropriate.'

'Listen, Ian. I know it's an imposition but you'd be doing us all a favour if you'd accompany Quentin and put him on the plane tonight.'

'Me?'

'Would you? I'm not sure he'd cope on his own.'

Ian sat back in his chair. What is this bloody game? Who's playing it? Only one way to find out.

He drew a deep breath. 'Of course.'

Chapter 47

'Did you get any sleep?' asked Kelly, as Colette joined her at breakfast next morning.

'Not much.'

'Nor me.'

'Kelly, when I was at the Embassy last night, before you arrived, Felix showed me a document – an internal memo, or something – which described the possibility of genetically modifying viruses like Ebola and Marburg to make them more contagious.'

'As if they're not bad enough already,' muttered Kelly. 'Where did the document come from?'

'He wouldn't say. But it suggested inserting some of the infectivity genes of influenza into the genome.'

'Is that feasible?'

'Theoretically, yes. Whether or not it could be done in practice, I don't know.'

Kelly busied herself with the kettle. 'Coffee?'

'Please.'

She passed Colette a mug. 'Cereals and fruit on the side. Anyway, to answer your question. As far as I could tell on the basis of no previous experience, the two Marburg cases seemed normal, showed most of the symptoms described in the literature.'

'I don't want to be alarmist, but I suppose we won't know if the present strain or strains— You're having them typed?'

'Yes.'

'So we won't know if they're more virulent or more contagious—'

'Don't say it, Colette. Just get Pete back as soon as possible, so we can get antiserum into the contacts – assuming we can trace them.'

'And into you.'

'Into both of us.' Kelly gave a bleak smile. 'Phone's out there in the hallway.'

Colette went through, returning to the kitchen a few minutes later. 'I think he was sitting by the phone. He's on his way.'

'So are we. Sorry about your breakfast. Grab some at the hospital.'

***

Pete-B was on his own this time, pacing up and down, when Colette and Kelly arrived.

He rushed up to them. 'How's Helen?'

'You've not heard?' said Kelly.

'Heard what?'

'She's on the mend.'

'You mean that?'

'She should make a rapid and normal recovery.'

Pete swallowed. 'That's, that's great. Huh…Can I see her?'

Kelly smiled and laid a hand on his arm. 'Later. First we need to collect more blood from you for… In case we need to treat in-contact people.'

'Sure.' He gave a rueful grin. 'Pete insisted I restore my fluid balance yesterday evening.'

'Come on, then,' said Kelly. 'I'll get you set up, then prepare the patient for your visit.'

'You sure she's going to be okay?'

'Positive.'

Pete snatched his wallet from his pocket and thrust it into Colette's hand. 'Go to the shop there and buy the biggest bunch of flowers you can find.'

'You old softie.'

***

'We're keeping Helen in an isolation ward for a few days, as much for her protection as anything,' said Kelly, as she and Colette made their way to the top floor of the hospital. 'It'll take a while for her immune system to get back to normal.'

Colette nodded.

'Put these on.' Kelly passed her a disposable facemask and gloves. 'In here.' Kelly opened the door into a small room with subdued lighting. A single bed stood in the middle, with the customary cabinets on either side, one of which bore the pot-plant which had been delivered earlier. There was a hand basin in one corner, and beside the bed was a drip-stand holding a plastic pack of clear fluid, which was infusing into the patient via a tube connected to a needle in her arm.

Colette noticed none of these details. Her attention was focused on the patient who lay asleep. Helen's face was still flushed but had lost much of its angry redness.

Hearing the door close, she opened her eyes and smiled. 'Hello.'

'How you feeling, Helen?' asked Kelly.

'I slept well.'

'This is Colette,' said Kelly. 'She knows about Marburg.'

Colette gave a nervous smile beneath her facemask. 'Hi.'

'Take a seat, Colette, while I give Helen a quick check over.'

Colette sat clasping and unclasping her hands in her lap.

'All looking good,' said Kelly, a few minutes later. 'We'll get you into a normal ward as soon as possible.'

'Then I can start living again?'

'Sure thing.'

'I'm so glad you're going to be okay, Helen,' said Colette.

'I gather I owe my life to a friend of yours.'

'Pete. He asked me to give you these.' She laid the flowers on the bed.

'They're lovely.'

'Yes, aren't they?'

'I'll ask one of the nurses to put them in water.'

'Yes, they need water.'

God, can't I think of anything sensible to say?

'Please thank Pete.'

'Yes, I will.'

'He's here at the hospital,' said Kelly. 'He would like to come and see you.'

'What? All horrible and blotchy?'

'Can I go get him?'

'As long as you warn him.'

'Sure.' Kelly patted the bed covers. 'Back shortly.'

Colette sat with her eyes wandering round the room.

'I'm so pleased to meet you,' said Helen. 'Sean told me all about—'

'Sean?'

'He came to see me earlier.'

'Oh.'

'That trouble at Tandala and at Franco's place sounded dreadful.'

'I suppose it was. I didn't really have time to think about it.' She briefly closed her eyes and wondered if Sean held Helen in the way he'd held her. She couldn't help the sigh that escaped.

'Are you all right?'

'Yes. Sorry. Just reliving some of the things that happened.'

'Do you want some water?'

'No, I'm fine.'

'Sean said how impressed he was by the way you helped that sick hunter. And that Somali girl. That was incredible, sewing up her face.'

'I guess my professional training kicked in.'

'I couldn't possibly have coped.'

Colette gave a half-mast smile.

'I'm afraid I don't get out to the ranch much these days,' Helen was saying.

'Sorry?'

'Not since our daughter—'

'Is someone looking after her?'

'Looking after who?'

'Your... your daughter.'

Something was wrong – terribly wrong.

'Didn't Sean tell you?' Helen whispered.

'Tell me what?'

'About Tanya?'

Colette sat frozen but managed a slight shake of her head.

'It was... was malaria. We'd been at the coast and were meticulous about giving her the anti-malarial syrup.' She gave a ragged whimper. 'But people didn't then know about, about chloroquine resistance.' Her voice was so quiet Colette could barely hear. 'By the time the doctors realised, it was, it was too...' She buried her head in her hands.

Colette found herself with her arms round Helen all thoughts of Marburg forgotten.

'She was so beautiful.' Tears poured down her cheeks and formed a damp patch on the covers.

'I'm so, so sorry. Oh, God!' Colette dashed a hand across her face and struggled to hold back her own tears. Her facemask fell onto the bed. 'I'd no idea. Helen, I'm so sorry.' She crumpled up the mask and flung it on the floor. 'Why am I such an awful person?'

'You weren't to know. How could you?'

'Yes, but, but...'

'It was my fault. I didn't realise there was a hole, a hole in the mosquito net.' Helen's expression was bleak as she looked up. 'You know the big acacia near where Sean parks his plane?'

Colette nodded.

'At the foot of the tree is where we, where we...' Her lower lip trembled and she sank her head into her hands again.

Colette hugged her.

Helen looked up, her eyes imploring. 'Sean blames me, I know he does.'

'No!'

She gave a desolate smile. 'Now you know why I can't go back.'

'Helen, there's no way Sean would blame you.'

She seemed to gather her composure. 'Can you pass me the tissues?'

Colette reached out a hand for the box, lifted Helen's anguished face and wiped the tears away.

'Thank you for understanding. Thank you so much.' Helen gazed into Colette's eyes. 'I so want to kiss you but Kelly would be appalled.'

'Kelly!' Colette leaped up. 'Quick!' She straightened the bed clothes, threw the crumpled mask and tissue in the waste-bin, grabbed another mask from a box beside the bed and tidied her hair.

The door opened and Kelly stuck her head round. 'I hope Colette hasn't been wearing you out.' She peered at Helen. 'You all right? You look a bit, a bit flustered.'

Helen smiled. 'I'm feeling better, thanks. So much better.'

'Hmm.' Kelly frowned and glanced at Colette who sat with a demure expression as she gazed out of the window.

'Anyway, Pete's here, can I bring him in?'

Helen laid her hands over the damp patch on the bed covers. 'Yes, of course.'

Kelly ushered a terrified-looking Pete into the room and introduced him.

He gestured to the flowers on the bed. 'I hope you like roses.'

'From you, I gather? They're lovely.'

'Yeah. Colette chose them.'

'I'm going to get a nurse to put them in water.'

'Right.'

Helen studied Pete's face. 'I gather I owe you my life. If it wasn't for—'

'Right.'

'Pete, thank you so much.'

'That's— Oh, shit. I'm so bloody hopeless at…' He rubbed his hands over his face.

Colette offered him her chair.

'Thanks.' He sat staring at the floor. 'Sorry. I guess I'm not very good at this sort of thing.'

'Come on, guys,' said Kelly, beckoning to Colette and Pete. 'Helen needs rest.'

'Yes. Right.' Pete stood up. 'Can I come and see you again?'

'I'd like that.' Helen smiled and blew him a kiss.

'I'm not always like this. I... I can be almost normal.'

'Almost,' said Colette, taking Pete's hand. 'Sometimes.'

'Here's your wallet, Pete,' said Colette, as they left the room.

'Thanks.' He stuffed it into his pocket. 'What the hell must Helen have thought of this weirdo with two left feet?' He kicked savagely at the wall.

'Pete, she owes you her life.'

'Does she? Anyone could have given their blood.'

'What rubbish and you know it.'

They lapsed into a tense silence as they made their way out of the hospital to the car park where the Pete's Land Rover was waiting.

'Can I give you a lift to the hotel,' he asked.

'The hotel?'

'Sean's staying at our hotel and wants to see you.'

Chapter 48

'The paper you ordered, sir.'

Ian looked up. 'Sorry?'

'You asked for a copy of the Daily Nation, sir,' said the waiter.

'Oh, right. Thanks.'

'Anything else, sir?'

'More coffee, please.'

'Yes, sir.'

Ian stared unseeing at the paper, still reliving his surreal meeting with the High Commissioner who had just departed. Was the Old Man losing his marbles? Being unhinged by the worry over his daughter? Ian felt like a pawn in some bizarre game of chess with crazed players moving him around the squares and cancelling out or contradicting each other's moves. And who else was playing the game? He sighed. When all else fails, stick to facts. And try to sort the true facts from the imagined facts.

His mobile rang.

'Ian, it's Grace. Have you seen the paper?'

'No, I...' He scanned the front page. 'Damn!'

'How soon can you get here? Police HQ.'

'Ten, fifteen minutes.' He checked his watch. 'On my way.'

The waiter made a rude gesture at Ian's departing back and threw his coffee out of the window.

***

Thanks for calling me about the Marburg cases,' said Grace, as Ian entered her office. 'Any further developments?'

'Not that I've heard.'

'We'll hear soon enough if there are.' She indicated the newspaper on her desk. 'What did you make of Walter's article?'

'Does he know something or is he guessing?'

'Let's hope he's guessing.'

Ian read the headline. '*Third anniversary of Embassy bombing.* I see Walter tries to make a link between the anniversary and his earlier article about Marburg.' He glanced up. 'Surely he can't have heard about the two cases.'

'I haven't told him anything, but even if he'd heard from some other source, there wouldn't have been time to get anything into

257

today's paper.'

'We need to get Walter in and give him our side of the story before he hears and starts guessing,' said Ian.

'I've set it up.'

A young plain-clothes officer put his head round the door. 'We're ready, Grace.'

'Thanks, Sammy. Coming.' She introduced Ian.

'Hi,' said Sammy.

Ian waved. 'What is all this?' he asked, as he followed her out of the office.

'You'll see.' She led the way along a corridor, down some steps and into a darkened room where she motioned Ian to a seat facing a large plate glass window which looked out onto a brightly-lit but bare room.

'Get them in, Sammy,' she said.

Eight men filed into the room on the other side of the glass and stood facing the hidden onlookers. Two were African, two middle-eastern, two Asian and two were European. Each held a card bearing a number.

Ian tensed.

'Do you recognise any of them?' asked Grace.

'No.'

'Number four?'

'Still no.'

'Okay.' Grace got to her feet. 'Let's go back.'

'Why the identity parade?' asked Ian, when they were back in her office.

'We brought in number-four last night.'

'Why?'

She smiled. 'To help us with our enquiries.'

'Is he?'

She seemed to consider the question. 'Not really. He's making a lot of noise, though, asking to see his lawyer and threatening us with his ambassador.'

'Who is he?'

'Faisal Malik. Also known as Qasim Chaudhry.'

'Malik! How did you find him? I thought he went off on safari with Richard Omar.'

'He did, but the kids have been watching Fedha Towers and Amos saw Malik yesterday evening go into the building and alerted me.' She began arranging paperclips on her desk. 'In view of our suspicions, I wanted him out of the way on the anniversary. I've told Felix.'

'Any sign of Omar?'

'No. Which could mean he's still at Lokinang, or simply that Amos and his helpers haven't see him.' She swept the paperclips into a drawer. 'Only problem was, the press was there when we picked up Malik.'

'How come?'

'I'm guessing, but I think that was friend Walter keeping an eye on Viktor who was staying in the Six-Eighty round the corner. He probably doesn't trust Viktor any more than we do and asked his friends to keep an eye on him.'

'Bit of a scoop then.'

Grace sniffed. 'I hope it doesn't backfire.'

Sammy appeared in the doorway. 'Felix is here.'

Grace waved him in.

'Hi, folks, how you doing?' Felix had abandoned his military top in favour of a T-shirt promoting the attractions of Mombasa Beach Hotel. To enhance his anonymity, he wore shades and a baseball cap.

'Bring us some tea, Sammy. Then come and join us.'

'Sure.'

'You seen the paper?' asked Felix. 'All this anniversary stuff.'

'We reckoned it was Walter trying it on,' said Ian.

'Could be. Let me show you something else, though.' Felix turned to an inside page. 'Read that.'

Ian glanced at Grace. '*The USS aircraft carrier, Harry S. Truman, which recently completed its deployment in support of Operation Southern Watch, including a UN-sanctioned strike on Iraqi-integrated-air-defence-system sites earlier this year, arrived off Mombasa yesterday for a goodwill visit and joint training exercise with the Kenyan Navy. The President said…* blah… blah…'

Ian closed the paper. 'I didn't know you had so much influence.'

Felix shrugged. 'I guess the Ambassador agreed that it would be handy to have some hardware around on the anniversary of the bombing, just in case.' He tossed a photograph of Malik onto the desk. 'Thanks for sending that over, Grace. The sonofabitch got my fellows kinda excited. You still got him, I hope?'

Grace smiled. 'We'll be pleased to get rid of him. He's making too much noise.'

'What's going to happen to him?' asked Ian.

'We're going to offer him a cruise round the Indian Ocean on old

Hairy Ass.'

'Excuse me?' said Grace.

'The Harry S. Don't know whether he'll accept the offer but guess he don't have much choice. If that guy so much as farted near the Embassy, I want to know.'

'When's the pick-up?' she asked.

'The Blackhawk's due at twelve. You've cleared with air traffic control?'

'They're giving you a deserted part of the airport near the freight terminal for landing, refuelling and—'

'Quick, come and see this,' said Sammy, sticking his head into the office.

They hurried out and across to a TV screen set high on the wall at the end of the general office. Other staff, already there, cleared a space for them.

'… *Russian reporter staying in the Six-Eighty Hotel opposite the building,*' read the newsreader. '*According to eyewitnesses the man arrested was a Pakistani business man…*'

Muttering round the room as a picture of Malik, Grace beside him, appeared on the screen. A second picture showed a hooded figure being hustled into a police car. A third picture showed people milling round the entrance to Fedha Towers.

'*It is understood the police received a telephone call warning of a bomb planted in the building.*'

The picture changed to live transmission and showed a reporter, microphone in hand, standing in front of a crowd outside the building. '*The police are still not allowing people in, but there are unconfirmed reports that a bomb has been found.*'

A phone rang.

Sammy snatched up the receiver.

Everyone in the room watched.

'Hold the line, please. I'll check.' He covered the mouthpiece. 'It's a reporter called Walter Cheriyot. He's just seen the news flash and is asking for you, Grace. Can you speak to him?'

She snatched the receiver from Sammy. 'Listen, Walter, what the hell's going on?'

Ian watched her face of thunder as she shot questions down the line – the first time he'd seen her lose her cool.

'If you two are not here within the hour, I'll throw the book at you.' She slammed the phone down. 'Where's that tea, Sammy?'

She gestured Ian and Felix to return with her to the office. 'So much for a low-profile arrest.'

'What was that about a bomb?' asked Felix.

'I've no idea. If that was Walter I'll…' She tapped her biro on the desk.

'Can we get Kelly along to this meeting?' asked Ian. 'She's the doctor from the hospital. Be a chance to give Walter and Viktor the true story about Marburg. Get ahead of the game, if you like.'

'What game are we talking about?'

'Sorry. Not a good word-choice.'

'No.' Grace threw her biro down. 'As long as she sticks to the facts and no speculating.'

'It's okay we've already briefed her.'

'I'm sorry?'

'Felix and I have briefed her.'

'I see. And who else do you propose to invite to this party?'

Ian frowned. 'I know you've had a long night, Grace, but don't take it like that.'

'You haven't answered my question.'

He took a deep breath. 'It would be good if Colette Fraser was at the meeting. She's a specialist on monkey viruses.'

'I know Colette.'

'Better those reporters get the proper story than making one up,' said Felix, playing the peace-maker.

Grace gave a resigned sigh. 'Go on then, Ian, set it up.'

Sammy arrived with three mugs of tea. 'Inspector down at Fedha Towers is asking if the bomb-scare is over yet?'

Grace glowered. 'I want to know how that rumour started. Get on to it, Sammy.'

'That, er, won't be necessary.'

'What do you mean?'

'I was the one who, um, suggested it.'

'On whose authority?'

'I had to think fast and thought it might divert attention from—'

'You what?'

'Take people's minds off the real reason for the arrest.'

Grace slumped back in her chair. 'You're right, Ian. It has been a long night.' Her faced relaxed into a smile. She chuckled. 'Well done, Sammy. Call the inspector. He can let people back in but no one goes onto the top floor until we've cleared out the Blessed Flowers office.

Tell him to put some officers outside, and if anyone who works there shows up, he should send them here for questioning.'

'And the press?'

'Tell them we'll be issuing a statement shortly. Nothing more. And, Sammy.'

'Yes?'

'Thanks for the tea.'

Grace sat staring at her desk after Sammy had departed. 'Are we missing something?'

'Like what?' asked Felix.

'Everyone's on high alert – our people and yours, Felix – and what's happened? Nothing – except a bomb hoax which we instigated.'

'You have picked up Malik, though,' added Ian.

'We got lucky.'

Felix leaned forward. 'Listen, even though Malik's out of the equation, all these other sleepers have been woken up. They're going to be thinking August seven – today. The third anniversary.'

'So's the rest of Kenya.' Ian sniffed.

'Yeah. So everyone's a bit twitchy, tightening security, that kinda thing. Mostly thinking bombs, I guess. Then nothing happens. What then?'

'We breathe a sigh of relief?' said Ian.

'Sure, *we* do, but what about the sleepers, the ones who've been woken up? They feel cheated and start thinking: hey, perhaps those guys running the show ain't so good after all.'

'Maybe they're planning to choose another day,' said Grace.

'No. Having wound these sleepers up, the top brass ain't going to let the symbolism of August seven slip.'

'So far so good,' said Ian. 'But the top brass, as you call them, are looking for something big. Right?'

'I guess so.'

'Which would hardly have come from Malik and his pals trotting round Nairobi inviting people to pop vitamin pills or sniff bottles – even if one or two of them do go down with Marburg.'

Felix sighed. 'This is all ass-about-face. We've gotten a motive but no crime.'

'Yet,' said Grace.

Chapter 49

Sean and Pete-A were seated at a table beneath a striped umbrella, eating a late breakfast.

'Hi,' called Sean, as Colette and Pete-B approached.

'Great news about Helen,' said Pete-A.

Colette could only nod.

'Send her my very best wishes.' Pete pushed his plate away and got to his feet. 'Now, if you will forgive us, dear people, I fear we must return to the coal-face.'

'For how long?' she asked.

'As long as it takes, dear lady. We owe that to Kimani.'

'I've still got the specimens Colette and I salvaged from your camp,' said Sean.

'You're too kind. We'll drop by sometime.' Pete-A applied a cheerful veneer to a bleak expression. 'I guess this is it then. We put up the shutters, turn out the lights and lock the door behind us.'

'Oh, Pete,' she said.

'Thank you, dear lady. But, as the walrus said: the time has come to… And all that bollocks. Let's go, Pete.'

'See you, guys,' called Sean, as they walked away.

They gave perfunctory waves but didn't turn.

Colette ran after them. 'You can't just bugger off like that.' She hugged and kissed them both. 'Thanks for everything you've done.'

'A mere trifle,' said Pete-A.

Pete-B turned away. 'Be seeing you.'

She watched until they disappeared inside the hotel, then returned to Sean.

'They all right?'

'I hope so.' She sat down and stared at her feet in their open sandals. Decision time. She felt a sudden emptiness. Sean has a beautiful wife who's recently cheated death. He doesn't need me around.

'When did you arrive?' she asked.

'I flew into Wilson Airport last night.' He gave his lop-sided grin. 'It's great to see you.'

She smiled and averted her eyes.

'Have you eaten?'

She shook her head.

'Buffet breakfast. Help yourself, over there.'

'Thanks.' She made her way to the buffet and tried to gather her thoughts which kept flitting off. She took some food at random. 'Just do it,' she murmured.

'That's an interesting mix,' said Sean, when she returned to the table.

She looked ruefully at the fruit salad and scrambled egg. 'Sean, I've decided... decided I should...'

'Should what?'

She stared at the mess on her plate. 'Should go back.'

'Back? Back where?'

'To London. I've finished the work Jeff wanted me to do here. Things will be building up there. I need to liaise with Alan Davies at Porton. My dad's not well and—'

'What about the vaccine work at Lokinang?'

'They'll have to manage without me.'

He studied her face with his blue eyes. 'Are you sure you're doing the right thing?'

'Yes.' *No.*

'Do you have to go back yet?'

Don't do this to me.

'I'll check the flights later on today.' She couldn't bring herself to look at him.

He busied himself with his breakfast then looked up. 'I saw Helen earlier.'

'I know. I'm so glad she's going to be okay.'

He nodded.

'Any news about Samira?'

Sean pulled a face. 'None. She hasn't come back. No one knows what's happened.'

'That's all my fault, Sean.'

'No way. She chose to run off. There's nothing you or anyone could have done, short of imprisoning her. Samira's a grown woman. She can take care of herself.'

'I do hope she'll be okay.'

'We all do. You can't blame yourself.'

'I suppose not.' She gave a rueful smile. 'I need to come to terms with myself. To grow up.'

'What's that supposed to mean?'

'Sean, I'm nearly thirty. I need to… God!'

'What?'

'I am thirty! Oh, shit and I forgot.'

'You forgot your birthday? When was it?'

'It's today.'

'Happy Birthday, you.' He mouthed her a kiss. 'Right. I'm taking you out to lunch, somewhere special. You'll at least let me do that before you leave.'

'You're such a lovely man.'

They looked up as one of the waiters approached their table. 'Excuse me, sir, you have a telephone call in reception.'

'Thanks.' Sean got to his feet.

She toyed with her coffee while he was gone.

The twenties are now behind you and you embark on the next decade of your life. Don't be so bloody pompous. All right, then; the rollercoaster of your hormonal years is – should be – behind you, so what's the next decade – year, even – going to bring? What are you going back to?

She was suddenly conscious of things: sights, sounds and smells which threatened to overwhelm her senses. The raucous call of an ibis. A brightly-coloured ball floating on a turquoise swimming pool. The scent of parched soil being revived by water from a sprinkler. Rainbow droplets pattering on leaves. A hoopoe probing the lawn – frightened off as Sean returned.

She closed her eyes but the vision remained, burned into her brain: a fauve canvas of bewildering exuberance, colour – and uncertainty.

'That was ole-Tomeno,' he said. 'He wants me to join him in Isiolo first thing tomorrow.'

'Why?'

'I don't know. He wouldn't say but it means going back today. I'm afraid the birthday lunch will have to wait. He also wants you to come.'

'Me? Why me?'

'Something to do with the proposed vaccine work I imagine.'

'Sean, I'm not going to get involved.'

'Surely a few days' delay won't matter?'

She sighed. 'I suppose not.' She studied the Samburu bracelet on her wrist. 'Helen told me about Tanya,' she whispered, squeezing the words past the lump in her throat.

Sean checked, his coffee cup half way to his mouth. 'What about her?'

'Sean, I'm so sorry. I wish I'd known.'

He returned the cup to its saucer. 'She was just beginning to walk.' He stared across the garden. 'I know Helen blames herself but... I should have checked the net before I packed it.'

Colette took his hand, not daring to look into his face. 'Neither of you can blame yourselves.'

'Yes, but—'

'Sean, you need to—'

'*Ciao, signora*,' said a voice.

She looked up. 'Franco!'

'Is good I find you here.'

'How are you?' She slipped her hand away from Sean's but sensed Franco had noticed.

'Doc, he say I have to wear this slink.'

'Sling.'

'*Si, si*. Is no so bad.'

She scrambled to her feet and pulled out a chair.

Franco dropped into it with a contented sigh. '*Kahawa tu* – just coffee,' he said, to the approaching waiter.

'Tell us what happened, Franco, after the Flying Doctor plane picked you up,' said Sean.

'Doc at Embassy, he sew me up, give me pills and put bandage. Felix from American Embassy he ask lot of questions. Then he say, you got place to stay in Nairobi? I say for sure. I stay with Larry... You know Larry?'

'Of course. The pilot.'

'So Larry, he say welcome. We have party and... Sean, my friend, I hear you got spare seat in your plane?'

'How did you know I had my plane here?'

Franco shrugged then rubbed his injured shoulder. 'Bush telegraph. Jungle drums. Is no matter.'

'Tell us.'

'Very nice place this.' Franco waved a casual hand. 'You swim?'

Sean chuckled. 'You don't change, do you? Franco, who told you I was here?'

'You know Solomon from New Paradise?'

'In Isiolo?'

'*Si*. He call my mobile and say big *bwana* want you back here.'

'Big *bwana*? Which big *bwana*?'

Franco looked furtively around then leaned forward. 'Ole-Tomeno. Grace told him you were here. Is how I find you. I think his PA, Maria, she help.'

'I see. Did Solomon tell you why ole-Tomeno wants us back?'

'He no say.'

Sean frowned. 'What's ole-Tomeno doing in Isiolo, why does he want *us* there, and why the urgency? Are you holding something back?'

For once, Franco was tongue-tied.

'Okay, I won't push it. You got a bag, any luggage?'

'He in reception.'

'I'll be right back,' said Sean. 'I need to pay my bill.'

Colette gazed after him until he disappeared inside the hotel.

'So, *signora?*' cried Franco.

She turned to him and tried to smile. 'I've decided to go back to London, Franco. As soon as this meeting with—'

'You mad?'

'I've made up my mind. It's bad enough screwing up my own life. I can't screw up two others as well.'

'Why you talk like that?' he growled.

'Franco, I'm in the way here. Sean doesn't need...' She was conscious of twisting her bracelet. 'I saw Helen earlier today and she told me about their daughter, Tanya.'

'Oh.' He studied his hands.

'Franco, that was so awful what happened.'

'*Si.* I was... how you say? Her godfather.' He looked up, his eyes misting. 'I no have children of my own.'

She couldn't trust herself to speak. She pressed his hand to her lips.

'I sorry I not thirty years younger,' he muttered.

'You understand why I have to go back?'

Franco stared morosely into his coffee.

'As soon as ole-Tomeno's meeting's over, I'll book my flight.'

Her mobile rang. She scrambled to her feet and moved out of earshot. 'Hello.'

'Colette, it's Ian. Any chance you could get over to police headquarters?'

'When?'

'Now. Those two journalists are coming in and we'd like you here as well to field any technical questions on Marburg – what we talked about last night at the Embassy.'

'Ian, I'm really sorry, I can't. I'm going back with Sean. I was going to call you.'

'I see.'

'Ian, don't be like that. I can't. Ole-Tomeno wants Sean back in Isiolo and—'

'Ole-Tomeno does what?'

'He wants him… him back in Isiolo.'

God, perhaps I shouldn't have told him.

'Why?'

'Why what?'

There was a sigh down the phone as though he was dealing with a recalcitrant teenager. 'Why does ole-Tomeno want Sean in Isiolo?'

'I don't know.' Her small voice.

Silence down the line.

'Are you still there, Ian?'

'Yes.'

'We're leaving shortly.'

'Right.'

'What about Kelly? Couldn't you get her along, like we discussed?'

'She's already coming. You also agreed to come, if you remember.'

'I know.' She rubbed a distracted hand over her face. 'Ian, I'm really sorry but it was before this other thing—'

'Is that it, then?'

'I've got your Landy here, at the New Hibiscus Hotel. I'll leave the keys at reception. Thank you so much for loaning it to me.'

He rang off.

The next decade hadn't started too well.

Chapter 50

Walter Cheriyot and Viktor Levkov sat on either side of a table in the briefing room looking bored.

'Sorry to keep you waiting,' said Grace, little suggestion of apology in her tone as she led in Ian, Felix, Kelly, Sammy and two uniformed officers. She took her seat at the head of the table, making no effort at introductions. 'Right, Walter, what have you been doing?' She tossed a copy of the Daily Nation onto the table.

The reporter's face was expressionless. 'My job.'

'Stirring up rumour and speculation is your job?'

'My job is selling papers.'

'By writing sensationalist stories?'

'I seem to have achieved my aim.'

'Meaning what?'

'Getting people like you to think about what I wrote.'

'Don't try and be clever.'

Ian's respect for Grace racked up a notch.

Walter and Viktor exchanged glances. One or two people shuffled feet.

'Shall we start again?' Grace sat back. 'Sammy, go and organise tea and biscuits, please.'

'Ah.' Walter mirrored Grace's fake smile. 'The standard refreshments of police TV drama.'

She shrugged. 'Tell me why you phoned requesting a meeting.'

'Viktor's pictures. Let's say the photograph of a senior police officer – you – arresting a Pakistani business man in the middle of the night was something out of the ordinary.'

'It was a bomb-scare.' Perhaps a little too hastily.

'Ah, a bomb-scare on August the seventh. Is there a connection?'

'Unlikely.'

'I'll take that as a yes, then.'

Grace glowered. 'What do you know about Marburg that you didn't tell Ian and me when we last met?'

Walter extracted a reporter's pad from his briefcase and flipped some pages. 'Nothing new, except I understand that local hospitals have been warned to look out for possible cases of the disease.'

'Anything else?'

'The US aircraft carrier, Harry S. Truman, has arrived off Mombasa on a courtesy visit. Pity I didn't hear about that in time to include it in my article.'

'What's that got to do with Marburg?'

'You tell me.'

Grace seemed to make up her mind. 'We agreed, when we met in the Park, to give your respective papers priority over breaking stories. In return, you—'

'A deal is a deal,' said Walter.

Viktor yawned and took a notepad from his jacket pocket.

Grace sniffed. 'Okay, so don't go making things up.' She paused while they located pens. 'Following recent speculation about Marburg disease, two cases have come to our attention: a man and a woman. The man died. The woman recovered. We are still trying to establish the source of infection but have notified local hospitals. Dr Kelly Ryder, here, treated the cases. She can give you the details.'

Ian sat, his chin resting on his hand, his eyes darting between Kelly and the reporters scribbling away.

'Your side of the bargain, Walter,' said Grace, when Kelly finished, 'is to report the facts and to alert your readers to the possibility – I emphasise possibility – of other cases occurring and to be on the look-out for the signs. Straight facts; nothing sensational. No *maneno* about killer-bug hits Nairobi.'

He thought for a minute. 'Sure. Any evidence of criminal activity?'

'We're seeking to establish the source of infection.'

'In my book that translates as: criminal activity cannot be ruled out.'

'What have I just said?' – steely ice.

'Okay, okay. I'm simply wondering why Special Branch is involved.'

'I'm not saying any more.'

'Yes, of course.' He smiled, put his pen away and closed his notebook. 'We appreciate what you've told us.'

Grace gave him a doubtful glance and passed him a sheet of paper from her folder. 'This is the information we've sent out to the various authorities.'

Walter slipped it into his briefcase. 'Thanks.'

'Final point, Walter: no names.'

He seemed to consider the request. 'Sure.'

Sammy arrived bearing a tray of disparate mugs from which tea was slopping. Behind him came a policewoman with a plate of biscuits.

Grace waved for people to help themselves.

'Now,' said Walter, 'perhaps I can give you something in return.' He took a small tape recorder from his brief case. 'This message was phoned into the newspaper this morning.' He pressed the play button.

Crackling and hissing was followed by a muffled voice: '*My name does not matter but I would like your paper to remind the people of Kenya of the anniversary of the great struggle against the oppressors of Islam. Njia Mpya will not let this day pass without recognition of our brothers who died as martyrs on this great day three years ago.*'

'Is this genuine?' asked Grace.

'We think so. It was preceded by a coded message.'

'What message?'

'I'm sorry, Grace, that goes beyond the terms of our agreement.'

'I could take out a court order against your paper.'

'You could, but we both know you won't.'

Grace scowled. 'Any thoughts, anyone?'

'I'm no linguistics expert,' said Ian, 'but it sounds like someone who speaks excellent English but it's probably not his native language.'

'Anyone else?' she asked.

Heads shaken.

'When did you receive the message, Walter?'

'Nine fifteen this morning.'

'Leave the tape, please.'

'Sure, we have the original.' Walter flipped open the tape recorder.

'In the interests of national security, I'm requesting you not to publish the message. It serves no public interest.'

Grace gathered her papers and stood up. 'And remember, Walter, don't you dare step off the track. Now if you'll excuse me, some of us have another appointment.'

***

Two cars pulled out of the yard at the back of Nairobi's police headquarters followed by a nondescript Toyota four-wheel-drive. A tall figure with a blanket over his head was squeezed between two police officers in the back seat of the unmarked lead car. In the second – a regular police car – officers, apparently on normal patrol duty, had their weapons hidden from the view. The Toyota followed

271

at a discreet distance. The three vehicles merged into the traffic on Uhuru Highway.

Felix, who was driving the Toyota, tapped the steering wheel and hummed tunelessly. Ian sat beside him trying not to imagine all the things which could go wrong. Grace was in the seat behind.

The twisted barrier, pitted walls and shredded trees near the Football Stadium still provided stark reminders of an event Ian struggled to forget.

'I wish to hell they'd clear up that mess.'

Felix grunted.

They passed the fortified citadel of the American Embassy, its flag at half-mast. Another reminder of the event three years ago.

Ian checked his watch.

They were half way through August the seventh.

Felix's mobile rang. He grabbed it from the shelf in front. 'Yeah, 'bout twenty minutes.' He returned the phone. 'Some smart ass from the Harry S says the eagle has landed.'

The cars in front began to speed up as the dual carriageway came clear of the city.

Two cars overtook them. Then a motorbike.

Felix moved to the outside lane to prevent other vehicles passing.

A Mercedes full of Asian ladies in saris came up on the inside. The driver, a turbaned Sikh, gesticulated angrily at the Toyota.

Felix waved two fingers. Remained in the outside lane. The Mercedes dropped back. Came up on Felix's tail. Began working the horn.

Ahead, the carriageway was blocked by two ponderous lorries driving side by side. All the traffic slowed.

The motorbike, or perhaps a different one, dropped back. Ian glimpsed two unidentifiable figures in helmets and black leathers.

'Next left,' said Grace.

Felix forced his way back to the inside lane. The Mercedes gave way. Then shot forward in the outside line. More gesticulations and horn.

The lorries continued to trundle towards Mombasa. The lead police car swung left, followed by the second car.

The Mercedes tried to cut in front of the Toyota.

Felix closed the gap.

Ian turned in his seat and gave a cheery wave to angry faces.

The service area and freight terminal of the airport came into view

272

about a mile ahead.

'What do we do about the bloody Merc?' muttered Felix.

'Forget it,' said Grace. 'But don't let it pass.'

Felix eased into the middle of the road. Another blast of strident horn.

The road ahead was empty. The driver of the Mercedes held the horn down, pulled onto the dirt shoulder of the opposite lane, engine snarling, and disappeared in a cloud of dust, enveloping those behind.

Felix swore.

A motorbike flashed past on the inside.

Gunfire.

Grace yelled into her radio.

The dust cleared.

The motorbike, with its two black-clad figures, raced away across the open plain. The Mercedes sped into the distance. The second police car followed, blue lights flashing.

The car containing Malik, its boot and rear window riddled with bullets, veered off the road. Smashed into a tree.

Felix pulled off the road. 'Fuck!'

The driver's door of the police car opened. The driver rolled out and lay groaning.

Grace and Ian leaped out of the Toyota. Ran across.

The man was oozing blood.

Felix arrived, clutching the vehicle's first aid pack. He ripped the man's shirt open. Hurled the pack away. 'He needs more than fucking sticking plasters.'

He and Ian used strips of the man's shirt to staunch the flow of blood.

Ian gritted his teeth. At least it wasn't another bloody bomb. At least there was no girl called Charity.

'I'll check the others.' Grace ran to the vehicle.

'What's the score?' called Felix.

'Two seem okay.' She hustled them out of the vehicle. They slumped to the ground.

'Malik?'

She whipped the blanket off his head. 'He's unconscious but still breathing. Covered in blood – impossible to tell whose. I think the other policeman's dead.'

She called the airport's police and emergency services on her radio.

'Ambulance is on its way. How's the driver?'

Ian got stiffly to his feet. 'I think he'll be okay. What about Malik?'

'I'm not a medic.'

'So what's plan B?'

Grace kicked savagely at the dirt. 'There isn't a plan B.'

'Yes, there bloody is!' Felix scrambled to his feet. Ran to the Toyota for his mobile. Bawled into it. Then ran back. 'Chopper's on its way. This scumbag's not getting off that lightly.'

He'd hardly finished speaking before the Blackhawk lifted off from beyond the freight terminal and sped towards them skimming low over the ground. It arrived with a deafening clatter of rotor blades and touched down some hundred metres away in a pall of dust which obliterated everything. The rotors had barely stopped before a door opened. Two US marines jumped out and ran across carrying a stretcher.

'Which one's Mr Smith?'

'Back of the car,' shouted Felix.

'Yes, sir!'

A third individual in immaculate navy whites emerged from the helicopter and sauntered towards them. 'Goddam it, Felix Rossi.'

'Chuck, you old coyote. How you doing, man?'

'Might've known you'd be in the middle of any shit being thrown around.' He noticed Grace. 'Begging your pardon, ma'am.' He stuck out his hand. 'Chuck Wallicker.'

'Pleased to meet you,' she said primly.

'We played in the same football team.' He jerked his head at Felix. 'Best quarter-back we ever had. Say, you see the score of last week's game?'

Before Felix could respond, an ambulance arrived, siren sounding and lights flashing. It pulled off the road and stopped.

Grace ran and spoke to the paramedics.

Ian joined the men attending to Malik. 'How is he?'

'We've saved worse,' said one, setting up a drip into Malik's arm.

The two marines then eased him out of the car, laid him on the stretcher and secured him in place with some serious strapping. They jogged back with him to the helicopter.

Waiting hands whisked him inside.

'You make damn sure that one lives,' Felix called after them.

'Don't you worry, man,' said Chuck.

'Hang on,' said Felix, running back to the Toyota and returning with a package. 'Papers from the guy's office. Name's there on the label. For someone called Howard something-or-other. You know him?'

'Sure, I know Howard.'

'Tell him to let us know what he finds.'

'Will do. I guess we'll get going. Nice meeting you folks.' He shook hands all round, returned to the helicopter and climbed aboard.

The rotors started.

Chapter 51

Colette was content to sit quietly beside Sean in the cabin of the small plane and gaze at the scenery slipping away beneath them: the dark green of coffee plantations, the blue green of pineapple fields and then, higher up, the green of tea bushes speckled with the bright clothing of tea-pickers. Then it was the neat *shambas* – smallholdings – of the Kenya highlands before the majestic peaks of Mount Kenya came up on their right, poking out of a collar of cloud which shrouded the forest below. They flew over the town of Nanyuki and the vegetation became sparser, the land more arid. This was where space began with the seemingly endless bush rolling away into the distance. Where sky, land and dust merged into a haze of emptiness. She had a brief insight into the pioneering spirit Karen Blixen must have felt, and wondered if she'd flown this way with Denys Finch Hatton in his biplane.

Am I stupid to be going back to London?

'What are you thinking?' shouted Sean, above the noise of the engine.

'Out of Africa.' She smiled at his bemused expression.

He pointed to a tiny speck in the distance. 'Tandala.'

She twisted round to Franco who was stretched across the two rear seats, sleeping off the previous night's party. The three of them were cocooned in a timeless world of their own: tiny, isolated and immune – at least transiently – from the rest of mankind.

She turned back to study the speck as it gradually crept nearer. All of a sudden, it rushed towards them. Sean brought the plane lower and buzzed the house. A figure came running out and waved. Leah? And surely that was Suni with her.

Sean banked round and prepared to land.

The sandy strip rushing to meet them, the nose of the plane coming up, the wheels touching down with a spurt of dust, then rattling over the hard ground before the plane finally coasted to a halt. It was beginning to feel so familiar.

'Welcome back,' said Sean, switching off.

Franco stretched and yawned. 'Now I start living again. Nairobi too much noise, too many people, too much *maneno.*'

What about London? Colette briefly recalled her sad little house.

'Let's go, guys.' Sean opened his door.

They climbed out. The smell of dust mingled with acacia blossom. The sound of birdsong, the sound of buzzing insects, the sound of peace. She tried to banish conflicting thoughts. Sean was busy unloading their bags from the back. Sensing her attention, he turned and smiled. 'Come.' He beckoned.

'What?'

'I want to show you something.' He took her hand. Led her through the trees. His face tense.

Suddenly she knew.

'Oh, God,' she whispered, as he pointed to the faint letters TP carved into the bark of the tree. 'And that... that...?' She indicated the distressingly small mound at the tree's base.

A slight nod.

'Sean, that is so sad.'

'Sorry we imposed this on you.'

She raised her anguished face. 'I'm so glad you did.'

'I like to think of her spirit soaring up there.' He pointed to a lone bateleur eagle sailing overhead.

'What a lovely thought.'

'Let's go.'

'You go on.'

He squeezed her hand. 'Sure.'

She stood staring at the tiny mound, her mind overwhelmed by desolation and grief. She moved to the tree. Hesitant fingers touched the initials carved into the trunk. 'I'm so glad I met you, Tanya,' she whispered. 'Mummy and Daddy love you very much.' She closed her eyes and bowed her head. Perhaps she prayed. She didn't remember.

She brushed the tears from her eyes. Looked into the heavens. The bateleur still circled. '*Kwa heri*, Tanya. To happiness.' She gave a slight wave.

A sound made her look round. Suni was bounding towards her with whines of delight. Colette picked her up. 'Suni, it's so nice to see you.' She tried to keep the frantic tongue out of her face. 'Let's go and find the others.' She set the little dog down and ran after her.

It took her a moment to recognise the wiry man, dressed in a T-shirt and ragged shorts, who was talking to Sean and Franco.

'Dima?'

He came over and smiled. '*Ndiyo, mimi* Dima.' He clasped her hands. '*Sasa nimepona kabisa.*'

She turned to Sean.

'Dima says he's now completely cured.'

'I cannot believe he recovered so quickly.'

Sean shrugged. 'I guess you have to be tough living in the bush.'

'*Kabisa*,' repeated Dima, and continued his outpouring of news.

Colette recognised a name. 'What's he saying about Samira?'

'Somehow, he met her and—'

'He met her! So she's all right?'

'Seems so. He says her face was very bad,' said Sean.

'I'm not surprised.'

'But now okay,' said Franco.

'Just like that?'

Dima nodded emphatically, picked up their bags and set off.

'Give him time,' said Sean, as they followed Dima back to the house. 'No rush.'

'What do you mean?' she said.

'Dima has announced that he now works for me.'

'What? No interviews, no references, no cvs?'

'What for?'

Why can't my life be as uncomplicated?

They came clear of the trees to see Leah standing on the steps of the veranda.

'You are all most welcome,' she said, smiling.

'Is all well, Leah?' asked Sean.

'It is well. That man has come.' She pointed disapprovingly at Dima who was seated on a nearby log paring his toenails with his *simi*, supervised by Suni.

'And Jotham?'

'He stays at Franco's place.'

'Is good,' said Franco.

'Any more trouble, Leah?'

'No trouble.'

'We'll go and join Dima,' said Sean. 'Could you bring some tea?'

Dima's earlier volubility had deserted him and he now sat wiggling his newly manicured toes like piano keys, embarrassed to be the centre of attention. Gradually his story emerged and Sean translated for Colette.

'What does he say about Samira?' she asked.

'He was very impressed by the way you sewed her face but it seems the wound got infected.'

278

'I'm not surprised. She needed antibiotics.'

'Dima says he gave her a home brew he concocted.'

'What sort?'

'I've no idea but I've heard that some of these bush remedies get infected by moulds which produce antibiotics.' Sean turned to Franco.

'*Si, si.* I also hear.' Franco sat nodding. 'Sean, my friend, can we… can we…?'

'What?'

'Can we pass my house?'

'Sure. We'll have a quick bite then drive over.'

'Is no so good, I think.'

***

Dima, as Sean's self-appointed employee, insisted on travelling on the roof of the Land Rover as a look-out.

Franco was slumped in the passenger's seat beside Sean who was driving. Colette sat in the seat behind with Suni on her lap.

'Franco, I was so sorry to learn about your house,' she said.

'Is only a home, I think.' He sniffed and lapsed once more into silence.

'I hope you didn't lose anything too precious.'

Perhaps the rattling of the vehicle muffled her words.

Sean turned off the main track and they continued in silence.

They came through a clump of trees and Franco cried out in amazement. 'My house. Sean, you say he was burned down.'

'It was.' Sean stopped the vehicle and they stared at the pristine building.

Two men, who were on the roof putting finishing touches to the thatch, waved. A door opened and a woman emerged.

'Samira!' Franco scrambled out of the Land Rover. Ran and hugged her. Sean, Colette and Suni followed, while Dima remained on the roof of the Land Rover grinning.

Samira came shyly forward and shook Sean's hand. '*Bwana.*' She then turned to Colette, who couldn't restrain herself and hugged her.

'Samira, it's wonderful to see you. You look so well, and your face. Let me see.' She held the smiling girl at arms' length.

Samira took Colette's hand and held it to her face. 'Is now good, I think.'

'*Dawa nzuri sana,*' called Dima from the roof.

'He says it was very good medicine,' said Sean.

'It certainly was.' Colette studied the suture line and tried to suppress the emotion welling up. Samira's face would probably always look slightly lop-sided but the effect on her beauty would be negligible once the swelling subsided and the scarring was replaced by normal tissue.

'Those sutures should soon be absorbed,' said Colette. 'Can you translate that, Sean? And tell Samira not to smile too much.'

'She says it's impossible not to smile,' said Sean. 'She is so happy now. And she is happy that Franco is well.'

'It'll take a while for things to settle and she may always have some restriction of movement.'

'You were bloody brilliant,' said Sean.

She pretended not to hear as she studied a beetle scurrying across the sand.

The two men scrambled down from the roof and began explaining everything to the bewildered Franco.

'What are they saying?' she asked.

'They say that Franco has done so much to help the local people,' said Sean. 'Now it was their turn to help him. Come, they want to give us a conducted tour.'

When they emerged from the little cottage, Franco ripped off his sling and threw it aside.

'I no longer need this slink. This is wonderful. I only need small house, simple house, a bush house. Is *perfetto, nzuri kabisa!*'

Chapter 52

The askaris on duty at the High Commissioner's residence were clearly expecting Ian. As soon as his vehicle turned into the leafy avenue, they opened the gates. He drove in, pulled up in front of the pillared portico and switched off.

The door opened and Quentin peered out – a spider preparing to exit a drain. 'Ah.'

Ian responded with a cool: 'You all set, then?'

'Just coming, old boy.'

The door closed, and Ian sat waiting and wondering whether he would get any sense out of Quentin. As he sat tapping the steering wheel, a well-upholstered woman strode up. She wore a flowered dress, sensible sandals and white socks, a floppy straw hat and yellow washing-up gloves.

'I won't let them touch the fuchsias,' she announced, in a voice normally reserved for calling recalcitrant hounds to heel. 'These chaps have no feeling when it comes to pruning fuchsias.' She brandished the secateurs she was clutching.

'I see,' said Ian. 'How are you, Lady Gilmore?'

'Call me Cynthia. You've come for Quentin, I suppose?'

'Yes. I understand he's being posted back to London.'

'Stupid nonsense. Aubrey's too soft.' She swooped on an inoffensive shrub to snip off an errant branch. 'What's this thing called? Lovely scent.'

'*Brunfelsia*. Same family as the deadly nightshade.'

'Oh!' She recoiled as though expecting it to entwine her.

'And the tomato,' he added.

'What a fount of knowledge you are, Ian.' Her voice dropped to her version of a whisper. 'Tell me, have you had a chance to see Fiona?'

'I, er, plan to go in tomorrow.'

'Can't think why she refuses to see us.'

'It sounds as though she's had a rough time.'

Lady Cynthia whirled her arms. 'Bloody *dudus*,' she muttered in Roedean vernacular, as some insect strayed into her air-space. 'I put it down to the diet.'

'I'm sorry?'

'Too much carbohydrate. All these fellows seem to eat is maize meal. No wonder they're—'

'Ah, here's Quentin.'

The furtive figure sidled out of the front door and came over to the Land Rover. 'Goodbye, Lady C.' He placed a dutiful kiss on the downy epidermis of her cheek.

'Goodbye, Quentin. Make sure you get some proper food inside you. Brace up a bit.'

He gave a watery smile and climbed into the passenger's seat clutching a small bag.

'Where's your luggage?' asked Ian.

'Already booked in. I didn't want to incommode you.'

'I see.' Ian put his head back out of the window. 'Goodbye, er, Cynthia.'

'Goodbye, Ian,' she boomed. 'Tell Fiona to eat lots of fruit and get plenty of fresh air.'

'Right, I will.'

As Ian drove out of the gate, the High Commissioner's wife strode purposefully towards an oleander which seemed to cringe before the advancing secateurs.

'Terribly good of you to do this for me, old boy,' said Quentin.

Ian grunted. Make the bugger sweat a bit.

'I took your advice, you know.'

'What advice was that?'

'Keep a low profile and—'

'Tell me, Quentin, what exactly happened at your house the other night?'

'Ah.' He fiddled with the zip on his bag then seemed to make up his mind. 'Frightful business. Hordes of them.'

'Hordes?'

'Seemed like it. I tried to fight them off, you know. Spirit of the— Did you go to public school, Ian?'

'No.'

'Right.' Quentin lapsed in silence.

'What happened to Fiona?'

'Don't know, old boy. I was overpowered and dragged off. I think she escaped.'

'I hear she's now in hospital.'

Quentin changed tack. 'I blame Stanley, you know.'

'Why Stanley?'

'All that Mau Mau stuff.'

Ian pulled up at some traffic lights and stared across at his colleague. 'What are you talking about?'

Quentin shifted in his seat. 'He's a Kikuyu. They were the ones at the centre of all that emergency kerfuffle. House servants letting the Mau Mau in at night to beat up the *wazungus*, that sort of thing.'

'That was fifty years ago, for God's sake.'

'In their blood, though.'

The lights changed and Ian moved off. 'Did you hear what happened to Stanley?'

Quentin either misheard or chose to ignore the question. 'It all happened so quickly. A few cuts and bruises but I gave one or two of them something to think about.'

Ian tried a different line. 'What do you think was the motive for the attack?'

'Unfinished business.'

'What sort of unfinished business?'

'That night when you were kidnapped from the house. You remember?'

'What about it?'

'Thing is, I believe they got the wrong man.'

'You think they were after you?'

Quentin nodded and stared ahead.

Ian sighed and tried not to notice the American Embassy coming up on the right-hand side for the second time that day – its flag still at half-mast. He checked his watch: six hours to go before he could start relaxing.

'Did you know today is the anniversary of the Embassy bombing?' asked Quentin.

'Yes. It was in the papers.'

'Wonder what those fellows are planning for tonight?'

'You think something will happen?'

Quentin shrugged. 'Wouldn't be surprised. Think they own the world.'

'Who do?'

'The Americans. Always throwing their weight—'

A motorbike roared past and Ian had a tense flashback of an earlier event that day, but the bike disappeared into the distance.

'I don't envy you chaps staying here. I won't be able to relax until I'm on that plane.'

283

Ian glanced across. 'The stuff you cleared from my office; what happened to it?'

'Oh, my lord. I should have told you.' Quentin clapped a hand to his forehead. 'All stolen in the raid. Can't think why anyone would want to take it.' He looked keenly at Ian. 'Was there some hush-hush stuff in there? Official secrets, that sort of thing? Material that could be used by an enemy of the state?'

'Expenses claims, you mean?'

'I jest not.'

Ian had to stop as a Maasai herdsman, emerged out of the approaching gloom and halted the traffic. Two others hustled a herd of cattle across the road.

'Peasants,' muttered Quentin.

Ian ignored him.

The road was now clear and traffic was moving again. As the lights of the passenger terminal came into view, Ian turned on the radio and wished he hadn't. He didn't need reminding about the anniversary. He switched off. Five minutes later, he pulled up outside the British Airways departure terminal.

'Goodbye, old boy,' said Quentin. 'I doubt our paths will cross again.' He shook Ian's hand, picked up his bag and climbed out of the vehicle. 'Thanks for the lift. Good show.'

'Goodbye, Quentin. Tell me something.'

'What's that?'

'Why have you been telling me a load of complete garbage this evening?'

Quentin gave a slight smile. 'I doubt you will ever know, old boy.' He emphasised the last two words, turned on his heel and walked away without looking back.

Chapter 53

It was mid-afternoon before they could get away from Franco's. Sean had just crossed the boundary into the ranch when Dima called from the roof.

Sean stopped and stuck his head out of the window. 'Dima says there's a vehicle coming this way,' he said. 'Let's see.'

He and Colette climbed out of the Land Rover and watched the dust plume draw gradually nearer. Some ten minutes later, the Petes drew alongside.

'You've have made good time,' said Sean.

'Thanks to the lonesome road,' cried Pete-A, giving a gesture encompassing Africa.

'Where are you heading?'

The flamboyance evaporated. 'To pay our last respects to Kimani.'

'Can we come with you?' asked Colette. 'Would that be all right, Sean? I'd like to… to see the place again.'

'Sure.'

'Dear lady, you'd be most welcome.'

'Do you know the short-cut?' asked Sean.

Pete-A shook his head. 'Lead, kindly light. We'll follow.'

Sean explained to Dima, and his expression clouded over.

After a couple of miles, Sean turned off the main track. The open plain quickly gave way to an escarpment with a barely-visible track across its rocky surface. This led to a series of steep inclines with the Land Rover grinding ever upwards like some willing work horse. They entered the forest and the cooler air was a welcome change from the heat lower down.

Colette looked round to see the Petes' vehicle following. Pete-A gave a languid wave.

'He's going to miss this,' said Sean, sensing her thoughts. 'They both are.'

'Do you think they'll come back?'

He looked across to her. 'You did.'

Why did he have to say that?

There was a faint tap on the roof and Sean stopped.

Dima's upside-down head appeared in Sean's window, a finger to its lips.

'What is it?' she whispered.

'Dima says it's a—'

A magnificent chestnut-coloured antelope, with vertical white stripes on its body, emerged from the bush and stepped onto the track in front. It had large ears and twisted horns, and was only slightly smaller than the greater kudu Colette had seen that first day on the ranch. She caught her breath.

Suni's ears were almost vertical with amazement.

'Bongo,' whispered Sean. 'First time I've seen one in this forest.'

The animal flicked its ears and briefly regarded the vehicles before disappearing into thick bush on the opposite side of the track.

'Wow,' she breathed.

'Quite something, hey?'

'It certainly was.' She turned to see Pete-A giving a thumbs-up and Pete-B clicking away with his camera.

'Let's press on,' said Sean. 'We're nearly there.'

She hunched in her seat and stared ahead, remembering that awful encounter with Kimani's remains.

They came clear of the trees and into the open area above the forest, stopped and climbed out of their vehicles. Dima jumped down from the roof. All of them silent.

An iridescent blue-black butterfly with twin tails on each hind wing settled on the bonnet of Sean's Land Rover.

'*Charaxes nandina*,' said Pete-A in a flat voice. 'Quite rare.' He kicked aimlessly at a tuft of grass and the butterfly flew away.

Suni wandered off sniffing. The two Petes followed.

A disturbance in the trees caused them to look up. A large male colobus monkey peered at the intruders in his territory. Satisfied they were not a threat he tore off some leaves and began munching them. The rest of the troop appeared.

Sean passed his binoculars to Colette.

'Not sick,' said Dima, sensing her interest. 'Before, very bad. Now better.'

She smiled.

'Over here.' Pete-B was on his hands and knees scrabbling in the grass. He held up a small bottle and peered at the label. 'It's that undescribed *Anopheles*, Pete. From the tree canopy on our last mosquito collection.'

Pete-A ran across and joined his colleague. 'Another bottle here.'

For a moment, the two of them immersed themselves once again in the science of the forest fauna.

Sean and Colette joined them. 'Most of the stuff's back at the house,' said Sean, 'but looks like we missed a few things.'

'I'd have been gutted if we'd lost these,' said Pete-B.

'If, as my distinguished colleague avers, this is truly a new species,' said Pete-A, 'we will name it *Anopheles kimanii*.'

'I think that's really nice, Pete,' she said.

'Yes, well.' He looked away.

They fanned out across the area and found a few more specimen bottles as well as some poignant reminders of the Petes' former camp: a pair of crushed sunglasses, a half-empty toothpaste tube and a sock with a hole in the toe.

'What do you want to do?' asked Sean. 'It'll be dark in an hour or so.'

'Where did you find Kimani's... find his body?' asked Pete-B.

'Through the trees there.' Sean pointed. 'Dima can show you.'

'Right.'

There was an awkward silence.

The two Petes looked at each other.

'I guess we won't camp here,' said Pete-A. 'I wonder if...'

'Come back to the house. Bring Dima with you,' said Sean. 'You know the way?'

'Yes. We've, we've a few things to finish here first. Thanks.'

'We'll go on ahead and put some beers in to cool.'

'Sounds good.'

There was a flash of gold as a black-headed oriole swooped across the clearing and into the trees on the far side, and began its melodious liquid call.

'A requiem for Kimani, I think,' said Pete-A.

Chapter 54

'All quiet last night?' asked Ian, as he and Grace sat down with Felix at the American Embassy's roof bar which was now serving breakfasts.

'At least the building's still standing,' growled Felix. 'But I don't think many of us got much sleep. What about your side, Grace?'

'Nothing.'

'So did our friend get it wrong?' asked Ian. 'Njia Mpya will not let this day pass without recognition of our brothers who died. Or whatever.'

'Perhaps the guys missed the bus,' said Felix.

Grace sniffed. 'So what would you do?'

'Excuse me?'

'If you'd missed the bus?'

Felix glowered. 'I guess I'd catch the next one.'

'Right. Only problem is we don't have the timetable.'

'Great. Thanks for that.' Felix jerked his head towards the bar. 'Self-service. Let's go grab some breakfast.'

They returned with their respective trays and Grace began peeling a banana with surgical precision. 'Have either of you had a chance to reread the report of the ninety-eight bombing?'

'I guess we've been too busy for light reading,' said Felix.

'Why do you ask?' said Ian.

Grace, having skinned her banana, executed a mid-line incision. 'Names.' She speared an excised morsel and popped it into her mouth.

'Names? What names?'

'Come on, Felix. We've both got the same list: the names of people involved in the ninety-eight attack and who are known to be still at large or unaccounted for. The sleepers who are waking up, *bwana*. Have woken up.'

'Hold on.' Felix went to the bar to use an in-house phone. 'On its way,' he said, returning to his seat.

'Anything back on Malik or the stuff you took from his office?' asked Ian.

'Still waiting to hear from the Harry S.'

'Nothing from my side,' said Grace. 'It'll take them a while to sort out.'

'And the motorbike which shot up the car?'

Grace shook her head.

'Most we can expect is a burnt-out wreck,' said Felix.

'How about the people in the car with Malik?' asked Ian.

Grace resumed her surgery. 'One died at the scene, as you know. The driver's going to be okay. The other two were unharmed, but unable to add anything.'

'And the Merc?'

She gave a slight smile. 'Some very frightened people but let off with a warning for dangerous driving. Unlikely to have had any involvement but we can follow up if necessary.'

Felix grunted. 'What's bugging me is how those ass-holes knew about the transfer.' He spooned some maple syrup onto a waffle. 'That Melhuish friend of yours, Ian; he been shooting his mouth off?'

'No way! One: he's not my friend. Two: I wouldn't even tell him the time of day. Three: he's out of our hair now. I've packed him off to UK – last night's BA flight.'

'Why?'

'I think the High Commissioner felt he was becoming a liability.'

'You can say that again. I get hot flushes whenever that guy's name's mentioned.'

'He was beginning to lose it, Felix. Talking complete garbage last night as I took him to the airport.' Ian looked up from his bacon and eggs. 'You know he beat up his wife?'

'No kidding? She the one who came to the Settlers Club the other night?'

'That was soon after it happened. I'm seeing her later.'

'Say hi from me.'

'Do you know her, Felix?'

He shrugged. 'Say hi, anyway.' He mopped up some maple syrup with his finger. 'Going back to Malik, Grace; any moles in your system?'

'Meaning what?'

'Who tipped off who about Malik being taken to the airport?'

'Listen, Felix, thanks to all the publicity, most of Nairobi would have heard about Malik's arrest.' Having finished her banana, Grace laid down her knife and fork side by side. 'There are always plenty of bystanders outside police HQ, anyone of them could have been watching.'

'Then as soon as they see a car driving out and someone with a blanket over his head, they call up the cavalry,' said Felix.

'Something like that.'

'Excuse me, major.' A young marine approached their table. 'The list you requested. Also, sir, Squadron Leader Hollis is here.'

'Thanks. Bring him up.'

'Yes, sir.'

'What's Tim doing here?' asked Ian.

'He's finalising his report on your bomb.'

'It's not my bloody bomb, Felix.'

'Figure of speech.' Felix flapped a paw. 'Leastways, he's asked me to check the draft. You ought to read it as well.'

Ian scowled and said nothing.

Felix turned to Grace. 'Learn anything?' He gestured to the printed sheet on the table.

She smoothed it out, took a pen from her bag and ticked off names. 'Twelve possible sleepers. Six are in custody, either here or in the US.' She crossed out the names. 'That leaves six others. These two blew themselves up trying to plant a home-made device.'

'And the other four?' said Felix.

'This one, we think is in Pakistan. Which leaves: Faisal Malik whom we've already picked up.'

'And who's now cruising the Indian Ocean,' added Felix. 'Who else?'

'Rashid Omari and Abdul Jamal, both of whom carry Kenyan passports.'

'Muslim names,' said Ian. 'Does that mean the coast?'

'Could be,' said Grace. 'Or possibly Somalia – Njia Mpya. Go back to your records, Felix and dig out any photos. Also, see if they carry other passports. I'll do the same.'

'Will do.'

The young marine returned with a stocky moustached figure in RAF uniform, who introduced himself to Grace. He then greeted Ian and Felix.

'You want some breakfast, Tim?' asked Felix.

'No thanks. Here's the draft, Felix. Grateful for your comments.' He turned to Ian. 'How's tricks?'

'Still tricky.'

'So where are you based?'

'I'm not. I spend my time pestering Grace and Felix. I can't go back to the High Commission.'

'Hmm. Still staying at the Settlers Club?'

'Yes, and going up the wall.'

Tim stroked his moustache. 'How about coming and staying back at my place?'

'I couldn't do that. It wouldn't be fair on your wife.'

'No problem. Mandy's just gone back to the UK. I put her on the plane last night. Sorting out the arrangements for when young James starts his new school next month. Means I'm on my own for a few weeks. Be good to have the company.'

'Are you sure?'

'Absolutely. Also you could probably use Mandy's office in the British Council. I'll check with her and she can call her boss.'

'Sounds good. Thanks, Tim.'

'Right. I've got your mobile number. One other thing: Sir Aubrey told me you were putting Quentin on last night's flight.'

'I did. I dropped him at the airport and waited until he went inside.'

'I see. What time was that?'

'Probably about seven.'

'That's strange, then.'

'What is?'

'It's simply that Sir A asked Mandy if she'd keep an eye on him, worried he might be heading for a nervous breakdown. Mandy phoned me this morning to say she'd arrived but said there'd been no sign of Quentin. She checked the passenger list with BA. He wasn't listed on the flight.'

Chapter 55

They set off early next morning for ole-Tomeno's meeting. Sean driving and Colette beside him with Suni on her lap, Dima in the seat behind.

The previous evening with the Petes had been sociable but subdued. They planned to leave that morning then spend the next few days sorting out the Nairobi end of their project before putting up the shutters. Colette thought they would spin things out in Kenya as long as possible. Was she doing the same?

'You're very quiet,' said Sean.

She applied a smile and remained staring ahead. 'Look! Oryx.'

Sean stopped and passed her his binoculars.

She made a pretence of studying them. I have made the right decision. I do have to go back.

She returned the binoculars. 'Thanks.'

As they continued their journey, the abundance and variety of the wildlife once again captivated her: zebras, more oryx, impala, warthogs, giraffe, dik-dik, baboons, quite apart from birds and butterflies.

Their journey became constantly punctuated with stops to study a bird, identify a new plant or scrutinise tracks – and even rocks. Was Sean doing this deliberately – trying to get her resolve to weaken?

I will come back – one day. But it will be as a friend.

They reached the dusty and unlovely outskirts of Isiolo. The township seemed hardly more than a village, with a single main road through the middle and a few side streets leading, as far as Colette could tell, mostly off into the bush. A scruffy gateway to the remoter eastern, northern and lawless regions of Kenya.

They pulled up at the back of a building which had once been white but had now taken on the terracotta colour of the surrounding dust which pervaded everything in the region.

They climbed out. Sean passed Suni to Dima who carried her onto the roof of the Land Rover where they settled down to acts as askaris.

Sean and Colette were about to enter the building when an open Land Rover pulled up, Franco at the wheel.

'How's your new house?' she asked.

'Is very okay,' said Franco, grinning. 'Come.' He led them through the back door, nodded briefly to the two women inside, who smiled doubtfully at the three people filing past, then led them up some stairs before knocking on a door at the end of a corridor.

The door was opened almost immediately by a smiling ole-Tomeno. '*Hamjambo, wote*,' he cried. 'Dr Fraser, so good of you to come.'

'Not at all.'

Why had she allowed herself to be talked into this?

'*Karibuni* – come in. Solomon some tea for our guests,' he called to the scowling proprietor, who'd followed them up the stairs.

Franco gave Solomon a playful punch. 'And plenty of biscuits, you old baboon.'

'Baboon yourself.' Solomon's face broke into a grin of brown-stained teeth.

'Please be seated, my friends.' Ole-Tomeno gave his shark-like smile and gestured to seats with garish covers displaying rampaging elephants. 'While we wait for Solomon, let me explain why I am here and why I have asked you good people to meet me. Dr Fraser, I include you in that welcome.'

'Thank you.' She tried not to be mesmerised by the self-congratulatory smile. 'Please call me Colette.'

He nodded graciously. 'As the MP for Isiolo District and patron of the Condor Programme, I have become increasingly concerned by some of the stories I am hearing about this area. I was appalled to hear of the attack, not only on your work premises, Franco, but also on your house. I understand, though, that the local people have rallied round to repair at least some of the damage.'

'They rebuild my house,' mumbled Franco. 'Is now very good.'

'That's splendid news. I also understand that one of your people, Sean, has been keeping an eye on the project premises.'

Sean nodded. 'I plan to pick him up after this meeting.'

'Good. Now to Condor. It is clear to me that the programme cannot be implemented while my own constituency, a major wildlife area, is in turmoil – hardly an appropriate model for the programme as a whole. I'm sure you agree.' He paused while the women from downstairs delivered tea and biscuits.

Franco winked at Solomon, who scowled back.

Ole-Tomeno sipped his tea and studied them.

Colette found his scrutiny unsettling and wondered how much of

293

his rhetoric to believe.

Ole-Tomeno finally turned to Sean. 'While I address the political issues, I'd like you to put on your Condor hat, Sean, and visit Lokinang.'

'May I ask why?'

'People tell me that the trouble in the region seems to emanate from there.'

'Forgive me, Daniel, but shouldn't it be the police or army who go and investigate?'

'Ah, but that's the point. You're going there as a conservationist looking at the wildlife potential of the area and how the needs of local people can be better integrated with those of the wildlife. While you're there, you keep eyes and ears open. See if there is any substance to the whisperings. If I were to send in the army or police, the local people would clam up, not say anything and they would know nothing.'

'Aren't Grace and Ian already covering that aspect as part of their remit on the security task force?'

'Yes, of course. Coming at things from a different angle, though, would complement their work.'

'I wouldn't want to tread on their toes.'

'Of course not. Just keep a low profile. That man Dima, whom I met, knows the area well. Take him with you.'

Sean frowned. 'Did you put him up to this?'

'I understand he was looking for work. It struck me that his local knowledge would be invaluable.'

'I see.'

'Franco, you may also want to, shall we say, assess the impact of your aid programme in the area.'

'I not understand,' said Franco, still mumbling.

'Your man, Khalif, can explain. We discussed earlier. The sooner we can establish the cause of the rumours and unrest in the area, the sooner we can decide how to proceed.' He paused to sip his tea, beaming round the gathering as he did so. 'Let me know how you get on.' He turned to Colette. 'I believe Jeff mentioned to you a vaccine development programme – some exciting prospects, it seems. I'd be interested in your views as to its feasibility.'

'I'll need to think about it.'

'I'd appreciate that. Talk it through with Jeff. What a wonderful triumph for Kenyan science – a vaccine for AIDS.' Unctuous smile.

'Kenya would forever be indebted to you, Colette, if you could see your way to helping with the programme.'

Her mind began to wander as conversation flowed back and forth. Sometimes in English. Sometimes Swahili.

Ole-Tomeno looked at his watch. 'Goodness, is that the time? More tea, anyone?'

'For me, beer,' said Franco.

Ole-Tomeno was briefly wrong-footed but quickly recovered. 'A splendid idea. It's never too early for a beer. Solomon, bring beers, please.'

Solomon glared at Franco and shambled out of the room.

'I go help.' Franco scrambled to his feet and hurried after him.

Ole-Tomeno frowned. 'While we wait, Sean, tell me if you've come across someone called Rashid?'

Sean shook his head. 'Where have you heard the name?'

'I wouldn't want to prejudice any thoughts you might have, but I believe it is a name we should keep in mind,' he intoned.

'That's not very helpful, Daniel. Can you give me the context?'

'You've heard of Mlala?'

'The sleeper. Only whisperings. I don't know whether to take them seriously.'

'Think of Rashid in the same context. Ah, here are the beers.'

Franco and Solomon entered clutching bottles which they handed round.

'You must excuse our Kenyan custom, Colette,' said ole-Tomeno. 'We prefer to drink straight from the bottle. Good health. Let me propose a toast to Condor.'

The others muttered.

Colette had the feeling that Sean and Franco shared her relief when they were finally able to escape.

'Keep me informed of progress, Sean,' called ole-Tomeno.

'Sure.'

'You too, Franco. You can always contact Maria if I'm not available. Thank you so much for coming at such short notice.'

They trooped down the stairs and out into the bright sunlight. 'What was all that about?' asked Sean.

'I not know,' said Franco. 'Perhaps a waste of time. Perhaps not.' He hugged Colette and seemed about to say something but changed his mind.

'We'll follow you, Franco,' said Sean. 'I need to collect Jotham.'

295

'Is good.' Franco clapped Sean on the back, climbed into his Land Rover and clattered off down the dusty road.

Sean returned with Colette to their Land Rover. 'Is all well, Dima?'

'It is well. Those men have come.'

'Which men?'

Dima pointed with his chin to a Toyota Land Cruiser beside which stood two men. They waved.

'Jeff, Richard!' cried Colette, running over to them, 'You're back?'

Jeff's smile was tense.

'What?'

'Bad news, I'm afraid. Maria told us you'd be here. We thought we might catch you.'

'What news?'

'About your father. The High Commission contacted me to say he's taken a turn for the worse, and you need to return to England.'

'No!'

'I'm so sorry,' said Jeff. 'You're booked on tonight's plane.'

'But I…'

'We have to leave now. It's a long drive.' He waved to Sean who was still talking to Dima.

'Leave now?' she echoed.

'If we're to get to the plane on time.'

'Oh, God!' She ran back to Sean. 'I'm so sorry, Sean, I didn't want it to happen like this.'

'What?' His expression mirrored hers.

'It's my dad. I just hope I'll be in time. The High Commission has booked me on tonight's flight.'

'What do you mean?'

'I've got to go back to England. I nearly didn't come because of what I feared. And now it's happened.'

She glanced at the other two. That smug look on Richard's face – surely imagined.

Jeff came and joined them. 'I hate being the bearer of bad tidings.'

'You're leaving now?' said Sean.

Jeff nodded. 'Where are your things, Colette?'

'My passport's back at the house at Tandala and I have a case in store at the Fairview.'

'We'll pass by the house on the way.'

'I'm so sorry, Sean,' she said.

'Why don't I fly you down? Be a lot quicker.'

296

'That's very good of you, Sean,' said Jeff, 'but we've got to go back to Nairobi.'

'It's no trouble.'

'I'm sure you've got more than enough to do here. Save you a journey. Provided we leave soon, we'll be in good time.'

'Let's go, Jeff,' she said, her face empty. 'It's best this way, Sean. You promised Franco you'd fetch Jotham.'

He said nothing.

'I'll write,' she whispered, kissing him on the cheek.

'Sure.'

She turned and walked to Jeff's vehicle. This wasn't how it was supposed to end. She didn't dare look back. A page of her life had been torn from the chapter she'd not yet read.

Chapter 56

'Darling, how lovely to see you,' cried Fiona, as Ian entered her room. She was sitting up in bed. A floral turban now replaced the bandages previously round her head. 'You've brought a ray of sunshine to my humdrum existence.'

'I've also brought these.' He proffered the package he was holding.

Fiona tore off the wrapping paper. 'Milk chocs, my favourite. Come here, you lovely man.'

He approached cautiously and received a passionate kiss.

She drew back, slightly breathless.

'How are you?'

'Miserable. You can't imagine.' She stuffed in a truffle surprise. 'The only people I see are nurses and that American doctor, Kelly. No one else comes.' She explored the inside of her mouth with her tongue to ensure she'd got her money's worth.

'That's probably because you tell them not to.'

'Oh.' Fiona screwed up the wrapping paper, then held out the box. 'They're very nice.'

He shook his head.

'You're being very masterful, Ian. So it's not simply a social call?'

'No.'

'Oh dear. Why have you come, then?'

'A number of reasons. One is that your father asked me to.'

'How is Daddy?'

'Shall we say, he's unsettled.'

Her gaze wandered round the room as though pursuing swirling thoughts she was unable to catch. 'Oh,' was all she could manage.

'He talked about having a word with the Permanent Secretary – someone called Halliwell – to try and—'

'Quentin used to call him ET.'

'Why ET?'

'The Everlasting Typist. He also looks like an alien.'

'I see. Anyway, your father said he'd speak to him, see if he could fix Quentin up with a quiet post in Montserrat, Vanuatu or similar.'

Fiona glowered and smuggled another chocolate into her mouth. 'I don't care.'

'Why?'

298

'I'm not going anywhere with him. We're finished.' Words churned in a mixture of emotion and caramel delight.

Ian studied her. Probably the truth. 'But it won't happen,' he said.

'What won't?'

'A backwater head-of-mission post.'

'Why do you say that?'

'Because I took Quentin to the airport last night to catch the plane to London but he never arrived. In fact, it appears he didn't get on the plane.'

A look of alarm passed fleetingly over her face. She hastily swallowed the caramel delight and pulled the bed covers up to her chin – a nervous filly peering over its stable door. 'Do you know what happened?'

'No. Do you?'

'Me?'

'I wondered if you and Quentin are playing silly buggers, stringing me along.'

'No! Why do you say that?'

'I've now been given three versions of what happened that evening you came stumbling into the Settlers Club: one from you, one from your father and one from Quentin who was babbling away as I drove him to the airport last night. I suspect none of them is true.'

Tears began to trickle down her face.

He remained unmoved – even when she began to sob.

Finally, she wiped her face on the bed covers and gave a faint smile. 'That didn't work, did it?'

'Fiona, you're incorrigible.'

She brightened. 'You have such a wonderful way with words.'

'So do you.'

'How can you say that, darling?' She began to wilt under his gaze. 'What?'

'Can I ask you some questions.'

She whipped off the turban to reveal her partly-shaved scalp bisected by a line of sutures streaked in gentian violet. 'How do you like my punk hairstyle?'

'It looks nasty.'

'It was.'

'That's partly what I've come to ask you about.'

She fitted her turban back on. 'What is it you want to know, darling?'

'Shall we start with the truth?'

'The truth? *Quid est veritas* – what is truth?'

'Shall we try this for starters? Stanley's dead.'

A hand flew to her mouth. Probably genuine shock. 'Stanley, who works for us?'

'Stanley, who used to work for you.'

'What happened?' Her eyes were imploring, wanting it not to be true. Was she hoping, so she could walk away from truth?

'You've heard of Marburg disease? It's been in the papers recently.'

'That horrible thing people can catch from monkeys?'

'Stanley didn't catch it from monkeys. He caught it from a bottle of vitamin pills – except they weren't vitamins.'

'How awful.' A string of emotions chased across her face.

He watched dispassionately, wondering which were genuine and which were the actress.

'Poor Stanley. It shouldn't have happened like this. It's gone all wrong.'

'What has?'

She seemed to gather her resolve and sat up in bed. 'What can I tell you, Ian?'

'You've already asked me that question and I've already answered.'

She nodded bleakly.

'In case you've forgotten, let me give you the list. What exactly happened that night you were beaten up? What was Quentin's involvement? Why wasn't he on the plane? Why do you refuse to see your parents? What happened to Stanley? That's a start. I'll probably think of others.'

She stared straight ahead. 'It's Daddy, you know. All I've been doing is trying to protect him.'

He went over to the window, his back to her. The American Embassy looked ugly and impregnable in the distance. 'Yesterday was an anniversary – the third, to be exact,' he said. 'I can't help thinking that in some obscure way these events may be connected.' He spun round. 'Are they?'

If his intention had been to catch her off guard, he didn't succeed. She still had the expression of bleak despair. He suddenly felt sorry for her. Pulling up a chair beside the bed, he sat down, took her hand and kissed it. 'Tell me.'

She buried her face in his neck and wept. Finally, she gave a great sigh and looked up. 'Please don't hate me, Ian.'

He didn't reply.

'I can't blame you if you do.' She brightened. 'Have a chocolate.'

He grasped her shoulders and looked into her face. 'Just stop. Okay?'

She held his gaze for a moment then seemed to crumple. 'All right.' She took a deep breath. 'Remember what I told you about Pakistan?'

'Some of it.'

'It seemed to start soon after Daddy got his knighthood and Quentin got nothing.'

'What started?'

'Quentin's bitterness. Please don't breathe a word of this, Ian.' Her eyes were imploring. 'Particularly to Daddy.'

'I can't make any promises. But I'll respect your confidences.'

'I suppose I can't ask for more.' Her hand hovered over the chocolates as though contemplating a difficult exam question. But she changed her mind. 'When Quentin first got to Pakistan, about twelve years ago, he had to travel all over the region. Anywhere ending in "stan" and he seemed to visit: Afghanistan, Uzbekistan, Kazakhstan, Tajikistan and the others. I can't remember all the names now. He became very good at the languages. I suppose it was his acting background – having to learn his lines.'

'Why did he go to those places?'

'As a sort of roving emissary; that was the official line. You know how funny he can be at times, and flippant. I think the local people regarded him as a harmless buffoon and he played on this.'

'He was a spy?'

'No! Spy's a dirty word. Spies are seedy men in grubby raincoats who hang around street corners and sleazy night clubs. Quentin wasn't like that.'

'Okay, but he used his position to gather intelligence?'

'I suppose so.'

'What sort?'

'He didn't, of course, tell me. But, at first, I think it was about the Russians and their weapons programmes. After the Cold War ended, it was more to do with Pakistan and the rise of extremism against the west, particularly through the Taliban in Afghanistan.'

'How did he get involved in that?'

He spoke fluent Urdu – like a native. Very few people realised. Even Daddy didn't know, although I think he may have suspected.

When they went to political meetings, the official proceedings were always conducted in English, but the Pakistanis would whisper among themselves without realising Quentin could understand every word. It meant that Daddy's reports back to London were always much more revealing than the Pakistanis could have realised.'

'And that's why he got his K?'

She nodded. 'I've probably said enough.'

'I'm sorry, Fiona, but all you've told me is that Quentin is good at languages and travelled a lot when he was in Pakistan. It answers none of the questions I've asked you.'

'You don't give up, do you?'

'No.'

'What will you do, if I don't tell you more? Put me over your knee and spank me? That would be fun.'

He regarded her coldly. 'I think you would have quite a lot on your conscience.'

Chapter 57

Dima and Jotham sat together on the roof of the Land Rover, Suni between them, as Sean drove unhurriedly back to the house.

'He is a good man, that one,' said Dima.

Jotham nodded. 'He is good. He understands us Africans.'

'He understands us.'

Suni seemed to nod in agreement and the two men laughed.

'That Khalif told me about the attack on his uncle's *duka*,' said Jotham.

'That was very bad.'

'Khalif says you rescued him from those Njia Mpya people.'

'That one is very brave but those ones are not good.'

'They are not.'

They continued in silence for a while, Dima absorbing his surroundings and considering the implications of his new life. 'Would Sean let me bring my family here?' he asked.

'It is possible. My family stays here. I have two sons.'

'For me, the same,' cried Dima. 'They need to go to school. There is no school where they stay.'

'There is no school here.'

They lapsed into silence again.

'Do you know Samira?' asked Dima.

'That one, I know. Khalif told me how you cured her when she had that sickness.'

'*Kwele* – true.'

'You are a good man.'

Dima began stroking Suni's ears. 'Samira told me she was a teacher in her country. Would Sean let her start a school here?'

'You must ask. It may be possible.'

'Our sons can then go to school together.'

'Perhaps.'

***

Sean pulled up outside the house. 'There is no vehicle,' he said. 'Did you see the Toyota?'

'We did not see,' said Dima.

Jotham shook his head.

The two of them climbed down from the roof of the Land Rover,

Dima carrying Suni. He set her on the ground and she scurried off.

'I will ask Leah,' said Jotham, going into the house.

While they waited, Dima drew random patterns in the sand with a toe. 'Is it possible that I can bring my family here, Sean? Here is a very good place and I can do good work for you.' He stood staring at the patterns.

'Where does your family stay, Dima?'

'It is very far. A place called Lokinang.'

'Lokinang?'

He nodded.

'I have to visit that place,' said Sean. 'If you come with me we can ask them.'

Dima looked up, smiling. 'They can stay here?'

'Of course. But are you sure they will want to leave their home?'

'*Bwana*, that is not a good place. Life is very hard. Often, no food. It is so hot maize cannot grow. My wife has to walk very far to find water. Here is a good place, a very good place.'

'We will go there and bring them back and you can help me build a house for them.'

'You are a good man.' He clasped Sean's hands.

'We must wait to hear about those men who are taking Colette; then we can leave.'

'Those men.' Dima returned to his patterns in the sand.

'What about them?'

'That African man—'

'He is called Richard.'

Dima shrugged. 'I think that one is not good.'

'Why do you say that?'

He drew another pattern with his toe. 'There is a place at Lokinang, a bad place, a place where they take dead monkeys—'

'Dead monkeys? What do they do with dead monkeys?'

'I don't know. That man, I saw him there.'

'When?'

Before Dima could respond, Jotham appeared on the veranda. 'Those ones have not come. Leah has been here and has not seen them.'

'The vehicle must be broken – perhaps a puncture,' said Sean. 'We will wait for some time then go and look. Jotham, ask Leah to prepare us some food.'

***

Dima sat beside Sean in the cabin of the tiny plane, not daring to move anything but his eyes. The engine started. The noise! He wanted to cover his ears but was paralysed.

'*Tayari* – ready?' called Sean.

Dima remained rigid.

The noise became even louder and the plane began to move forward. The trees at the end of the track rushed towards them.

Dima closed his eyes. His stomach fell down inside him. He waited for the trees to come crashing into the cabin.

Nothing.

He opened an eye. Then both eyes. All he could see was sky. '*Aieeh!*'

'Now you are a bird,' said Sean.

Dima risked a glance out of the side window. 'The ground is very far.' The plane began to turn, lying on its side in the air. He clutched the seat fearing he would fall.

Sean smiled and pointed. 'See the house,' he shouted.

'It is so small,' cried Dima. 'I see Suni. She is like an ant.' As he realised the plane was not about to tumble out of the sky, he relaxed, and even began to enjoy the flight. 'I am a vulture. I can see very far. I see many things.'

Sean indicated ahead. 'See, that is Isiolo. We will go there then follow the road back.'

'It is so wonderful to see everything from such a high place. See there,' cried Dima. 'It is a rhino.'

'Your eyes are very good.'

'They are good.' He pointed to tiny vehicles in the distance. 'They are *siafu* – safari ants.'

'That is the main road from Isiolo. See down here; this is the road we must follow. Watch for that Toyota.'

Dima concentrated on the track below them. He saw some zebras and nearby some giraffes. He used to wonder what it would be like to look over the trees like a giraffe and see far. Now he was a vulture and could see everything. They flew over some huts. Some children waved. He waved back. More giraffes over there. And there elephants. But no Toyota. 'That *gari*, I cannot see,' he shouted.

Sean frowned. 'What has happened?'

'Perhaps they went another way.'

Sean took the plane higher.

There is the sacred mountain of Ololokwe. There the forest where the monkeys live. There, surely a tiny plume of dust. He pointed it out to Sean, who shook his head. *Wazungus* had poor eyesight. Dima was content to wait while the dust crept nearer.

'I see,' cried Sean finally.

'It is the one.'

'But why is he going this way?'

'Perhaps he is lost.'

Sean frowned.

The vehicle drew rapidly closer and Sean went so low he almost touched the trees. He flew over the vehicle and then soared back into the sky. An arm came out and waved.

'Is that the *gari*?' asked Dima.

Sean nodded. 'But where is he going?'

'Perhaps to Lokinang.'

Sean turned the plane. 'Today is late. We will go tomorrow.'

Chapter 58

Ian returned to Fiona's room with a cup of coffee he'd purchased from the hospital canteen.

'You sure you don't want one?'

'No thank you, darling.'

'I forgot to tell you; Felix said to say hi.'

'Felix? Do I know a Felix?'

'He's my counterpart in the American Embassy.'

'Is he good looking?'

'Much better than me. He's in the US marines.'

Fiona's eyes widened. 'Send him a kiss and tell him to come and help me convalesce.'

'I'll think about it.' Ian settled in the chair beside her bed, conscious of her regarding him with the large brown eyes of the nervous filly.

'Is it inquisition time?'

'No thumb screws. I promise. Was it Quentin who beat you up?'

'I don't think so,' – small voice.

'Earlier, you said it was.'

'I was wrong. It all happened so quickly, I thought it must have been him.' She fiddled with the box of chocolates still lying on her bed. Seeming to make a decision, she closed the lid and put the box on the bedside table. 'One thing about being stuck here is that I have time to think things through.'

'Or make up stories?'

'Don't be so beastly! If you're going to question everything I say, I'm not going to tell you what happened. I was knocked unconscious, you horrid man. How can you expect me to remember all the details?'

'Sorry, Fiona, but it's my job.'

'Huh!' She yanked her top down to show her chest and shoulders covered in bruises. 'He also did that to me. Sorry I can't remember whether he had a mole on his cheek or what after-shave he used. I was too busy trying to survive.' She covered herself again and glared. 'And before you ask. No. He didn't do *that* to me.'

'I said I was sorry. Sorry I have to play a bastard at times, but some of the things I have to deal with can be quite unpleasant.'

'I know.' The nervous filly nodded.

'Who attacked you?'

'Let's call him Mick.'

'Why Mick, in heaven's name?'

'Because Mick's easy. And before you interrupt; I'm not playing silly buggers. I just can't remember his real name except that it began with M. At least, I think it did. It's something like Majid, Massouk. It was either him or someone working for him.'

'Could it have been Malik?'

'Why? Do you know a Malik?'

'It's another Pakistani name beginning with M.'

'I suppose it could have been.'

'Someone you knew in Pakistan?'

'I didn't know him. Quentin did.'

Ian was content to wait, hoping this version of the story would approach the truth.

Fiona leaned back and closed her eyes. 'You know about *madrassas*, Ian?'

'Schools for Islamic studies. What about them?'

'Quentin was invited to lecture at one of them on, what were called, "western values." Daddy thought it was a splendid idea.' Her eyes remained closed. Had she fallen asleep?

After a pause, she resumed. 'It seems the scheme might have backfired.'

'How?'

'I think, rather than instilling western values into them, Quentin might have been the one who was influenced.'

'And converted to Islam?'

'He grew a big bushy beard while we were there. I said it made him look like Rasputin.'

'Was this when you began to have doubts about him?'

'I suppose so. When Daddy's knighthood came through, I think Quentin began to look at ways to get back at the establishment which had overlooked everything he'd done. Outwardly he remained the same – jovial and witty – but I could see a change.'

'You believe he became radicalised and went over to the bad guys?'

'The bad guys? I sometimes wonder who they are.'

'Hell's bells, Fiona. You know who I'm talking about. People who blow up American Embassies, for Christ's sake. And tried to blow me up, for that matter. The people whose anniversary we celebrated yesterday. Except not many of us did.'

'Oh, God! You think Quentin might have been involved in that?'

'I don't know. I'm asking you.'

'And I don't know either. If you don't stop interrogating me as though I was responsible, I'll call a nurse and get you thrown out.' She dropped her gaze and the anger faded from her eyes. 'Sorry, Ian.'

'Here.' He passed her a drink from the table beside the bed.

'You're very kind. I like people who are kind.'

He waited.

'Soon after we arrived here, I got a phone call at the house from a man who said something like: "*this is Mick – except he didn't say Mick – tell Abdul I'm back in Kenya.*" I told the man he had a wrong number but when I mentioned it to Quentin, he became very angry and said I'd been spying on him. If he'd dismissed it, I would have forgotten all about it.'

'You think Abdul could be the Islamic name Quentin used?'

'Have you ever been attacked like this, Ian?'

He shook his head.

'It can be quite hard to remember things. It's called amnesia. And before you start thinking that's convenient for her...'

'I wasn't.'

'I'll probably remember more as my memory comes back.' She challenged him with her eyes.

He didn't respond.

'Someone came to the house that night. Quite late. I could hear Quentin talking to him in the hall. They seemed to be arguing and your name was mentioned.'

'Mine?'

'Something about the bomb, I think, and why things hadn't been sorted out.'

'What was that supposed to mean?'

'I couldn't hear everything – only when their voices were raised. Remember I said Quentin thought you and I had been... had been doing things that night you came to our house?'

Ian tried to keep his face expressionless.

'He was furious. I don't know whether he accepted that nothing happened, but I think he felt I was partly responsible for your kidnap, rescue, disappearance, whatever it was. Informing the enemy, if you like.'

'So this was payback time?'

She shrugged and a hand strayed to her turban. 'Then the arguing stopped and Quentin came into the sitting room to say he had to go out, something urgent, not to wait up. I heard the front door close and decided to get an early night. I went into the hall and... and I don't remember much until I woke up lying on the floor in a pool of blood. I called for help but no one came. Eventually, I managed to recover sufficiently to clean myself up. I knew you were staying at the Settlers Club and... and the rest you know.'

'Any idea who attacked you?'

'No.'

'No. Is that it?'

'Stop being a pig.'

'You're sure it wasn't Quentin. Both of them, even?'

She glared at Ian. 'I don't know.'

'Could it have been one of these people whose name begins with M: Majid, Massouk, Mick or whoever.'

'I suppose so.'

'The man who was arguing with Quentin?'

'Ian, how much longer is this going on for?'

'Fiona. We've got to sort this out.' He got up, wandered to the window then turned back. 'Why haven't you told your parents?'

'Daddy would never believe me. He thinks the sun shines out of Quentin's backside.'

'Your mother then?'

Fiona gave a rueful smile. 'Mummy would say I should brace up, eat lots of fruit and get plenty of fresh air.'

He returned the smile. 'Seriously, though, you should let them come and see you. They're really worried.'

'Would you tell them?'

'Sure.'

'But don't tell them any of the things we've talked about, darling. I'll make up something.'

'That shouldn't be difficult.'

'Beast!' She stuck out her tongue then lay back against her pillows. 'Oh what a tangled web we weave when first we practise to deceive. Do you know where that comes from?'

'Macbeth?'

'Most people think Shakespeare, but it's from Marmion by Sir Walter Scott.'

'I see. And is that what you're doing?'

She sat up, her eyes blazing. 'If you're going to stoop so low, you can bloody well get out!'

'I'm sorry, Fiona, that was uncalled for.'

'Too right.'

'Sorry. Am I forgiven?'

'I haven't decided.'

He watched a plane passing over the American Embassy on its way to the airport. 'So why didn't Quentin get on the BA flight?'

'I've no idea.' She folded her arms and glowered. 'Have you stopped being a pig?'

'Yes.' He returned to the bedside.

'Hmm. You know Quentin had a diplomatic pass for the airport?'

'For meeting and greeting dignitaries?'

'And escorting them through immigration.'

'Right. So he could have used that to get through and then boarded a different plane – assuming he had a ticket – or simply waited until I'd left and come back out?'

'I suppose so.'

'He's not tried to make contact?'

'He wouldn't dare.'

'I'll take that as a no, then.'

She rubbed her eyes. 'You're still being a bit of a pig, Ian, and I'm beginning to feel quite tired.'

'I won't grill you much longer. Tell me about Stanley, though.'

'Is it true what you said, about him, about him catching that disease?'

'Yes. It's what Helen had; only she's on the mend thanks to Kelly.'

Fiona stared forlornly into space. 'He went with the house.'

'Stanley did?'

'I think we were the fourth set of High Commission staff to be accommodated there. By the time we arrived, Stanley probably felt he owned the place. He certainly seemed to run it to suit himself. Took no notice of what I said. Provided I let him do things his way, he was fine. If I queried anything like petty cash missing or sugar disappearing, he would get stroppy. In the end I decided to overlook his pilfering: booze, tea, biscuits and so on. He probably regarded them as perks which went with the job. And he was a terrible hypochondriac.'

'In what way?'

'Always complaining about things wrong with him – probably to shirk his work. And always asking for medicines and pills.'

'Which you gave him?'

'Sometimes. Mostly, though, I think he helped himself from the cabinet in the bathroom.'

'Without really knowing what he was doing.'

'Probably.' She gave a slight smile. 'I think he went on taste. The fouler it was the greater its efficacy. Does any of that help?'

'Possibly.' Ian stared at a pied crow which had settled on the window sill outside and was peering into the room.

'Go away, you beastly bird.' Fiona waved her arms.

The crow flew off.

'That's not an omen, is it? We were talking about Stanley.'

'Bit late for that, I'm afraid.' Ian paused to gather his thoughts. 'We think Helen caught Marburg from some vitamin pills that had been doctored in some way—'

'That's terrible. But how?'

'We don't know. It's possible Stanley was infected in the same way but we can't see a link.'

'Quentin had some pills.'

Ian checked. 'He what?'

'In a brown bottle. They were among some papers he brought back from the office one day. I pulled his leg about them and he got very cross, telling me to mind my own business.'

'Did you read the label?'

'He wouldn't let me.'

'What happened to them?'

'I think he burned them, along with the papers. He said he was having a clear-out at work.'

'Could they have been my papers?'

'I don't—'

There was a perfunctory knock, the door opened and a harassed-looking Kelly came bustling in. 'Sorry to barge in, folks. Bit of an emergency and we need to free up some space. We're bringing someone else in here, Fiona. Hope you don't mind.'

'So long as he's tall, dark and handsome. Nothing personal, Ian.'

He shrugged. 'Do you want me to leave, Kelly?'

'No. You're fine.' She smiled at Fiona. 'Sorry to disappoint, but she's tall, fair and beautiful.' She stuck her head out of the door. 'In here.'

'Helen!' cried Ian, as a group of hospital porters wheeled in a bed, a bedside table and a trolley of personal effects.

'How is everyone?' She gave a regal wave as she was wheeled into place. 'Sorry to impose, Fiona, but I've been kicked out of isolation.'

'You beautiful person. You can tell me all the latest scandal.'

'I'm a bit out of date, I'm afraid.'

'Now don't you two go wearing each other out,' said Kelly. She waited while the porters finished arranging things to her satisfaction. 'I must be getting along. Remember what I said.' She followed the porters out.

'Welcome to my humble abode,' said Fiona. 'I can't offer you a G and T but would you like a chocolate? Ian, be a darling and do the honours.'

'No thanks.' Helen shook her head. 'I'm afraid you're going to be a bit cramped in here now.'

'No, it's lovely to have someone to talk to. I've been going up the wall. I'm not sharing this gorgeous man with you, though.'

'Don't take any notice, Helen,' he said. 'I go with the furniture.'

'It's all part of the service,' said Fiona. 'I wish.'

He regarded the two of them giggling. 'I think it's time I left.'

'Come back soon, darling.' Fiona gave him another passionate kiss. He leaned over and kissed Helen's cheek. 'Take care.'

'You too.' She gave a wistful smile which he couldn't fathom. 'Did you send me that?' She indicated the orchid on her bedside table. 'I remember you told me it's called *Phalaenopsis*.'

'No. Must be one of your other admirers.' Ian picked up the card. '*To Helen Paterson, who liked orchids*.' He frowned and passed the card to Fiona. 'Do you recognise the writing?'

'Yes, of course; it's Quentin's.'

Chapter 59

Colette sat between Jeff and Richard – the latter driving – pleased that neither tried to engage her in small talk. She gazed forlornly out of the windscreen and imagined the worst. She should never have come rushing out to Kenya. Would never forgive herself if she was too late.

They passed some huts. Then some zebras, which gazed incuriously at the vehicle. More huts. 'Are you sure this is the way back to the house?'

'Short cut,' said Richard, without taking his eyes off the track.

They went through a dried up riverbed.

'I'm sure Sean didn't come this way.'

'Soon be there,' said Jeff.

What was it between her and Jeff? She suddenly snapped. 'Where are you taking me? Is this another of your stupid fucking schemes?'

'Stop,' he said.

Richard glanced across and coasted to a halt.

'Now what? Why are we stopping?'

'Over there.' Jeff pointed out of the side window.

She leaned forward. 'What is it? I can't—'

Strong arms pinned her to the seat. A hand was thrust over her mouth. A sharp prick into her arm as she thrashed around trying to break free. The last thing she remembered was, was… She couldn't remember.

***

The nightmare began to fade. She tried to reach out. Couldn't move. She turned her head. Faint light seeping into the place showed a blank wall. She turned the other way. Also blank. She took a gasping breath. She was strapped to some sort of bed. Tried to sit up. Couldn't.

Don't scream.

Think. Remember.

Don't scream.

She closed her eyes. Think. Think and remember.

She remembered. Her father. Would she be in time? You're going the wrong way. Another of your stupid fucking—

'JEFF!'

314

A light snapped on. A door opened.

She twisted her head. Couldn't see anyone. Strained against the bindings. 'Who's there?'

Heavy breathing.

'Jeff?'

Breathing getting nearer.

'Richard?'

Don't scream.

Breathing becoming ragged.

Something was thrown over her face. A cloth that smelled of stale sweat and wood smoke.

A hand touched her arm.

Began exploring

Panting. Sewer breath.

Don't scream. Don't scream. Don't scream.

Both hands.

Investigating.

Groping.

'GET AWAY!'

A shout. A curse. A crack followed by a groan and a thud.

Someone released the bindings and sat her up.

She snatched the thing off her head, and caught a glimpse of a man being dragged out of a door. An African in combat fatigues. An African with a pink puckered scar on the side of his head. An African with—

A cloth was bound over her eyes. Her hands were yanked behind her back and tied.

She was pulled to her feet and frog-marched.

No words spoken.

Smooth hard flooring, probably concrete. A corridor? A corridor of darkness. Leading where?

Dread and despair unbearable.

Sand. Sunshine and a slight breeze. A door opened. More flooring. Another door.

She was pulled down into a chair.

She sensed a person, people.

'Jeff? Richard?'

'Good morning,' said a voice. A man. Not Jeff. Not Richard. Cultured. British?

'Who are you?'

Question ignored. 'I do apologise. That One-Ear has his uses but he can be such an animal.'

'Where am I?'

'If you don't mind, I'll ask the questions.'

Her earlier terror was replaced by savage stubborn resolve. She'd put Samira's face back together. She could handle this. Yes, but Sean had been there then. Think of Sean. Ian had also been there.

'I understand you have some very special skills— No, don't interrupt. Special virological skills. I and my colleagues have need of those skills. You, my dear, could be famous. You could contribute to one of the greatest projects the world has ever...'

The man's voice rose.

Colette shut her mind.

The tirade stopped.

'Do you work for Jeff?' she snapped.

A pause. 'No. I most certainly do not work for Jeff.'

She was pleased. She'd riled him.

'Professor Jefferson Carter works for *me*.'

'For you?'

'Does that surprise you?'

Keep quiet.

The rustle of papers. 'Ah, here we are. Sean Christopher Paterson.' A pause. 'What an interesting person. I can understand why you're—'

'What about him?'

'Excuse me, I'm asking the questions.'

'Tell me.'

'What an impetuous young lady you are. We'll make a good team.'

Say nothing.

Silence.

The creak of a chair.

Silence.

'Sean won't—'

She couldn't help the scream.

He was beside her, his face close to hers, his breath sickly, sweet, stale.

'I understand his injuries are not life-threatening.'

'What do you mean?'

A sigh. 'As I said, that One-Ear does get carried away sometimes. I really will have to have words with—'

'What's happened to Sean?'

'Shall we say, he's our insurance policy? A deposit, if you like, to be refunded on satisfactory completion of the project.'

'What project?'

He moved away. She sensed him prowling the room. She tried blinking her eyes to loosen the blindfold. No joy.

'My colleagues told me you were an impulsive young lady.' The voice behind her. 'I can see they were right. Head-strong, stubborn are words I also heard.' Now at the side. 'This led me to believe you might need some, er, persuasion to work on our programme.' Now the other side. 'No, not torture – so uncivilised, don't you think?'

She gritted her teeth. Still that sickly breath. Candy floss. Brighton beach, wasn't it? A hundred years ago.

'His injuries could always become life-threatening if you are foolish enough to resist cooperating' – almost chatty. 'Terminal even.'

A door opened.

'How remiss of me. I should have asked earlier. Is it tea or coffee?'

The shutters came down.

'Oh well. Shall we say coffee, then? With biscuits?'

'What's your name?' she shot.

'My name?'

'Yes.'

'Why do you want to know?'

'My parents always taught me to be polite and introduce myself.'

'How quaint.'

'So what is it?'

'You can call me Abdul.'

'Why Abdul? You don't sound like an Abdul.'

'How dare you!' Heavy breathing. 'So that's it?'

'What's it?'

'You're trying to provoke me.'

'Why should I want to do that?'

'Don't forget, young lady, we are holding Sean.'

'I think you're bluffing. You don't hold Sean. He'd never let himself be caught by—'

The blow was shock rather than pain.

'Don't test my patience.'

'Is that your style? Knocking defenceless women about?'

'You pathetic little bitch.' The rasping breath by her ear.

A rattle. A metal tray?

'On the table, please.'

The door closed.

'Enough of this nonsense. I have better things to attend to. Others more versed in these matters will explain your duties.'

A pause.

She tensed, expecting another blow. It didn't come.

'I should warn you, others may not be as patient as I am.'

Her hands were untied. Before she could remove the blindfold, the door opened and closed.

'You haven't got Sean!' She ripped off the blindfold. 'I know you—' The room was empty. A few chairs. A table. A mug of coffee and a plate of biscuits on the table.

She hurled the mug at the closed door. It smashed. Coffee splattered over the door. She waited for her ragged breathing to settle.

Listen. Watch.

A spider appeared above the door, watching back. Spinning, weaving, plotting?

A CCTV camera high in one corner. On a schoolgirl impulse, she waved a savage V-sign.

Bars on the windows. She peered through them.

A building opposite obscured all but a view of sand and sky.

She tried the door. Locked? Not locked. Did she dare? She opened it a crack and squinted out.

A man sat on a stool, his back to her. A gun across his knees. An African. An African with two ears. Probably as loathsome.

Should she run? Run where? She eased the door shut.

The spider ran off.

Chapter 60

Ian, having spent the night at Tim Hollis's place, drove with him next morning and parked near the British Council.

Tim chatted over his shoulder as he led the way into the building. 'All arranged. Head of the Council is happy for you to use Mandy's office. I'll take you up.'

They went to the second floor and Tim unlocked a door at the end of a corridor. He handed Ian the key and led him into a tidy functional office. 'You should have everything you need. If not shout. This is Mandy's password if you want to use the computer.' He scribbled on a piece of paper. 'The green phone is a direct outside line. The other goes through the switchboard. Anything else?'

'No, this is great.'

'You've got my mobile number if you need to contact me?'

'Yes and thanks again, Tim.'

After his colleague left, Ian spent a few minutes prowling round the office and opening drawers. He then sat down at the computer and drafted a note to one of his contacts in MI6, heading it Urgent.

Grateful you run check on Quentin James Melhuish, recently First Secretary, British High Commission, Nairobi. Current whereabouts unknown, but possibly still in Kenya. Previously posted (approximately 1985-1997) to High Commission, Islamabad, where he may have been involved in information gathering (?MI6 and/or CIA) regarding Russian weapons (?bio-weapons) programmes and later Taliban activities in Afghanistan and elsewhere. Reliable information (Ian wondered about the adjective) *suggests he may have converted to Islam and become radicalised adopting the name Abdul. Accomplices in Pakistan and Kenya may include an individual by name of Majid, Malik or Massouk. Grateful for information on movements with respect to possible involvement in bombings of US Embassy in Kenya (August 1998), and current anti-west activities, including possible use of bio-weapons. Individual is assumed to be still active and a threat to British, US and Kenyan interests.*

He reread the message, printed it out then deleted it from the computer. He locked the office and headed for the American Embassy.

Instead of being taken to Felix's office, he was surprised to be shown into a large room where a meeting was in progress. He recognised most of those present including Grace, Felix, Kelly and the large comfortable Afro-American woman at the head of the table, who could have been Felix's elder sister. She passed the cat which was on her lap to the man beside her and rose with a jangle of bracelets. 'Good to see you, Ian.' She held out a firm hand.

'Morning, ambassador.' His puzzlement clearly conveyed itself.

'Sorry to spring this on you but we've gotten a problem which needs some action. You may be able to help.'

'I'll do my best.'

The Ambassador settled into her chair, retrieved the cat and turned to Kelly. 'Over to you again, doctor.'

Kelly pushed untidy hair out of her face and addressed Ian. 'It's happened. What we feared.'

He waited for her to continue, taking in the shadows under her eyes and the tension in her face.

'Four cases last night – one of which has already died – and three suspects this morning.'

'Marburg?'

'Systems here can't cope. I can't cope.' She gave a ragged intake of breath. 'The authorities asked me to approach the Embassy for help and the Ambassador has been kind enough to call this meeting.'

'You're welcome,' said the Ambassador, absent-mindedly stroking the cat. 'You reckon there are going to be more cases?'

'In a word: yes.'

'What sort of isolation facilities does Kenya have?' asked the Ambassador. 'Inspector, do you know?'

Grace studied her hands before looking up. 'Madam, we have nothing which could manage an outbreak of Marburg.'

'By bringing patients into local hospitals, we're creating a focus of infection which will only make things worse,' said Kelly.

The Ambassador tapped her fingers on the table. 'Seems like we might not have escaped August seven after all.'

'That's my fear, ma'am,' growled Felix.

'Okay, so what can we do to help?'

'Is there a vaccine available?' asked Ian.

'No,' said Kelly. 'A: I don't think there is a vaccine. B: even if there is we don't have any. C: vaccine won't help clinical cases.'

It was Ian's turn to tap fingers on the table. 'Do you know how these people became infected?'

'Probably contacts with Stanley, the man who died.'

'My people are looking into this,' said Grace. 'At the moment, that seems to be the situation.'

'That's something, I suppose,' said Ian.

'What you saying?' asked Felix.

'I'm saying that if these are in-contact cases, there may not be a link to the seventh.'

'That doesn't help me,' muttered Kelly.

'You confirmed this is Marburg?' asked the Ambassador.

Kelly glowered. 'The symptoms are identical to the two cases I saw earlier. One recovered and one died.' She added 'ma'am' as an afterthought. 'We'll have confirmation shortly.'

'I've arranged to get samples tested on the Harry S,' said Felix.

'Good.' The Ambassador wobbled her jowls in what Ian took to be a nod.

'I'm sorry,' snapped Kelly, 'but it doesn't matter to me whether it's Marburg or friggin' chickenpox. I've gotten people dying of a contagious disease which could infect half of Nairobi.' She rubbed trembling hands over her distraught face.

'That bad?' said the Ambassador.

'Yes.'

'So what do you need?' asked Ian.

'A miracle.'

'Apart from that?'

'You want the list? Isolation facilities, trained staff – medics and nurses – life-support systems, drugs. That's for starters.'

'You treated Helen, though?'

'Ian, that's one case, for Chrissake! She got lucky. Can't you see, we need those facilities, and better, repeated ten times over – probably more? Where am I going to find that?'

'The Harry S. Truman.'

'Excuse me?'

'The aircraft carrier, stationed off Mombasa.'

'How does that help? We put these people on the bus to Mombasa and they swim out?'

'No. You bring the facilities to them.'

'Goddam it, Ian!' cried Felix. 'They've gotten mobile hospitals geared up for biological warfare, nuclear, humanitarian disasters. The works, man.'

'You think they could help?' The first sign of hope showed on Kelly's face.

'Too damn right they could.'

The Ambassador held up her hand. 'Don't get too carried away, Felix.'

'Ma'am, those guys probably itching for something like this.'

'Maybe but we'll have to clear it.' She turned to the man sitting beside her recording the minutes of the meeting. 'Joe, get me the Secretary of State on the line.' She checked her watch. 'If he's in bed, wake him up.'

'Yes, ma'am.' Joe passed his notepad and pen to Felix and left the room.

The cat looked up briefly, yawned and settled more comfortably into the ample lap.

'If we're planning to bring US military personnel into Kenya,' continued the Ambassador, 'we also have to get presidential clearance.' She looked down the table towards Grace.

'The President is currently out of the country, madam,' she said.

'But can be contacted?'

'Yes, of course. I think, though, we could work through Minister ole-Tomeno.'

'Is that wise?' asked Felix.

Grace ignored the question. 'If you agree, madam, I'll contact ole-Tomeno's PA and she can arrange for him to call you.'

'Sure. Go ahead,' said the Ambassador.

Joe returned and whispered in her ear. 'Okay, folks,' she called. 'We'll take a comfort break. Reconvene in half an hour.' She rose, tucked the cat under her arm and left the room, followed by Grace.

As soon as the door closed, Ian buttonholed Felix. 'I hope I'm not wasting people's time,' he said, 'but could you send this through your secure system?' He passed Felix the note he'd prepared for MI6.

'Sonofabitch.' Felix's eyebrows rose higher as he read. 'Where's this "reliable information" from?'

'Fiona, Quentin's wife.'

'Getting her own back on hubby, then?'

'Look, Felix, what she said was plausible and parts we know are true. It's worth following up.'

'I'll run it by my folks as well.' Felix tapped the paper. 'This Quentin guy got it in him?'

'What do you mean?'

'He strikes me as an ass-hole, not some Mr Big. Has he got the balls to be running a terrorist network?'

'Hell, Felix, I don't know. All I know is he's a good actor. Most of the time, he plays the fool – all that "old boy" stuff – but he's a dark horse. And he seems to have been in the right places at the right times; some of them, anyway.'

'You got his picture?'

Ian delved into his briefcase and handed Felix a folder. 'Apparently he used to have a beard. Fiona said it made him look like Rasputin.'

'He al-Qaeda?'

'It doesn't matter.'

'Okay, but don't hold your breath.'

'Felix, it's worth a try. We haven't got a lot else going for us right now.'

Felix grunted, then as Grace returned, handed her Ian's message. 'Take a look at that.'

'Interesting,' she said. 'How reliable are these names: Majid, Massouk and Abdul?'

'The Abdul is probably correct,' said Ian. 'The others could be names plucked out of the air. Fiona seemed pretty vague except it was someone whose name began with M.'

'Fiona's the wife?'

'Yes.'

'Could the name have been Malik?'

'I suggested that but it didn't seem to ring any bells. He would fit the bill, though.'

'Abdul, Abdul.' Grace tapped her chin. 'Felix, that list of names we looked at yesterday, have you got it with you?'

'Sure.' He extracted a sheet from his papers and spread it on the table.

'Here.' She pointed. 'Two names of people linked to the ninety-eight attack but not yet located. One of them is an Abdul: Abdul Jamal. Perhaps Fiona was right. It could also explain why my people couldn't find Quentin Melhuish listed on any flight out of Nairobi last night – international or domestic.'

'If he's calling the shots, guy like that probably has a spare passport in his back pocket as well as a couple of immigration officials,' muttered Felix.

Grace jabbed at the paper. 'I'll get my people to check the flight lists again. See if Abdul Jamal appears.'

'And while they're at it, the other name as well,' said Ian. 'Rashid Omari.'

323

Grace didn't appear to hear but snatched her mobile from her bag and moved out of earshot.

Ian and Felix glanced at each other.

She returned looking thoughtful. 'Maria says that Richard Omar went on a British Council scholarship to Pakistan under that name, having changed it from... Rashid Omari.'

'Holy cow,' muttered Felix. 'So Britain paid for that scumbag to go train in Pakistan? And sure as hell, that wasn't needlework and cookery.'

'I don't suppose it was.'

'Quentin, alias Abdul, was in Pakistan at the same time,' said Ian. 'And if Fiona's correct, he wasn't doing needlework and cooking either.'

Chapter 61

Dima helped Sean load the Land Rover: boxes of food, containers of water, cans of petrol, a great case of medicines, tents, cooking pots, vehicle spares and Sean's gun. No wonder he needed a vehicle to carry everything.

This time, Sean would not let him travel on the roof. 'We have to go far. And I need to drive fast.'

Dima, who normally followed elephant and other game trails, took a while to adjust to the speed.

Sean was quiet. He was probably worrying about that *mzungu* woman.

Dima stared through the windscreen as places rushed past. 'We should visit Emunyu,' he said, after they'd been driving for a while.

'Who's that?'

'He is a friend who knows many things. Perhaps he will have news.'

'Is it far?'

'Not far.'

They continued their journey in silence. Dima's thoughts turned to his little gazelle. She would not be able to share the new life on Sean's place.

'Turn by that tree,' he said.

A *manyatta* came into view. Sean pulled up. Some dogs ran out barking. Dima shouted at them. One of them sauntered forward, sniffing the air, hackles raised. Satisfied the newcomers were harmless, it cocked its leg against the Land Rover in a gesture of welcome.

'Emunyu's wife makes very good beer,' said Dima.

He and Sean climbed out and walked towards the beaming Samburu man, still wearing his only wardrobe.

'Dima, you are welcome,' he cried.

'*Asante*, Emunyu. This man is my friend, Sean. He is an African like us.'

Emunyu shook Sean solemnly by the hand. 'You are most welcome, *bwana*. Come. I will call for beer.'

Dima caught Sean's eye and shrugged.

'So tell me the news, Dima,' said Emunyu, as the three of them settled on the log beneath the acacia tree. 'That Samira, is she well?'

'She is very well. Her face is nearly cured.'

'That one is strong.'

The three men nodded.

One of Emunyu's wives arrived with a gourd and passed it round. 'This is very good beer,' said Sean.

The woman dropped her gaze and smiled. '*Asante, bwana.*'

Emunyu put two fingers in his mouth and gave a piercing whistle. A boy came running out of the bush and bowed his head before the men. 'You remember Namunak?'

'I remember,' said Dima. 'You are now cured?'

'Yes, sir.' The boy turned to show the residual scars on his body.

'This one was shot with a gun and wanted to die,' explained Emunyu, 'but Dima saved him. He is a good doctor.'

'He is very good,' said Sean.

The boy grinned. 'I can go now?'

'Wait,' said Dima. 'You can sit.'

Namunak looked questioningly at his father.

'Stay,' said Emunyu, 'and hear what Dima has to say.'

The boy sat on the log beside Sean, excited to be invited to join the men.

'Do you have news of the place of the monkeys?' asked Dima.

'That place is not good,' said Emunyu.'

'Sir, that place is very bad,' cried Namunak.

'Have you been there?' asked Sean.

Namunak glanced at his father. 'No, sir, but I have sometimes been to the big fence.'

'I think this man's woman has been taken there,' said Dima.

Emunyu shook his head in sympathy and offered the gourd to Sean who declined.

'Is it possible to pass through the fence or to cut it?' asked Sean.

'Sir, that fence is very strong and there are many askaris,' said Namunak. 'I think it will not be easy to enter.'

'I also have been to that place,' said Dima. 'I know it will not be easy but we must find a way.'

Namunak whispered in his father's ear. Emunyu frowned and shook his head. The boy persisted. Eventually Emunyu sighed. 'This boy wants to take you there.'

'*Asante*, Namunak,' said Dima. 'We will find that woman.'

Sean muttered something in a language he didn't understand.

'It is good that I can help you,' said Namunak. 'This is a very fine vehicle.'

'You must take us by a way so those askaris don't see us,' said Dima.

'I know a way.'

'Also we must not pass Molito's place. You know Molito?'

'That one I know. He has a son who is sick in the head.'

'I think that boy works for those people at the place of the monkeys,' said Dima.

'That is true,' said Namunak.

Most of their journey was across a flat sandy plain interspersed with dried up water courses and thickets of thorn scrub, but as they drew nearer to Lokinang Mountain the ground became more rocky and Sean was forced to slow down.

'See that hill,' said Namunak. 'I think you can drive there and we can hide and see the fence.'

Sean forced a way up the rocky slopes, through scrub and onto a small open area just below the top and out of sight of the compound.

'We can stop here,' said Namunak. 'And bring your special glasses.' He indicated Sean's binoculars. 'We must be very quiet.'

They eased the Land Rover doors shut and followed Namunak along a game trail which led to the top of the hill. They settled down among a jumble of rocks and looked at the scene below.

'See, there is the fence,' Namunak whispered. 'It is very strong. And over there is the gate where cars can pass. See they have askaris always there. I think they stay in that house at the side.'

Sean studied the fence, the gateway and the area through his binoculars. 'See on those poles,' he said, 'they are special cameras which watch the fence and tell the askaris if someone is trying to enter. And that wire on top, I think it is electricity.'

'*Aieeh*,' said Dima. 'This place is very difficult.'

'Tell me, Namunak,' said Sean, 'do they have lights here at night?'

'So many lights.'

Sean peered once again through his binoculars. 'See how those cameras turn,' he said. 'It might be possible to cut the fence when they are turned away.'

'Perhaps,' said Namunak.

'I will go and see.' Dima slipped noiselessly away.

A few minutes later he was back, beckoning to them. They

followed him along a game trail below the skyline and came to a cleft between two rocks.

'See,' he said, grinning. 'That is how we can pass.' He pointed to a large warthog scrabbling at the base of the fence. Even as they watched, it gave a final thrust with its snout and squeezed under the wire.

They waited for shouting or alarm bells. All they heard was birdsong from the surrounding trees and bushes.

'That is the way,' said Sean. 'We will come back when it is dark. Now, Namunak, we will return to your *manyatta*.'

A shout of laughter made them turn. Molito's son stood on the skyline gibbering at them. Before they had time to move, the crazed boy ran down the hill towards the gate shouting.

The askaris looked in their direction. Then one went into the gatehouse and returned with special glasses and began searching the hillside.

'Back to the *gari*,' hissed Sean.

They ran back to the Land Rover, and Dima scrabbled inside for his bow and arrows. 'Sean, take Namunak. Then return and wait. I will become a warthog.'

He didn't wait for a response.

Chapter 62

'OK, folks, let's resume,' called the Ambassador, as she returned to the room with Joe, but without the cat, and took her place at the head of the table. 'I've spoken to the Secretary of State, who wasn't best pleased to be called in the middle of the night. Anyway, he's agreed we should involve the Harry S. Truman. One of his people will contact the Captain. Felix, who's your contact on the carrier?'

'Guy called Chuck Wallicker, he's commander of the SEAL troop on board.'

'Brief him about what's happening. He'll know the set-ups they have for this sort of thing?'

'Sure, he can liaise with the medics. Just be a case of deciding where to locate.'

'That's being arranged,' said the Ambassador. 'Minister ole-Tomeno called me. Thank you for setting that up, inspector.' She nodded down the table to Grace. 'He's given clearance and suggests locating the facility near the freight terminal at the old airport.'

'Sounds ideal,' said Kelly.

'He'll also contact the Minister of Health to get cooperation from the medical authorities. I've said that you, Kelly, will be the link person between them and the Embassy.'

'Fine.'

'I think that's it then. Meeting closed. I'll leave you folks to sort out the details. If you need anything else from me, I'm around for most of the day. Just contact Joe.' She departed bracelets jangling. Most of the others followed, leaving Ian, Felix and Grace behind.

'I ain't happy bringing OT in on this,' said Felix.

'Why?' asked Grace.

'Why? I'll tell you why.' He leaned across the table. 'I ain't sure we're singing from the same hymn-sheet.'

'Meaning what?'

'Meaning, I think he may well have a different agenda. That's what.'

'I think he has.'

'What! Why in hell's name didn't you say so?'

'Because I don't think it's relevant.'

'Not relevant?'

'What's not relevant, Grace?' asked Ian.

She drew a breath. 'I believe ole-Tomeno plans to run for the presidency at the next election.'

'And is using the Condor Programme to get brownie points?'

'I think so.'

'And why he buys everyone beers in Isiolo?'

'Perhaps.' Grace turned to Felix with an innocent expression.

'I know that look,' he growled. 'What is it this time?'

Her smile became almost angelic. 'The Minister wonders if we – if you – can organise a plane to get him back here to coordinate the operation.'

'Jeez.' Felix slumped back in his chair.

'Could you?'

'Where from?'

'Isiolo.'

'Where in hell's that?'

Grace retained her seraphic smile. 'The pilot will know.'

Felix rose to his feet. 'Give me a break, you two. I got work to do.'

'Thanks, Felix. I'll tell Maria to call you.'

'Grace, you sure know how to influence people without making friends.'

***

Ian found himself squeezed in the back of a police car with Grace and Sammy, and two burly officers in the front.

'I presume you have a search warrant?' he said.

'No,' said Grace. 'That's why I brought you.'

He scowled. 'What was it Felix said about influencing people?'

'Ian, I have a job to do. If it means cutting corners sometimes, that's tough.'

He sniffed.

'Maybe Melhuish's place isn't technically British soil. Maybe it is. If it is, you'll have to sort things out.'

'Great.'

Sammy glanced from one to the other. The officers in front stared fixedly ahead.

'Go in there and stop.' Grace indicated the car park of the Settlers Club.

The driver pulled up and the three in the back climbed out.

'Wait here,' she said to the driver. 'I'll call you if we need you.'

The man grunted and began exploring his nose. He and his

colleague settled back in their seats.

Sammy retrieved a backpack from the boot. Ian led the way across the road to Quentin and Fiona's bungalow. They peered through the wrought-iron gates which were secured with a padlock and chain.

Grace called out. No response.

'They've gone away,' said a woman, dressed as an *ayah*, who was wheeling a Barbie-doll child in a pushchair.

'There's no one there,' added Barbie doll in an American accent.

'Thank you.' Grace waited until they were further up the road then nodded to Sammy who had already extracted an appropriate implement from his pack.

The padlock clicked open and the three of them slipped through the gate. Sammy closed it behind them. They skirted round to the back of the bungalow. A man was hacking at the edges of a flowerbed with a machete.

Grace called to him and he sauntered over.

'Are you the gardener?' she asked.

He nodded.

She showed her police ID. 'This man—' She indicated Ian, '—is a friend of *Bwana* Melhuish and has come to collect...' Her voice trailed off as a tall stooped figure appeared from behind a hedge.

'Sir Aubrey!' exclaimed Ian.

'Good Lord,' said the High Commissioner. He had the look of a small boy caught scrumping apples. He came towards them and peered myopically at Ian. 'Do I know you?'

'Ian Sinclair, sir. I was formerly—'

'The bomb man?'

'I suppose so.'

'Ah, yes.'

'Could I ask, sir, what brings you here?'

'I was, er, keeping an eye on the place. While Quentin's away, poor fellow. You know Quentin?'

'Yes, I took him to the— What news of him? Did he arrive safely?'

'Yes. Absolutely fine.' The High Commissioner stared fixedly at some colourful birds pecking at the lawn. 'Fine. Absolutely fine.'

'Would it be possible to make contact? I need to ask him about the things he cleared from my desk.'

'Your desk?' – vaguely.

'Yes.'

'No.' The High Commissioner shook his head. 'No. He's, he's

331

staying with… with an aunt.'

'An address, perhaps?'

'Somewhere in Wiltshire. He didn't give the details. Said he didn't want to be disturbed. He's had a difficult time, you know.'

'I see. A phone number then?'

'Eh?' The High Commissioner's gaze followed the birds as they flew to a different part of the lawn. 'Are you a bird man? Tell me, what are they?'

'Superb starlings.'

'Most attractive. I must— Who are these people?'

'We're police officers.' Grace showed her ID. 'We were told there'd been a… a break-in.'

'Break-in, eh?'

'Yes, sir.'

'Well, I won't detain you. Have you seen Quentin?'

'No.' Ian caught Grace's eye. 'I thought you said he was in England.'

'Did I?'

'Something about an aunt in Wiltshire?'

Sir Aubrey seemed to ponder this. 'Oh well. You'll let me know if you see him.'

'Of course.'

'I live next door. Gap in the hedge. Comes in handy sometimes.' He shambled off with the air of a care-worn camel. Turned round and came back past them. 'It's this way.'

'Is he all right?' whispered Grace.

Ian pulled a face. 'I'll try and have a word with his wife.'

Grace looked doubtfully at the departing figure. 'We must get on.'

While she and Sammy went to quiz the gardener, Ian wandered off to inspect the "gap in the hedge". He could make out Lady Cynthia – brush poised – peering at an easel set in front of a flowering shrub. Sir Aubrey tiptoeing past.

Ian set off to explore the garden. The flowerbeds offered little of interest but he was intrigued to see the windows on the guest house were boarded up. He continued to the back garden. Beyond the vegetables, the remains of a bonfire. Fiona mentioned something about Quentin burning papers. He poked through the ashes with a stick. The chink of broken glass. A scorched and broken picture frame.

Why the hell did he have to burn that?

He stared forlornly at the remains of the ravaged photo of Colette bottle-feeding a young cheetah. 'Bastard!' He kicked his former life back into the ashes.

He continued scratching through the heap. Mostly amorphous ash with the occasional metal clip from a binder file or a partially-burnt piece of cardboard. Something else. The melted remains of a plastic screw-cap bottle. No sign of the label but he knew it would have read: "*one to be taken morning and evening.*" The day took on a sudden chill.

There was a call from Grace.

'Here,' he called.

She and Sammy joined him. 'Have you found anything?'

He poked the misshapen bottle with his stick. 'I suspect it will have contained vitamin pills laced with Marburg.'

'The ones which infected Helen and Stanley?'

'That's my guess. Did you learn anything useful?'

'Let me show you.' She led Ian round the side of the bungalow. 'What are those flowers?' She pointed to a small greenhouse filled with flowering plants.

'I think you probably know.'

She went in and sniffed some of the blooms.

'Most orchids don't smell,' he said.

'This man is awful. Using these beautiful flowers as a signature for all the horrible things he does.'

Ian realised why he had so much respect for Grace. 'Was the gardener able to tell you anything?'

'He says his work is the garden. He doesn't know what happens in the house.'

'Does he stay here?'

'No. He comes in by *matatu* each day.'

'Wasn't he the one who took Stanley to the hospital?'

'Yes. I don't think they were the best of friends, though.'

'Why?'

'He said he was a miserable old baboon.'

'The gardener's not been ill?'

'What do you think?'

The man was wielding his machete with malicious enthusiasm as he attacked the edges of the flowerbeds. He showed no interest in the visitors.

'Did he say anything about the High Commissioner?' asked Ian.

333

'He thinks that one is not right in the head. Apparently he often wanders in here mumbling to himself.'

'Has anyone else been around?'

'The gardener says not.'

'Who pays him?'

'He says he's paid at the end of the month. If no one appears, I imagine he'll stop coming.'

'Over here,' called Sammy, who was standing beside the open door of the garage.

'Is there anything he can't open?' muttered Ian.

'Not that I've found.'

They walked over and peered into the garage.

'Well, what do you know?' Ian bent down to inspect the dust-covered motorbike being careful not to touch it. 'Is it the one, do you think?'

'Could be,' said Grace, crouching beside him. 'I'll get forensics to check it. No number plates. Did the one which shot up Malik have plates?'

'I didn't notice.'

'Nor did I.' She stood up. 'What sort of car does Melhuish have?'

'A white Range Rover, I believe.'

'Registration?'

'It has red diplomatic plates starting with 22 CD – same as the Land Rover which was blown up near the Stadium.'

'So, possibly the same hit-men.'

'At least they'd know the score.'

'Come on.' She turned towards the house. 'Let's see what other surprises we can find. Sammy, lock up here then we'll go inside.'

'Put these on.' Sammy handed them each a pair of disposable gloves and some overshoes. 'I've already opened the front door.'

Grace gave a faint smile, led the way to the front of the bungalow and gently pushed open the door. They stood in a hallway tainted by menacing shafts of light and waited for their eyes to adjust to the dim interior. A table stood at one side with a phone and a magazine on it. A chair beside. A potted plant on the window sill.

'Another orchid?' said Grace.

'*Phalaenopsis*, the same as the one sent to Helen.'

'This man is sick,' she muttered. 'Anything else before we go in?'

'That seems to confirm at least part of Fiona's story.' Ian pointed to a dark stain on the hall carpet.

Grace lifted the edge of the carpet and peered at the underside. 'Forensics can see if they get a match.' She dropped the carpet back and stood up. 'You know the layout, Ian, lead the way.'

As the three of them trailed through the rooms, the only thing Ian noted was the two single beds in the main bedroom rather than the usual double. He didn't comment. None of the other rooms seemed to offer much of interest to the sharp eyes of Grace and Sammy, except one, and that was locked.

Sammy knelt down and shone a torch in the keyhole then sucked his teeth.

'Cooee, anyone there?' called a voice.

'Damn. Stay here. I'll get rid of her.' Ian pulled off his gloves and overshoes, stuffed them in his pocket and hurried out to the front door. 'Lady Gilmore, good morning. How are you?'

'It's Cynthia. And it's afternoon,' she announced, with a look which threatened to blister the paintwork. 'What's going on, Ian? Aubrey came back with some cock-and-bull story about people looking for Quentin.'

'The police were told there'd been a break-in.'

'The police?'

'Yes, they asked me to come with them.'

'I see. And who informed the police?'

'They, er, wouldn't say.' He manoeuvred himself to hide the stained carpet from the eagle-eyes sweeping the place. 'How is Sir Aubrey? We, um, met him in the garden. He seemed a bit confused.'

'He needs to pull himself together,' she snorted. 'I'm making sure he eats plenty of avocadoes – rich in riboflavin.'

'I'm sure that'll help.' He steered her outside where the gardener was still attacking the borders. 'That man keeps the place looking nice.'

'Fiona won't let him touch the shrubs. Quite right too.'

'How is Fiona?'

'Coming out tomorrow. Silly girl thought she'd upset us. That's why she didn't want to see us. We had a long chat on the phone this morning.'

'I'm glad she's on the mend.'

'I'm insisting she stays at the residence. I need to keep an eye on her. Plenty of fresh air and fruit is what she needs.'

'Absolutely.'

She shot him a glance. 'Yes, well. I've told Fiona that the Helen girl should also come and stay. Young girls these days simply don't know how to look after themselves. Don't touch that,' she boomed, as the gardener approached an unsuspecting bougainvillea. The poor man scuttled back to his hacking. 'One needs eyes in the back of one's head.'

His attention was caught by Grace waving to him from the front door. 'Excuse me, er, Cynthia.'

'Who's that?'

'She's from the police.'

'She looks awfully young.'

'Won't be a moment.' He ran across. 'Did Sammy get the door open?'

'Eventually,' said Grace.

'And?'

'Empty, except for a desk and some chairs. No books, no papers, no safe, nothing in the drawers.'

'So what do you want to do?'

'Sammy wants to take the place apart.'

'Why?'

'Because he has a bad feel about it.'

Ian frowned.

'Listen, Ian, I respect Sammy's judgement – his sixth sense, if you like. If he says he's unhappy that's good enough for me.'

'Suit yourself.'

'Thank you. I will.'

They glared at each other.

'Okay.' He sighed. 'What do you want from me?'

'Tell that old cow, we're going to be here for a few days. Make up some story.'

He glanced over to Lady Cynthia, standing hands on hips watching over the hapless gardener. 'That old cow happens to be the wife of the British High Commissioner.'

'I know.' Grace smiled. 'We still want her out of the way and the *bwana mkubwa*. Until we give the all-clear, this is a crime scene and we don't want them tramping around. Don't worry. We'll be discreet.'

'I hope so. How long do you think you'll—' He snatched his mobile from his pocket. 'Yes?'

'Ian, Felix. Go tell Grace to pack her snorkel and flippers – you too. We're off to the seaside.'

Chapter 63

Dima lay concealed in a thicket close to the place where the warthog burrowed under the wire. The bush was too thick to see what was going on inside the compound. He studied the cameras which turned slowly back and forth, the sun glinting off their glass eyes.

A snuffling sound. The warthog was returning. It came to the gap under the fence, snorted a couple of times, squeezed underneath and ran off.

Dima picked up his bag, his bow and arrows. Checked the eyes were looking away. Scurried across the open ground. Squeezed under the fence and into the bushes inside the compound. He lay waiting for alarms to ring, men to come running.

Nothing.

He followed the track made by the warthog. Came to a large tree. Impossible to make out more than a suggestion of low buildings. Away to his left, the bushes thinned out and the great mountain of Lokinang rose above the surrounding area. The fence finished at a cliff-face.

He detected a deep resonance. Too low to hear but unmistakable. Wind weaving through the rocks and trees? Possibly, but it seemed to come from the mountain itself.

He came clear of the trees and reached the cliff-face. Drawn towards the sound, he moved along the base of the cliff and reached a place less steep. Climbing with the assurance, nimbleness and speed of the *mbuzi ya mawe* – the klipspringer – he scaled the cliff and looked around. Ahead: the mountain rising into the sky. Below: the tops of trees, buildings, a road, a vehicle driving on the road, the fence surrounding the compound.

He resumed his climb. The sound grew nearer, stronger, recognisable.

Elephants.

He stopped on the edge of a great hole and peered into the darkness below. The scent and sound of elephants drifted upwards. These elephants had come from far away to scrape salt from the walls of one of its many tunnels. He could make out shapes moving and rumbling in the darkness. He called to them in the language his father had taught him – a language which, from the dawn of time,

337

enabled man to communicate with elephants.

Silence from below. He could sense the elephants listening. He called again.

An answering rumble. 'Come, friend.'

He moved down the rock-fall of what had once been the roof of a massive tunnel inside the lava mountain. His eyes adjusted to the darkness. The elephants resumed their gouging of the tunnel wall with their tusks, rumbling contentedly to each other and to their visitor.

He settled on a ledge and studied the scene below.

A ledge?

He ran his hands over the rock wall. A crack. A crevice. He reached in and extracted a… a tin. A tin of special paste used by his father. A tin placed there many years ago. Placed there the day he, Dima, became a man. He turned the tin, felt its shape, its rusted surface. He returned it to its place of concealment and wondered if he would ever hold it again.

When he was here all those years ago, there was no hole in the roof of the tunnel. But there were times when the mountain was as a restless giant turning in its sleep shaking the tunnels with his snoring. Once he had seen and smelled his acrid breath as it emerged from a crack in the ground. Perhaps it was on such an occasion the roof fell in. He hoped the giant was now sleeping.

He banished fanciful thoughts and became the hunter-tracker. He was in a tunnel in a mountain, but would use the same craft as if it were the bush.

He called again to the elephants. Heard their reassuring rumbling replies. He scrambled down to the floor of the tunnel. Air blowing towards him. Carrying a smell from inside the mountain. Not the breath of the sleeping giant but a chemical smell – like the chemical used on cattle to kill ticks.

He crept through the space between the rock-fall and the tunnel wall – a space too narrow for elephants. Ahead, a faint light. Not sunlight. He moved towards it, his bare feet seeking out the firm rocks.

His foot touched something. Not a rock. Not an animal. Not a plant. He reached down. Felt it. Picked it up. A book. Why a book? He slipped it into his bag and continued.

The mountain was like the honeycomb of bees with its tunnels and holes, many of which he and his father had explored. Near here should be a side tunnel leading into the heart of the mountain.

He came round a corner. The side tunnel was as he remembered. The light ahead, brighter now. Coming from a large hole. When here as a boy, the hole was a cavern of darkness. Now it was brightly lit. He crept forward and peered in. People dressed in green like the man he saw that day he came with the dead monkeys. People working at benches. People doing things with bottles inside glass cupboards. People preparing medicines for *uchawi*.

Was this a dream?

The alarm bell wasn't a dream.

A man, as from a radio, called out in a loud voice. The people stopped their work and began to leave. One of them looked up.

Sean's woman? Surely not.

He ducked down.

The alarm bell continued.

He scurried back down the tunnel.

The elephants were leaving in haste. Fluttering above their heads were bats – bats also obeying the call to leave the cave.

He joined the exodus. Emerged from the tunnel and watched the elephants ambling off. The bats flying in confusion in the afternoon sunshine.

Time to return to Sean.

A rattle of stones. He hid behind a rock.

Three men appeared. A *mzungu* and two Africans with guns. One man had lost an ear.

At last. He unwrapped the protective binding and notched an arrow into the bowstring.

The men came nearer.

He raised his bow. A clear line of sight.

He pulled back on the bowstring and… and lowered his bow.

Who was he to pass sentence on this man?

This man, whatever bad things he had done, was still a man. He, Dima, was also a man. *Mungu* would decide how and when this man would die. He re-wrapped the arrowhead in its binding and returned the arrow to the bark quiver. Time to—

A volley of shots rang out. He threw himself down. Another volley.

The elephants fled in panic down the hillside. Several of the swirling bats tumbled out of the sky.

First dead monkeys. Now dead bats. What sort of *uchawi* was this?

Chapter 64

Despite her apprehension, Colette had dosed off. She heard the door open and woke up. Jeff looking awkward. Richard looking smug. Both in white coats.

'What the bloody hell's going on?' she yelled.

'Ah,' said Jeff.

'Is that all you can say?'

'What I want to say—'

She turned her back on them. 'Bugger off!'

'We'll, er, come back later.'

'Don't bother.' She found a star-shaped stain on the opposite wall profoundly interesting.

She waited, tense, listening. No sound of a door closing. No breathing sounds. No people sounds.

She glanced over her shoulder. The room was empty. She was about to get up and look out of the window. A knock on the door. She focused again on the star. A gecko scuttled down the wall to inspect it.

'In case you're hungry.' Jeff's voice?

She studied the star through half-closed eyes. It became a diamond. The gecko became a crocodile.

Something being placed on the concrete floor. A plate? The scent of curry wafted towards her.

The door closed.

The star, diamond, whatever it was, lost its interest. The gecko hoofed off.

She got to her feet, glared at the camera high on the wall and picked up the plate together with the spoon and fork. The pieces of broken mug had been removed. She crossed to the table, plonked the plate down, drew up a chair, sat with her back to the camera and discovered how ravenous she was.

So what if it was drugged? She dug her spoon into the rice and stirred in the curry. She was—

The words leaped out from a scrap of paper hidden under the rice: "*Trust me, J.*"

What? She peered again. "*Trust me, J.*" Apart from a slight curry smudge, the writing was clear. J was presumably Jeff. But trust him?

Why? Why the hell should she after the way he'd treated her?

Was this supposed to mean she could trust Jeff but not Richard? Why should she trust either of them?

She hunched her shoulders round the plate so the camera couldn't see, scrabbled the paper into a ball with her spoon and fork, buried it in some rice and popped it into her mouth.

Wasn't this what spies did?

Yes, but their messages were written on rice paper, not bloody cardboard. She eventually macerated it sufficiently to swallow and just managed to avoid gagging.

Trust me. Did she have an option?

She finished the food and, in defiance of parental upbringing, licked the plate. She sat facing the camera, leaned back in her chair, stuck her legs out and twiddled her thumbs. Every now and then curled her lip and made snarling expressions for the benefit of anyone watching.

She was going mad.

She got up and crossed to the door. Locked this time. 'I need the loo,' she shouted. 'The *choo*, the bog, the can, the john, the… the convenience.' She couldn't think of any more words for toilet.

Nothing happened.

She went and slumped back in her chair.

'Knickers!' The rudest word from her vocabulary when she was four.

Shit. I *am* going mad.

This time the door did open.

A woman entered. A woman who, when she wasn't beating up defenceless girls, wrestled gorillas. She jerked her head. 'Come.'

Colette wasn't in defensive or gorilla mood and followed meekly.

Sunshine.

There had been a time when she doubted she would ever see it again. Sunshine and fresh air. Over there, a ten-foot fence with strands of electrified wire above. Should she summon up the inner Wonder-Woman, hope she could remember how to throw gorillas, and go for it?

As if reading her thoughts, the two-eared guard who'd been sitting outside the door, prodded her with his gun and followed behind. Any minute she expected him to start snapping at her heels.

She returned Wonder-Woman to the reserves' bench and studied her surroundings. Dominating the view was a great volcanic cone.

She presumed Lokinang. She hoped extinct.

Franco had said something about people getting their arses shot off at Lokinang. Her buttocks clenched, deflecting imagined bullets. She glanced over her shoulder, relieved to see the guard's gun pointing skywards.

The man leered and made an obscene gesture with the barrel.

Charming.

They approached a cliff face, set into which was a pair of enormous steel doors.

Gorilla-Woman spoke into the grill of an intercom. A side-door opened. Richard emerged.

'Thank you, Primrose.' He beckoned Colette inside.

Primrose!

Richard closed the door behind them.

She was relieved to have got this far with her backside still intact. Now what?

'Where are we going?'

'This way,' he said, avoiding her eyes.

You little shit!

He led her along a passage and into a room with two doors leading off.

Richard indicated the right-hand door.

She was now on home-territory. She used the toilet. Changed into hospital greens and moved to the exit door. Please God, it's the quarantine facilities at the Zoo; not the isolation unit at Nairobi Hospital.

She fitted the disposable hat and facemask, pushed open the door and stepped into... into a modern microbiological laboratory. No sick monkeys, no Marburg patients. Incubators, pH metres, laminar-flow cabinets, water-baths, centrifuges; all things, and more, she had in her laboratory at the Zoo. A few people, similarly clad to her, were peering down microscopes, pipetting fluids, setting up assays. They looked up incuriously as she entered.

Was she, were they, really standing on the brink of the greatest development in AIDS research since Robert Gallo and Luc Montagnier identified the causative virus? An HIV-3 virus which caused a mild disease in monkeys and rendered them immune to the virulent HIV-1. A potential vaccine for AIDS. Was it that simple? If so, why the kidnap, the blackmail, the strong-arm tactics, the... the bloody bloodiness?

Richard, clad in green, emerged from the adjacent door and indicated she should follow him.

They passed down the side of the laboratory to a glass-fronted office at the end where Jeff was seated at a computer. He smiled. His eyes were frank and transparent but conveyed something more pressing. Was it his trust-me look?

She kept her face expressionless.

He fitted his facemask and rose from his chair. 'Come, I'll show you round.'

As they walked along the different benches, Jeff chattered away about introns, RNA splicing, polymerase chain reactions, nucleotide sequencing; about T-cells, MHC antigens, adjuvants, monoclonal antibodies; things she doubted Richard had a clue about. He took culture flasks from incubators, placed them under inverted microscopes and pointed out cytopathic effects, vacuolation and cellular hypertrophy. He showed her radio-immuno assays, electron micrographs. He pointed out the complex of cables and pipes above their heads which carried power and water and controlled the internal environment.

'What's that?' She pointed to a dark hole high in the cave wall.

'One of the tunnels. The mountain's riddled with them. Makes a cheap and efficient extraction system. We keep a positive pressure in here and the air flows out there, wafting away any bugs.'

She'd never known him this garrulous. Was he trying to rebuild the bond, the trust there had once been between them, while excluding Richard who trailed along at the back?

'We used to have a problem with bats,' he said.

'Doing what?'

'Doing what bats do. Not conducive to a clean working environment.'

'No, I suppose not.'

'Then we installed that.' He pointed to what looked like a guitar amplifier high in the roof. 'It emits ultra-sound. We can't hear it but it blocks the bats' echolocation systems and those guys keep away. Clever, eh?'

Wonderful, amazing, stunning, fantastic. She didn't voice any of these facetious thoughts.

None of the workers in the laboratory seemed to share Jeff's enthusiasm. Instead they gazed with indifference, hostility even, as the three of them walked round.

'Why was ole-Tomeno so keen for me to come here?' she asked.

He didn't appear to hear, or else chose to ignore her question. 'Something else to show you.' He led her to a door at the far end of the laboratory and punched in a code on the keypad at the side.

She couldn't help noticing the sequence – probably coincidence – 0708: the day and month of her birthday. And of the Embassy bombing.

He opened the door and led the way down a darkened corridor, the ever-present Richard trailing behind.

Jeff stopped opposite a small plate-glass window. 'This is the clever stuff.'

She peered into a room containing a pressurised class III biosafety cabinet with three work stations – what she disparagingly referred to as a glove-box. The nearest station was vacant and the gloves stuck out like the arms of a drowning swimmer. At the other two stations people, with their hands and arms inside the gloves, were tipping capsules from stainless-steel trays through funnels and into small brown bottles.

'What are those capsules?' she asked.

'The vaccine. More specifically, vaccine antigen inside nano-bubbles embedded in uniquely constructed gelatin capsules composed of lipid bi-layers.' He could have been reading from a script. 'The cabinet is pressurised with nitrogen to prevent premature release of the nano-bubbles.'

She glanced at him. 'Not sure I can get my head round that.'

He touched her arm and pointed to a control panel beside the window. 'We control all the environmental conditions of the room from here – temperature, air pressure and so on – as well as sterilizing procedures and chemical decontamination. After each cycle we sterilize everything with ultra-violet light. This switch here. Zaps anything inside.'

'Ultra-violet for ultra-sterile?'

'If you like.'

Why is he telling me all this?

'Come.' He led her further down the corridor.

'What's through there?' She pointed to a door at the end.

'The mountain. Emergency escape route in case we get a fire or something in the lab. We've never had to use it, thank goodness.'

'Why, thank goodness?'

He studied her briefly. 'You have a choice of a quick death by fire or a slow death from starvation lost in the tunnels. This, though, is what I want to show you.'

He led her to another plate-glass window. 'This is what the programme is all about.'

She was reminded of the window she and the Petes had peered through to observe Helen. This time, she was looking into what appeared to be a dimly-lit hospital ward. There were some twenty beds, all but one occupied. Most of the occupants appeared to be asleep, but one or two gazed with bored expressions at the ceiling. One man was prowling round the room as though looking for a door or window, of which there appeared to be none. In one bed, the occupant was completely covered with a sheet. Wasn't that what they did when people died?

She gave an involuntary shiver.

'These are some of our vaccine volunteers,' said Jeff, a little too brightly. 'They all come from Somalia. As you know it's a poor country and these people can earn good money.'

'So what happens to them?'

'They're given the experimental HIV-3 vaccine. Those capsules, a unique oral formulation—'

'Oral? Since when can you—'

'We monitor their antibody levels each day. Some good responses, but variable.'

'Then what?'

'We challenge them, but that's some way off yet.'

'Challenge with what?'

'HIV-1, the AIDS virus. As I said, good results in monkeys. These volunteers are the lucky pioneers. They'll go home rich men.'

He was staring fixedly ahead. An oral vaccine for AIDS? Did she believe it? Did *he* believe it?

She glanced round the room. Why no windows, no natural lighting, no fresh air? Why no –?

A door, set flush into the wall at the side of the ward, opened.

'Time to go,' said Jeff, moving her away, but not before she'd seen someone enter in a biohazard suit with built-in respirator.

For AIDS research? No way!

She followed Jeff down the dim passageway, into the laboratory and back to his office.

'So,' he said, removing his facemask and sitting down behind his desk, 'you've seen the sharp end of the research. What do you think?'

Was it his trust-me look again?

Could she really trust him after that babble of science and pseudo-science? What was its purpose? To impress her? Impress Richard? Confuse one or both of them? All that stuff about nano-bubbles and lipid bi-layers. And an oral vaccine for AIDS?

She leaned back against the wall and folded her arms. 'Jeff, you've given me the grand tour, now perhaps you can tell me what it is I'm supposed to—'

Her words were cut off by the strident sound of alarms bells, and a tinny voice exhorting people to leave the building.

'Not again,' groaned Jeff.

'What is it?'

'Come on.' He led her and Richard out of the office. 'We get around four or five a week. False alarms. Elephants and other animals wander into the tunnels and set off the alarms.'

'We must leave,' said Richard. The first words he'd spoken during the whole tour.

Colette took a last look round then at the hole, high in the wall. That wasn't an elephant. When she looked again, the face had gone.

Chapter 65

It was dark by the time Dima returned to the Land Rover.

'What news?' asked Sean.

'The news is good.' He gave an account of his findings.

'And that woman you saw in the cave? Was it Colette?'

'I think.'

Sean squeezed his arm. 'You are a good man, a brave man. Tell me, is she well?'

'She is well, but I think she is with those ones from Isiolo, the ones who took her in their *gari*.'

'Jeff and Richard?'

'I think.'

Sean muttered something Dima didn't understand.

'And I found this.' He passed Sean the book he'd found in the tunnel.

'Wait.' Sean fetched a torch from the Land Rover. 'A bible!'

'It was on the ground.'

Sean opened the cover. 'Here is a person's name: Huw Williams. Do you know a person called—'

'I know that one. He was a man of God. He stayed at the place where my mother worked. I think he was killed by that One-Ear.'

'Killed? How?'

'Shot with a gun. That one also killed my parents.'

'Dima, I am so sorry.'

'Thank you. Now One-Ear works here.'

'You're sure?'

He nodded.

'Why do you call him that name?'

Dima was silent for a moment. 'I bit that one's ear.'

'You bit his ear?'

'Because he wanted to attack my mother.' Then, for the first time, he recounted to another person all the things that happened on the night he became a man.

'You have had a hard life, a very hard life,' said Sean.

'That is true.'

'Tell me, this One-Ear, what does he do here?'

'I think he is a guard. That one is very bad. Today I could have

347

killed him. But *Mungu* told me it was not for me to do that thing.'

Dima was conscious of Sean watching him.

***

Next morning, they both woke before sunrise. Sean jumped down from the roof of the Land Rover and Dima emerged from a shelter among the rocks. They finished the remains of last night's food then Sean locked the Land Rover.

Dima led the way over the brow of the hill and down to a place among the rocks where they could hide and watch.

When the sun rose behind them and lit up the compound, the security lights went out. The two of them remained in the shadow of the hill. The monkeys were beginning to wake in their cages.

Sean, who was looking through his special glasses, said there were three kinds: colobus, Sykes and vervet.

Dima shrugged. A monkey is a monkey, even if some have valuable skins and others don't.

A man appeared pushing a wheelbarrow. The monkeys began screeching and rattling their cages. Following the man, a guard carrying a stick, his gun slung over his shoulder.

Dima hissed. 'That is One-Ear.'

Sean looked through his glasses. 'Yes, I see. He has no ear on this side. I think you were very angry when you bit that one.'

'I was a leopard.'

Sean smiled. 'True.'

The men came to the first cage, and while One-Ear poked the monkey through the bars with his stick, the other man opened the door, threw in some food and slammed the door shut. Slowly they worked their way down the lines of cages. Most of the monkeys cowered back when One-Ear poked them but some, particularly the big ones called Sykes, attacked the stick with screams of anger. When the food was thrown in and the door shut, One-Ear poked them again as punishment and their screams became those of rage and fury.

An idea began to form in Dima's mind. Would that be a way to rescue Sean's woman? He studied the other buildings and the fence line. 'Sean, you see that place where we warthogs pass?' He grinned and pointed to the gap under the fence. 'I will pass there and look in the houses. Perhaps I will find Colette. I will tell you when it is ready for you to pass that way.'

'How will you tell me?'

348

'Perhaps I will come. Perhaps I will... I will think of a way.' He studied the compound once more. The monkeys had settled down to eat their food. The only people in sight were two guards on the entry gate.

'I go.' He touched Sean's arm. Ran off through the cover. Paused until the glass eyes turned away. Wriggled back under fence. He hid his bag, bow and arrows near the big tree. Then crept through bushes until he was close to the monkey cages.

He had promised *Mungu* he would never again hunt monkeys. He hoped they would understand. When he called to them, some shouted in alarm but he managed to reassure them and they settled.

He studied the area. Two guards at the gate were smoking cigarettes. No one else in sight. He called again to the monkeys. This time, their responses were friendly. He checked the guards were looking away. Slipped out of his hiding place. Ran down the line of cages opening the doors.

He ran back to his hiding place, satisfied he'd not been seen.

He was wrong.

Molito's crazed son was running down the hillside, shouting to the guards and pointing towards Dima's hiding place.

One of the guards hurried into the guard house. A siren sounded, loud and strident in the still morning air.

Dima ran back to the big tree, retrieved his things, climbed up and settled among its great branches. Although the sun was shining on him, he was safe. People rarely looked up.

Molito's son was plucking at the guards' clothing, waving his arms, pointing where Dima had been hiding. They tried to push him away.

The monkeys were edgy. Some, bolder than the others, emerged from their cages and sat on top. Some ran off.

Still the siren.

A scream. Molito's son clubbed with the butt of a rifle. Another blow. Another scream. The boy collapsed. Lay still. One of the guards kicked him. Kept kicking him.

More shouts. This time from the buildings.

People who had just woken up, struggled into their clothes as they rushed out of the buildings expecting fire. Seeing no flames, they were uncertain what to do.

The siren was turned off.

One of the guards on the gate shouted and pointed.

People fanned out and moved towards the bushes.

One-Ear appeared struggling with the belt of his trousers.

The monkeys saw him. Screamed.

He shouted back.

A big Sykes monkey jumped to the ground. Stood glaring at him. Bared its teeth. Two more joined it. All three screamed.

One-Ear shouted back. Struggled to hold his trousers with one hand, get his gun off his back with the other.

Another monkey arrived.

Four monkeys circling.

Two more monkeys.

One-Ear's shout became one of fear. He freed his gun. His trousers fell to his feet.

A monkey darted in and bit his leg.

He swung his rifle butt. The monkey lay senseless.

Another monkey closed.

One-Ear whirled round.

A monkey leaped onto his shoulder. Bit his neck.

One-Ear screamed.

More monkeys. More screaming. Guards milling round. Afraid to shoot for fear of hitting One-Ear.

He tried to run. Fell.

The monkeys became leopards. Ignored One-Ear's beating arms and kicking legs. Ignored shouts, screams and shots. They leaped. Slashed, ripped, tore.

Another shout.

The man called Jeff was dragging a hose. He turned the tap and the blow of water scattered the monkeys. They fled screaming. Some to the bushes. Some to the fence to fall back senseless from electricity. Some returned to their cages and sat whimpering.

Jeff turned off the hose and closed the cage doors.

Two monkeys scampered into Dima's tree, screeched in fear but were calmed by his soft words.

Jeff went and—

Dima suddenly remembered and realised. Jeff was the one with the special glasses for seeing birds. The one who had saved him when he was left for dead at that place with the bones. The one who gave him one thousand shillings. This must surely be a good man. A good man among many bad men.

Jeff joined the crowd gathered round One-Ear. He knelt down and turned the man over. Started back. One-Ear no longer had a throat and the sand was soaked with blood.

Mungu had decided the man's time had come.

Dima watched and waited.

Two men tried to stuff the body into a sack. The sack was too small. So they dragged the body away. Some people followed the snake-trail of blood in the sand.

Dima looked for Sean's woman. No sign. Too many people for him to search without being seen. He needed Sean's help. He delved into his bag and drew out his tin of poison; the tin with its surface rubbed smooth. He pointed the base of the tin towards the sun and tilted it. A speck of light – too small to attract attention – appeared on the hillside. He moved the tin, and the speck wandered across the trees and bushes.

Steadying his hand against a branch, he guided the speck to where Sean was hiding.

He looked up.

Twice, Dima moved the speck across him. The third time, Sean gave a cautious wave.

They met at the foot of the tree and climbed back into its branches.

People were still rushing round the compound. Someone shouted to find the person who'd released the monkeys.

Dima caught Sean's eye and grinned.

'Have you seen Colette?' asked Sean.

'No. I am thinking you will know what to do.'

'Are you?' Sean drew a breath. 'Where do—?'

'Someone comes,' hissed Dima. He scrambled onto a higher branch. A man in a white coat was moving slowly through the trees. The man looked up. Dima waited for the shout but the sun was shining in the man's face and he couldn't see those in the tree. Dima could see. This was the man called Richard.

Dima dropped back down to Sean. 'Did you see?'

Sean nodded.

He indicated his bow and quiver hooked over the branch but Sean shook his head. 'Wait. See if others come.'

The man came slowly nearer, following the warthog track.

Dima unsheathed his *simi*.

Sean whispered in his ear.

He nodded.

No sign of anyone following.

The man would pass directly beneath the tree.

Nearer.

Sean touched Dima's arm. The two of them dropped from the tree. Sean onto Richard. Dima to the side, his *simi* ready.

The man had no time to cry out. No time to defend himself.

Sean pushed his face into the sand while Dima ripped off the man's white coat. Slit his jeans with the *simi* and made bindings for his arms, his legs, a blindfold and a gag.

'Listen,' hissed Sean, in the man's ear. 'Where's Colette?'

The man shook his head.

'I'm going to loosen your gag,' said Sean. 'You will tell me where we can find her. If you shout we will kill you. Do you understand?'

Richard shook his head and gave a muffled cry.

Sean nodded to Dima, who drew his *simi* slowly down the man's arm, watching with interest the line of blood which emerged.

Richard shuddered.

'Good,' said Sean. 'My friend has some interesting poison he can rub into that wound if you need more encouragement.'

Richard whimpered.

Sean loosened the gag. 'Where is she?'

'She … she… Go to the laboratory. I think she is there.'

'Where's that?'

'In the mountain.'

'Are you sure?'

'Yes, yes.'

'Good.' Sean tightened the gag. 'We will hide you here and come back later when we have found her. If we fail to find her, we…' He left the sentence hanging.

Richard tried to say something.

They ignored him.

Sean picked him up, threw him over his shoulder and followed Dima to a place deeper in the bushes. They tied Richard's arms behind a tree. Patted his cheek. Left him.

Dima and Sean climbed back into the big tree.

People were no longer rushing round the compound. Some were returning to the buildings. Some stood and shouted at each other. Others peered into empty cages. Looked for missing monkeys.

The two monkeys in the tree with Dima and Sean sat in the highest branches, quiet and motionless.

Still no sign of Colette.

352

The red snake which wound across the sand and disappeared behind a building, had darkened.

Dima and Sean had a whispered discussion. Dima nodded, reached into his bag for his fire sticks, dropped to the ground and checked the direction of the wind.

Small hesitant flames crept into the dry grass. They quickly grew in size and confidence. Raced off through the bushes, snapping and crackling to each other.

It was a brief distraction which would soon burn itself out.

The siren sprang to life again.

Dima put on Richard's white coat – too big for him. Checked his *simi* was hidden underneath. Waved to Sean and set off, hoping his bare feet weren't too conspicuous.

Chapter 66

Ian and Tim Hollis set off for the airport soon after daybreak. They picked up Grace on the way and continued down the dual carriageway out of Nairobi, the three of them preoccupied with their own thoughts.

Even at this hour, people were streaming from the shanties into the city in pursuit of their livelihood: guards, maids, clerks, mechanics, cleaners, shop assistants, layabouts, pick-pockets, prostitutes and con-men, along with the idlers, the spongers and the desperate-for-work. The flow would reverse in the evening as people returned to their shacks to repeat the process the following day and the day after and the day...

'Next turn left,' said Ian.

The sinister profile of a Blackhawk helicopter came into view, its rotors idling.

Tim stopped at the security gate. Grace showed her pass to one of the armed policemen who waved them through.

Tim pulled up close to the helicopter. Felix appeared from inside and came across. 'You guys all set?'

'All ready,' said Grace.

'Thanks for the lift, Tim,' said Ian, and followed Grace and Felix into the cabin where they found Kelly already seated.

'Hi,' she said.

'I didn't realise you were coming,' said Ian.

'The sooner we can get set up the better I'm going to sleep.'

Further conversation was interrupted as the door was slammed shut and the whine of the engines increased.

'Seat belts on?' The pilot turned to check. 'Harry S here we come. Be around two hours, folks. Can't get more than about one-eighty out of this old bird.'

Their flight path took the helicopter south-east, more or less following the Nairobi-Mombasa road; one Ian had driven many times. Away to the south, the twin peaks of Mount Kilimanjaro could be seen poking out above the clouds: the snow-covered dome of Kibo at over six thousand metres and the slightly smaller, but no less impressive, craggy peak of Mawenzi. Further on, the Tsavo National Park.

Ian peered ahead for his first glimpse of the Indian Ocean.

Soon, the line of deep blue and turquoise came into view, redolent of coral sands, palm trees and balmy tropical seas – the reality of which rarely disappointed.

Grace pointed through the cabin windscreen. 'That is so huge.'

The pilot turned. 'Two-hundred-forty-four feet high, ma'am.'

She looked suitably impressed.

'You don't want to fall off the side.'

'I have no intention,' she said.

Ian caught her eye and smiled.

From their aerial perspective, the aircraft carrier seemed to tower over the town of Mombasa, looking distinctly menacing, despite its goodwill visit.

The pilot skirted north of Mombasa then out to where the great vessel was moored well beyond the fringing reefs which laid ribbons of white surf along the coastline.

As they approached the carrier, the pilot continued his commentary of need-to-know information: 'The Harry S – also known as Hairy Ass – is one-thousand-ninety-some-feet long and two-five-seven-feet wide. We carry around eighty aircraft – choppers and fixed-wing. Deck is some four-point-five acres, bigger than two football pitches.' He turned to Grace. 'That's American football, ma'am.'

She smiled sweetly.

'Displaces almost ninety-seven-thousand tons. That's one hell of a weight to drop on your toe. Ha, ha. It can accommodate over six-thousand crew members and produce around eighteen thousand meals a day. Don't reckon you'll go hungry. Ha, ha.'

Grace looked at Ian with a pained expression.

'You folks had breakfast?' asked the pilot.

'No,' said Grace.

'Hope they haven't run out when we get there.' He turned in his seat. 'Don't worry, folks, that's a joke.'

'Ha, ha,' said Grace. She gave a slight smile and turned to look out of the window.

Notwithstanding the pilot's rhetoric, Ian couldn't help being impressed by the scale of the vessel and the might and power of the US navy. But can might and power defeat Marburg?

The pilot turned again. 'Seat belts fastened?'

The helicopter touched down, the door was opened and they

climbed out. They barely had time to smell the sea before they were escorted to an elevator and plunged inside the great vessel. Except for the armed escort, front and rear, Ian felt they could have been in a shopping mall or plush hotel, rather than an instrument of war. After a number of corridors and stairways, they came to a panelled wooden door.

'Party to see the Captain,' said their lead escort into an intercom speaker.

'Enter,' came the tinny reply.

The man opened the door to show a large meeting room with three people seated at the end of a highly-polished table, papers spread out in front of them.

The only one in uniform rose, his easy-going manner belying the shrewd eyes which studied them.

'Good morning, folks. Hope you had a good trip.' He shook each of them by the hand. 'Captain Wendall Murphy.'

'Morning, sir,' said Felix, and introduced his three colleagues.

'Buffet breakfast over there,' said the Captain. 'Help yourselves then we'll get started.'

The other two men sat on either side of the Captain. One was small and fidgety, the other large and comfortable. They were not introduced and made no effort to introduce themselves but sat regarding the newcomers with... Was it indifference, hostility, distaste?

When they were settled, the Captain glanced at the papers in front of him, then looked up.

'Welcome aboard, folks.'

Murmurs of thanks.

'As we all know,' he continued, 'August seven was the anniversary of the Embassy bombing three years ago. The fact that the Harry S has been around for the last few days is, I'm sure you realise, no coincidence. We were on red alert at the time but I then reduced that to green. Following the call from the Secretary of State's office, readiness has been raised to yellow and I requested the Ambassador to mobilise you folks and bring you here.' He turned to Felix. 'So that's where we are. Major, perhaps you could tell us your side.'

'Thank you, sir. It's our opinion that a bio-terrorist attack using Marburg virus was planned for August seven but was postponed because we took out the main operative.'

'The man Malik?'

'Yes, sir.'

'But you believe the threat persists?'

'Affirmative, sir.'

'Can I ask why?'

'Perhaps I can answer that,' said Ian. 'The man whom we believe is behind the operation calls himself Mlala – Swahili for sleeper. We don't know his identity but we have a number of suspects, one of whom is – or was – Malik.'

'Who's now out of the loop,' added Felix.

The Captain nodded. 'Who else?'

'A British subject by the name of Melhuish,' said Ian. 'He converted to radical Islam when he was in Pakistan and took the name Abdul Jamal. We know he was in contact with Malik, either directly, or through an intermediary name of Rashid Omari, who is also at large. We also believe Melhuish – Abdul whatever we call him – tried to have Malik killed. Presumably to stop him talking.'

The Captain peered over his glasses. 'I heard that someone shot up the car he was in.'

'We believe at least two people were involved. We found the motorbike they used, in Melhuish's garage. I can't see him riding it, though,' said Ian. 'It was probably hired hit-men.'

'I see,' said the Captain. 'And the other two you mentioned?'

'We think they're still in Kenya,' said Grace. 'My people have checked all the recent international flight lists. Neither their names, nor their possible pseudonyms appear.'

'So the terrorist threat presumably remains?'

'Yes, sir,' said Felix. 'Although these guys missed the first bus, we reckon they'll be on the second.'

'Explain.'

'We believe part of the strategy is to use a group of Somali extremists as the operatives.'

'These…' The Captain consulted his papers. 'These… How do you pronounce this?'

'Njia Mpya, sir,' said Grace. 'It means the new path or way.'

'Right.'

'We reckon they've been on alert for a while,' continued Felix. 'And are itching to be let out of their kennels.'

'And where are these so-called kennels, major?'

'Probably centred round a place called Lokinang.'

'Which has been on our radar since satellite pictures showed some

357

abnormal activity in that area. Correct?'

'Yes, sir. We believe the main operation may be taking place inside caves in an extinct volcano. That's why the satellites don't pick it up.'

'And what is this main operation?'

'Production of Marburg virus as a bio-weapon.'

The Captain rubbed his hands over his face. 'And the evidence is credible?'

'Yes, sir.'

The Captain looked round the table. 'In view of what you've told me, major, should the Harry S remain on yellow alert?'

Felix took a deep breath before replying. 'Affirmative, sir. We know those—'

'Thank you, major. That's all I need to know.' He looked to the men on either side of him. 'Any questions, gentlemen?'

The smaller man addressed Kelly. 'About the request for provision of mobile hospital facilities.'

'Yes?'

'You're sure this is Marburg?'

'Certain.'

'On what basis?'

'Clinical symptoms, laboratory tests and a second expert opinion.'

The man sniffed.

Kelly turned to the Captain. 'We're very grateful for your offer of help, sir. The sooner we can get mobilised, the sooner we can get this thing under control.'

The man leaned across the table to face Kelly. 'I'm not sure that the death of a couple of African natives really justifies—'

'I understand the Secretary of State approved the deployment of resources from the Harry S. Truman.' Kelly applied a fixed smile and stuck out her chin.

The man's mouth was a thin line. 'No more questions.' He gathered his papers and rose to his feet. 'Excuse me, captain; I have more pressing matters to attend to.'

The Captain waved a languid hand. 'Would you mind telling the Senior Medical Officer to come and see us?'

The man gave a terse nod and left the room.

The larger man leaned back in his chair. Scratched himself. Yawned. Frowned through bushy eyebrows. 'So, Major Rossi, what gives?'

'In what respect, sir?'

'You tell me.'

Felix was rescued from his floundering when the door opened and Chuck Wallicker, the man they'd last seen at the shoot-out of Malik's car, entered.

'Sorry I'm late, captain,' said the newcomer. 'Felix, you old coyote, so they got you out here at last?'

'Good to see you, Chuck. You remember Ian and Grace?'

'Hi folks.'

'Kelly, she's the doc dealing with this Marburg thing,' added Felix.

'Morning, ma'am. Say, Felix, what an ass-hole, that Malik guy.'

'Has he been singing?'

'Loud and clear – once we told him we weren't sure we could treat his injuries.'

'What did he tell you?'

Before Chuck could answer, the door opened and a fresh-faced man entered. His enthusiastic manner suggested a vicar or sports master. 'I was told you wanted to see me, captain.'

'Thanks for coming, doc. This is Dr Kelly Ryder.'

'Ma'am.' He shook her hand. 'I'm Dr Coates, the SMO. Say this Marburg thing sounds real interesting. Be great if it's genuine.' His voice had an eager boyishness and Ian half expected him to add "super".

'It is,' said Kelly.

'No kidding.'

'I guess you two need to talk technical,' said the Captain. 'No sense in keeping you hanging around here.'

'Thank you, captain.' Dr Coates nodded to Kelly. 'Shall we go down the medical centre?'

'Sure.' Kelly got to her feet. 'Thanks for the breakfast, sir.'

'You're welcome,' said the Captain.

When they'd left, the large man seated beside the Captain leaned forward. 'You haven't answered my question, Major Rossi.'

'Excuse me,' said Grace. 'Before Felix answers, I have some questions I would like to ask.' She counted them off on her fingers. 'Is there anything in the papers from Malik's office? What can *you* tell us about the man called Quentin Melhuish also known as Abdul Jamal. And his colleague Rashid Omari? And what has Malik told you? That's a start.' Smile applied.

Stunned silence.

'Remind me who you are,' said the man.

'Inspector Grace Kiptagat, Special Branch, Kenya Police. This ship is currently moored in Kenyan territorial waters.' Her smile still lacked humour. 'I'm told this is a goodwill visit.'

Forty love to Grace. Ian's respect for her racked up a couple more notches.

The man folded his arms. Sat back. Glowered. Thumped a fist on the table. 'Goddam it!' His mouth creased into a smile. 'We can do business.'

Game, set and match, Grace. Bloody brilliant.

Chapter 67

Colette stood at the barred window mesmerized by the hungry fire. People rushed around shouting, waving and throwing buckets of water. Someone operated the hose but it was too short. Smoke drifted across the buildings. The monkeys resumed their screaming, drowning out the siren.

The second time this morning there'd been sirens and panic. The first had been horrific with that guard being savaged. Now this.

The first could have been an accident – someone inexperienced looking after the monkeys. But two such incidents?

A man in a flapping white coat ran bare-foot past the hut, shouting, waving and opening doors. He tried her locked door. Ran on.

Dima?

Dima!

If he was here, Sean should be nearby. What could she do? Not stand helpless, looking out of the window, that's for sure.

She pushed at the door. Jiggled the handle.

No joy.

She glanced round the room. Gorilla-Woman had neglected to leave crowbars and explosives when she'd locked her in last night. But there must be something.

A table, a bed, two chairs. That was it.

Great.

The room wasn't built as a prison cell. No CCTV camera. But it still had barred windows and a locked door – even if that door did open outwards.

She tugged at the bars. Nearly pulled her arms from their sockets. Threw herself against the door. She couldn't decide which was more painful; the dislocation or the impaction.

'Bugger!'

She prowled round the room kicking things. Nearly broke her toes.

The bed moved. What? The bed moved.

So what?

It's on wheels. That's what's bloody what!

She wheeled it against the wall opposite the door. Readied herself then raced the bed across the room. Smashed into… into the door frame.

'Shit!'

Try again.

The aim was better. Something cracked.

'Go for it. Third time lucky.'

The door smashed open.

She leaped across the bed, into billowing smoke. Ran clear and round the end of the building, coughing, her eyes stinging. Collided with someone.

They both fell to the ground.

She tried to scramble to her feet and run. Someone grabbed her ankle pulling her down. She kicked out. Struggled to break free. This person was strong.

'*Jambo*,' said a voice.

She twisted her head.

'Dima? Thank God.'

He helped her up. '*Kuja* – come.'

They raced round the building, along the back, cross to the next building. The great doors into the mountain lay ahead. People running out of the side door.

Hide behind some bins.

Dima's face split in huge grin. 'I have found you.'

'Where's Sean? How is he?'

'He is well. See.' He pointed to a big tree she could make out through the smoke. 'See, he is high in that tree.'

'I can't see. He is not sick?'

'He is—'

A shout. Gorilla-Woman brandishing a pickaxe handle. Her version of have-a-nice-day.

Colette caught Dima's arm, raced with him across the open space. Pushed past the people running out of the mountain. Led him through the side door. Slammed it shut. Pounding on the metal-work confirmed Gorilla-Woman's intentions.

Colette kept hold of Dima's arm. 'This way.'

No time for sensitivities. She led him into the female changing area. Ripped off his white coat. Gave him a set of hospital greens.

She smiled at his bemused expression. 'Like this.' She slipped similar clothes on over her T-shirt and jeans.

A startled woman came from within the laboratory where the

alarms were still ringing. 'We must leave.'

'Just coming,' said Colette.

She waited until the woman had gone.

'Forget about the clothes.' She dragged Dima into the lab. The pounding on the outside door had stopped. Soon there would be a gorilla wielding a pickaxe handle, rampaging along behind them.

Hide somewhere and hope the gorilla won't find us? Think of a way to overpower her? Hope she takes early retirement? All unlikely.

Nowhere to hide. She hurried Dima down to the door at the end.

The code? The bloody code?

How the hell could she forget her own birthday?

She punched in the numbers. Opened the door. They slipped through into the faintly-lit corridor. Waited for their eyes to adjust to the gloom.

She led Dima to the first window. All three sets of gloves in the glove-box were doing their drowning-man impressions. Trays of capsules lay inside the sterile chamber together with racks of bottles. Could she do it? She glanced at the control panel. Remembered Jeff's words. Time to abort the greatest advance in AIDS research. She threw the u.v. switch. A momentary delay. Then the whole room was bathed in purple blue light.

'*Aieeh!*' exclaimed Dima.

The faint sound of shattering glassware confirmed that rampaging gorillas and laboratory equipment were not a good mix. Thank God, they hadn't tried to hide in the lab.

A deep menacing rumble echoed along the corridor.

'What's that?' she hissed.

'It is the mountain,' said Dima. 'It is waking.'

Another rumble, louder.

No more shattering glass. Instead a great crash of tumbling something. Rumbling shaking the ground, the walls, the mountain. A hundred lorries playing dodgems in the lab. The sleeping mountain stirring.

The rumbling died away. The mountain sighed and settled.

She rushed to the door they'd come in by. The tumbling, rumbling, crumbling something had blocked it. Not even her bed would shift this lot.

She ran back to Dima. He was peering in horror through the second window. He kept repeating the word *uchawi*. She'd no idea what it meant.

She looked over his shoulder into hell.

Some of the AIDS "volunteers" were too weak to move from their beds. Others were scrabbling round the walls – some on hands and knees – looking for a way of escape. She barely noticed, because – faces pressed to the glass – were three zombies with blood-red eyes and slavering blood-stained mouths, scratching and tearing at the glass with broken fingernails.

Hell on earth was not "the greatest advance in AIDS research." It was Marburg, a category-A bioterrorism agent. A nightmare of revulsion and horror.

The implications could wait.

'Come.' She dragged Dima to the door at the far end of the corridor – the one Jeff said led into the mountain. Their only hope.

Please God, it's the same code. Punch it in. Pull the door handle.

Nothing.

'Come on!'

She heaved. Hinges creaked.

Dima joined her.

The door groaned open revealing an abyss of blackness.

A rumble emerged from the bowels of the abyss.

The lights went out.

Chapter 68

The mutual suspicion had dissipated by the time the group settled in Chuck's cabin and spread out their various files, folders and laptops on the table.

'Sorry it's a bit cramped, folks,' he said.

'Great view, though,' said Ian, looking out across the flight deck to Mombasa in the distance.

'I try not to let it distract me.' Chuck turned to the large comfortable man. 'Over to you, Howard.'

The man, who clearly felt on the same wavelength as Grace, addressed his remarks to her. 'Where's the money come from?'

Grace frowned. 'What money?'

'To run this caboodle. This bio-weapons thing they're cooking inside the mountain. Don't reckon we're talking pocket-money.'

'I don't suppose we are.'

'Right. So where's it coming from?'

'I've no idea. Have you?'

'Nope.' Howard sat back and chuckled. 'You're smart.'

Grace glowered.

Howard shuffled his papers and studied his notes. 'These Ninja people brought in to help with the cooking.'

'What about them?'

'They got any money?'

'No. They're an—'

'Yes, they bloody have!' cried Ian.

Heads turned.

'Explain,' said Howard.

'Grace, correct me if I'm wrong,' said Ian, 'but in their spare time, don't they go round hijacking oil tankers for ransom money?'

'We think it's the same group.'

'Jeez,' said Felix. 'You reckon, not only is Mlala getting these Ninja jerks to do his dirty work, he's getting them to pay the bills?'

'Could be,' she said.

'Damn right, it could.'

Two jets streaked off the carrier with a roar which shook the cabin and made speech momentarily impossible.

Howard shifted his ample weight. 'Tell me, Grace, you had any recent contact from Prairie Dog?'

She looked baffled.

'Sayed Farouk,' said Felix. 'The one we know as Jeff Carter. Prairie Dog's his codename.'

'I see. No. We've not met but I understand he was seen in Isiolo about a week ago.'

'Who says?'

'A man called Solomon. He runs a bar up there. He keeps his ears and eyes open for me.'

'That so?' Howard unrolled a map of Kenya. 'Show me.'

'Here.' Grace pointed. 'That's Isiolo.'

'And this is Lokinang, right?' He indicated a red circle on the map.

'Right.'

'And the distance is one fifty miles?'

'About that.'

'So, three hour's drive?'

Grace laughed. 'More like six or seven. You haven't seen the roads in that area.'

Howard drummed his fingers.

'What's bugging you, Howard?' asked Felix.

'What's bugging me is that we haven't heard from Prairie Dog for over a week now.'

'I thought you'd given him a long leash.'

'Not that long.'

'You reckon he's been rubbed out?'

'Could be.' Howard looked round those seated at the table. 'Or else he's gone off the rails.'

'What does that mean?' said Grace.

'Gone over to the other side. Vamoosed. Jumped ship. Skedaddled. It's been known.'

'Why would he do that?'

'Because...' Howard stared out of the window. 'Because he and Malik were buddies on the Russians' bio-weapons programme back at Stepnogorsk.'

'We know they worked together,' said Felix. 'But who says they were buddies?'

'Friend Malik. That ass-hole told us quite a few things. That was one of them.'

'And you believed him?' said Ian.

'Man, we don't believe nothing he tells us. It's just that it squares with what we know.'

'But I thought Jeff – Prairie Dog – was working for you people,' said Ian.

'So did we. Don't mean he can't jump ship. He's a Muslim. Same as Malik. Brotherly loyalty, if you like.'

Felix looked up from his laptop. 'You reckon Prairie Dog could be this Mlala guy who seems to be running the show?'

Howard shrugged. 'Dunno. Not sure Malik knows, or if he does he ain't saying. Perhaps he's too scared.'

'Felix and I made the link before,' said Ian.

'Between PD and Mlala?'

'Yeah,' said Felix, 'but we couldn't get it to stick.'

'Okay,' said Howard, 'put that on ice for the moment, but keep him in mind, along with…' He consulted his notes. '… with this Quentin-Abdul person and Rashid Omari.'

Ian leaned forward. 'Howard, anything in Malik's papers?'

Howard wrinkled his nose. 'Not a lot; orders for laboratory equipment consistent with a biohazard lab. Some religious-type tracts urging true followers to do this and that – the usual garbage.'

'One of which was sent to a Kenyan newspaper,' said Grace. 'Rallying call for August the seventh.'

Howard nodded. 'Any idea who sent it?'

'We think it was the one who now calls himself Rashid Omari—'

'Since when?' said Felix.

Grace gave a slight smile. 'A colleague of mine, Maria, who worked with him. I played her the tape. She thinks she recognised the voice.'

Felix grunted. 'That figures. Anything else in Malik's papers?'

Howard rubbed his chin. 'The main thing of interest to our boys was a plan to beef up this Marburg thing by crossing with influenza virus – something like that. Kinda scary.'

'We've seen a copy of that document,' said Felix.

'How come?'

'Your people sent it me.'

'Why?'

'You'd better ask them.'

Howard scowled. 'What you make of it?'

'Where did the document come from?'

'You haven't answered my question.'

'And you haven't answered mine.'

367

The two men glared at each other across the table, words buzzing like hornets round the room. Howard then threw his hands in the air. 'Hell, Felix, we're supposed to be in the same team. Seems like Prairie Dog got hold of the document when he was in Stepnogorsk but as far as we know the Russians never followed up on it.'

'We were told the proposal was credible,' added Felix.

'Who by?'

'A, er, colleague of mine,' said Ian. 'A virologist who specialises in monkey viruses.'

'What did he say?'

'It's she. She said the premise was sound, but didn't know if it would work in practice.'

'Pretty much what I heard.' Howard shifted again. 'Could they be cooking this thing up at this Lokinang place?'

'That's what we fear,' said Felix.

'And that's why you want the Harry S kept on yellow alert?'

'Yup.'

Ian's attention was caught by a small twin-engine plane coming in to land on the flight deck: a rabbit among wolves.

'Let's move on, folks,' said Felix. 'That shopping list of names I sent you, Howard, anything else come up?'

Howard opened a file in front of him and gave his lazy smile. 'You'll be pleased to know that Ian Sinclair and Grace Kiptagat appear to be clean.'

'You bugger, Felix,' muttered Ian.

'Like I said...' Felix waved a dismissive hand. 'You know what I said.'

'Yes, but I didn't think you'd stoop that low.'

'What about the other names?' snapped Grace.

Howard avoided her venomous gaze. 'We've dealt with the Quentin guy. We've not come up with anything new on him, nor has MI6. We confirmed his conversion to radicalism and his trips round Pakistan and similar places, which ties in with what you folks have told us, except...' He glanced at Ian.

'Except what?'

'Except most of the info he gathered was useless to the extent my people think it was probably deliberate misinformation.'

'Hmm. Any harm done?'

'Probably not, but like you, we'd sure as hell like to know where he is now.'

'And the others?' said Grace.

'That Tarzan guy got us interested.'

'Who?'

'The one who lives out in the jungle.'

'Sean Paterson?'

'Yeah, him.'

'Why's he interesting?'

'Because, he lives out there where much of the action is.'

'You could say the same about Franco,' said Grace.

'Sure, but we know that one works for us. Paterson, though—' He tapped the folder. '— from what Felix tells us, he seems to get around and be in the right place at the right time.'

'I think that's probably coincidence,' said Grace.

'Coincidences make me nervous. Also we don't know diddly-squat about him.'

'I'm sorry?'

'Nix, nothing, zilch.'

'Does that surprise you?'

'No. It bugs me.'

Grace looked doubtful.

'Okay, okay, I know. But it's my job.' Howard sat back and studied her then patted his pockets. He eventually located some gum, unwrapped it and popped it in his mouth.

She frowned. 'So who else makes you nervous?'

'This one.' He underlined a name and passed her the file. 'You know him?'

'Ole-Tomeno? He's the Minister for Environment and Conservation. What about him?'

'Another joker who seems to get around.'

Grace plonked her elbows on the table and glared at Howard. 'I don't know what all this is, but I cannot see how the Minister, or Sean Paterson for that matter, can have anything to do with this Marburg plot. You have some perfectly good suspects without going off to... to fairyland to find others.' She glared round the table. 'We're wasting our time coming out here. I am, anyway.'

'Don't take it like that, Grace. It's only that we'd like to look into these people a bit more.'

'And you think we haven't?'

Howard held up his hands. 'Don't get me wrong. It's just we may be able to put a different slant on things.'

'How?'

'Dunno. But it'd be good to have a chat.' Howard shifted the gum to the other side of his mouth. 'Real friendly like. Chew the fat together. You know?'

'No, I don't.'

'Excuse me a moment,' said Ian, getting up and peering out of the window. 'I don't know who's on your side, Howard, but it looks as though your wish could be granted.'

'How you mean?'

'If I'm not very much mistaken, ole-Tomeno has just arrived on a Flying Doctor plane and is being escorted somewhere.'

The others crowded to the window.

'Felix, is this your doing?'

'Yeah, well. Grace did say she wanted him picked up. Larry said he could…' Felix shrugged.

'Let me go find out what's going on,' said Chuck. 'Carry on here, folks. I'll get some tea, coffee sent up.'

'Sounds good,' said Felix.

Before Chuck could leave, there as a knock on the door and a naval rating entered. 'Excuse me, commander, this just came in.'

Chuck scanned the note. 'Well, what do you know?'

'What is it?' said Felix.

'Prairie Dog's a-calling; that's what. His PLB's been activated and—'

'His what?' said Ian.

'His personal locator beacon. Only thing we have to get a fix on him.'

'So where is he?'

'Howling out there in the prairie.'

Chuck's phone rang. He snatched up the receiver. 'Sir?'

The others watched and waited.

Chuck replaced the receiver and a slow smile spread across his face. 'Looks like it could be show time, folks. Captain says report to his quarters now. Follow me.'

The cabin that Chuck led them to, reminded Ian of the lounge bar at the Settlers Club.

Ole-Tomeno and the Captain were seated in comfortable armchairs with cups of coffee at their elbows. Seated in the background at a small table, Larry, the Flying Doctor pilot, was tucking in to waffles and maple syrup. He waved a spoon and called 'hi' as they entered.

Ian waved back.

Ole-Tomeno rose to his feet, came to greet them then checked. 'Ian? Ian Sinclair?'

'Yes, sir.'

'But I thought…'

'Shall we say the account of my death was an exaggeration.'

'Sir, we felt it might help our investigations if those responsible for the bombing thought they'd succeeded,' interjected Grace.

'I see.' The Minister regarded the two of them coldly. 'Well, I'm sure you acted in what you judged to be everyone's best interests.'

'Yes, sir.'

'Grab some seats, folks. Coffee, tea and refreshments over there,' said the Captain. 'Help yourselves.'

Once they were settled, ole-Tomeno seemed to regain some of his composure. 'My apologies, captain, a slight misunderstanding.'

'Sure.'

'Now that we are all assembled, can I thank you, captain, for receiving me – all of us – so warmly,' said with the sincerity of royalty invited to open a canning factory.

'Our pleasure, sir.'

'I, in turn, would like, on behalf of the Kenyan government – a little belatedly perhaps – to welcome you, your crew and your magnificent ship, to Kenya.'

'Thank you, sir. Much appreciated.'

Polite murmurs and nods.

The Captain resumed. 'You've seen the message, Chuck, what's your thinking?'

'I think we should go get him, sir?'

The Captain turned to the CIA man. 'And you, Howard?'

'Prairie Dog's one of our best operatives, sir,' said Howard, licking syrup off his fingers. 'I've had my doubts about him at times but he always comes up with the goods in the end. This is for real.'

'Meaning what?'

'Meaning, if he's activated his PLB, he's not simply wanting a lift home, he needs the cavalry sent in.'

'You know the political implications of what you're saying?'

'Yes, sir.'

The Captain picked up a bowl of roses on the table in front of him and sniffed them. 'I guess these come from Kenya, minister?'

'Undoubtedly, flowers are one of our main exports.' Ole-Tomeno beamed round the room.

'I didn't know that. I love roses.' He replaced the bowl on the table. 'As you can see, sir, we have a problem. We have—'

Ole-Tomeno held up his hand. 'Allow me stop you there.' He glanced round the group. 'As you good people probably gather, my arrival here is not entirely fortuitous. When your Ambassador spoke to me, captain, she intimated some of her concerns. I consulted my people, not least Inspector Kiptagat.'

Grace studied her finger nails.

'Needless to say, we share your concerns over this current threat. None of us will forget that appalling attack on your Embassy three years ago.' He paused, inviting comment. When none was forthcoming, he continued. 'I have to confess that I was led to believe the research being conducted at Lokinang concerned a vaccine for AIDS. If, as it now appears, this is a front for bio-weapon's research, I have to say I am appalled.'

He rose to his feet and crossed to the window. 'What a magnificent view.' He fell silent for a moment then turned back to the gathering. 'I for one have no intention of allowing our beautiful country to be ravaged by fanatics and fundamentalists with extremist beliefs and radical ideologies. With that in mind, captain, may I request you, on behalf of the Kenyan Government, to assist us in exterminating this cancer from our midst? You are perhaps familiar with our own paramilitary force, the General Service Unit or GSU. They will provide you ground support if you would be kind enough to mobilise whatever forces you feel may be appropriate.'

The Captain rose and shook ole-Tomeno's hand. 'Thank you, sir.'

'Can I suggest, captain, in the interests of international diplomacy, that any reports of the mission to appear in the press could, er, perhaps play down the role of the US?'

'I'm sure that would be possible, minister.'

'Probably best that way.' Ole-Tomeno smiled as he agreed with himself.

The Captain pointed to a flag mounted on the wall, which depicted crossed cannons on a scarlet background with the words "*Give 'em Hell*" emblazoned across it. 'That, sir, is the battle flag of the Harry S. Truman.'

'Indeed? I can only endorse its sentiments. May you all return safely.'

The Captain turned to Chuck. 'What are we waiting for, commander? You heard what the Minister said. Operation Lion Tamer is go!'

'Yes, *sir*! Let's go kick ass.'

Chapter 69

Some thirty minutes later, Ian found himself sitting between Grace and Felix on uncomfortable canvas seats in the rear of a Blackhawk helicopter. Howard stayed on the carrier: 'for a nice cosy chat with OT.'

Ian and Grace qualified for US combat operations on the dubious basis they were the only ones who knew what Jeff, Quentin and Richard looked like. Additionally, Grace could act as interpreter. Their hastily-borrowed uniforms were identical to those of Felix and the accompanying SEALs but Ian doubted anyone with hostile intent would discriminate on the grounds that he and Grace carried no weapons or clip-on radios.

In the seats immediately in front were four SEALs, one of whom was Chuck. The pilot and navigator occupied the front two seats, and behind them, two more SEALs manned machine guns mounted in the openings of the two side doors. One of the men was ogling over the pictures in a girlie magazine, much to Grace's disapproval.

Ahead of them, the other Blackhawk had a complement of ten SEALs.

Grace leaned across to Felix. 'What are SEALs?' she shouted above the noise of the engines and the rushing wind.

'Acronym for Sea, Air, Land teams, ma'am.'

'Oh.'

'US special forces, like our SAS,' said Ian.

'Only better,' said Felix, and grinned.

'Better than our GSU?' Grace gave a slight smile and turned to look at the scenery passing beneath them.

The noise level precluded further conversation.

The pilot's voice came crackling over the intercom. 'Mount Kenya visible over on our port side, folks.'

Ian gazed morosely out of the side window. Despite all the US gung-ho, this was no schoolboy adventure. People could be killed. He could be killed. They all could. Perhaps Njia Mpya was better armed and prepared than any of them thought. It only needed one trigger-happy Ninja with a shoulder-fired missile launcher to knock their ponderous craft out of the sky. Perhaps Jeff really had gone over to the other side and Operation Lion Tamer was flying straight into the lions' den. Perhaps *this* was to be Mlala's – Jeff's – celebration of August the seventh.

A voice came crackling over the intercom. 'Lion-One to Lion-Two.'

'Go ahead, Lion-One,' answered the pilot of their helicopter.

'Some ass-hole just taken a pot-shot at us. Keep your eyes peeled.'

'Copy that, Lion—'

The transmission was drowned by staccato firing of the two machine guns.

Ian's thoughts about missile launchers began to seem less fanciful.

'You ever been duck shooting?' shouted Felix, above the clamour. 'I guess I now know how those guys feel.'

'Them or us?' shouted Ian.

'Whatever.'

The machine guns fell silent and the man went back to his girlie magazine.

'Lokinang, straight ahead,' called the pilot, a while later.

Apart from a slight bracing of shoulders and the man tucking his magazine away, there wasn't much change in the level of preparedness of the already alert SEALs.

Despite his own impotence, Ian felt reassured.

'Lion-One to Lion-Two. Over.'

'Go ahead, Lion-One.'

'We'll go in, secure the target. You give us cover.'

'Copy, Lion-One.'

The engine noise increased. The Blackhawk swept round in a wide arc.

Ian caught glimpses of the mountain, the tree-speckled summit, the compound, buildings, people running in panic, a large fence, people throwing themselves to the ground. Two men raised guns. Dived for cover as the machine gun in front opened up.

Lion-One hovered above the ground. SEALs poured out from each side. The helicopter then rose and joined Lion-Two circling slowly overhead watching the SEALs deploy across the compound.

Ian was impressed.

A few minutes later a call over the intercom.

'Lion-One to Lion-Two. Ground force reports target secured.'

'Copy, Lion—'

A great cloud of dust and ash emerged from the mountain.

'The bloody thing's erupting!' yelled Ian.

The two helicopters rose away from the danger.

'Lion-Two to Lion-One. What's your take on the mountain? Is it erupting?'

'Negative. Vibrations from the choppers caused partial collapse. Prepare to land, Lion-Two. We'll go first. You follow when we give the all-clear.'

'Copy, Lion-One.'

Chuck turned and grinned. 'Like taking candy from kids.'

'I wonder,' murmured Ian.

Their helicopter touched down and the pilot came on the intercom: 'Over to you, commander.'

'Go, go, go!' shouted Chuck.

They scrambled out into the heat of the afternoon sun.

'You wait here with the chopper,' said Chuck, to Ian and Grace. He and Felix ran off, sending groups of SEALs in different directions searching buildings, rounding up people, attending to the injured, and on the lookout for any counter-attack.

'I think Felix is enjoying this more than his desk job,' said Grace.

Ian smiled. 'I almost wish I could join him.'

One of the SEALs came running up to them. 'Commander says he needs your help. This way.'

They jogged after him and rounded a building. A disparate group of people, watched over by four SEALs, sat on the ground showing varying emotions: fear, anger, relief.

'You recognise any of them?' asked Chuck.

'That's Jeff, the older one sitting on his own. The one you call Prairie Dog,' whispered Ian.

Chuck pointed. 'You, over here.'

Jeff clambered to his feet and came towards them, his face expressionless. He was quickly frisked by one of the SEALs, then stood to one side under the man's watchful gaze.

'Anyone else?' asked Chuck.

Most of the group kept their eyes downcast as Ian and Grace wandered among them. They returned shaking their heads.

'No sign of Quentin or Richard,' said Ian.

'GSU should be here soon,' said Grace. 'They can take these people into custody and we'll interrogate them later.'

'Sure.' Chuck called to one of the SEALs. 'Okay, sergeant, be nice to these folks, give them some food and water and treat anyone who's injured. But keep an eye on them.'

'Yes, sir.'

Chuck turned to Grace and Ian. 'Let's go have a look round. You too.' He jerked his head at Jeff, who followed them round the building.

When they were out of sight of the others, Chuck extended his hand. 'It's an honour, sir.'

Jeff smiled. 'That was quite a show, commander. Ian, how are you? And Grace – Grace Kiptagat isn't it?'

She smiled.

'Where can we go talk?' said Chuck.

'Let's sit under that tree over there,' said Jeff. 'Best we stay in the open.'

'Sure.' Chuck called to one of the SEALs to bring chairs. 'Tea, coffee?'

'Tea, please. Be great,' said Jeff.

'Same for you guys?'

Ian and Grace nodded.

Chuck shouted further orders.

As soon as they were seated, Chuck turned to Jeff. 'First question we gotta ask: you know the whereabouts of... Remind me, Ian.'

'Quentin Melhuish alias Abdul Jamal, and Richard Omar alias Rashid Omari.'

'In a word, no,' said Jeff.

'Can you be a little more specific?' growled Chuck.

'With respect to their current whereabouts, no.' Jeff regarded him thoughtfully. 'I should perhaps explain, commander. The arrival of your circus was not – how shall I put it? – the only excitement in town today. As you can see there has recently been a bush fire – quite an impressive one. Thank you,' he added as he was handed a mug of tea. 'I have every reason to believe it was started deliberately to create a diversion.'

'Was that when you activated your PLB?'

'I can't keep track of all your acronyms, but if you mean my personal locator beacon, yes. It was clear that things were getting out of hand. The release of the monkeys didn't help.'

'What monkeys?'

'Over there.' Jeff indicated the cages. 'Monkeys being used to test experimental vaccines. Some enterprising person released them and they took exception to a singularly unpleasant guard we have here – or rather had.'

Chuck raised an eyebrow.

'The monkeys saw fit to remove his throat.'

'Jeez.'

'It wasn't very pleasant, I can assure you.'

'What was the diversion for?' asked Ian.

Jeff stared into his tea. 'Almost certainly to rescue Colette.'

'Colette! What's she doing here?'

'It's a rather complicated story.'

'Is she all right?'

Jeff looked up. 'I don't know.'

'You must know something,' said Ian.

Jeff pointed. 'Colette was locked in that room there last night.'

'The one with the smashed door?'

'Yes. Colette, as you know, is a very resourceful and determined young lady.'

'She did that?'

'Undoubtedly.'

'Bloody hell.' Ian frowned. 'Why was she locked in?'

'As I said, it's complicated.'

'Come on, Jeff, what can you tell us?'

'That's all I know. I can only hope the diversion served its purpose and she was rescued or—'

'Who by?'

'I can only assume it would have been Sean Paterson?'

'You've not seen him, though?'

'No.' Jeff stared at his feet, his face bleak.

'If she wasn't rescued?'

'God, I don't know. She could have been in there – there where the lab was. Where the lab was until you people with your helicopters and your go-get-em kick-ass mission, caused the mountain to collapse.'

'Shit,' whispered Ian.

'Succinctly put.' Jeff paused. 'There is also a third option.'

'Which is?'

He brushed trembling hands over his face. 'Why the hell did I get into all this?'

'What's the third option?'

'She's been kidnapped by the one you call Quentin Melhuish, whom I know as Abdul Jamal.'

'What evidence?'

'No evidence – a hunch. The man has disappeared.'

'So you reckon this joker saw his number was up and legged it?' said Chuck. 'How did he go?'

'I don't know he did.' Spittle was collecting at the corner of Jeff's mouth. 'If he did, I don't know how he went. And I don't know where he went. Got that? Don't know!' He glared at Chuck then seemed to crumple. 'Sorry, commander, the last few days haven't been that great.'

'Sure.'

'For all I know, they could both be buried under that lot.'

A garbled voice came over Chuck's radio. He flicked a switch. 'Please repeat, Felix.'

Slightly less garbled this time but still too scrambled for Ian to make out.

Chuck drew a breath. 'Felix says they found this Omari person – what's left of him.'

'Meaning what? Lions, hyenas, what?' said Jeff.

'No.' Chuck paused. 'Felix says it was ants.'

Chapter 70

Dima held Colette's hand. Peered into black nothingness. Waited for lights to come back on.

They didn't.

She was trembling.

'Be strong,' he whispered.

He held a hand in front of his face. Total blackness. He knew the blackness of night when there was no moon, and stars were covered by clouds, but never blackness like this.

He turned his head back and forth. Not a glimmer. Not even the faintest speck. He couldn't see. But he could hear. He could feel. He could smell. How often had he relied on those senses when he was hunting at night? And he could detect the spirit of the great mountain – a comforting and reassuring presence.

But Colette wouldn't know how to use smelling and hearing, nor would she detect the mountain's spirit. Her breathing was ragged.

'We must check the way we came.' He wasn't sure why he whispered. Perhaps he didn't want to disturb the sleeping giant.

As if in reply, another rumble echoed through the mountain.

She shuddered.

'Come.' He held her hand tighter and they edged back past those windows towards the door they'd come in by.

No light or sound from those bewitched men. No strange light from the dying arms.

They came to the door. He felt for the handle. Turned. Pushed.

Harder.

Both of them straining.

They could have been pushing against the side of the mountain for all the impression they made.

'There is only one way,' he said.

'No!' She hammered on the door and screamed.

'Stop!' He pulled her away.

She stood panting.

'There is a way.' He gripped her hand. 'It *is* possible. We cannot see but we can hear, we can smell and we can feel.' She probably didn't understand but, at least, her breathing was settling.

They edged back to the door that led into the mountain.

He stood on the threshold, listening. Listening for echoes. Listening to the stones and rocks. Listening to the solid sounds of tunnel walls and rock floors. And the hollow sounds of emptiness and silence.

'Come.' He stepped with her into nothingness.

He held one of her hands and used his free hand to feel along the wall. They edged deeper into the mountain. He smelled the giant's breath and felt it brush his face. He smelled something else. Elephants. If they could keep moving towards that scent they would be saved.

He stopped. One hand still held Colette. The other hand felt nothing.

He edged back and found the tunnel wall again. He listened to the solid sounds and the empty sounds.

'We must turn here. Keep close.' He led her round the corner and the floor started to rise steeply.

The stones beneath his feet were loose.

The tunnel became steeper.

Colette fell, pulling him down.

They slid back down the slope. For a moment, he feared they would fall for ever. As he sometimes did in dreams.

She gave a sharp cry as they stopped at the bottom and he landed on her.

'Are you hurt?' he asked.

'No!'

He was pleased. She was going to fight this. But she must fight with purpose – not panic.

'We must keep close to the wall. It is not far – *si mbali.*'

Do I really know that?

They started up the slope again. This time, he felt for every rock, every stone, waiting until he had a firm footing and handhold before inching forward.

The steepness became less. They reached a solid wall and edged sideways.

His foot felt nothing. He moved it back until it touched the rock floor. He let go her hand and knelt down. He groped forward – forward into emptiness. Ahead, the hollow silence of nothing.

He was glad he couldn't see the great hole in front of them. Glad she couldn't see it.

He drew a breath. 'We must go back – *enda nyuma.*' He squeezed past and took her hand again.

The scent of elephant wafted towards him.

'It is the way,' he said. 'I will—'

An angry rumble erupted. Became a roar. A wind rushed up the tunnel blowing dust and giant's breath.

They clung to the rock wall. To each other. Listened to tumbling rocks. Then silence. More rock falls. Another silence. Some stones falling. Silence waiting, listening, hesitating, then wandering off into darkness and back to them. Silence unsure of itself.

Dima felt the dampness of sweat on Colette's hand. Smelled her fear. He led her forward, creeping, edging, feeling, checking.

Something struck his head. He staggered. Stopped. Felt the rock-face ahead.

'We must go low.' He crouched down and crept into the narrow tunnel, guiding Colette's head down below the roof.

They crawled on hands and knees. The tunnel getting narrower. Creeping deeper into darkness. Now wriggling on his stomach. She held his foot.

He turned a corner.

Light.

But faint light, distant light.

They crept forward, the roof getting lower.

Still distant light.

They squeezed through a narrow gap. The tunnel opened out. The light had gone.

A faint rustling above their heads.

'What's that?' she whispered, her voice raw and hoarse.

'It is bats.' He didn't think she understood.

They were back in eternal darkness. The smell of bats mingled with the smell of elephants.

Follow the elephants.

He checked. Listened. Listened to the mountain's spirit encouraging him, encouraging her.

He felt along the rock wall. Edged forward.

Darkness. Darkness, rocks, silence and the scent of elephants and bats.

Another corner.

Light again.

He tried to move faster.

More light.

She urged him on.

Sunlight.

A jumble of rocks ahead of them. They squeezed past.

On. On. On towards the light.

Another rock heap.

They scrambled up it. Out into the open. Out into sunshine and freedom.

They tumbled onto parched spiky grass.

Colette slumped onto her face.

He reached out a hand and patted her arm then lay on his back, gazed into the heavens and gave thanks to *Mungu*.

His daughter's face appeared. She smiled.

Dima wept.

Chapter 71

Colette sat up, wiped her face on the sleeve of her green top and breathed in beautiful fresh air. She turned her face to the sun, letting its warmth and light flood into her body and drive out the darkness.

'How are you?' he asked.

She turned to him. 'I'm bloody marvellous.'

Dima didn't understand the words but he clearly understood the sentiment. Her faltering Swahili was quite inadequate to express her feelings. But the radiance in her eyes told him everything.

'Now we go to Sean,' he said, pulling her to her feet.

Sean? Is he really all right?

'I shan't need these things.' She ripped off the torn and filthy hospital clothes, and stuffed them under a rock. As she did so, she noticed a small brown creature – dead.

'What's this, Dima?' She moved it with her foot.

'It is called *popo*.'

'A bat – but quite big. The big ones are fruit bats, aren't they?' The Swahili translation eluded her.

'Those ones shoot them.' He gestured with his chin in the direction of the compound.

'Shoot them? Why?'

He shrugged.

Colette turned it over with her foot. 'I wonder.'

'Another here,' he called.

On sudden impulse, she retrieved the hospital clothes, and using a stick, lifted the dead bats on and wrapped the clothes into a tight ball.

'Just a hunch. One I can't begin to translate.' She smiled at Dima's mystified expression.

'*Tuende* – let's go,' he said.

She followed him along the contour of the mountain. Still slight tremors beneath their feet and the occasional rumble.

'*Aieeh!*' exclaimed Dima.

She ran to catch up. Two helicopters, their rotors idling, were in the middle of the compound; people running back and forth. What transfixed her gaze, though, was the great hole in the mountain where once there had been a laboratory doing hideous things with Marburg. She shuddered at the memory of those zombie faces at the window and at the thought she might have been made to work on "the greatest advance in AIDS research." She never wanted to see Jeff and Richard again and hoped they'd perished when the mountain collapsed.

The rotors on one of the helicopters speeded up. A few moments later, the sound of the engines reached them. The pitch increased, and as the helicopter lifted off, thudding reverberations shook the mountain.

'Come.' Dima grabbed her hand and ran with her down the slope, off the trembling mountain.

They reached the perimeter fence of the compound. She stopped to recover her breath. The helicopter was now a speck in the distance.

'This way,' he said.

She followed him along the fence and up the rocky slope away from the compound, ducking under branches and skirting boulders. Her legs felt weak. Her heart was pounding. But was it simply the exertion of the climb?

A short way down the other side of the hill was Sean's Land Rover. Two men sat on the roof. They looked round and waved when Dima called.

One was Sean. The other was... was some sort of soldier.

She didn't have time to wonder. Sean had jumped from the roof and was running towards her.

'Thank God you're safe,' he cried.

She clung to him.

Dima watched with an amused expression.

She broke free. 'Who's the other man?'

'His name's Butch. He's a SEAL,' said Sean.

She sniggered. 'He doesn't look like a seal.'

Sean explained. 'I rather think our American friends thought I might do a runner.'

She shook her head. 'I'm lost.'

'We'll go and join the others then things will become clear.' He noticed the green bundle by her feet. 'What's that?'

'Dead bats.'

'Bats?'

'I'll explain later. Have you got a plastic bag they can go in?'

He rummaged in the back of the Land Rover. 'This do?'

'Perfect.' She dropped the bundle in and tied the top. 'Don't let me forget them.'

'No chance. The smell will remind us. Let's go.'

She waved to the man on the roof.

'Howdy, ma'am,' he called.

Sean held the passenger door open for her.

Dima scrambled onto the roof beside the other man.

Sean went round to the driver's side and climbed in. 'Are you—'

She couldn't hold back. She felt the strength and safety of his arms. The warmth of his body. She closed her eyes.

I shouldn't be doing this.

She pulled away breathless. 'Can we go?'

He studied her for a moment, before starting the engine. 'Are you okay?'

'Not really,' she said, as life caught up with her.

'Not really what?'

'Not, not... Dima was absolutely bloody brilliant. I would never have, have...'

'You're safe now.' He squeezed her hand.

Don't do this to me. I've got to go home – home, back to England. I don't belong in Kenya. Don't belong in your life.

'Tell me what happened.'

She stared down at their hands, fingers entwined. 'Thinking of you kept me going,' she whispered.

He glanced across. She wasn't sure he'd heard.

He released her hand and changed gear as they came over the brow of a hill. The second helicopter was still there, its rotors now stationary. Various figures were moving around and a couple of tents had been set up. What a contrast to the morning when smoke was billowing, sirens wailing, monkeys screaming, people shouting and rushing about.

Sean turned into the entrance gate of the compound. They were briefly stopped by two SEALs who joked with their colleague on the roof. Then Sean drove on past the monkey cages, many of which were empty. He stopped in the shade of an acacia tree.

Colette looked around what was now a tranquil scene. Seated with their backs to a building, was a disconsolate group of people being watched over by two armed SEALs; among them, the lecherous guard with two ears. She shuddered when she recalled what had happened to his one-eared colleague.

'How you doing, folks?' said a voice at Sean's window.

'Felix!' she cried and scrambled out.

'Evening ma'am. Good to see you're okay.'

'Thanks.'

'Steak, fries and cold beers any use?'

'You beautiful man.' She failed to get her arms round his chest.

'I guess that's a yes then.'

'Hi, Colette.'

She turned to see two figures running over. Both dressed as SEALs. She wasn't sure she could get used to the acronym. One was Grace and it took her a moment before she realised the bearded man was Ian.

'Wow, this is quite a welcome.' She hugged both of them, pleased there was now no awkwardness with Ian – just warmth.

'We've been desperate ever since Sean told us what happened,' he said.

She was conscious of him studying her. 'What?'

'I've been worried sick,' he whispered.

She stared at her feet. 'I was also quite worried. But now…' She looked up and waved an arm round the compound. 'This is wonderful.'

She called Dima to come down from the roof of the vehicle. He stood staring at the ground.

She took his hand and drew him into the circle. 'This person, this marvellous person, is the one I have to thank for saving me. Can you translate that, Grace?'

Dima made random patterns in the sand with his toe.

As soon as Grace had finished, he slipped away.

'Hello, Colette.'

She turned to see Jeff standing on his own. Her look of anger turned to one of puzzlement. Surely not. His cheeks seemed wet. It must be a trick of the light.

'So?' she snapped.

'Did you find my note?'

She gave a terse nod.

'And?'

Her heart speeded up. 'I bloody nearly choked on it.'

'You what?'

'I ate it. Isn't that what I was supposed to do?'

'I don't believe it.' He began to chuckle.

'You bastard!' She rushed up and pounded her fists on his chest.

'Don't you ever, ever, do something like that to me again. Ever!' She dropped her hands and stood panting and glaring. 'I suppose I did trust you.'

'Thanks.'

She gave a rueful smile. 'I wouldn't be here now, if I hadn't.' She glanced round the others. 'Shit. Why's everyone looking at me?'

Before anyone could respond, a SEAL came running up to Felix and saluted. 'The lorries are here, major. Guys in maroon berets.'

'That'll be the GSU,' said Grace. 'I'll organise them. Back shortly.' She ran off to the gate with the marine, who struggled to keep pace with her.

'I guess that'll about wrap things up,' said Felix. 'Now folks, I think I hear the chink of cold beers.'

Chapter 72

Colette was enjoying the warmth and companionship of another campfire in the middle of Africa, and thinking the US military do these things rather well. She was sitting on a camping chair beside Sean, a cold beer in her hand, the conversation flowing round her.

The only people in the group she'd not met before were a friend of Felix's – Chuck something-or-other – and a major called Ben Ndegwa from the General Service Unit, who, as an Olympic teammate of Grace's, had only managed a bronze medal. The two of them were quietly chatting – perhaps reliving times of former glory.

The lone helicopter stood near the boundary fence, looking hostile and menacing, its crew lounging nearby. The smell of roast goat wafted in the air as the GSU used the occasion to host Dima who was the centre of attention. Colette could just make out his animated expression and beaming face lit up by the fire around which the group was sitting.

'It's your turn now,' whispered Sean.

'What is?' She was conscious of the others looking at her.

'We want to know what happened to you. Jeff has told us some, but we need you to fill in the bits.'

She sat staring into the fire and recounted the factual parts of her ordeal. 'And that's about it,' she concluded lamely. 'Dima was the real hero, though.' She called and he waved his beer bottle.

The group round her waved back and Dima looked away.

'He was bloody marvellous.'

'Another beer?' asked Felix.

She was vaguely aware of the question. 'Sorry?'

'Another beer?'

'Please.'

One of the SEALs hurried across with a bottle. 'Food's ready, major.'

Colette waited until everyone was settled with their food then said: 'Who exactly is Abdul?'

Glances were exchanged.

'I can probably best answer that,' said Ian, taking a sip from his bottle. 'His full name is Quentin James Melhuish. He's English and worked at the British High Commission in Pakistan and most recently as First Secretary in Nairobi and—'

'What an earth was he doing out here?'

'That, I'm afraid, is another of these long stories,' said Ian.

'So? I've told you mine.'

'Fair enough.'

She sat with her eyes closed and tried to take in what Ian was saying. 'It sounds terribly complicated,' she said, when he'd finished.

'That's why it's taken us so long to work out.'

'So what's this place? This compound? And why Marburg? I assume that's what it is.'

'Let Jeff tell you,' said Ian.

Jeff set down his cutlery. 'It is Marburg, and it was being developed here as a bio-weapon to attack the US Embassy.'

'My God! And they so nearly succeeded?'

'Yes.'

'And Helen?'

'That was a test run,' said Ian, 'aimed at... at me.'

'At you! That *and* the bomb?'

'I'm trying to forget the incidents.'

Someone else who'd been to hell and back. She stared at her food. 'Jeff, that day I was kidnap— The day you picked me up. What were you doing lurking in the backstreets of Isiolo?'

'Solomon told us you were having a meeting with ole-Tomeno, so we decided to wait.'

'And cook up that story about my dad being ill?'

Jeff gazed out into the darkness. 'Worst mistake I ever made was recommending Richard to ole-Tomeno to help with the Condor Programme. I would never have forgiven myself if—'

'Where is Richard?' She was conscious everyone had stopped eating. 'What have I said?'

'You've not heard?' said Jeff.

'Heard what?'

Jeff took a deep breath. 'He died. He was killed by ants.'

'Ants? Safari ants?'

Jeff nodded. 'Must have been pretty grim.'

'So much noise, I guess no one heard his screams.' said Felix.

'How awful.'

'Perhaps he had it coming to him,' said Ian. 'He was bad news.'

'He was a good person once,' she whispered. 'So who corrupted him; ole-Tomeno?'

'We thought so for a while,' said Ian. 'Quentin kept dropping hints. Called him Dodgy Dan and such like. We even thought ole-Tomeno might have been this Mlala person and was using Condor as a cloak under which to hide.'

'We discovered he *was* using Condor,' said Grace, 'but it was to gain respect from fellow politicians and donors in his bid to run for President in the next election.'

'I see.' Colette thought for a moment. 'Richard, though, was also able to use the Condor cloak, but for a different reason?'

'Yes,' said Jeff. 'Ole-Tomeno supported the work here at Lokinang because Richard persuaded him it was to develop a vaccine for AIDS. In view of the global potential for such a vaccine, ole-Tomeno was keen to keep everything under wraps so Kenya could reap the glory, and he could further enhance his bid for the presidency.'

'He knew of rumours relating to security problems around Lokinang,' added Grace, 'but Richard told him the so-called problems were security guards keeping local people away so they couldn't learn about the work at the laboratory.'

'And he accepted that?'

Grace nodded. 'Until he spoke to the American Ambassador and she referred him to me.'

'And?'

'I explained the situation.'

'He then authorised deployment of US forces on Kenyan soil,' said Felix.

'I see – I think.' Colette, finally remembered to start eating. 'Jeff, you haven't explained how you got into all this – at least to me.'

'Ah.'

'Who's for another beer?' said Felix, getting to his feet. 'Colette?'

She shook her head.

'Anyone else?'

'Coke for me,' said Jeff.

Felix signalled to a couple of the SEALs.

'So,' said Felix, sitting down with a fresh beer. 'You heard what the lady said, Jeff.'

Jeff held up his bottle of Coke and studied the bubbles rising. 'Question is: where to start?'

'The beginning?' suggested Colette.

'Hell, do I have to go back that far?' He was clearly unsettled. 'Okay, then. Let me start by offering you an apology, Colette.'

'I thought you already had.'

'This is different.'

She sniffed. 'How?'

'You as well, Sean.' Jeff appeared to choose his words carefully. 'Jefferson Carter doesn't exist. He's a figment of my imagination.'

He held up his hand as Colette was about to interrupt. 'Like I said, I'm sorry I've had to string you along all this time, but I hope the reasons become clear.'

'So who *are* you?' she snapped.

'In a manner of speaking, I suppose I am Jeff Carter, director of research at the London Zoo and, more recently, coordinator of the Condor Programme. It's in the former capacity, Colette, that I've obtained your funding and supported your research, which I believe has gone pretty well.'

'Don't patronise me, Jeff, or whoever you are. And you haven't answered my question.'

'And you haven't let me finish.'

They glared at each other across the fire then she dropped her gaze. 'Sorry.' She gave a nervous laugh. 'Is it all right if you're still Jeff with me?'

'I'd like that.' He turned to stare into the fire. 'My real name is Sayed Farouk. My birthplace was Cairo. My mother was American and my father Egyptian. I went to medical school in Cairo then got a scholarship to go to the States to study primate viruses. Hence my later links with the Zoo. As a good Muslim, I don't drink alcohol, and as a good American, I subsidise American industry.' He held up his Coke bottle. 'I also chose a staunch patriotic name: Jefferson Carter, in honour of two distinguished presidents.'

'That still doesn't explain why you were drawn into all this,' said Colette.

'It was my job.'

'Your job? What does this have to do with Condor – or the Zoo, for that matter?'

'My other job.'

'I'm lost.'

'Tell her, Felix.'

'Jeff works for CIA,' said Felix.

'Doing what?' Her eyes were wide.

'I'll rephrase that,' said Jeff. 'I worked for the CIA. No longer after this. From now on I'm Jeff Carter, the coordinator of Condor.' He raised his bottle. 'To Condor.'

No one responded.

'Yeah, well. You know, Colette,' he continued, 'the hardest thing I've ever had to do in my life was that subterfuge about your dad needing you back, and then kidnapping you.' He searched her face. 'Can you forgive me?'

She stared ahead. 'Not sure.'

'It was either suffering the pain of your anguish or the possible burden of a bio-terrorist attack with Marburg – one I was in a position to prevent.'

'So what *was* your CIA job?'

'Put on my Condor cloak and delve into the murky world of terrorism and extremism in East Africa, particularly as it related to the ninety-eight attack on the American Embassy and more recent incidents.'

'The bomb that nearly killed Ian?'

'Is an example.'

She sat, for a moment, listening to the sounds of the night. 'Tell me, Jeff, all that bollocks about HIV-3 being a vaccine for AIDS; where did that come from?'

'That wasn't entirely fantasy. The premise is true, and such a virus has been isolated – here in Kenya.' He gave a brief smile. 'That's part of the irony. The work's not published so can't be verified but it seems Malik did isolate such a virus from one of the monkeys which hunters were bringing in here.'

'Malik, the one who's currently in US custody?'

Jeff nodded. 'He was the virologist on the team. When Richard heard about the HIV-3 story, he realised he could sell it to ole-Tomeno and this would give the Lokinang lab an air of respectability – an alibi, if you like. Richard arranged for Malik to meet ole-Tomeno and got me along as well. The two of them did a pretty good job at persuading him and I think he got a bit carried away, wondering if we could incorporate the research into Condor and suggesting you, Colette, might become part of the team.'

'What you and Richard told me, that morning you came to the ranch?'

'Exactly. We came here to Lokinang first and dropped Malik, then back to Tandala to see you.'

'And that's when you disappeared from our radar?' growled Felix.

'I presume so.' Jeff nodded.

'If the real work here was ever discovered,' said Grace, 'ole-Tomeno would be seen as the one who'd approved it. I doubt anyone would believe he didn't know about Marburg and he'd be held responsible.'

'Did he?' asked Colette.

'Did he what?'

'Know about Marburg.'

Grace sighed. 'We don't think so.'

'But you're not sure?'

Grace didn't answer.

'You know, Colette,' said Jeff, 'you have a great knack of going to the heart of a problem. Probably why you're such a good scientist.'

She glowered. 'I asked you not to patronise me.'

'Sorry.'

'And the nano-bubbles? That has to be off the wall.'

'No,' said Jeff. 'I don't know where the technology comes from, but that was something else Malik picked up.'

She stared into the night. 'So why was I brought here? You, Jeff, know as much about simian viruses as I do?'

'I'm not as up to date, though.'

'Even so?'

Jeff sighed. 'The reason I asked you to come to Kenya, as I said originally, was to investigate the disease the Pete's had found in forest monkeys.'

'That doesn't explain why I was dragged up here.'

'I would never have called you to Kenya if I'd known what was developing.' He studied her for a moment. 'With Malik in custody, Mlala had lost his virologist and—'

'Richard thinks: hey, perhaps we should follow up on ole-Tomeno's suggestion; why don't we kidnap Colette and tell her unless she collaborates, Sean's the one who's going to suffer?' Her knuckles were white on the arms of the chair.

'Something like that.'

'Bastard.' She sat back and glared. 'You sure it wasn't your idea, Jeff?'

'No, Colette. It wasn't mine.'

'Why did you go along with it, then?'

'I had no choice.' He stared into the fire. 'At the time, I was running with the foxes and hunting with the hounds.'

'Stop these bloody riddles and just tell me!'

'It means the good guys thought I was on their side, and the bad guys thought the same.' He sat back in his chair and linked his hands behind his head. 'I knew some of the good guys and I knew some of the bad guys. Problem was, there were some guys in the middle I couldn't figure out whether they were foxes or hounds. It wasn't until I got to Lokinang that I found out the truth. I knew Richard, Rashid, whatever we call him, was bad news but I soon learned he wasn't Mlala. But I reckoned the only way we'd get to Mlala was through Richard, so I was forced to stick with him if I was going to see this thing through.' He poked the fire with his boot. 'Latterly, I think Richard suspected something, particularly when you arrived. That's why he'd never leave the two of us alone.'

'Hmm.' It seemed to her that the two of them were enclosed in a bubble of firelight with a hazy circle of onlookers outside. 'I still think you're holding something back. What is it?'

'Why do you say that?'

'You're evading the question.' She gave a slight smile. 'So, I'm right.'

Jeff regarded her through half-closed eyes, his chin sunk on his chest. 'Okay, but don't take this the wrong way.'

'Bit late for that, isn't it?'

He ignored the retort. 'In brief: if I came to work on the programme here, I would be missed and you wouldn't.'

'What's that supposed to mean?'

'It means that if Jeff Carter, the coordinator of the Condor Programme, is not around coordinating, contacting donors and being nice to the press, people might start asking questions. His absence would be noticed. Whereas, Colette Fraser—'

'Is a nobody and no one would notice her absence. Is that it?'

'No! Don't get me wrong.'

'What then?'

'Colette Fraser, as far as her family and friends in England know, has gone to Kenya to investigate monkey diseases. She's out in the bush and can't be contacted. Her friends and colleagues in Kenya, though, have heard she's been called back to England because her dad's ill, and don't want to disturb her at this difficult time.'

'So I could disappear off the face of the earth and no one would notice?'

'I wouldn't put it quite like that.'

'I'd notice,' whispered Sean, from outside the bubble.

'Me too,' said Ian.

She didn't respond.

'I'm afraid there is another reason,' said Jeff.

'Apart from my being here and being expendable?'

'Apart from those considerations, yes.' Jeff sighed. 'Malik was aware that Marburg is not readily transmitted by aerosol, except under conditions of high concentration and, despite being classified as a category-A bioterrorism agent, is not the ideal bio-weapon. He began to wonder about—'

'Hybridising the virus with influenza to make it as contagious as—'

'You know about that?'

'I've seen the draft.'

'When? Where?'

'It doesn't matter.' She looked into his face. 'So it was either do the work, or Sean's life?'

He avoided her eyes.

'So Malik wrote that draft – the one about hybridising with influenza?'

'Yes, back when he worked in Kazakhstan. He wanted to get approval from the Russian authorities for his work on Marburg.'

'Did he get it?'

Jeff spread his hands and gave a wry smile. 'I don't know, but I do know he'd already done the work and—'

'He'd already made the construct?'

'Yes. And tested it.'

'He what?'

'Unwittingly, I think. One of his technicians died – probably a laboratory accident. It happened around the time I was leaving. I don't know the details.'

'Was that Olga Levkova?' asked Ian.

Jeff nodded. 'She and I never hit it off. I think she resented my US background.'

'How well did you know that Boris person?' asked Felix.

'Borishenkov?'

'Yeah, him.'

Jeff shrugged. 'He was the boss of the set-up at Stepnogorsk. Our paths didn't cross much.'

'Why do you think he defected?' asked Ian.

Jeff stared into the fire. 'I think he began to get a conscience about the bio-weapons research programme. Malik's draft followed by

Olga's death was the wake-up call.' He remained staring. 'CIA brought me in to work alongside him when he defected, but I learned very little – even though I claimed an interest in orchids.'

Colette suddenly sat up. 'Are you Mlala?'

'No,' he said quietly. 'I'm not Mlala.'

'How can I be so sure?'

'You trusted me before.'

She slumped in her seat. 'Shit, I don't know.' She tried to sip from an empty bottle but didn't want to break the bubble by asking for another beer. 'So Mlala is this Abdul-Quentin person, who happens not to be around at the moment?'

'Seemingly.'

'And he was the one responsible for those poor people in that, that hell-hole?'

A log rolled off the fire and Jeff kicked it back.

'Have you heard about a group called Njia Mpya?' he asked.

'You haven't answered my question.'

'Bear with me and answer mine about Njia Mpya.'

'Aren't they a group of disaffected youths causing problems on the Kenya-Somali border?'

'That's how they started but then Mlala recruited them to wage holy war against the west – at least, that's what he told them. The main targets being the States and the UK, the two countries that have been so welcoming to me.' For a moment he seemed to be talking only to her. 'It saddens and angers me that such people manipulate religion – my religion – to justify their extremist ideologies.'

'And you joined the CIA to fight back?'

'I suppose I did.'

'So these Njia Mpya people thought they were waging holy war but instead were being recruited as guinea pigs to test a Marburg bio-weapon?'

'Pretty much. Although they were also used to cause trouble locally and keep people away from Lokinang. I believe they also started a rather lucrative pastime of hi-jacking oil tankers for ransom. I think Mlala was able to tap into the money to fund this operation.'

'That's horrendous.'

'Yes.' He rubbed his hands over his face. 'I had to go along with all the subterfuge in order to find out exactly what was happening so I could hopefully put a stop to it.'

Colette was silent for a moment. 'So where is he now; this Mlala-

Quentin-Abdul person?'

Felix jerked a thumb towards the mountain. 'In there, we hope.'

She looked beyond him towards the mountain, silent and brooding in the bright African night. 'And if he isn't?'

Chapter 73

Colette was the last to wake next morning. She lay for a moment staring at the canvas above her head. Like everyone else, she had slept in the clothes she'd been wearing and felt hot, sticky and dirty. Better than feeling dead.

She ran her fingers through her hair, emerged from the tent and joined the others who were sipping mugs of tea round last night's fire, which had been brought back to life.

'Morning, ma'am.' Felix handed her a mug.

'Thanks.' She chose an empty chair between Grace and Sean.

'If your snores were anything to go by,' said Grace, 'you must have slept pretty well.'

'I hope I didn't keep you awake.' She noticed Grace had relinquished her SEAL uniform in favour of running things. Ben was dressed similarly. 'Where have you two been?'

'We decided to run round the mountain,' said Grace.

'Whatever for?'

'Exercise.'

'Glad you didn't ask me to come.'

Grace smiled briefly. 'You know what you said last night, Colette, querying whether Mlala is in there?' She nodded towards the mountain.

'Yes. What about it?'

'Ben and I don't think he is.'

'Why? Where is he?'

'We found fresh tyre marks in the sand – very recent. They came from a cave in the mountain that seems to have been used to hide a vehicle. Also a fuel store there with tyres and spares.'

'An escape route?'

'It looked like it. There was a tunnel at the back which appeared to head through the mountain in this direction.'

'Looks like friend Mlala did a runner when the balloon went up,' said Felix.

'Fled the country?'

'Who knows? I've radioed the Harry S to send out an alert to Kenyan police and our guys in the Embassy.'

'The sooner we're back in Nairobi,' said Ian, 'the sooner we can

399

mobilise resources.'

Colette winced at the army-speak. 'So is everyone leaving?'

'The GSU will be here for a few days tidying up,' said Grace. 'The rest of us are returning in the helicopter. And you?'

'I, er…'

'I wondered if you'd like to help me,' said Sean, returning from the mobile kitchen. 'There you go.' He handed Colette one of the two plates he was carrying. 'Unless you need to get back to Nairobi for anything.'

She slashed open a sausage and stared at her plate.

You've made your decision, stick with it.

'I do need to go back.' She looked up brightly. 'Life's far too exciting out here for a city girl like me.' Her attempt at humour flopped onto the sand and her forced smile failed to revive it.

'Are you sure?' said Sean.

Of course I'm not bloody sure! I don't want to go back to that grotty little house and the pathetic remains of my former life.

'What's going to happen to the monkeys?' she asked.

'We need to sort them out. Be good if you could help before you leave.'

'What needs doing?'

'We check those which are left. Any sick ones, I guess will have to be put down – I've got stuff in the Landy. Then I'll come back later with a truck for the others and release them in a more appropriate habitat.'

'And the ones which have escaped?'

'They'll have to take their chance. Quite a few, though, have already returned to their cages. I think they've been quite traumatised.'

Not the only ones.

'Ben says the GSU can look after them until I get back.'

One of the SEALs – she remembered his name was Butch – came up to Felix and saluted. 'Sir, the report you asked us to prepare.'

'Thanks.'

The others watched as he read.

'Could have been worse,' he said. 'Could have been much worse.'

'Can you share it with us?' asked Ian

'Sure. One SEAL with a broken ankle – he jumped out the chopper too soon. Otherwise the task force is clear. Five fatalities: two guards, some local woman built like a tank—'

'Or gorilla?' said Colette.

Felix shrugged. 'Could be. Leastways, it took three guys to nail her. Then she blew a fuse – probable heart attack. Seems she was overweight.'

'She certainly was.'

'You know her?'

'We met a couple of times. They weren't social occasions.'

'Yeah, right. Then there was a boy – a teenager – found by the gate.'

'That'll be Molito's son,' said Sean. 'A local herder. His son, poor lad, wasn't all there and the set-up here used him as a kind of look-out. He didn't deserve that.'

'And the other was Richard?' said Colette.

'Yeah. The guys couldn't get to him until they zapped all the ants that were tucking in.'

That's not how I want to remember him. He was a friend until... Until what? She felt saddened.

'Excuse me, sir,' said Butch, who was waiting nearby. 'Commander says can we leave soon as possible?'

'Sure,' said Felix.

Colette jumped up, put her plate on her chair and ran to Sean's Land Rover. She returned carrying a small package which she handed to Felix.

'What's this?' he asked.

'Dead bats.'

'Excuse me? These are dead bats?'

'The people here were shooting them.'

'They probably believed they were evil spirits,' said Sean.

Colette lifted her plate off the chair and resumed her cold breakfast. 'Could you get them sent off to Fort Detrick, Felix?'

He rubbed his cheek. 'Not sure they go in for that sort of thing.'

'Sorry?'

'Witchcraft, evil spirits. Not sure Fort D can help on that.'

She found herself blushing. 'I'm sorry, Felix. I haven't explained it very well.'

'Are you thinking rabies?' asked Jeff.

'Rabies?' said Felix. 'You want these tested for rabies?'

'No, for Marburg,' she said.

'I'm lost.'

'I'll let Jeff explain.' She suddenly found cold fried egg profoundly

401

tasty.

'If Colette's hunch is right,' said Jeff, donning his lecturer hat, 'the bats here may be carriers of Marburg, just as some species of bats are carriers of rabies in the States. Mostly, they don't show signs but they do excrete virus which can build up to high aerosol levels inside the caves where they roost. A number of people have gotten rabies without being bitten – simply by entering bat-infested caves.'

'You think the same could be happening here?' said Sean.

'It's worth checking,' said Colette. 'There were loads of bats flying around in the tunnel where Dima and I were.'

'Maybe the folks on the Harry S can check them out,' said Felix. 'If not, they can send them off.'

'Thanks,' she said. 'Next question to you, Sean: do monkeys go in caves?'

'Baboons do a bit, but… You're thinking, how do monkeys get infected if they don't go in caves?'

She nodded. 'My epidemiology lectures tell me it would be unlikely for monkeys to be the natural host of a disease which so readily killed them.'

'Because the disease couldn't maintain itself?' said Jeff.

'Exactly.'

Sean indicated the package. 'Those are fruit bats, right?'

'They're quite large and have foxy faces.'

'Probably the Egyptian fruit bat. We get the same species in the forest where the colobus were dying.'

'Surely bats and colobus don't have much contact with each other,' said Jeff.

'Could well do. The bats roost – often in large numbers – in hollows and crevices in the big trees there, particularly figs.'

'Voila!' cried Jeff. 'The epidemiology of Marburg sorted. You and Colette should write a paper.'

'Hang on, Jeff.' Colette laughed. 'We haven't identified virus yet.'

'Bravo. There speaks the true scientist.'

She scowled. Why is he always so bloody patronising?

'Can we get ready to leave folks,' called Felix.

'Is there time for me to help Sean with the monkeys?' She shovelled in the last scraps of congealed breakfast and wished she hadn't.

'Yeah, sure.'

'I'll get my kit from the Landy,' said Sean. 'Meet you at the cages.'

She was glad that two of the GSU, who were farmers' sons, offered to help. It avoided any awkwardness between her and Sean, and the men proved surprisingly adept at restraining the monkeys without getting bitten.

She insisted they all wore facemasks and gloves, and hoped none of the monkeys was infected. Three seemed lethargic. To be safe, she decided to put them down.

'Thanks, guys,' said Sean, when they'd finished.

'No problem, chief,' said one of the men, and they sauntered off.

'When I come back with the truck,' said Sean, 'I'll bring Dima to—'

'Dima,' she cried. 'Where is he?'

'He's gone home.'

'Oh no! And I never said goodbye.'

Sean stared at the ground. 'It's probably best that way. You said your thanks.'

'I know but—'

'Did you know he's asked if he can move his family down to Tandala?'

'Why?'

'He says it's hard living here.'

She gazed round the barren landscape with its black lava rocks and sun-scorched sand. 'I can see what he means.'

'I'll pick the family up on my way back.'

'How far away is it?'

'From Dima's description, I guess about twenty miles.'

'Couldn't you have given him a lift there?'

'I guess he wanted to warn his family in advance.'

'He'll have walked all that way?'

'Run, probably.'

'That man is amazing.'

Why are we pursuing this pointless conversation? Is Sean trying to spin things out – me too?

She turned away. 'I'd better go.'

He caught her arm. 'Are you sure you're doing the right thing?'

She didn't trust herself to look at him.

'Stay a few more days and we could do some proper safaris – Out-of-Africa style.'

She gave a bleak smile. 'I don't look much like Meryl Streep.'

'Nor me Robert Redford.'

'Sean, I've got to say this.' She took a deep breath. 'Helen is such a lovely person, there is no way I'm going to screw up your marriage.' She turned and impatiently brushed away a tear. 'There, I've said it.'

'What if things were to change?' His eyes were searching, imploring.

'Sean, stop it!'

He let go her arm.

She kissed his cheek and ran back to the others. Sean followed. She couldn't risk letting him hold her again.

The helicopter was ready to leave, its rotors idling. Jeff stood in the doorway. 'Sean don't forget the High Commissioner's bun fight in a week's time,' he called. 'I want all the task force leaders there, which includes you. That's when we finally get Condor started. Put all this behind us.'

'I'll be there.' Sean waved.

'You ready, ma'am?' asked Chuck who was waiting to help her aboard. 'You gotten your luggage, ticket and passport? Only joking.'

'My stuff!' she cried. 'It's all at…' She ran back to Sean and explained.

'So what do you want to do?'

Was that hope in his eyes?

'Could you bring my things when you come down for Jeff's meeting? I'll be at the Fairview.' She didn't wait for his reply, ran back to the helicopter and scrambled aboard.

Chuck showed her to a window seat.

She sat down conscious of her ragged breathing and stared out of the window, unaware she was twisting her bracelet.

The lone figure, who waved, was lost in the dust cloud as the rotors speeded up and the helicopter lifted off.

Chapter 74

Colette could see a small village of tents, set out in neat rows, as their helicopter came in to land near the freight terminal at the old airport. Teams of US marines and Kenyan GSU were unloading another helicopter parked nearby.

'We radioed ahead, major,' called the pilot, as he switched off. 'There should be transport waiting for you.'

'Thanks,' said Felix. 'And thanks for the ride.'

'You take care now,' called Chuck.

They disembarked and found Kelly waiting. 'Welcome to Camp Embakazi.'

'Wow,' said Colette. 'This is quite a set up.'

'Early days,' said Kelly, 'but let's say I'm a lot happier than I was at the beginning of the week. Jim Coates is here with some of his people. They were keen to see the real thing.'

'And have they?'

Kelly pulled a face. 'I'm afraid so.'

'What's the score, honey?' asked Felix.

'Three confirmed cases, one of which is terminal, the other two should recover. One death already.'

'Doesn't sound too good,' said Ian.

'Could be so much worse. We would never have coped without this set-up.' Kelly waved her hand round the encampment. 'Helicopters coming and going all the time; through the night as well.'

Jeff stuck out his hand. 'Hi, Kelly, I'm Jeff. I came for the ride.'

'We found him out there howling in the prairie,' said Felix.

'Excuse me?'

'Don't take any notice of him,' said Jeff, laughing.

She smiled uncertainly. 'Would you folks like some coffee? Be good to bring you up to speed.'

'Sure,' said Felix, 'I'll go tell the driver.'

They made their way to one of the tents which was set up as a canteen and settled at a table where they were joined by Jim Coates.

'Marvellous opportunity this,' he enthused. 'Must say, I never expected to see the real thing. No amount of simulation can replace first-hand experience.'

'No, I suppose not,' said Colette.

'Fingers crossed,' said Kelly. 'So far, all the cases are people who had contact with Stanley Wambugu, the first fatality. If the outbreak is limited to—'

'Would you like some help?' blurted Colette.

'Sorry?' said Kelly.

'It's just that I'll be in Nairobi for a few more days and I'd like to... to help.' She was conscious of twisting her bracelet. 'That's if you could use me, Kelly.'

'We certainly could – another professional could be very valuable.'

'Tell me what I can do.'

'Sure. We'll keep you out of the hot zone, which means you won't have to stay on site.'

Colette hesitated momentarily. 'This time I will stay at the Fairview, Kelly. You've got far too much on your plate to worry about a house guest.'

'You sure?'

'Positive. I left my case there when I went... when I arrived.'

'Fair enough, then. We can drop you off. We have minibuses doing the rounds several times a day.'

'I can start straight away if you like.'

'Sure.' Kelly checked her watch. 'Let's get you started.'

'I guess we should also get going.' Felix set his cup down and got to his feet. 'Thanks for the coffee, honey. See you back home.'

***

The minibus stopped at Police Headquarters to drop off Ian and Grace.

'Anything comes up, we'll be in touch,' said Felix. 'Jeff and I'll be at the Embassy.' He closed the door and the minibus sped off.

Grace led the way to her office. As soon as she and Ian arrived, Sammy stuck his head round the door.

'Good to see you back. How was it?'

Grace studied her hands. 'It was interesting, Sammy. Interesting. Any contact from the aircraft carrier?'

'Yes, we got their message about Mlala and have set up check points and alerted the airports. If we find him, we only stop him if he tries to leave the country. Otherwise we keep him under surveillance. Correct?'

'Thanks, Sammy. I want to see where he leads us.'

'I've also had his picture – the one you gave us, Ian – faxed out to all forces.'

'Anything back yet?' asked Grace.

'Not so far,' said Sammy. 'Oh, and Maria says to call.'

'What about?'

'She wants to know you're safe and also if you'd give her a list of people ole-Tomeno should invite to the formal opening of the Condor Programme next month.'

'You can help me on that, Ian,' said Grace.

'Sure.'

'If Maria calls back, Sammy, tell her—'

Grace's mobile rang. 'Yes.' She continued in Swahili, too rapid for Ian to follow. At one point she snatched up a pen and scribbled on a notepad.

She finished the call, tossed the phone onto the desk and sat for a moment tapping her fingers. 'That was Solomon.'

Ian raised an eyebrow.

'Mlala went to the New Paradise for breakfast.'

'He what!'

'He left Isiolo about an hour ago, having filled up with fuel, including spare jerrycans.'

'How does Solomon know Mlala?'

'I'm not sure he does,' said Grace, 'but he knows a man he calls Mlala, who's been using the New Paradise as a meeting place with Njia Mpya. Remember how scared Solomon was when I asked him about Mlala that time I took you there?'

'So can we assume this was Quentin? The timing would be right in terms of driving from Lokinang.'

Grace nodded.

'Does Solomon know where he's going?' asked Ian.

'He thinks towards Nairobi. And the man he gave a lift to was someone called Clive Upton.'

'How on earth does Solomon know that?'

'Because, as a hotelier—' She gave a slight smile. '— he has to record details of any foreigners who stay there.' She tore the sheet off the notepad. 'Those are the man's passport details. It seems he's a backpacker who'd hitchhiked down from Ethiopia, stayed the night at the New Paradise and met Quentin, Mlala – whatever we call him – over breakfast. Solomon thinks it was a chance meeting – just someone wanting a lift. The only luggage the man had was a backpack with a British flag on the back.'

'Very patriotic.' Ian tapped the note. 'This worries me.'

'Why?'

'Somehow, I don't see Quentin giving a backpacker a lift out of the goodness of his heart.'

'Perhaps he wanted someone to talk to on the long journey.'

Ian frowned. 'I'm not convinced.'

'Sammy, show us where the police check points are,' she said.

He crossed to a large-scale map of Kenya on the wall. 'Isiolo is here and Mount Kenya here. We've set up checks at the Meru turn-off here, and then one in Embu in case he goes round the east side of the mountain. If he goes on the road to the west, which is faster, he'd have to pass check points at Nanyuki, Nyeri and Sagana, and the last one here at Thika.'

'What sort of check points?' asked Ian.

'Just a police car, with two officers,' said Sammy, 'parked by the road and noting the traffic going through.'

'Would he get suspicious?'

'In most cases he probably won't notice them.'

'Right, Sammy,' said Grace, 'work out the likely timings when this vehicle can be expected to pass those check points and alert the people on them. They shouldn't stop the vehicle; just note the time it passes and whether there are any passengers. You've sent out details of make, colour and registration?'

Sammy nodded.

'Also send out descriptions of the two men. According to Solomon, this Upton person also has black hair but is quite a bit shorter. Not much to go on, I know, but it could help. The rucksack could be distinctive.'

Sammy was about to leave the office when a uniformed officer knocked on the open door. 'Excuse me, inspector, report in from Nanyuki. A white Range Rover with red CD plates passed through the roadblock five minutes ago. That's the registration number.' He passed her a slip of paper.

'How many people?'

'Two. Probably *mzungus*.'

'Good. That means they should reach Nyeri in about an hour. Warn the people there. Same procedure: note the time but don't stop them.'

The man nodded and left.

'Perhaps we'll have some tea, Sammy,' said Grace.

'Two? One without sugar?'

'Good memory, Sammy,' said Ian. He turned to Grace. 'What's your plan with Quentin?'

'As soon as he reaches Nairobi, he comes under maximum surveillance.'

'Why not arrest him?'

'I need to know if he has any contacts here; safe houses he uses.' She stared at pictures of Quentin, Malik and Richard pinned on the opposite wall. 'I don't want to take out one person and then find others have become sleepers to re-emerge three or four years later.'

'A bit risky isn't it?'

'Yes, and it's why I won't get any sleep until he's in custody.' She got up and ripped the pictures of Malik and Richard off the wall, then tapped Quentin's. 'What are we missing, Ian?'

'In terms of?'

She shrugged. 'We've had some luck with Solomon. Let's hope it continues.'

Sammy returned with the tea and set the mugs on the desk.

'Tell me, Sammy,' said Grace. 'anything more at Omar's house?'

'No. He'd gone through and cleared every scrap of paper. He probably suspected we'd search it. But we've got a twenty-four-hour watch in case he comes back or anyone visits.'

'He won't be coming back,' said Grace.

'Why?'

'*Siafu* got to him.'

Sammy's eyes widened. 'He was killed by safari ants?'

'I'll give you the details later. Tell me about the Melhuish house.'

'I've heard of *siafu* killing—'

'Sammy, the Melhuish house.'

'Yes, sorry. We spent most of yesterday there. We took the motorbike, and forensics have also taken the hall carpet to check the blood stains.'

'Anything else?'

'Nothing we didn't know about. The only thing of possible interest was... Hold on, I'll get it.' He left the office and returned with a dog-eared paperback. 'We found this in the loft in a box of old books.'

'*No Orchids for Miss Blandish*,' she read. 'The author is someone called James Hadley Chase.'

'It's an American thriller,' said Ian. 'I read it ages ago when I was at school.'

'I thought that might have been where the idea about orchids came from,' said Sammy.

'Could be.' Grace leafed through the pages. 'Not my thing.' She tossed the book onto the desk. 'Sammy get on the phone to Walter Cheriyot, the reporter at the Nation, tell him to come here at two o'clock if he wants exclusive stories on how the GSU saved the day at Lokinang and how ole-Tomeno masterminded the overthrow of a terrorist plot.' She smiled. 'Something like that.'

Sammy grinned. 'I think I get the picture.'

'Anything else at this end?'

'Mrs Melhuish asked if she could move back into her house. I said that would be all right.'

'You're keeping it under surveillance, though?'

Sammy nodded. 'Plain-clothes officers, changed regularly.'

'Could you warn them I'll drop by later on?' said Ian. 'I'm not happy Fiona being there on her own while Quentin's still on the loose.'

'Will do,' said Sammy.

Ian rose to leave. 'I should get going.'

'Keep your mobile switched on,' said Grace. 'I'll call as soon as the next report comes in. And, Ian.'

'Yes?'

'It was quite a trip. Thanks for your help.' She smiled.

He couldn't help noticing the warmth.

Chapter 75

Ian returned to his borrowed office at the British Council and negotiated the loan of a Council car. Then he called Felix.

'Good news, Ian. Keep us posted. Grace gotten things under control?'

'We hope so. The next few hours will tell.'

'See you.' Felix rang off.

Ian checked his emails. He sent MI6 a request to check Clive Upton's passport details – not that he anticipated learning anything of significance. Still nothing back on his earlier request to them to check on Quentin. He shrugged. Things had moved on a bit since then. When two hours had elapsed and still nothing from Grace, he called her.

'Still no news from Nyeri,' she said.

'They couldn't have missed him?'

'Not a distinctive vehicle like that.'

'Has he broken down? Stopped to eat something? Turned off a side road?'

'They're all possible. I've told Nyeri to send a car to Nanyuki and check back along the road. I'll let you know as soon as I hear anything? If necessary, I'll send up a Police Air Wing helicopter.'

'Thanks, Grace.'

A clerk entered the office with the mail. Ian leafed through it. A letter sent via the diplomatic pouch to Colette. He turned it over and studied it. No indication of the sender.

He called her mobile.

'Hello, Ian.' She sounded slightly breathless.

'You okay?'

'I'm fine.'

'I've got an official-looking letter for you, sent via the pouch. Shall I drop it in the Fairview?'

'You can open it, Ian. It's probably Alan Davies from Porton. The report on the samples.'

'Hang on.' Ian opened the envelope and scanned the contents. 'It is from Porton. Lot of technical stuff but the bottom line seems to be that it was Marburg that Pete Barnsley had.'

'Thanks, Ian. That's good to know. Anything else?'

'I, er, was wondering if, rather than you eating on your own, I could take you out to dinner tonight.'

There was a pause and Ian could feel his heart beating.

'Thanks, Ian. I'd love to come. Tell me where and I'll get a taxi.'

'No. I'll pick you up.'

'Are you sure?'

'Shall we say six-thirty at the Fairview?'

'That would be nice.' She rang off.

Nice? He sat frowning at the phone. Quite a few bridges to repair. Don't screw up this time. He was about to go back to his emails when the phone rang.

'Ian, Grace. The police have found the car.'

'What happened?'

'Not good news. They found the vehicle down a ravine some fifteen miles from Nyeri. It seems it went off the road on a bend and caught fire. It's still burning and they can't get near it. Be at least half an hour before the fire service can get there. Some locals, though, are trying to help with buckets of water but... The other thing, Ian, there's a body inside.'

'My God. Just one?'

'As far as they can tell.'

'I'll come over.'

As soon as Ian reached Police Headquarters, he was shown into Grace's office. She was on the phone and waved him to a seat.

She finished her call and put the phone down. 'They've got the fire out.' She paused and gazed out of the window.

'And?'

'They think it's the right vehicle. It matches the description but the number plates have been removed.'

Ian frowned. 'And the body? Was it just one?'

Grace fiddled with a pen. 'Burned beyond all recognition. The police think it was doused in petrol before the vehicle was set alight.'

'That's horrendous.'

Grace wiped a hand over her a face and nodded. 'Presumably to prevent us identifying it.'

'So, what now?'

'I'm arranging for the vehicle and its... its contents to be brought to Nairobi. It'll be a while, though, before they get it out of that ravine.' She stood up. 'Come on, Ian, I'll buy you lunch in our canteen. It won't be great but it'll take our mind off things for a while.'

Ian selected a bottle of Coke and a cheese sandwich with curling edges. Grace chose a banana and a glass of milk; then led Ian to a table reserved for senior staff.

Sammy came hurrying into the canteen. 'Can you take a call in my office, Grace?'

'Back in a minute,' she said, and followed Sammy out.

Ian peered inside his sandwich, clearly past its sell-by date. He pushed it aside and studied the decor.

Grace returned looking thoughtful. 'Some good luck, hopefully.'

'What?'

'Some switched-on officer in Nyeri had come off duty and was walking down the main street when he saw a *mzungu* carrying a black hold-all and a backpack with a British flag on it.'

'Clive Upton?'

'Possibly.'

'But how would he get from the burnt-out vehicle and into Nyeri in that time?'

'*Matatu* – local minibus. There are plenty along that road. They'll stop anywhere if someone waves them down.'

'I see. And what was this person doing when he was spotted in Nyeri?'

'He was going into a car-hire firm.'

'Was he just?'

'Some fifteen minutes later, the officer saw the man drive out in a Datsun. He made a note of the number and then went into the office and spoke to the woman on duty.' Grace paused while she finished her milk. 'The car was hired out in the name of Clive Upton and paid for with a credit card in that name. The car-hire people took the details from his passport.'

'Are you thinking what I'm thinking?' said Ian.

'I'm thinking, what motive would Clive Upton have for killing Mlala and setting fire to his vehicle?'

'On the other hand?'

'On the other hand... I suspect Mlala is now heading to Nairobi using a new identity and travelling in a car which won't attract attention. I've alerted officers here and also told Amos to spread the word.'

413

Chapter 76

'How are you, sir?' said a voice at Ian's elbow, as he walked past the city market on his way back to his office.

His hand went instinctively to his wallet anticipating a pick-pocket attempt. He turned to the speaker – a girl of ten or eleven.

'Do you remember me, sir?'

'Charity?'

'Yes, sir. How are you?'

'I'm very well, and you?' He released the hold on his wallet.

'Now, sir, I am very better.' She showed him the pink scar on her arm. 'How is Inspector Grace?'

'She is also well.'

Ian was aware of a number of passers-by giving him strange looks talking to a street-girl.

'There is Amos,' she cried, beckoning the boy over.

'*Jambo*, Amos,' said Ian. 'What news?'

'Sir, we have seen that car. Inspector Grace told us to watch for a Datsun.'

'You've seen it?'

'Yes, sir. It is not far.'

'Where? Wait.' Ian noticed a dingy café in a side street. 'Come. We'll go there.'

He ordered the children some food – probably the only meal they would eat that day – and a cup of tea for himself. The proprietor, a taciturn and monosyllabic Asian of uncertain age, took no interest in his only clients, other than to overcharge Ian. As soon as he'd served the food, he returned to watching the Bollywood soap on a television beside the counter.

'Now,' said Ian, 'you saw the car Inspector Grace asked you to watch for?'

'Yes, sir. This one.' Amos showed the number scratched on his arm.

'It is on the big street near here,' said Charity. 'The driver went to buy food in the market.'

'Well done, guys.' Ian took out his mobile and called Grace.

'I think, sir, Inspector Grace will be pleased,' said Charity.

'She is very pleased. You two have done really well.'

'Thank you, sir.' Amos grinned. 'Unofficial police force very good.'

'Very good, Amos. Did you see any people in it?'

'We only saw one, sir: a—'

The door opened. Ian looked up expecting Grace. Instead, an Asian man slouched in, wearing a shirt-like smock and grubby turban.

'When Inspector Grace comes,' said Ian, 'you can show—'

'Hello, old boy.'

'Quentin!' hissed Ian. The pistol under the smock was pointing at his chest.

'My name is Abdul Jamal. No. Don't get up.' The pistol jerked. 'I must say I wasn't expecting our paths to cross again but there won't be another occasion.'

Ian was conscious of Amos and Charity aware something was very wrong.

'You do keep strange company these days, old boy.'

'Cut out the old-boy stuff,' snapped Ian. 'What do you want?'

'To see you and your colleagues get what you deserve.'

Ian glanced over Quentin's shoulder to the street outside. Still no sign of Grace.

'The genie's out of the bottle. No putting it back.'

'What's that supposed to mean?'

'You don't seriously expect me to explain.' Quentin's mouth shaped a smile. 'A pity we haven't perfected the hybrid virus yet but the one I have is still extremely unpleasant and very—'

The door opened. This time it was Grace.

Quentin was momentarily distracted.

Ian hit him. No more than a glancing blow as he had to reach across the table.

Quentin reeled back.

The gun went off. The television set exploded. The proprietor yelled.

Quentin kicked a chair away. Rushed past the proprietor. Fled out of the back.

'Look after the kids, Grace!' Ian was briefly aware of curry smells as he raced through the kitchen, thrusting portly Indian women aside. Into the deserted alleyway.

A shot.

He dived into a doorway. Peered out.

Another shot. A piece of brickwork shattered above his head.

415

He grabbed his mobile. 'Grace, get help as soon as—'

'On their way,' she shouted. 'Try and see where he goes.'

'Will do.' Ian peeked out again in time to see a turbaned figure turn the corner. He raced after him. '*Mwivi*!' he shouted. 'Thief!'

Doors were flung open and people peered out.

'*Mwivi*!' Ian pointed along the alleyway.

Mutterings. The cry was picked up. Several youths joined the chase.

Ian turned the corner into a busy street.

Quentin dodging between cars. '*Mwivi*!' he cried, pointing ahead.

A rabble was forming. Several men carried machetes.

Quentin glanced over his shoulder. Tripped on the curb. Fell heavily. His turban rolled off.

'*Mwivi*!'

The rabble was in danger of turning into a lynch mob.

Quentin scrambled to his feet. '*Mwivi*!' He pointed down a side street.

The mob hesitated.

The cry was picked up by those in the side street. The mob surged forward. Traffic came to a halt.

Ian swore.

The spontaneous combustion engine which had sprung to life flowed past him, smashing shop windows and car windscreens. There was little doubt Quentin would get away. Ian hoped no innocent bystanders were in the wrong place.

The wail of sirens filled the street. Riot police arrived adding to the chaos.

Pied crows squawked approval from the roof of the city market.

Ian called Grace on his mobile and walked away.

Chapter 77

That evening, as Colette waited in reception for Ian, she realised she was sitting behind the same potted palm as all that time ago. On that occasion, she was agonising about going off alone with Sean to Tandala. Now she agonised about meeting Ian when he would probably try and revive their relationship – again. She didn't want that, didn't need that. But she had to try and build a friendship. She at least owed him that. Her decision to return to London was the right one. Better to go now than leave a trail of shattered relationships in her wake. She could then repair her life. Perhaps return to Kenya and work with Jeff on Condor when things had settled and wounds had healed. She gave a wry smile remembering her savage response when Ian had suggested the idea.

A man went up to reception. She peered through the screen of palm leaves.

It wasn't Ian.

She returned to her agonising.

'Dr Fraser?'

She looked up. 'Yes?'

'I'm sorry to intrude. Maria told me you were staying here.'

'Maria?'

'Minister ole-Tomeno's PA. One real smart lady.'

'Can I ask what this is about?' She tried to keep her expression friendly. The man was late thirties, early forties, well dressed. Quite good looking in a smarmy sort of way.

'Real coincidence. I'm also staying at the Fairview.' He held out his hand. 'Clive Upton.'

'Hello,' she said. 'I'm sorry but I don't think I know the name.'

'May I?' He gestured to the vacant seat beside her and sat down. 'We've heard about your work with monkey viruses and would—'

'We?'

'Tropivax. We're based in Gainesville, Florida.'

She shook her head. 'It's not a company I know.'

'We're building quite a name in bio-engineered vaccines for tropical diseases.' The man signalled to a passing waiter. 'What are you drinking, Colette? You don't mind if I call you Colette.'

'Fresh lime, please.'

'Same for me, waiter.' He turned back to her with a toothpaste smile. 'So much easier to be on first-name terms, don't you think? Call me Clive.'

Colette frowned. 'I don't want to appear rude, er, Clive, but I don't know you, I don't know Tropivax and I'm not sure why you've accosted... approached me.'

The man laughed and she caught a faint whiff of sickly-sweet breath.

'I guess I'm getting carried away. Let me put my cards on the table.'

'Yes. Please do.'

'HIV-3.' The smile on his lips didn't extend to his eyes.

'I'm sorry?'

'My company's heard about the HIV-3 virus that's been isolated from monkeys in Kenya and how it might protect against AIDS.' Sickly-sweet breath again.

'Who told you that?'

'Minister ole-Tomeno. We've been discussing setting up a joint venture.'

The blindfold, the smug voice. 'Do you know someone called Richard Omar?' she shot.

'Richard who?' An imperceptible hesitation – possibly imagined – then the man shook his head. 'No can't say I do. Why do you ask?'

'Candy floss? Brighton beach.'

'Excuse me?'

'Richard was eaten by safari ants.'

This time, there was no mistaking the uncertainty that flickered in his eyes.

'I know who you—'

He grabbed her wrist. 'Stop playing the fool and listen to me.' All trace of an American accent had vaporised.

She tried to pull away but he was too strong.

The waiter arrived with their drinks and smiled seeing them holding hands.

Colette knocked the drink's tray over, tore herself free and rushed over to reception. 'Call security! That man tried to...'

'Which man, madam?'

She turned. 'The one over...'

He'd gone.

Ian entered.

She rushed up to him. 'Thank, God.'

'Hey. What's all this?'

'Candy floss. Brighton beach,' she babbled.

'What are you talking about?'

'Ian that was... was Abdul, Mlala—'

'What was?'

'The man who accosted me. We were sitting over there.' She rushed back to the waiter. 'I'm so sorry, *bwana*. It was an accident. Let me pay for the drinks.'

'That is quite all right, madam,' he said, retrieving pieces of broken glass. 'May I get you another one?'

'What's going on?' said Ian.

'I'm going to have a scotch, Ian. What do you want?'

'I'll, er, have the same.'

She turned to the waiter. 'Two whiskies, please, *bwana*. Large ones.'

'Yes, madam. And the other gentleman?'

'He, he had to leave. His wife's having... having a baby.'

The waiter's face lit up. 'Please send the family my best wishes, madam. My name is Bartholomew.' He showed her the badge pinned to his jacket.

'I'll wish them well,' she said. 'If it's a boy, I'll tell them to call it Bartholomew.'

'Thank you, madam.' The waiter departed, his face wreathed in smiles.

'What on earth is all this?' said Ian. 'Whose wife's having a baby?'

'I'm sorry, Ian. I had to think fast.'

'And what was that about Mlala?'

'Ian, he was here. Don't forget, I've never seen him but I'm sure it was him. I recognised the voice. He pretended to be an American calling himself Clive something-or-other.'

'Upton?'

'Yes. He said he represented a vaccine company called Tropivax – one I've never heard of.'

Ian snatched his mobile from his pocket and studied Colette while he waited for an answer.

'Grace, it's Ian. I'm at the Fairview. Quentin was here a few moments ago. I didn't see him, but he confronted Colette.' He frowned. 'Yes, certain. He used the name Upton. Fine, we'll wait for you in the lounge bar.'

'Sorry to panic,' said Colette, when she and Ian were settled with their drinks. 'But for a moment I was reliving that hell at Lokinang when, when I...'

'Tell me,' he said.

'I already have.'

'There were probably bits I missed.'

She stared into her drink. 'Thanks, Ian.' A sympathetic ear could help erase some of the pain. When she'd finished, she was relieved he didn't offer platitudes or try and take her hand. He just sat back, sipped his whisky and studied her with his brown eyes. Sean had blue eyes.

'What are you thinking?' she asked.

Before he could respond, Grace hurried into the bar. '*Jambo*, Colette.'

'Hi.'

'Where was this man?'

'He came into reception. We were talking out there but then he disappeared.'

'Which way did he go?'

'I didn't see.'

'Right.' Grace ran out. She returned a few minutes later and briefly put a hand on Ian's shoulder before dropping into the vacant chair.

'I've got Sammy out there with a couple of officers. They're questioning the security guards but it seems that a man matching Mlala's description drove off just after you arrived, Ian.'

'What sort of car?' said Ian.

'A dark-coloured one.'

'A Datsun?'

'But not the one he hired in Nyeri; that's still parked where Amos and Charity saw it. I suspect he realises we're watching it.'

'That's unfortunate.'

'I don't suppose there's any doubt that it was Quentin?' said Grace.

'None,' said Ian. 'Question is how did he know Colette was here?'

Grace paused. 'I think Maria probably told him.'

'How did she know?'

'Because I told her.' Grace pulled a face. 'Remember, she wanted a list of names of people for ole-Tomeno to invite to the launch of Condor. The list you and I prepared, Ian.'

'Shit,' he whispered. 'And when a smooth-talking American from a firm called Tropivax calls Maria and asks whom he could contact about a new vaccine venture she's conned into giving out names.'

'Any news of the baby?' said a voice.

Colette turned to see a beaming Bartholomew. 'No, it's too soon.'

'I hope all is well, madam.'

'Er, yes. I hope so. Grace, what are you drinking?'

'Fanta.'

'Yes, madam.'

'What was all that about?' said Grace, as the waiter departed.

'A misunderstanding. It's not important,' said Colette. 'Do you know why this Upton, Mlala man wanted to contact me?'

'I can only guess.' Ian waited while the waiter served Grace's drink and Colette signed the chit. He then waved the man away before there was any more baby talk. 'I still think of him as Quentin. My guess is that he realises we're closing in on him and wants to take as many people down as possible – particularly targeting those he feels have thwarted him.'

'I wish I hadn't asked.' Colette swirled the drink in her glass. 'So now what?'

'We mobilise resources,' said Ian, 'and hope to apprehend him.'

Colette groaned. 'Mobilise resources? What does that mean?'

'Well, it... Let's hope we can keep ahead him.'

'Have you been over to his house yet?' asked Grace.

Ian finished his drink and got to his feet. 'I'll go now. Do you mind if we delay dinner, Colette?'

'No, so long as I can come with you.'

They were about to leave when Sammy came in and joined them. 'Hi,' he said. 'We've checked the hotel register, Grace, nothing there.'

'The man said he was staying here,' said Colette.

'Probably lying,' said Ian. 'Comes easily to Quentin.'

'Anything more on the car?' asked Grace.

'The askaris in the car park say it was a small car, probably a Datsun or Toyota but they weren't sure.'

Grace sat slumped in her seat and rubbed her eyes. 'It looks like being a long night. Put a team together, Sammy, and start with the hotels in this area then work outwards. Give them copies of Mlala's picture and see if we come up with anything. Omar's place is still being watched?'

Sammy nodded. 'And the Melhuish house.'

'Colette and I are on our way there now,' said Ian. 'Can you let your people know so they don't arrest us?'

'Sure,' said Sammy. 'Does that cover everything?'

'Probably not.' Grace got to her feet and led the way out.

Chapter 78

Ian parked in the Settlers Club car park, nodded in the direction of a nondescript Volvo, then he and Colette crossed the road and peered through the wrought-iron gates of Quentin's bungalow. Lights were on inside.

A torch shone in their faces. 'Have you come to the party?' said a voice.

'Er, yes,' said Ian.

There was the rattle of a key as the askari opened the gate. '*Karibuni*,' he said. 'You go there.'

'Thanks,' said Ian.

Colette realised she had her arm linked through his and hastily disengaged. As they drew near to the house, they could hear faint music and the sound of voices, but curtains were drawn and it was impossible to see in.

Ian knocked. The voices stopped. The music was turned down.

A few moments later there was the sound of bolts being drawn. The door opened.

'Dear lady!'

'Pete!' cried Colette. 'What are you doing here?'

'I could ask you the same question.'

'I was, er...'

'Pete and I were summoned by the call of damsels in distress. We mounted our trusty steeds and here we are.' He held out his hand. 'You must be the famous Ian.'

Ian grinned and shook his hand.

'Who is it, darling?' called a woman's voice from inside.

'Jehovah's Witnesses,' said Pete-A.

The owner of the voice emerged from the sitting room. 'Ian!' She wafted across the hall, floral kaftan billowing, and embraced him. 'How are you, darling?'

'I'm well, Fiona.'

'Lovely to see you, but I simply can't keep pace with all your lady friends. Who is this one?'

'I'm Colette. Ian's told me a lot about you.'

'My dear, how tiresome.' She checked. 'Did you say Colette?'

'Yes.'

'Not *the* Colette?'

'I'm not sure about that.' Colette smiled. 'Are you feeling better now?'

'I am, thanks to this beautiful man.' She took Pete's hand and kissed it.

'Your wish is my command, dear lady,' said Pete, giving a sweeping bow.

'He's so chivalrous. Mummy adores him.'

Pete seemed slightly startled.

'Come through,' said Fiona, 'and we'll do introductions.'

'Before we do,' said Ian. 'Can I ask you a question?'

'A question?' Her brow clouded.

'I don't want to spoil the evening, but can I ask if you've seen Quentin recently?'

'Quentin? Do I know a Quentin?' She fiddled with a potted plant on the window sill then turned on him. 'How dare you spoil my homecoming.'

'I'm sorry, Fiona. We won't stay but I do need to know.'

'Darling, throw this beastly man out,' she cried, urging Pete forward.

'No,' said Pete. 'It's what we talked about earlier.'

'Oh,' she pouted, then seemed to crumple. 'You men are so masterful.'

'What *were* you talking about?' asked Ian.

'Come.' Fiona took Colette's hand and led her into the sitting room.

'Helen!' cried Colette. 'How lovely to see you. And Pete!'

Pete-B let go of Helen's hand and came and embraced Colette. 'Hi. You look great.'

'You too,' said Colette. 'What a lovely surprise.'

Helen held out a hand. 'Excuse me if I don't get up, Colette. I'm still a bit wobbly.'

'You're looking so much better.' Colette kissed her warmly.

Helen smiled. 'We're getting there. The Petes have been brilliant.' She waved. 'Hello, Ian.'

He came and kissed her cheek.

'Have you met Pete?' she asked. 'The one who saved my life.' She reached out and took Pete-B's hand.

'Drinks?' cried Pete-A.

'Something soft, please,' said Colette.

'Same for me,' said Ian.

Fiona crossed to a CD player and put in a disc – not at all what Colette would have expected. She felt a momentary twinge as she was transported back to a log fire in the bush and a man playing Bach on the guitar. Someone touched her arm.

'Mango juice,' said Pete-A. 'I hope that's okay.'

'Thanks, Pete.'

'You all right?'

She gave a tight smile. 'I'm fine.'

He studied her face. 'Sure?'

The smile tightened.

'Grab seats everyone,' he said. 'An inspector calls.'

Ian held up a protesting hand. 'I'm not going to ruin your evening and I promise we won't stay but I gather you might have been talking about Quentin?'

'What about him?' said Fiona.

'You tell me.'

'He was here earlier – before we arrived.'

'How do you know?'

'Ian, this third-degree is a bit tiresome. Can't we get on with our lives.'

'Not until we've sorted out this mess.'

'You're very determined.'

'Yes.'

'Tell him, Fiona,' said Pete-A.

She gave a theatrical sigh. 'The gardener said the *bwana* had come for his motorbike and was very angry when he learned the police had taken it.'

'So what happened?'

'Quentin threw a wobbly, accused the gardener of stealing it and said he was going to the police.'

'I doubt that,' said Ian. 'Then what?'

'Quentin left, scarpered, vamoosed, went.' She glared at Ian. 'And no, I don't know where.'

'When did you lot get here?'

'Around the middle of the afternoon,' said Fiona. 'We'd been staying at the residence but it was becoming a pain so we decided to move in here – like being students again.'

'By which time, Quentin had long gone?'

'I suppose so. Ian, do we really have to—?'

The phone rang in the hall. Fiona went through to answer it while the others managed desultory small-talk.

'That was Mummy. She said, why hadn't we arrived for dinner? Had we forgotten? I said we hadn't forgotten, but there would be two extra.' She took Ian's hand. 'I hope that's all right, darling. Sorry I was grotty.'

'I'll lead the way,' cried Pete-A, jumping to his feet. 'We'll sneak through the hole in the hedge.'

***

Colette followed Fiona into the sitting room. The place had a claustrophobic feel – the legacies of different high commissioners and their wives: crocheted cushion covers and embroidered samplers, watery colour paintings of fuchsias and canna lilies, cups for polo and flower arranging, and sepia photographs of men trying to look eminent and foresighted in Panama hats.

'Come and meet Mummy and Daddy,' said Fiona.

'Sherry, my dear?' asked Sir Aubrey.

'Er, could I have something soft, please?' said Colette.

'There you go,' said Pete-A, who appeared at her elbow with a glass.

She smiled her thanks.

'And G and T for you, your Grace,' he said to Lady Cynthia.

She gave a tinkling laugh. 'I'm not a countess yet, you know.'

Pete winked at Colette.

'These boys have been simply marvellous,' boomed Lady Cynthia. 'Isn't that right, Aubrey?'

'Which boys?'

'The Petes.'

'Oh, yes. Rather. Thoughtful of them to have the same name.'

'Can't think how we could have coped with these girls without their help.'

'Come off it, Mummy, Helen and I are perfectly capable of looking after ourselves.'

'Nonsense. You've both had very difficult times.'

'That's what I tell them, your Grace,' said Pete.

'Stop it, you naughty boy.'

The High Commissioner looked vaguely round the room. 'Is Quentin with you?'

The temperature plummeted.

'No, sir,' said Ian. 'He, er, had a previous engagement.'

426

'Pity. I need some help with this Condor thing. We're hosting a reception here later in the week, you know.'

'Daddy, for goodness sake!' cried Fiona. 'Quentin was the one who had me beaten up.'

'Was he?' The High Commissioner sniffed the air. 'Pity about that. He was a good egg.'

'He was a thoroughly rotten egg.'

'If you say so, my dear.'

'I do. Daddy, you *know* the Petes are helping with Condor, and I'm sure Ian and Colette can help as well.'

'Good show.' He turned to Colette. 'I don't think we've met.'

'No, sir. My name's Colette.'

'Is that Irish?'

'I think it's French. My mother's mother came from France.'

'Is that so? I knew a Coleen once. She was Irish.'

'She was American,' said Lady Cynthia. 'Anyway, this girl is Colette.'

'Wonder what became of her?'

'Who?'

'Coleen.'

'She became an alcoholic and committed suicide. I sometimes wonder if—'

'Mummy, can we go through to dinner?' said Fiona. She took her father's hand and opened the door into the dining room.

'May I escort you, Lady C?' said Pete-A, offering his arm.

'You do spoil me,' she twittered. 'Come along girls.'

The High Commissioner dithered over seating arrangements. His wife gave counter instructions, and Pete-A settled people in their seats.

'Isn't he marvellous, Mummy?' said Fiona, giving Pete a passionate kiss.

'He's a brick.'

'Wonder what that makes me, then?' murmured Pete-B.

'You're a rock,' whispered Helen. 'My rock.'

Colette looked round the happy faces illuminated by the glittering light of a chandelier reflecting off silver cutlery and crystal glasses but all she could see was the twinkling light of fireflies and a camp fire in the bush. She stared at some tiny ants making their way, like arctic explorers, across the stark whiteness of the tablecloth. She was reminded of safari ants and of Kimani and Richard.

'Red or white?' said a voice in her ear.

'Er, white, please. Thanks, Pete.' The ants weren't *siafu*. Even so... She twisted the bracelet on her wrist.

When everyone's glass was filled, Pete-A tapped his with a spoon. 'With your Lordship's permission—'

The High commissioner gave a fruity chuckle.

'— I would like to propose a toast to these beautiful ladies in our midst. Firstly, our lovely hostess—'

Lady Cynthia's turn to chuckle.

'— and three very wonderful people who have endured, in different ways, unimaginable...' He swallowed and blinked. '... unimaginable hardship and suffering which few of us... few of us can conceive, and... Oh, bugger! To Colette, Helen and Fiona.' He finished, sat down and stared at his hands.

'Thank you, darling,' whispered Fiona and squeezed his arm.

'Bravo!' cried Sir Aubrey, as the men drank a toast.

Lady Cynthia rang a small silver bell beside her elbow. 'Time for the first course. I hope the—'

The lights went out.

'Not another bloody power cut,' muttered the High Commissioner.

'I'll see if I can sort it out,' said Pete-A.

'Stay where you are,' said a man's voice. 'Nobody moves.'

Colette grabbed Ian's hand.

The lights came back on.

'Quentin!' cried several people.

'Stay seated and put your hands on the table. That includes you.' Quentin brandished his pistol at Ian. 'I would like to remind everyone that my name is Abdul Jamal.'

'Poppycock!' snorted Lady Cynthia.

Quentin ignored her retort. 'I'm sorry the staff won't be responding to the bell.'

'Why?'

'I sent them home.'

'Quentin, old chap,' said Sir Aubrey. 'What's—'

'Shut up.'

'How dare you!' cried Lady Cynthia.

'Yes. I do, thank you, Lady C, you pompous old sow.'

She picked up her glass and threw it. It missed Quentin but the wine showered over him.

Colette recoiled at the fury raging on his face and the look of loathing in his bloodshot eyes as he struggled to control his breathing.

'What do you want, Quentin?' asked Ian.

'It's Abdul!' Quentin turned wild eyes on him. Then he seemed to compose himself and his fury abated. 'Hello, old boy. Fancy meeting again so soon.'

Colette risked a glance round the table. The High Commissioner was mumbling to himself in a daze. The others sat frozen, mesmerised.

Quentin seemed to gather courage from their paralysis. 'Just like an Agatha Christie plot.' He gave a mocking smile. 'All the cast assembled in the dining room for the *denouement*, how appropriate.'

'I can't imagine how I put up with you so long,' hissed Fiona.

He rounded on her. 'Bitch!'

'Why don't you put that gun down?' said Ian.

'For too long I've allowed myself to be pushed around by pathetic small-minded people. Not for much longer. The sleepers have woken and a day of reckoning is coming which will rock the world.' Quentin seemed to draw strength from oratory. 'Following this final act, you will learn where the path of righteousness leads.'

'Don't talk such drivel,' snapped Lady Cynthia. 'And give Ian that gun.' She rose to her feet.

'Sit down!'

Ian tried to pull Lady Cynthia back into her seat. She flapped at his arm.

The gun went off.

Fiona screamed.

Lady Cynthia collapsed in her chair.

'She's only fainted,' said Quentin, now calm. 'Next time, I won't miss.'

'What will you do when the security people arrive?' said Ian.

'They won't, old boy. I told them they could go off duty – same as the house staff. So now it's only the Agatha Christie victims and me, and once again I play the lead.' He held up a bottle which he'd taken from his pocket and showed it to Helen. 'How foolish to go sniffing those capsules meant for Ian. No!' He brandished the gun as Helen reached for the bottle. 'This is the prelude to the final act. When I unscrew the cap and release the pressure I have around two seconds to leave the room. You others will not be so lucky because—'

429

The chandelier exploded in a shower of incandescence.

The lights went out.

The door slammed. A key turned in the lock.

For a moment, the only sound was of popcorn.

Ian flung the curtains aside. Light from a full moon flooded into the room. He grabbed a chair. Smashed the window.

A burglar alarm went off. A red light started flashing on the roof.

Pete-A demolished the remaining glass with another chair, flung open the empty frame and scrambled out. 'Women and children first,' he cried, taking Helen in his arms as Pete-B passed her through the gap.

'There!' Colette pointed at a lone figure fleeing across the lawn. 'Be careful,' she yelled, as Ian set off in pursuit.

'Lady C next,' cried Pete-A.

She was still unconscious but showing signs of recovery as the two Petes heaved her out of the window.

'Like trying to move a bloody piano,' panted Pete-A.

They laid her on the lawn and Colette and Fiona scrambled out and attended to her.

Sir Aubrey insisted on managing on his own and had to be caught by Pete-A when he stumbled.

'Bloody bugger,' he muttered to no one in particular.

Ian came running back. 'He's gone. Had a car waiting. Everyone okay?'

'We think so,' said Pete-A.

'Go over to the other house,' said Ian. 'I'll call the police and hope I can get Grace. I'll wait here. I just hope everyone got out in time.'

Chapter 79

'You seen this Minister-uncovers-terrorist-plot crap?' said Felix, tossing the paper across his desk as Ian entered his office next morning.

'Is this friend Walter?'

'I guess so.'

'I know Grace arranged to brief him yesterday afternoon, but I don't suppose she had much say in what he wrote.' Ian skimmed the article. 'He's put the US in the back seat, I see. Otherwise... Are your people going to be upset?'

Felix shrugged. 'Leastways, it stops the folks back home worrying about terrorists targeting US interests abroad. The Ambassador will be able to play it down.'

'Morning, folks.' Jeff wandered in clutching a mug of coffee. 'Any news other than that?' He gestured at the paper.

'I have a bit,' said Ian. 'But what about your side?'

'Most of yesterday was spent debriefing,' said Felix, who was checking his e-mails. 'What's a PCR?' he asked, over his shoulder.

'Polymerase chain reaction,' said Jeff. 'It's a technique for amplifying small amounts of nucleic acid.'

'Viruses and things?'

'Can be. Why?'

'E-mail just in from the Harry S. They used this PCR thing and reckon that was Marburg in those bats Colette picked up.'

'Looks like her hunch was correct then,' said Jeff.

Felix grunted and swung his chair round. 'You gotten anything on Mlala, Ian?'

'Yes. We, er, brushed swords.'

'What's that supposed to mean?'

Ian glanced at his watch. 'Grace is due here soon. Let me fill in my bits while we wait. Hopefully, she'll be able to add a bit more.'

Felix sat with his chin sunk on his chest while he listened.

Jeff stared out of the window, his back to them.

'Jeez,' said Felix, when Ian had finished. 'That Quentin jerk's got some balls. Still an ass-hole, though.'

'He certainly is. Felix, he's lost it. He's totally flipped.'

'What's this day-of-reckoning crap?'

'I don't know. He may have some delusion about spreading those capsules around in a crowded shopping mall or at some meeting or other. I think it's more likely his imagination's running—'

'The launch of Condor,' said Jeff, turning from the window.

'What about it?' said Felix.

'That's the target.'

'You serious?'

'Completely. Think of the publicity: all the politicians, donors and other dignitaries going down with Marburg.'

'Holy shit!' – spoken in capitals.

'So all the hype about August the seventh was a red herring?' said Ian. 'Winding up the press and reminding people about the martyrs who gave their lives on the great day et cetera?'

'Probably,' said Jeff. 'Once the seventh passed off without any apparent incidents, people – us – started relaxing, leaving Mlala and his colleagues a clear field.'

'And we took our eye off the ball,' said Felix.

Jeff gave a humourless smile. 'Hindsight is a wonderful thing.'

'It all adds up.' Felix was nodding. 'At least we nailed Malik.'

'That, undoubtedly delayed, or even stopped, development of the hybrid virus,' said Jeff. 'But as we've seen, the existing form is still pretty unpleasant, even if it is less readily transmitted.'

'Certainly, if Helen Paterson's experience is anything to go by,' added Ian.

'Indeed.'

'Do you think Quentin has any stocks of virus left after we destroyed the Lokinang set-up?'

Jeff pursed his lips. 'We have to assume he has.'

'So.' Felix got to his feet. 'We pull out all the stops to nail the guy.'

'How?' asked Ian. 'One man in over a million is going to be pretty hard to find in Nairobi. Someone like Quentin could easily fade into the background.'

'No.' Jeff wagged a finger. 'A guy like him thrives in the limelight. Sooner or later he'll show his hand.'

'You think so?'

'From a psychological perspective, yes.'

Ian ran his hands through his hair. 'I suppose so. All that garbage about a day of reckoning.'

'Exactly. We just have to be there ahead of him.'

'Great,' muttered Felix. 'And how exactly do we do that?'

'I don't know,' said Jeff.

'Thanks.'

'Any chance we could postpone the launch?' asked Ian. 'At least until this whole thing is sorted.'

Jeff shook his head. 'Invitations have already gone out. Ole-Tomeno would never allow it. This is his big day. Let's hope it's not Mlala's as well.'

Felix rubbed his hands over his face. 'Guess I'll retire to the Rockies and raise chickens when this circus is over.'

'In the meantime?' said Ian.

'In the meantime.' Felix drew a breath. 'We up the security to maximum and—'

They all looked up as Grace entered and slumped into Felix's chair. 'Mlala's stolen a car.'

'The hell he has!' cried Felix.

'Looks like you may be right, Jeff,' said Ian.

'Showing his hand, you mean?'

'Yes.' Ian nodded.

'What details on the car, Grace?' asked Felix.

'Sorry?' Her eyes began to droop.

'What details on the— You want some coffee?'

'Tea, please.'

'I'll go get it,' said Jeff. 'You take sugar?'

'Two spoons.' She yawned, closed her eyes and appeared to fall asleep.

Ian and Felix waited.

'There you go,' said Jeff, returning. 'Plus some biscuits.'

She sat up and rubbed her eyes. 'Thanks.'

'Tell us about the car, Grace,' said Ian.

She dipped a biscuit in her tea and stared at the wall. 'I only heard after I saw you at the Fairview, Ian.'

'Heard what?'

'Police at Karen reported that a woman came in very distressed in the evening, saying her car had been stolen at gunpoint earlier in the day.'

'Any details?'

'It seems she was putting her daughter into her car near the central market in town when a man approached and threatened the girl. He made the woman drive out to a remote spot in Karen, where he dumped them and drove off.'

'Were they harmed?' asked Ian.

'No. Terrified, though, and it was more than an hour before they reached the police station.'

'But they're okay?'

'They've gone to spend the night with friends. I'm sending a welfare officer to talk to them but I don't expect to learn anything more.'

'And the man?'

'A *mzungu* who matches Mlala's description. He was well-spoken but the woman doesn't remember much more about him.'

'When was the vehicle stolen?'

'Soon after you caused that riot in town,' said Grace. 'A lot of complaints coming in about the damage caused.'

'Send Quentin the bill.'

'Any sign of the car?' asked Felix.

'The details have been circulated. Nothing back.'

'So we now know how Quentin got around to the various places where he was seen, including the High Commissioner's residence,' said Ian.

'And the Fairview.' Grace stifled a yawn. 'It also tells us he knows the car at the market is being watched.'

'Anything more on where he might be staying?'

'No.'

'Are you looking in the right places?' asked Jeff.

'Of course we're not! We would have found him if we were,' Grace stirred her tea causing it to slop onto Felix's desk. 'Sorry about that.' Little suggestion of apology. She wiped a savage hand through the mess.

'Where have you looked?' asked Jeff.

'Don't you think we've checked every hotel and boarding house in Nairobi?'

'I'm sure you have,' – placatory tone.

'Right. And we're still checking.'

'Perhaps he's high-tailed out of the country,' said Felix.

'We're watching airports and border crossings,' said Grace.

'He might try slip over the border into Tanzania or Uganda and fly out from—'

'No,' said Ian.

'Why so sure?' asked Felix.

'What we've just been talking about. His big day. The launch of

Condor.'

'Great. Thanks for that.'

Ian shrugged. 'Be my guest.'

'Mosques,' said Jeff.

'Excuse me,' said Felix.

'Grace, have you checked the mosques?'

'No. Why?'

'Because if he's as devout as he claims,' said Jeff, 'he would be praying regularly and perhaps even seeking sanctuary.'

For the first time since she'd entered the office, Grace's face showed a measure of hope. 'Can I use your phone, Felix? Mine's out of battery.'

'Sure, go ahead.'

She finished her call and pushed the phone back across the desk. 'Thanks. Sammy's getting onto it. We've got several Muslim officers based in headquarters.'

'Let's hope they come up with the goods,' said Felix. 'Come on, folks. Let's go topside. We need some fresh air.'

They settled at a table in the roof café and Felix ordered waffles and syrup. 'Hope you folks are feeling hungry.'

Ian helped himself then turned to Grace. 'Your people have secured the residence and sealed off the room?'

She nodded. 'We've also spoken to Kelly Ryder who's sending some people over to collect the capsules and decontaminate the place. She also suggested anyone at risk should be treated.'

'You feeling okay, Ian?' said Felix.

'Well, I haven't developed symptoms yet. If that's what you mean.'

'Yes, but—'

'No, yes-but, Felix. Let's wait and see. Okay?'

Felix scooped up some syrup with his finger. 'Just make damned sure you get to see Kelly soonest. You and the others.'

'Can we talk about something else?' Ian tried to ignore the others exchanging glances.

'Ian, your High Commissioner,' said Grace, 'is he all right? When I interviewed him last night it was impossible to get any sensible answers.'

'I think the poor guy's been unhinged.'

'How?'

'He regarded Quentin as his right-hand man, and now he's done the dirty on him and had his daughter beaten up it's all been too

435

much. His wife feeding him on avocadoes and telling him to brace up can't have helped.'

'I guess if it wasn't so tragic, that could be kinda funny,' said Felix.

'I suppose so,' said Ian.

'Will he be up to hosting the meeting of task force leaders at the end of the week?' asked Jeff.

'Most unlikely.'

'Right.' Jeff leaned back in his chair. 'We can't postpone the launch but we can postpone the task force meeting until the launch is out of the way. That'll give us a bit more breathing space.'

'Makes sense,' said Ian. 'By which time the— Excuse me.' He took out his mobile. 'Grace, it's for you. Sammy.'

She turned her back on the others. Then turned slowly round. 'They've found the stolen car.'

'Where?' said Ian.

'The, er, unofficial force found it near the Jamia Mosque. Come on, Ian. I've got a car waiting outside.'

***

The police car dropped Ian and Grace near the city market where they found Sammy chatting to some street children outside a pharmacy which sold footballs and fertilizer.

'We found the car,' cried Amos and Charity in unison, as Grace and Ian arrived. 'Unofficial police force very good.'

'Very good,' said Grace. 'Which one is it?'

'On the other side,' said Amos, 'in front of the white van.'

'It's the one that was stolen,' added Sammy.

'Please, Grace, no one has come to it,' said Charity.

Grace studied the two scruffy children and smiled. 'I am not giving you meal tickets this time. Instead, I am arranging a surprise.'

'What, what?' they cried.

'Something special, but first we need to find this man.'

'We will work very hard,' said Amos.

Charity nodded emphatically.

'We have two other officers watching,' said Sammy.

Ian noticed a woman window shopping and a man lounging against the bonnet of the Volvo he'd seen at the Settlers Club. Both were in plain clothes and wore trainers.

'Are they armed?'

'Yes.'

Grace checked her watch. 'Ian and I can't risk staying and being recognised. We'll go back to headquarters. The moment anyone comes for that car, bring them in, Sammy. Remember this man is a good actor and may well look different.'

'And he's probably armed,' added Ian.

Sammy nodded.

'Here is Njoroge,' cried Amos, as another boy came weaving between cars and people, clutching a piece of paper.

'How are you?' he cried to everyone, as he handed the paper to Grace.

'It's from one of the officers who's been watching the mosque,' she said. She briefly squeezed her eyes shut before staring vaguely along the bustling street congested with cars and people. 'Look at all those people; ten or more could be terrorists and we would never—'

'Grace, the note,' said Ian.

'Sorry. A *mzungu* collapsed at the mosque after morning prayers and was taken to Kenyatta Hospital. Let's go, Ian. The car's waiting.'

Chapter 80

Things were settling into a routine at Camp Embakazi and Kelly was able to join Colette for a morning break in the canteen tent and learn about the traumas of the previous evening.

'It sounds terrifying,' said Kelly.

'It was. The man's a maniac.'

'Any idea what happened to him?'

Colette shook her head. 'He's still on the loose and seems bent on causing as much mayhem as possible in pursuit of his twisted cause.'

'Which is?'

'Some rubbish about a day of reckoning.'

'What's that?'

'No idea. And I doubt he has.'

Kelly sipped her coffee. 'Tell me more about those capsule things.'

'I don't understand the technology, but it seems they're made of some sort of gelatin or polymer bi-layer which incorporates virus inside minute bubbles. On exposure to air, the capsules rupture and release virus. It sounds like popcorn going off.'

'And they create an aerosol of virus?'

'Pretty scary, eh? But I hope I inactivated them.'

Kelly's cup stopped in mid-air. 'You what? How?'

Colette recounted her nightmare in the laboratory and the details of the glove-box with the drowning arms. 'When Jeff showed me the capsule set-up, he also pointed out the system for sterilizing the room with u-v light. Later, I, er, had the chance to operate it. I just hope it worked.'

'Do the others know this?'

'It was all so hectic last night, I never had a chance.'

Kelly nibbled a biscuit. 'If the u-v didn't work and there was active virus in those capsules, what are the chances those of you in that room last night would have been exposed?'

'Pretty low, I think. The window was smashed almost immediately and everyone was out of the room within a couple of minutes. Even so...'

'I've spoken to Ian and agreed to give antiserum to those at risk,' said Kelly. 'We'll get onto it asap.'

'Excuse me, doctor,' said a nurse, who had just entered. 'Two people asking for you.'

'Pete, Helen. How you doing?' cried Kelly, pulling out chairs. 'Thanks for coming.'

'Hello, Kelly.' Helen sank into the chair. 'I do get tired quite quickly.'

'That's to be expected. Don't go overdoing it.'

'No risk of that. Pete won't let me.'

'Good for you, Pete.' Kelly looked up at the sound of distant sirens.

'Trouble?' said Helen.

'Could be. Anyway, you're both okay for us to take blood? Stocks of antiserum are getting low.'

'It's the least we can do,' said Helen.

The wail of the sirens grew louder.

'I better go see,' said Kelly. 'Back shortly.'

The sirens, which were making speech difficult, were suddenly switched off. A few minutes later, two figures in biohazard suits hurried past the open flaps of the tent.

'Doesn't look good,' said Colette. 'First time I've seen this level of activity since I've been here.'

Helen whispered to Pete who nodded. They turned to Colette, their expressions tense. 'Helen and I have been talking.'

'Yes?'

'Thing is…' said Pete. 'You're still planning to go back to UK?'

'As soon as Sean brings my passport and stuff from Tandala.' Which means I should be out of everyone's hair by the weekend.' She gave a nervous laugh which scuttled off in embarrassment.

'What we want to…' said Pete. 'Could you…?'

'Could we…?' said Helen.

'Could you what?'

Helen took an envelope from the bag on her lap. 'Could I ask you a massive favour, Colette?'

'Of course.'

'Could you give this letter to Sean?'

'Yes, but he's… I believe he's coming down in a couple of days.'

'Haven't you heard?' said Pete.

'Heard what?'

'The meeting of task force leaders has been postponed because the High Commissioner's not well.'

'Oh no!'

'Which probably means Sean won't be coming down.'

'So I won't be able to—'

'If you could manage to take the letter,' said Helen, 'you could pick up your things and still be away by the weekend.'

'Well, I'm not—'

'Would you give it to him? It would really help.'

Colette took the letter and turned it over in her hands. 'I suppose… But…'

'I would take it,' said Helen, 'but I'm not fit to drive there—'

'And I need to be here to look after her,' said Pete. 'And… and… Take my Land Rover. We've got Helen's car we can use.'

Colette stared at the envelope, which simply read "Sean". No "to" or "love from", or even "from". And no other name. Presumably he'd recognise the writing.

'The Landy's just been serviced,' said Pete. 'Running well.'

'Well, I'd have to ask—'

'Hi, guys.'

'Ian!' cried Colette.

'Mind if I join you?' He drew up a chair.

'So, were you responsible for that commotion outside?' she asked.

'Not responsible but I came with Grace in one of the police cars.'

'What's going on?' said Helen.

'A man was found unconscious in the Jamia Mosque this morning. He was taken to the Kenyatta Hospital, where he caused something of a panic.'

'Marburg?' whispered Colette.

'Almost certainly. That's why the police escorted the ambulance here.'

Colette felt a terrible sense of foreboding. 'Does this mean another focus of infection?'

'Probably, but this time we know the likely source.'

'Which is?'

'If your theory is correct, Colette, the source is the tunnels at Lokinang – presumably the bats.'

'Do I know the patient's name?'

'I think so.'

'God,' she whispered.

'I know him as Quentin,' said Ian, 'but he also uses the names of Abdul and Mlala. And he recently stole the identity of a man called Clive Upton.'

'That the madman who was at the residence last night?' said Pete.

'The same. History repeats itself.'

'What do you mean?' asked Helen.

Ian seemed to consider the question. 'If I recall correctly, there's good circumstantial evidence from a local missionary that a boy who entered the tunnels in Lokinang mountain, some twenty years ago, contracted Marburg and died. No definitive diagnosis was made but the symptoms described – fever, collapse, red eyes and so on – suggest it was Marburg. That right, Colette?' He touched her hand. 'Colette.'

'What?'

'Were you with me?'

'Red eyes.'

'I'm sorry.'

'Ian, that's it! Quentin's eyes were all bloodshot last night. With all the commotion, I didn't take it on board but—'

'You think he was showing signs last night?' said Pete.

'Yes. It also fits with his manic behaviour.'

'I reckon he's been living on the edge for a while,' said Ian. 'Would that speed up the development of the disease? It seems rather quick.'

'You'd have to ask Kelly,' said Colette, 'but stress can compromise the immune system and that would hasten things.'

'He was certainly stressed,' said Ian.

'You're telling me,' said Pete.

'Also, he may have caught Marburg before escaping through the tunnels,' said Colette. 'There was plenty of hot virus around at Lokinang.'

'And in the dining room last night,' added Ian.

'Probably not,' said Colette.

'What do you mean?'

She repeated what she'd told Kelly.

Ian leaned forward. 'Are you sure?'

'Optimistic.' She smiled. 'But Kelly's taking no risks. I've given her the list of those to be given antiserum – you included.'

Ian drew a breath. 'Things suddenly seem a bit brighter.'

Grace came in and slumped into a vacant seat beside him.

'You look shattered,' said Colette.

'Worse than the Olympic final,' she said smiling. 'But we've got him. At long last we've got him.'

Ian reached over and squeezed her hand.

'You've done an amazing job,' said Colette.

'Despite what Walter says in his article, this was an international effort,' said Grace. 'We couldn't possibly have managed on our own.' She leaned forward. 'You must be Helen. I've heard a lot about you.'

'I'm sure most of it's untrue,' said Helen.

'I'm sure it's not.'

'Does this mean the day of reckoning is over?' said Pete.

'Not for me it isn't,' said Kelly, joining the group and drawing up a chair. 'Listen, folks,' she said softly. 'You may not like what I'm going to say but I'm going to say it anyway. I'm a doctor, not a policeman, not a politician and certainly not a judge and jury. My commitment is to my patients. I make judgements on clinical symptoms and diagnostic tests, not on a person's character, nor on crimes they may or may not have committed. That's for others to decide.'

'What are you saying, Kelly?' asked Colette.

'I'm saying that I'm pulling out all the stops to save this man. That was the oath I took when I qualified. I'm as committed to it now as I was then.' She gave an awkward smile. 'Sorry for the speech-making.'

'We have to ask this, though,' said Ian. 'What are his chances of pulling through?'

'It's too early to make a judgement.'

'When will you know?'

'Give me twenty-four hours.'

'I must insist that he's under constant police surveillance,' said Grace. 'Can that be arranged without putting my officers at risk?'

Kelly nodded.

'In the meantime, I'm preparing a list of charges against this man.'

'Going to be quite a list,' murmured Ian.

'Yes. And I'll be adding the murder of a British backpacker. The preliminary forensic report says the man in the burnt-out Range Rover was shot.'

'Does that change your view, Kelly?' asked Colette.

'No.' Kelly got to her feet. 'If you'll excuse me, folks, I'm going to be kinda busy over the next few days.'

'Will you need me?' asked Colette.

'No, you've done a brilliant job sorting out the paperwork. That's been a massive help. When are you off?'

'Probably at the weekend, but I'll come and say goodbye.'

'Let's hope things have settled a bit by then. Take care, Colette.' She kissed her cheek. 'Come on Pete, Helen, let's get you set up.

Looks like we are going to need those extra stocks.'

'Pete, before you go,' said Colette. 'About that thing you asked me?'

'Yes?'

'Have you got your Landy here?'

'It's parked outside.'

'Could I have the keys?'

Chapter 81

Colette drove back to the Fairview after lunch, grabbed a few clothes, packed her suitcase with her memories and the rest of her things and left it in the hotel's store. Three hours later she found herself in the bar of the Naro Moru River Lodge wondering why she'd agreed to be a courier. Perhaps Sean wouldn't be there and she could drop the letter, pick up her things, leave him a quick note and get out of his life. If all went well, she could be back in Nairobi this time tomorrow and then off to UK the next day.

Having reassured herself and set her mind at rest, she ordered herself a beer, resisted a white farmer's attempt to chat her up and went through to the dining room where she had... She didn't remember. She *was* doing the right thing. This is best for everyone. And it would be a chance to see Mum and Dad. It would be good to get back to a normal life. Normal? Is that what my sad little house offers?

***

She went out to the car park next morning and a Samburu woman who was seated nearby selling tourist trinkets, waved to her. 'Lucky bracelet,' she called, tapping her wrist.

Colette smiled, waved, scrambled into the Petes' Land Rover and slumped her head onto the steering wheel. 'Lucky?'

She started the engine and moved off. Before long she left the tarmac and was onto the familiar dirt road. Memories of that first journey with Sean came flooding back. That was where they saw the greater kudu and a bit further on – she followed the track down into the tree-lined sand river – was where they met the Petes. Some vervet monkeys, foraging in the sand, looked up as she stopped; then scampered into the trees as she climbed out. She sat on the bumper sipping from a water bottle, listening to the monotonous tonking of emerald-spotted wood-doves and the soothing *kokwaarro* of mourning doves. An enormous eagle watched her with unblinking eyes, ignoring the protests of the weavers nesting in the branches below. She wasn't good on eagles and wondered which species. Sean would know. She would have to ask him when... She probably wasn't going to see him. She'd ask the Petes when she got back to Nairobi. She sighed, finished her drink and resumed her journey which was trundling towards its happy ending. Thirty years gone, only a few hours to go. Happy ending? Was this the easy way out: leaving bits of her life scattered around in Kenya, walking away from them, not bothering to retrieve them?

An hour later the familiar buildings came into view. There was Sean's plane. And that was the tree beneath which... A bird fluttered in her chest. No sign of any vehicles. No sign of Suni. Did it mean Sean was away?

Leah appeared on the veranda and waved.

Colette stopped, switched off the engine and climbed out. '*Jambo*, Leah.'

'*Jambo, memsabu.* You have come.'

'Yes. I've come. Where is, is Sean?'

'He is not here.'

'I've only come to collect my things.'

'They are still in your room.'

'Thank you, Leah. Can I get them?'

'I will unlock the door for you.'

Colette followed Leah and found her things exactly as she'd left them in the room. Her passport was still in the zip pocket inside her rucksack.

'Would you like some tea, *memsabu*?' asked Leah. 'I can make while you are packing.'

'Thanks, Leah, that would be great. I won't stop, though.'

Colette knelt down and began stuffing things into the rucksack oblivious to any order or method. All she had to do was get everything together and—

A whirlwind hurtled through the door, raced across the bed and jumped into her arms.

'Suni!'

The little dog was whining in ecstasy, her tail wagging so frantically it seemed in danger of falling off.

'Suni, it's so nice to see you,' cried Colette. She finally managed to calm the exuberance and put Suni down. She then got to her feet and...

He was standing in the doorway giving his lop-sided smile. 'You came back?'

'Hi, Sean.' The bird started fluttering again. 'The Petes lent me their Landy. I won't stop, though.'

He raised his eyebrows. They really were unusually fair.

'Leah says she's making some tea.'

'Sure.' He turned and headed back to the veranda.

Colette picked up the rucksack and followed.

They settled on either side of the table where the tea was waiting.

'What have you been up to?' he asked.

'It's been quite hectic. Lots happening.'

'Tell me.'

As he listened, she tried to avoid the blue eyes studying her, and ignore Suni who was lying across her feet. Were they conspiring against her?

'Sounds pretty hairy,' he said.

She nodded and sipped her tea. Fiddled with her bracelet, conscious of an awkward silence.

'You remember that time I took you and showed the tree where Tanya—'

'I'm so glad you felt you could share that with me.'

'Dima also lost a daughter,' he said softly.

Colette looked up, her face distraught. 'When? How?'

'An accident with a fire.' He gazed bleakly into the distance. 'She and Tanya would have been about the same age.'

Colette came round the table and held him against her body, feeling his warmth and strength. Pretended not to notice the tears. 'Time to move on,' she whispered and kissed the top of his head.

She turned at a rattling sound. 'What's that noise?'

'Colobus monkeys in their cages. This is the last batch from Lokinang. I'm taking them up to the forest this afternoon to release them. Dima and I have—'

'Tell me: how is Dima?'

'He's fine. He and his family are settling in well. Jotham is helping them build a house.'

'Just like that?'

'Pretty much. Franco and I gave them the materials and they're getting on with it.'

She returned to her place on the other side of the table. 'It must be so nice not having to worry about things like planning permission and estimates and... and...'

'It is.'

She looked down and studied her fingers which she was twisting together.

'You okay?'

She gave a bright smile. 'I'm fine.' She hoped he believed her words more than she did.

'Would you like to—'

'I nearly forgot,' she cried.

'What?'

'Hang on. I'll get it.' She jumped up and ran to the Petes' Land Rover, Suni on her heels. 'There,' she said, handing him the letter. 'It's from Helen. She asked me to give it to you.'

He studied the envelope for a few moments before opening it.

Colette made a fuss of Suni and tried not to watch. The fluttering bird was back.

When he'd finished reading he returned the letter to the envelope and slipped it in his pocket, a thoughtful look on his face.

'Everything okay?' she asked.

'Yes, fine. How is Helen?'

'Kelly expects her to get back to full fitness very soon.'

'That's good.'

Colette checked her watch. 'Gosh, is that the time? I really should start heading—'

'Would you like a last safari?'

'What do you mean?'

'Come to the forest to help me release the monkeys?'

'Sean, I'm not sure I—'

'Be good to have your help.'

'I need to return the Petes' Landy.'

'Knowing the Petes, I don't suppose a few extra hours will make much difference.'

'I don't know.' She began twisting her fingers again. She looked into his face. This time she couldn't avoid the blue eyes. She was losing her place in the script. She looked down at her fingers and nodded.

***

After a snack lunch, she helped Sean load the monkey cages onto a trailer which was hitched behind the Land Rover. They then covered the cages with a tarpaulin. Sean drove slowly along the rough forest tracks to avoid jolting the monkeys. Neither of them spoke. He finally pulled into a clearing, switched off the engine and they climbed out.

'Recognise that call?' he asked.

She listened to the melodious liquid call. 'Black-headed oriole?'

'There he goes.'

'That was what we saw when we came to the forest with the Petes? When we came to—?'

'Yes,' he said.

'That was so horrible.'

'Come on. You untie that side. I'll do this.'

They removed the tarpaulin, and the monkeys – after some initial cries of alarm – peered out of their cages at their new surroundings.

'Is this it, then?' she said.

'Yup. I hope they settle.'

'Are the resident monkeys likely to object?'

'I hope not. These are all youngsters so they should be accepted. Let's see.'

They opened the doors of the cages then climbed onto the roof of the Land Rover to watch.

'There's the oriole,' said Sean, handing Colette his binoculars and pointing at the black and gold image which swooped across the clearing and settled in another tree.

'It's beautiful.' Once again she was immersed in the magic of the forest. She didn't trust herself to look at Sean as she handed the binoculars back.

'Looking hopeful,' he said.

Two monkeys emerged from their cages. One hopped down to the ground to be followed by the other. The booming cry of a resident monkey rang out across the forest. The monkeys looked up, startled, and fled back to their cages. Almost immediately, they were out again and onto the ground, followed by three more; then the final two. All looking in the direction of the booming cry. One of them edged forward, then seeming to pluck up courage, raced to the nearest tree, scampered into its branches and began calling to the monkeys below. As though on some command, they all followed, then sat looking back at the two watchers before disappearing into the forest.

'That's it, then,' he said.

That's it, then. The end of a chapter? The end of the book? Time to open a new one. Time to…

'I should get going.' She jumped down to the ground and began folding up the tarpaulin and closing the doors of the cages.

He came and joined her. 'Can I show you something first?'

'What?'

'It's not far. Come.'

Swallowtail butterflies flitted ahead of them as he led the way along a game trail through the forest.

The sound of falling water. Growing louder. He took her hand and led her past a thicket of bushes.

'What do you think?'

She stood transfixed. 'I've never seen anything so beautiful,' she whispered.

A cascade of shimmering water poured over a ledge onto a rock some five metres below and into a pool. Swallows swooped in and out of the rainbow above the pool and dipped their beaks.

She knelt down and swished her hand through the water. 'It's lovely and warm and so clear.'

'See the fish? Over there.'

She was mesmerised. 'This place is magical. Does it have a name?'

'I'm told it's called *Kiziwa ya chatu*. I sometimes come here and swim.'

'Is it safe?'

Without waiting for his response, she peeled off her clothes and dived in. She swam a few metres under water then surfaced and climbed out onto the rock beneath the waterfall. She sat with her eyes closed letting the water cascade over her body, washing out the dust and sweat, and… and… Was it washing away the anguish and pain of the previous weeks? The doubts and uncertainties? The wavering and hesitation?

She opened her eyes and waved to Sean who was sitting on the opposite bank with his camera.

'You can't take pictures,' she called, 'I'm not wearing anything.'

'Really? I hadn't noticed.'

She stuck out her tongue then swam back across the pool with a powerful crawl.

'Here, give me your hand.' He reached out.

She grasped his hand, and with a sudden lunge, pulled him in on top of her.

For a few moments, the peace of the forest was broken with shouts and shrieks of two infants splashing each other.

He caught her arm. 'Where did the bracelet come from?'

'I bought it from a Samburu lady. It's lucky.'

He held her hand to his lips.

She tore free and swam to the waterfall, and back to his waiting arms. 'You've still got your clothes on,' she whispered.

The butterflies looked the other way.

***

'Time to wake up, princess,' said a voice in her ear.

'I've been having such a lovely dream.'

'Tell me.'

'No.' She sat up and looked around. The sun had sunk below the trees and taken the pool's rainbow with it. She leaned her arm onto his bare chest and placed a kiss on his nose. 'You never told me what it meant.'

'What?'

'The name of this place.'

'There.' He rolled over and pointed to a rocky ledge above the pool.

She could make out a large something on the ledge. A flurry of wind parted the branches and allowed a shaft of sunlight onto the something. She just managed to stifle the cry. 'But you said it was safe to swim.'

'You didn't give me a chance, but there's no way I would have let you go in if I hadn't seen him.'

'Is it a python?'

He nodded. '*Kiziwa ya chatu*, the pool of the python. My own private swimming pool. The local people keep well away.'

'So how could you be so sure it was safe?'

'You can see he's bloated – some poor duiker or bush pig which got chomped when it came for a drink. He probably won't move for a month.'

'Nor will I.' She lay back and closed her eyes.

'Are you going back to sleep?'

'Just to dreamland.'

'You're very beautiful.'

Colette smiled.

'Did Helen tell you what she wrote?'

She shook her head.

'Things weren't working out.'

She sat up. 'Sean, I feel so terrible. She must hate me.'

'No, this was well before you came. We tried to make things work, but…' He put a finger on her lips as she was about to interrupt. 'She and Pete will make a great couple.'

'Sean, I'm so sorry?'

'What for?'

'For, for…' A range of emotions chased each other across her face. 'I don't know.'

'You said you wouldn't move for a month. Would you like to make it a bit longer?'

She lay back on the grass, closed her eyes and felt a greater peace than she had ever known. 'I don't know. I'll have to think about it.'

***

It was nearly dark when they reached the house and found a beaten-up Land Rover waiting, with two figures sitting inside.

'Franco! Dima!' she cried, running up to them as they climbed out. 'Dima, how are you?'

'I am well. Here is a very fine place.'

'And your wife and children?'

'They are very happy.' He scuffed the sand with his foot. 'You stay here now?'

You stay here now. Was it a question or a statement of fact – a directive, even? Her future life defined so succinctly. Perhaps she would have a chance to read that page after all: the one torn from her life the day in Isiolo when she was abducted by— She blanked out the memory. 'I stay here now,' she said.

'I go to see Leah,' said Dima, running off.

'So, *signora*, you come back?' Franco's face was wreathed with happiness.

'I finally followed your advice,' she said, hugging him.

He stood back and studied her. 'He was good advice, no? I can see by your eyes.'

She dropped her gaze and nodded.

'So, Franco,' said Sean, coming to join them, 'what brings you here?'

'I come with Dima to borrow… to borrow…'

'To borrow what?'

Franco threw his hands in the air. 'I forget.'

Sean gave him a playful punch. 'I'll fetch some beers. You and Colette get the fire going.'

By the time Sean returned, the fire had been revived and the smell of acacia wood smoke drifted on the evening air. Colette settled beside him and rested her head on his shoulder.

Franco regarded them a slight smile on his lips. '*Salute.*' He raised his bottle. 'Sean, my friend, if I thirty years younger you stand no chance.'

451

Chapter 82

Although Colette was familiar with the Kenyatta International Conference Centre – Nairobi's most imposing building – today was the first time she'd been inside. She and Sean had barely entered before they were greeted.

'Do you remember me, Dr Fraser? Maria, the Minister's PA.'

'Please, it's Colette. Yes, of course.'

'Welcome. And you, Sean. You can get your badges and programmes over there. I'll get someone to bring you drinks.'

'Thanks,' said Sean. 'Are you well, Maria?'.

'I think so. I'll tell you once the launch is over. Excuse me, the American Ambassador.' She rushed off.

'Dear lady!'

'Pete. How are you?' cried Colette.

'Spiffing.'

'Is Fiona here?'

'Afraid not. Confined to barracks. Looking after his lordship.'

'How is Sir Aubrey?'

Pete pulled a face. 'Not great, but he seems happy. Getting a bit pissed off with avocadoes, though.' Pete suddenly sprang to attention and saluted.

'At ease, Acheson,' said a smiling Ian, resplendent in dress uniform.

'Ian, you've shaved your beard,' cried Colette.

He rubbed his chin and gave a rueful smile.

'It never really suited you.' She kissed his cheek then waved to a passing waiter, who brought them drinks.

'You two look well,' said Ian, glancing between Colette and Sean.

'We've just come back from a couple of weeks at the coast,' she said.

'All right for some, then.'

She suddenly felt awkward.

'Excuse me, I need to grab Maria a moment.' Ian gave a bright smile and moved away.

'Is he all right?' asked Sean.

'I hope so.' She pulled a face. 'Trouble is, he's too noble.'

'Noble? What's that supposed to—?'

'Hi, folks.'

'Jeff!' Colette hugged her former boss. 'This is the first time I've seen you in a suit and tie.'

'Not my scene.' He ran a finger round his collar.

Colette slipped her arm through Sean's. 'Have things settled down in Nairobi? We've been out of touch for a while.'

Jeff nodded slowly. 'We think so. That man died, you know.'

'That Quentin Mlala person?'

'Yes. He insisted, though, his name was Abdul Jamal. He hung on for a few days then died quite suddenly.'

'Did you go and see him?'

'Shortly before he died. The doctor told me she thought he'd pull through.'

'Was she upset?'

Perhaps he misheard her question. 'There were only two other cases – the men who took him from the mosque to the hospital – and they're both recovering.'

'Does this mean his predictions of a day of reckoning are out of the window?' asked Pete.

'For the moment.' Jeff's expression became bleak. 'But there'll be other incidents.'

'Do you know of something in the wind?' she asked, startled.

'No.' He stared into space. 'But I fear we have done no more than cut one head off a Hydra.'

They were rescued by the arrival of Maria who led Jeff away to introduce him to a dignitary who had just arrived.

'Phew,' said Colette. She placed her empty glass on a table, 'Let's go and get our badges.' She linked her arms through Sean's and Pete's and led them through the gathering throng. 'Are Pete and Helen here?' she asked.

'No,' said Pete, 'they've gone to the Mara, hoping to pick-up the end of the wildebeest migration – at least, that's their story.'

'Is Helen well?'

'Getting better all the time.' Pete smiled. 'Let's say Pete and I are thankful we didn't go rushing back to UK.'

'Amen to that,' whispered Colette.

Sean put his arm round her waist.

The harassed Maria came up to them. 'Could you take your seats, please? We'll be starting in a moment.'

'Is Grace here?' asked Colette.

'She's coming,' called Maria over her shoulder, and hurried off to chivvy others.

They settled into their seats and Colette studied the gathering of diplomats, politicians, donors and dignitaries assembled for the launch of Condor. There were times over recent weeks when she'd wondered whether the day would ever come. She was sure many others felt the same, not least Jeff who was welcoming a beaming ole-Tomeno, who had just arrived surrounded by security officers. Maria showed him to his seat, while the officers took up strategic positions at the doors.

Jeff stood up and crossed to the podium. 'Good afternoon, folks. My name's Jeff Carter and I have the privilege of coordinating the programme we are here to launch this afternoon. However, I'm not here to make a speech. Who said, thank goodness?'

Polite laughter.

'My very pleasant task is to introduce someone who is well known to all of you: someone who has been unswerving in his commitment to setting this exciting programme on course, and exceedingly generous in supporting those of us working at the coal face. There have been times when things have been tough, but this person has retained the vision when some of us lesser mortals had our doubts.' He paused to take a sip of water.

'He'll have him walking on water next,' whispered Pete to Colette.

She stifled a snigger.

'I guess that's enough from me by way of introduction,' said Jeff. 'Can I please ask you to welcome His Excellency Daniel ole-Tomeno, Order of the Golden Heart, Minister for Environment and Conservation, and Patron of the Conservation in Developing Regions Programme – better known as Condor.' He held up his hands and led the applause as the Minister made his way to the front.

'I'm sure I don't deserve all those accolades,' said ole-Tomeno, taking his place at the podium. He beamed round the gathering. 'Honourable Ministers, Excellencies, Distinguished Guests, Ladies and Gentleman, it is my pleasure to welcome you all on this beautiful afternoon to the launch of the conservation programme known as Condor. September is my favourite time of year in Nairobi. The long rains have finished, everything is green and lush, and soon the jacarandas will be coming into flower. It is a time of hope and the promise of new beginnings; an auspicious time to launch this exciting new programme.' Another all-encompassing smile. 'Firstly, can I thank Professor Carter for his kind words of introduction? Although he is the coordinator of Condor, he would be the first to acknowledge the help and support of numerous people and organisations who have contributed to bringing this about. I won't embarrass those concerned by mentioning names but you will find a full list in your programme.' He held up his copy of the glossy document, then glanced at Maria, who gave a slight nod.

'Good people, may I crave your indulgence while I digress for a few moments and use today's opportunity to promote another worthy cause.'

'What's he on about?' whispered Pete.

Sean shook his head.

Colette shrugged.

'There are two causes close to my heart,' said ole-Tomeno, 'one is Kenya's incomparable wildlife resource which Condor seeks to sustain; the other is our young people who are our hope for the future. They are the ones who will inherit the legacy of Condor. I hope it is something of which they will be proud and something they will continue to take forward.'

He drew a breath. 'It is a sad fact in a poor country like ours, that too many of our young people – through no fault of their own – are unable to achieve their aspirations or realise their potential. With that in mind, can I say how proud I was to be invited to be patron of the Mlango Trust. As you will know, *mlango* means door or gate in Swahili. This trust, which is supported by one of our great athletes, is opening the door to youngsters who have the potential to follow in her footsteps but are prevented from doing so through poverty or tragic circumstances. Thanks to her initiative, commitment and foresight, these children now have the prospect of attaining greatness and upholding this country's proud athletic tradition and achievement. Will you please welcome Olympic gold medallist Grace Kiptagat, and with her, the children of the Mlango Trust, some of whom, I have no doubt, will be wearing Olympic medals in the years to come.'

Maria opened the door and a smiling Grace entered. She was wearing her Kenyan tracksuit and holding hands with Charity and Amos, who were followed on each side by five boys and five girls, all wearing identical tracksuits. The children lined up on either side of Grace, faced the crowd, grinned and waved Kenyan flags.

The audience erupted in applause and rose as one.

'Isn't that bloody marvellous?' cried Pete.

Colette struggled to swallow her emotion, as Charity seemed to single her out for a special wave and smile.

Eventually, the applause died down and Grace and Maria led the children to reserved seats at the side. Grace then went and sat next to Ian. Colette was vaguely aware of ole-Tomeno speaking again. Did she imagine it or did Grace slip her arm through Ian's? She blinked the dewiness from her eyes and turned back to ole-Tomeno.

'… have faced difficult times over the last few months with threats to both our national security and the nation's health through the recent Marburg scare, which, I am pleased to hear, is at last being contained. It is perhaps invidious to mention names, but I would like to acknowledge the tremendous work done by the Ministers of Health and of Defence and their staff in bringing us through these difficult times.'

The ministers mentioned stood up, beamed at the audience and received desultory applause.

'Finally, I would be very remiss if I did not acknowledge two of our most valuable partners who have stood shoulder to shoulder with Kenya during these challenging times.' He turned to the American Ambassador. 'May I, excellency, thank you on behalf of our nation for the unstinting support the US has provided.'

'Thank you, minister,' she said. 'I will be pleased to pass on your kind words to my President.'

'Of the challenging times we have recently experienced here in Kenya,' continued ole-Tomeno, 'none has been more shocking than the terrible bomb which was detonated near the Football Stadium some six weeks ago. As you know there was considerable loss of innocent life and one of those reported killed was Colonel Ian Sinclair, the military attaché at the British High Commission. However, I am delighted to say, in this respect, the press was misinformed. Perhaps, Mr Cheriyot,' he said turning to Walter, who was smirking in a seat at the side, 'your paper would like to print a correction.'

'It will be a pleasure, minister.'

When ole-Tomeno turned back, Colette saw Walter wink at Ian who pretended not to notice.

'Britain is a steadfast supporter of the Condor programme and I would like to welcome Colonel Sinclair who has kindly agreed to stand in today for the British High Commissioner, who is currently indisposed.' He turned to Ian, who was sitting beside the American Ambassador. 'Please, Ian, convey our best wishes to Sir Aubrey and wish him a speedy recovery.'

'Thank you, sir, I will.'

'I don't wish to detain you good people for…' His voice trailed off as Felix slipped into the room and whispered in Maria's ear. Then moved over to talk to the American Ambassador.

'What is it?' whispered Colette, seeing the expression on the Ambassador's face change from disbelief to dismay to horror. 'Oh, God!' She was conscious of her tense breathing.

'Shit,' whispered Pete. 'Not the bloody day of reckoning?'

Time stood still.

The Ambassador rose and crossed to ole-Tomeno, who listened, his head bowed. He nodded, took a deep breath and faced the audience.

'Her Excellency the American Ambassador has asked if she can say a few words.' He relinquished the podium and invited her forward.

She consulted the slip of paper passed to her by Felix. 'Please excuse me, folks, for interrupting proceedings,' she said, her voice cracking with emotion. 'My colleague has handed me this note from our President. Let me read it you.' She put on her glasses. 'It is with deep sadness that I report a number of airliners were hijacked by terrorists and flown into the Twin Towers of the World Trade Centre and the Pentagon around nine o'clock US eastern time this morning. Casualties are not yet known but are expected to be many thousands. God bless America.'

She took off her glasses and stepped down. 'Thank you, minister.'

As she left the room on Felix's arm, the audience sat in numb silence.

Ole-Tomeno returned to the podium, his face bleak. 'Ladies and Gentlemen, can I ask you, as a matter of respect, to leave the room quietly.' He paused, struggling to retain his composure. 'We are staring into an abyss. Let us hope the youth of today do not follow the paths of their fathers and can lead us to a brighter morrow.'

457

By the same author:

HIGHWAY OF DARKNESS (literary fiction)

A young Kenyan boy from a Nairobi slum dreams of becoming a doctor. Only if he can escape poverty and destitution, and overcome the fear and challenges of The Highway, will he realise his impossible dream. A powerful coming-of-age story of youthful resilience and courage in the face of hardship, deprivation and suffering.

OPERATION FRUIT-BAT (humour)

The murder of a prominent member of the aristocracy in nineteen-sixty's England jeopardises a top-secret enterprise involving Britain and Kenya. Responsibility for rescuing the operation falls to the hapless Archie Bracegirdle and his more astute Kenyan colleague, Mwangi. A spiffing fast-paced spy thriller set in Kenya: from the backstreets of Nairobi, to the African bush and the Indian Ocean coastal beaches. The novel also provides a rare insight into the workings of FIDO, Britain's most secretive intelligence organisation.

COBRA STRIKE (teenage fiction - thriller)

Terrorists are smuggling uranium ore out of Tanzania to build nuclear weapons. The top-secret security organisation Cobra recruits teenagers Lucy, Kal, Ellie, and their Maasai friends Matata and Kiki to infiltrate the operation. Where is the ore coming from? Where is it going? Who is masterminding the operation? To answer these questions Cobra operatives must survive the hazards of mountain jungles, the African bush and shark-infested caves. Then they face the sinister Chui and his accomplices…

Cobra Strike was shortlisted for the Wells Festival of Literature Children's Story Competition 2016.

ABOUT THE AUTHOR

Tony Irvin qualified as a vet from Cambridge and spent twenty years in Kenya researching diseases of cattle and wildlife, working closely with internationals scientists and with indigenous people such as the Maasai. He was Director of Biosciences at the International Livestock Research Institute in Nairobi and, for a number of years, was a senior adviser in the aid branch of the Foreign Office. On return to the UK, he began writing fiction for adults and children, all of which is set in Africa. The nearest he now gets to an off-road vehicle, is a ride-on mower.

The terrorist bombing of the US Embassy in 1998 occurred while he was living in Nairobi.

<tonyirvin12@gmail.com>

ACKNOWLEDGEMENTS

While living and working in East Africa, I spent many weeks on safari and nights camping in the bush. My grateful thanks to those knowledgeable people who shared that passion, and from whom I learned so much about Africa, its remote places, its people and its spectacular wildlife, in particular: Ken Bock, Michael Gwynne, Lionel Hartley, Robin Newson, Peter Stevenson and their families. I am particularly grateful to Hilary Shepherd and Ann Jessett who read the whole draft manuscript and provided invaluable advice and critique. Other writer colleagues who offered shrewd commentary and encouragement are: David Axton, Barry Baddock, Carolyn Belcher, Julian Corbell, Pauline Emery, Claire Frank, Nigel George, Wilf Jones, Valerie Kershaw, Gill Mather, Rosie Phillips and George Wicker. Particular thanks to George Wicker for book production.

Printed in Great Britain
by Amazon

86099445R00267